GLASS HEARTS

GLASS HEARTS
TERRI PAUL

ACADEMY CHICAGO PUBLISHERS

Published in 1999 by
Academy Chicago Publishers
363 West Erie Street
Chicago, Illinois 60610

Library of Congress Cataloging-in-Publication Data

Paul, Terri.
    Glass hearts / Terri Paul.
        p.   cm.
    ISBN 0-89733-470-1
    I. Title.
    PS3566.A8269G58   1999
    813'.54—dc21   99-10242
                                                        CIP

In loving memory of my father,
ISADORE REUBEN GOLDBERG,
who taught me to believe in myself.

ACKNOWLEDGMENTS

This book would not have been possible without my aunt, Sarah Grossman (Szerene), storyteller par excellence, who told me about her life over many afternoons filled with laughter and sparked my imagination. I am very grateful to Jordan and Anita Miller for their faith in the novel and their efforts in bringing it to print. I wish to acknowledge the Ohio Arts Council for awarding me an Individual Artist's Fellowship while I was working on *Glass Hearts*.

The members of my writers' group—Kathy Matthews, Applewhite Minyard and Dan Mushalko—read the manuscript several times with unwavering patience and good cheer and helped to bring out my best effort. Every writer should be so blessed. Charleen Lewis, Jan Lindner, Roseanne Rini and Bee Vacca also reviewed the book at various stages and gave me the encouragement I needed to keep going.

Last, but certainly not least, my husband, Terry Paul, my first reader, my best friend, nudged me to start writing fiction in the first place and has remained my most ardent fan. There aren't enough words in the English language to describe what his support means. So I'll just say thank you.

HOME, 1913-1915

EXILE, 1916-1917

THE NEW WORLD, 1918-1919

Part One

HOME, 1913-1915

PAPA

Papa melted away one night, like the butter in Mama's frying pan. At least, that's what my brother Sam told me the following evening after Mama lit the Sabbath candles and said the blessing without Papa. Something she never did before in all my five-and-a-half years.

"You know how butter starts to bubble?" Sam asked. "In a little while, it has no color or shape. It's just steam rising in the air. Well, that's what happened to Papa, and you may be next."

"Why?" I asked.

"Because you ask too many questions."

Afterwards, I couldn't get that steam out of my mind. It was there when I carried in wood for the stove or hung wet clothes out to dry over our verandah railing or chased the geese in our yard for Mama to stuff with grain. Lying on the grass behind our house, I imagined the fringes of Papa's hair and the tips of his fingers and toes turning slowly to liquid. His arms and legs and ears and skin and coal-black eyes oozed together, until all that was left was a brown puddle. Pretty soon, the outlines of my own body began to shimmer in the bright sunlight so that I could hold my hand in front of my face and see the blue sky right through it. That made me laugh, which surprised me. All I ever wanted was for Papa to love me.

During those years right before World War I, he took care of animals in Galfalva, our village in Transylvania. He pried the old shoes off horses and served drinks in his beer-and-ale parlor to the men who

rode them. The tavern was connected to our house by a big open courtyard and had a blacksmith's shop attached to it. When he was in a very
good mood, which might happen two or three times a year, Papa shaped
a tiny bit of metal into a rough star or tree for me. I treasured these odd
little pieces, stuffing them into my straw mattress for safekeeping.

Once, he had to pull a horse's tooth. He poured liquor down the
animal's throat and drank a swig himself. When he threw his arm over
the horse's neck, the two of them looked like the best of friends. I stood
in the shadows watching, and the sound of my laughter escaped into
the heavy air before I could jam my fist into my mouth. Papa stared at
me with a frown so deep his eyebrows cut a thick black line across his
forehead, and I wondered what made him hate me so much.

A few days after Papa gave me that hateful frown, Mama let me
stir corn mush she prepared for dinner. I sprinkled cheese on top of it
and set the table, accidentally putting out meat instead of milk dishes.
I spooned helpings for everyone, and Mama, being too kind, didn't
point out my mistake. She didn't want to hurt my feelings. But not
Papa. He came inside just as I set the last bowl on the table and, once
he saw what I had done, threw the dishes out the window. He yelled
about how I'd committed a terrible sin in mixing flesh and milk and
breaking the kosher laws that went back thousands of years and made
us Jews clean in the eyes of God. Mama shook her fist at him and went
into the yard to gather up the broken dishes.

Sam said Papa acted crazy around me because I was the only one
in the family with blond hair and blue eyes, like the rich banker in our
town, Mr. Kosich, who was a Christian. My older sister Mina said Sam
better keep quiet because that was an awful way to talk about Mama. I
didn't understand what they meant.

Of course, there was a reason Papa melted, and that reason was
money. The mayor of our village pounded on the front door while we
were eating dinner one evening and asked for Papa. He said Papa owed
the grocer, the carpenter, and a man he'd hired to build us a new house
in Szereda, a village that was bigger than Galfalva and closer to my

grandparents' house. It also had a nicer synagogue, with a rabbi who was Orthodox enough to suit Papa. There were so many debts, in fact, that the mayor had come to throw Papa in jail.

Mama said she didn't know where Papa had gone. She said her own mama, who died on the day I was born, had warned her about the strange things men did.

"I named Serene after her," Mama said. "She is the exact image of her grandma."

(That was a lie. I saw her picture many times, and she was dark like the rest of the family.) Anyhow, Mama told him how Grandma Serene got it into her head to walk barefoot in the field on a chilly May morning and was bitten by an old corn husk left over from the year before. The bite made her toes swell up and poisoned her blood. Mama said that she couldn't possibly go to the funeral because she was in the middle of having me, but ever since then, her mother appeared in her dreams with a sorrowful, deserted look on her face.

"Come to the point, Mrs. Spirer," the mayor said. "Where is your husband?"

Mama shook her head. "My mama always told me men had a knack for vanishing. You could nail their nightshirts to the bedpost with them inside, and the next morning they'd be gone. Even my own father disappeared one evening right after my sixth birthday. Got thinner and thinner, until Mama could stick her arm right through the air where he was standing."

"That's ridiculous."

"Maybe so, but I was sure he died and chanted the *Kaddish*, you know, the Jewish prayer of mourning, inside my head every Friday night in synagogue until he came back about a year later. He just grew himself into his proper place in the bed. When he finally departed this earth for good, I kissed him good-bye before the village women took off his clothes, bathed him, put him in his burial cloth, and closed him in his coffin. To this day, though, I won't swear to you that he didn't escape before they put his body in the ground. Sometimes at dusk, if I look far enough up the dirt road that runs away from the village, I see him shuffling home for dinner."

"That's quite a story, but it still doesn't answer my question. Besides, it looks like your husband was plenty busy himself before he left—if he ever left at all." He nodded toward Mama's stomach.

He was talking about my baby sister, Kati, who was waiting to be born. I used to see her dark, pinched little face at night before I fell asleep. Mama was sure she would have a boy. She had already decided to call him Mishi, after her favorite brother, a traveling musician who came to visit us every summer. Someone found him dead in a ditch on the road to Budapest the last day of October, 1912, almost a year before Papa melted. I dreamed Uncle Mishi was attacked by wolves with yellow eyes that glowed in the moonlight. Mama said it was more likely he'd been killed by a greedy Romanian who sneaked across the border with murder in his heart toward all Hungarians.

"Mishi's soul is inside me," Mama said, whenever we talked about the new baby. "Waiting to be reborn."

After the baby was born, Mama named her after her Aunt Kati who, Mama said, was "also a traveler."

The last anyone ever saw of Aunt Kati she was riding bareback on a horse, behind a Gentile book salesman who had bewitched her into running away with him. That's what Mama's family always said. Mama loved her in spite of her going off like that with a non-Jew.

Mama faced the mayor with her hands on her hips and tears in her eyes. "I don't know where my husband is," she said. "He may even be dead by now. That's true."

I caught my breath and was about to step forward when I felt a pinch on my arm, like the ones Papa gave me when I made him angry.

"Papa?" I whispered under my breath. But it was only Sam.

"What was that, Serene?" the mayor asked.

"He's lost," I said. "None of us may ever find him again, except in our dreams and thoughts."

KADDISH

Market Sundays were especially busy for Mama after Papa disappeared. Our yard was crowded with wagons and peasants, some in their best white fitted wool trousers, embroidered vests, and shirts with long flowing sleeves. They greeted their friends and stopped for a refresher in Papa's tavern. Most days, Mama let me and Sam help her there. We spread fresh sawdust on the floor and rubbed it on our cheeks because we liked the gritty feel of it against our skin. We arranged Mama's round egg cookies with sprinkles of sugar on top in tiny plates on the bar. Of course, we sneaked a couple of cookies for ourselves and stuffed them into our pockets. We took pennies from the people who bought glasses of beer and *slivovitz*, plum brandy that made our eyes water just carrying it from one end of the bar to the other. Mama was a great believer in cash and never gave credit to anyone. Not like Papa. For each of his regular patrons, he sliced a stick down the middle, keeping one half for himself and giving the other to the patron. Every time the patron ordered a drink, Papa matched the two halves, cut a notch in both, and then counted notches and settled the bill at the end of the month, after many loud arguments and harsh words. Mama had no patience for such things. She needed to feel the coins in her hands and couldn't afford the mistakes Sam made when he collected money or the food I spilled when the dishes got too heavy. So on market Sundays, she rose before dawn, taking only Mina with her.

Some market days, Sam acted like an angel and picked me a four-leaf clover from the yard. He told me that it would protect me forever and that I was sure to lead a charmed life. Other days, he behaved like a devil. One Sunday, Mama reminded Sam to heat up a stew she had made the night before for our noon meal. I didn't know he had decided to be a devil.

"I'm the gentleman of the house," he said, when the two of us were alone. "I don't want to get my hands dirty carrying that old pot to the stove."

"You'd better," I said. "Mama told you it was your job." I cried because I was too little to carry the pot. Besides, Mama never let me near the wood stove inside our house unless she was there.

"Suppose some soldiers came and put you in prison and wouldn't give you anything to eat?" he asked. "Would you cry like a baby then, too?"

He was always telling me stories about how there was going to be a big war in Europe soon. He said the Russian army was going to march across our land and torture us with knives before shooting us right between the eyes.

I came after him with my fist raised and punched him on the shoulder. "No one's going to take me away," I said. Afterwards, I wasn't so sure. I got back into bed and pulled the covers over my head, but then I smelled that delicious stew cooking, and an invisible hand drew me toward the table by the stove.

"Uh uh," Sam said, as I moved closer. "I'm not going to give you any."

"Why not?" I asked.

"Because I put a spell on the pot. I knew you'd want to have some, but if you take even one bite, you'll be sorry."

My mouth watered, and I sat there while he ate most of the stew. He said the spell wouldn't bother him, since he was the one who made it up. He warned me I'd never be the same again if I took even one bite of the stew. I was so hungry, though, that the second he was finished and out the door, I reached my spoon into the pot, grabbed a tiny piece of potato, opened my mouth, and let it slide down my throat. My stomach gurgled with happiness. Next, I picked out a carrot and a sliver of meat, and before long, the pot was empty.

Sam was right. My life did change. I started dreaming other people's dreams. That first evening I dreamed I was in an underground cave like the one Sam used to tell me about at night when he wanted to scare me. There I was, running around inside my brother's skin, catching bats with my bare hands, and waving them at my little sister. I looked puny and weak, and the next morning I began to understand why Sam picked on me all the time. When he poked me after breakfast, I pinched him right back. That made him look at me for a long moment before he pushed me out of his way.

A little while later, I dreamed I was sitting in the Catholic church in our village, carried away by the priest's prayers for the soul of Magda, a young woman who taught school and died suddenly of influenza. Her casket was covered with red carnations, and the stained glass window with God's bearded face on it made me cry so hard that the collar of my dress got wet, although I barely knew Magda. That dream belonged to Mina, who loved to go to funerals so much Mama had a hard time keeping her out of church. Mama worried herself to sleep at night thinking Mina might take it into her head to leave the religion of her birth. Once Mama even tied Mina's leg to the wood stove to stop her from walking five miles to the funeral of a man who used to drink beer at Papa's tavern.

Another time, I dreamed something that must have been Kati's. It was all red and black curly lines, like what might go on inside a baby's head, especially one who hadn't been born yet.

The dreams that bothered me the most, though, were Mama's. For three nights in a row, I saw myself taking Papa's hand. He smiled at me, put his arm around my waist, and danced with me until I was out of breath. His eyes burned with excitement. Then I found myself with Mina at my side, holding baby Sam in one arm and baby Serene in the other. My eyes ached with tears, and Papa shrank to a tiny dot and vanished altogether. Except I didn't call him Papa. I called him Shumi, and just looking at him made me light-headed.

One morning I sat at the table peeling carrots for Mama. The night before, I dreamed I kissed Papa on the cheek, and his mustache stung my skin. Somehow that dream took away my appetite.

"How did you meet Papa?" I asked.

"Through a matchmaker," she replied.

"What's that?"

"A man who travels all over the countryside getting to know men and women so he can pair them up in a marriage."

"Oh."

"Our village matchmaker first talked to me about finding a husband when I was thirteen. He wrote down what I liked and brought me several men, but your papa was the best."

"Why?"

"I don't know. He was still in the Hungarian army back then, and he looked so handsome in his uniform."

"Did you like him?"

"Yes. You could say that. He came from a good family. He was the third of four sons. Papa's older brothers moved to a faraway place called America before you were born. Of course, I had a *nadan*."

"What's that?"

"A dowry. Money and jewelry or maybe land a wife brings to a marriage to help her husband get started. My family owned a farm. I suppose Papa's family thought we were all right, because they came down to our wedding in their fur coats to show us how rich they were. Still, that didn't stop Mrs. Spirer from trying to take my *nadan* away from Papa and give it to your Aunt Gizella, but that's a story for another day. The old devil. Bad luck she's your grandma."

I wanted to ask her if she missed Papa, but my tongue grew swollen and heavy, and the only words I could think of froze in my throat and wouldn't form themselves into the right question. Besides, Mama always changed the subject when I told her I thought Papa was dead and never let me come back to it, no matter how hard I tried. I bit down on my lip and went on building a mountain of orange carrot scrapings, keeping quiet until I couldn't stand the silence any longer.

"Mama, do I really look like that blond old man at the bank, Mr. Kosich?" I asked.

"What?" she asked. "Who put such an idea in your head?"

I shrugged my shoulders. "It's just that you and Sam and Mina and Papa are all dark, and I'm not."

She ran her hand gently across my face. "It's a funny thing, but once every generation or two, a blond-haired, blue-eyed person gets born into our family. My Mama told me that happened because we came here from Spain hundreds of years ago and carried in our blood a little of that part of the world. She said my great, great grandparents, many generations back, mixed with other European people who had light hair and skin. Now, the Spirers. They came from a place between Africa and Asia where everyone is dark, so naturally they don't like fair-haired people. Anyhow, this blond person is always smart, sometimes too smart for her own good, and asks a lot of questions. Unfortunately, she possesses a gift for making other people angry, maybe because she says whatever is on her mind. Who knows? So, you're this special one for your generation."

"But I hate being like this. I hate my name, too. Why didn't you call me Clara or Anna?"

"Oh. Such plain names."

"But I want to be plain and look like everyone else."

She wrapped me in her arms and whispered, "No you don't. Just wait. You're going to have a magical life. I can feel it every time I run my fingers through your hair or hold you close to me."

She sighed, and I thought, I'll change my name one day when I am old enough.

That night, almost before I put my head down on the pillow, I saw myself standing in a smoky room feeding flat pieces of wood into a big machine that turned them into perfect squares. I looked down at my hands, and they were strong, the kind of hands that could form metal into horseshoes. The nails were broken and had black half-moons of dirt underneath them. There were men all around me, speaking a strange language that sounded like a dog barking. It hurt my ears and made my eyes water, and I was lonely for Galfalva and the smell of fresh grass on slow summer mornings.

*M*y cousin Itzy—the son of Mama's oldest sister—came to our house once a month to say *Kaddish* in the synagogue at Galfalva. He wished to honor the memory of his father who died in America several months before we lost Papa, so his mama let him miss school, since his village was too small for its own synagogue.

Itzy was tall, with thick black hair and the beginnings of a mustache. He was ten years older than I, and I was in love with him, partly because he would talk to me for hours and partly because of Mama's bean soup. Itzy arrived on Thursdays and stayed until Sunday. Whenever he was expected for dinner, Mama made a big kettle of bean soup, my very favorite. She began cooking it after lunch and took it off the stove in the late afternoon so it could cool on the table for dinner. I always managed to dip my spoon in the pot three or four times before the meal, until Mama caught me and made me go outside and play in the yard.

That December, Itzy came right before Kati was born. Mama said she could tell the baby was going to arrive soon, because Kati had dropped way down in her stomach and was kicking and pushing and generally reminding Mama she was ready to come out. Lately, Mama had been letting things go. Not like before, when Papa was here and

Kati was resting peacefully inside her. Then she had eyes in the back of her head. Now she was too busy and, on that Thursday, didn't watch me or the soup as carefully as usual. I took a spoonful here and a spoonful there. Somehow or another, only half a pot was left when we all sat down to dinner, with me perched on the edge of my chair, my spoon in my hand, waiting for a bowl of that wonderful soup. Mama reached inside the pot with her ladle and stirred nothing but air. She stood and looked into the pot and laughed.

"Serene," she said. "You ate half the soup, and you act like you're starving and want more. I'm surprised you haven't exploded by now. I don't know. Sam? Itzy? Should we give her any more?"

"No, she's already had twice as much as everyone else," Sam said. "Besides, she's too fat."

"I don't agree," Itzy said. "Aunt Rosa, the cook should take it as a compliment when someone cherishes the food she prepares."

He and Mama laughed. Sam kicked me under the table, and I tapped his leg back twice with the tip of my shoe before he kicked me again, though not so hard this time.

The next morning Mama asked Itzy and me to get out of the way while she prepared our Friday evening dinner. We pushed open the front door and ran through the courtyard, past the woods in back of the blacksmith's shop until we came to a hill overlooking the tracks of the very first train to travel to our part of the country. We held hands and waited breathlessly for the distant sound of a whistle, but all we heard was the wind crackling through the branches of the bare trees. The temperature was almost freezing, and we shivered as we ran back to the shed behind the blacksmith's shop. Inside the shed was a large oven shaped like a dome. Mama fired up this oven with wood and baked bread in it. For a day or so afterwards, while the stone cooled down, the shed was as warm as toast. Sometimes in the winter, we brought our blankets out there and slept on top of the oven. Itzy and I climbed on the oven and pressed our backs against the wall. I felt safe and happy with Sam and Mina in school and my cousin all to myself.

"Itzy, why do you have to say *Kaddish* for your father?" I asked. "Why don't you just use your own words?"

"Oh," he replied. "My own words are so sad and small by comparison. Besides . . . It's hard to describe. The rabbi asks the mourners to rise. I stand and close my eyes and recite a prayer that goes all the way back to Abraham. I see myself holding my father's hand, and he's holding the hand of his father before him, and so on, back thousands of years. It makes me believe in the piece of us that never dies."

I moved away from him, wishing to hide the silly love smile that spread across my face. For a moment, I kept my eyes glued straight ahead and remembered how it was Itzy who told me there were angels at the window when it banged on cold nights and scared me awake. I liked this idea better than Sam's, that there were bats outside waiting to make a dinner feast out of my heart and liver.

"My papa's dead," I said.

"Who says?" Itzy asked.

"No one, but Mama never wants to talk about what happened to him." My smile vanished, and my teeth chattered so hard I was afraid Itzy would laugh at me.

"Oh, my poor Serene. He's not dead."

"Well, where is he?"

"Everyone in the family knows he took a boat across the ocean to America."

"No. No. That's not true."

"Yes, it is. Why, at this very moment, he's probably working in a factory making guns or barrels, thinking of us here warming ourselves by the oven, so happy with the smell of fresh bread."

I hit him in the face. "That's for lying to me. Papa would never leave Hungary. He told us a thousand times how much he loved Franz Josef, how this is the best place in the world for Jews, the only place where we can own land and earn a good living and go to school."

Itzy laughed and glanced over his shoulder. "I could have sworn that was Uncle Shumi talking, except I didn't know he had such a squeaky voice." He smiled at me and took my hand in his.

I didn't smile back. The thought of Papa there in the shed made my throat feel dry, and I wanted to tell Itzy to stop teasing me. I knew Papa was dead. I could see it every time I spoke his name to Mama and her back got stiff and tiny lines appeared at the edges of her mouth.

"His brothers went to America, and he called them fools," I said. "I heard him myself."

"I know he did," Itzy said. "I heard him, too. I'm sure he didn't want to go."

"I didn't mean to hit you." That wasn't the whole truth.

He shrugged. "That's okay. It didn't hurt much."

We hugged each other, but we weren't as easy together as we'd been before.

"Listen," he said. "Lots of people around here are pretty angry because Uncle Shumi owes them so much money. Now your mama is playing dumb."

"Mama's not dumb."

"Of course not, but if his creditors ask her for money, she can tell them honestly that she doesn't have any and doesn't know where your father is. With the war coming. And she has three, soon four, mouths to feed. Maybe she didn't say anything to you because she didn't want you to tell everyone."

"Yes, because I have blond hair."

He frowned and shook his head and then, as if he'd just remembered something very important, grabbed my arm. "You have to swear you won't say a word about this to Aunt Rosa." He squinted at me.

"What's wrong?"

"I never should have said anything about Uncle Shumi. What if they try to make Aunt Rosa pay his debts, and you tell them he's in

America? You and your mama and brother and sister could lose your house, and I won't be able to come anymore."

"I won't tell anyone. I promise."

Itzy jumped down from the oven and looked around until he found a sharp knife hidden on a shelf too high for me to reach. He pricked his finger and squeezed it until a drop of blood appeared. Then he pricked my finger, squeezed out a drop of my blood, and held his finger on top of mine so that our blood mixed together. I closed my eyes, trying hard not to cry out. I wanted to prove Sam was wrong. I wasn't such a baby after all.

"Repeat after me," Itzy said. "I swear before God."

"I swear before God," I said.

"Not to breathe a word of what Itzy told me today to another living soul."

"Never to talk about Papa again."

"Not even to Aunt Rosa."

I giggled.

"Finish it," he said.

"Not even to Mama," I said.

He pulled himself back up on the oven and rubbed his palms together and blew on his hands, satisfied for the moment that Papa's secret was safe with me.

"Itzy, will you do me a favor?" I asked. "Will you chant the *Kaddish* for me?"

"Oh, yes," he replied. "It's such a sad, sweet song." He began to sing in a low, rumbling voice. "*Yisgadal Veyiskadash Sh'may Rabbo Be'olmo Deevro . . .*"

I made him chant it for me over and over, until I memorized the entire prayer, though I didn't really know what it meant. I'd heard it often enough at the end of services. By then, I was usually tired and restless, trapped between Mama and the women on one side of the synagogue and wishing I could be with the men on the other side where there always seemed to be more room. Besides, the *Kaddish* was always right before the end of the Friday night service, or right before lunch on Saturday when my stomach growled and I was weak with hunger. So I never paid much attention to the prayer.

The sound of Itzy's voice echoed in my ears long after he said good-bye that Sunday morning and rode away on his horse with a lunch Mama packed for him to eat during his trip home. Before he left, he grabbed my arm again and, with his face so close to mine our eyelashes practically touched, said, "Don't forget."

"I won't," I said. "I promise."

He patted me on the shoulder and kissed me lightly on the cheek, as he always did the last thing before he left.

Of course, I didn't really believe Papa was still alive. If he was, he would never have left Hungary, the place he loved most in the world, and Mama and the tavern. Instead, I imagined the ship that carried Papa away was a coffin buried at the bottom of the ocean. The thought of him under all that water reminded me of the hands in my dream about standing in front of a machine and making squares out of wood. That wood went into a coffin, and those hands belonged to Papa. I'd seen them hundreds of times, pouring beer into a glass and hammering shoes onto a horse's foot. The longing in that dream and the loneliness that stretched out forever were Papa's too, and the dream was his soul crying out to me to save him.

So I began to pray for him, in spite of the black looks and angry words and broken dishes. "*Yisgadal Veyiskadash Sh'may Rabbo*," I whispered into my pillow each evening, until Sam overheard me and told Mama what I was doing. She said if I loved the *Kaddish* so much, maybe I should start taking Hebrew lessons from our rabbi when he came to help Sam study for his *Bar Mitzvah*. The idea of sitting with the two of them, puzzling over those funny-looking shapes on the page, made me dizzy, and for a few nights, I just recited the words inside my head. But soon my new little sister was about to be born, and in my excitement, I forgot all about the prayer for a while.

THE BULLET

Sam and Mina and I were lying under a scratchy, camel-colored horse blanket in the back of Grandpa's wagon. Grandpa sat in front where we couldn't see him, silently guiding the horse from Galfalva back to Marosvasarhely, where he and Grandma lived.

"There are huge worms beneath the floor of Grandma's house," Sam said. "And they come out at night." He rolled a sticky finger under the sleeve of my coat, and I jumped and pushed him away.

"Stop it," I said.

"Tonight. Squish, squish."

I put my hands over my ears and thought about Grandma's house with its one big room and the old pot-bellied stove in the corner. The stove almost went out every night. We had to sleep huddled together with Grandma, who snored like a rusty saw, and Grandpa and Aunt Gizella, the only one of Grandma's daughters never to get married, and Uncle Mihai, the youngest of Papa's brothers who was home visiting from the Hungarian army. And the cow that usually wandered in at night during a snowstorm.

It was late December, and we felt like orphans because Mama had sent us away so she could have her baby in peace. I dreamed about that baby for quite a while, with her olive skin and tiny feet and eyes so dark you could only make out the slightest trace of blue. In my dreams, she was hungry all the time and cried out for Mama, and I knew she would be born the day after the Gentiles observed their Christmas.

That was Mina's birthday as well. This was the first time we wouldn't all be together to celebrate Mina's birthday, and we weren't happy about it. Mina didn't like the idea of this new little thief stealing the most important day of her year.

"Why do we have to go there?" she asked Mama every morning for a week before we left. "Grandma makes me want to wring her skinny chicken neck."

"What a terrible way to talk about your own flesh and blood," Mama replied.

But she didn't like Grandma any better than we did. She often told us Grandma was such a terror because she was the only child of a wealthy couple and she married a Yeshiva boy, a Hebrew scholar who never worked a day in his life and made her spend all her dowry and her inheritance to feed the ten children he gave her. We could see by the way Mama frowned and pursed her lips when Grandma called her a farmer's daughter that she hated the sight of that old woman, too.

"She's your father's mother, so we have to be nice," Mama always said, shaking her head. "God bless your papa, though I've never understood how a son like him could come from someone like her."

Whenever we went to Grandma's, we stayed very quiet because Grandpa studied the writings of learned men like the great Hungarian rabbi Isaac Taub all day and all night and couldn't be disturbed. Grandma usually found a way to spill tea or soup on whatever page he was reading. That made him glance up at her with a hurt expression in his hollow black eyes, like the old dog that once stumbled into the courtyard behind our house looking as if it hadn't eaten in a month. She would shake her fist at him and throw her hands in the air when he buried his nose back in the dampened page.

Mina remained silent during the whole trip, and when we got there, she stuck her tongue out at Grandma, right in her face. At lunch, she spilled half of her beet borscht on the clean tablecloth on purpose and cracked the stale sugar cookie Grandma gave her on the edge of her chair so that all the crumbs fell on the floor.

"Don't, Mina," I whispered. She pretended not to hear me.

"Well, what else can you expect from a child without a father?" Grandma said. "That's all you get for lunch, Miss. One bowl of soup, no matter how much you spill, and one cookie."

Somehow, Sam managed to palm two extras into his pants pocket.

We tiptoed around Grandpa, who sat in his chair like a stone statue, and out the door, but not before Grandma told us not to go beyond the yard because she didn't have all day to spend chasing after us. Of course, Sam headed straight for the woods behind the house. I wanted to follow him, but Mina grabbed my arm and pulled me in the other direction, down a dirt road that wound toward the center of town.

"Come along with me," she said. "We have better things to do than throw stones at half-frozen squirrels."

"I don't want to go," I said.

Running around the woods didn't sound so bad to me. I dug my heels into the ground, but Mina was much bigger than I was. I had no choice but to stumble along after her, and I rushed to keep up, since she never once let go of me. We walked for quite a long time, turning this way and that, until I wasn't sure where Grandma's house was anymore.

"We're lost," I said.

I started to cry because my toes tingled from the cold and my socks were wet and the skin on the tip of my nose was starting to burn. I tried to pull away from Mina, but the harder I pulled the tighter she held on to my arm. I remembered the story Mama told me about the day Mina was born.

"Most babies take pity on their mothers and come out head first," Mama said. "Not your sister. She came out backwards, bottom first, and she's been contrary ever since. If I say turn left, she wants to go right."

My arm started to ache, and I thought about how handsome Uncle Mihai looked in his uniform. He picked me up and put me on his shoulders, right after Grandpa dropped us off in front of the house and drove the wagon toward the barn. Aunt Gizella cupped Mina's face in her hands and kissed her gently on the forehead. All the while, Grandma warned them to leave us alone before they spoiled us rotten. She searched through our packs and took away the few coins Mama sent along with us.

"Ouch," I said, as we made our way down an unfamiliar street. "You're hurting me."

"Be quiet," Mina said.

"But we ought to go back. Everyone will be worried."

"They won't worry. They won't miss us at all. If we're not there for supper, why, Grandma, she'll be just as glad to give our food to Grandpa or eat it herself."

She threw her head back, but her laughter was silent against the wind. Fat, heavy flakes of snow fell so fast they caked my eyelids and made it hard to see even a few inches in front of me. We stood by the gate of a pleasant cottage with a thatched roof and a verandah circling all the way around it. Mina reached over and pinched my cheek with her free hand. I screamed and started crying again, loud, angry sobs.

"Good," she said.

She unlatched the gate and dragged me toward the door. She only knocked twice before a young man opened it. I could see a big fire behind him and smell bread fresh out of the oven, and I was sure these things weren't lost on Mina either. She opened her eyes wide and let some big tears slide down her face, one at a time every few seconds. When I saw those tears, I made quite a few of my own, thinking about Mama bringing our new baby into the world. Pretty soon, my whole body was shaking right along with Mina's.

"Girls, girls," the young man said. "Come inside and warm your-selves by the fire. After you thaw out a bit, maybe you can tell us what is making you so sad."

Mina let out a loud wail. Her hand never loosened its grip on my arm, but I was the one who led the way into the house.

We took off our shoes and socks and sat down on the floor in front of the fire, warming our toes. The soles of our feet grew so hot we had to move back a few inches. The young man told us his name was Roka, and his wife's name was Yashi, short for Yadwiga. Mina said she was called Magda, and I was called Sarah. "Sarah," I whispered. The name was so much softer and prettier than my own and rolled off my tongue easily. I began to imagine myself as this new person, this Sarah, who came from a family with a mother and a father. They loved her and thought she was the most beautiful child in the world.

"You girls look hungry," Roka said. "Not much meat on your bones. Yashi!"

His wife appeared from nowhere with two large pieces of bread so hot they singed the tips of our fingers and steamed our faces pink. We blew on the bread and sucked in the sweet smell of the yeast before swallowing each doughy bite. When we finished, Mina licked her fingers and held them up in front of the fire to dry. A sad smile crossed her lips.

"It's been since before Mama died," she said. "She was giving birth to our poor dear baby brother, who only made it halfway out. It's been since then that I've never tasted such wonderful bread. Isn't that so, Sarah?"

I didn't answer because I was too busy thinking about how warm and full the bread made me feel. Mina poked me with her elbow.

"What?" I asked.

"Where's your papa?" Yashi asked.

"Dead," Mina said. "He ran away in the middle of the night and drowned in a boat on his way to America to make money so he could send for us." She wiggled her toes and sighed. "We're orphans."

I bit down on my lip to keep from crying real tears this time, because I wasn't an orphan now and never wanted to be one.

"It's true," Mina said. "Sarah whispers a special prayer for the dead into her pillow every night. One prayer for each of our parents. Would you like to hear it?"

"Mina!" I said. "I mean, Magda!" That prayer was supposed to be my secret.

31

Roka sat down beside us, looking at Mina and me and at Mina again. His eyes were so soft I was sure he was about to start crying too. Mina rocked back and forth and stared into the fire.

"My birthday is the day after Christmas," she said. "I'll be eleven, and there's no one to share it with, except Sarah."

"Don't you have any other family, aunts and uncles, grandparents?" he asked.

Mina told him we'd been sent to live with our grandmother, our father's mother, a nasty old woman who fed us leftovers from the dog and finally kicked us out of the house because there wasn't enough food to go around, though the dog himself got to stay. I caught my breath on that lie, because even Grandma wasn't that mean. Roka coughed and sat up with his hands on his thighs. He grinned at his wife.

"Well, I think we'd better find out exactly where these two belong," he said.

"You don't have to do that," Mina said. Her voice was pleading, and she studied him carefully. I stood up and stretched out in the direction of the table at the other end of the room, hoping for another piece of that wonderful bread.

"You know," Mina said. "We could live here with you. We're no trouble, and we're very good at helping around the house."

Yashi glanced at her husband, and he narrowed his eyes. "That doesn't sound like such a good idea to me," he said. "I'm sure someone is looking for you. But for now, since it's starting to get dark outside, why don't you girls stay the night with us? Tomorrow we can figure out what to do."

Mina nodded. "Yes," she whispered.

We were arguing about which one of us would get to sleep closest to the fire when there was a loud knock on the door. Roka opened it, and there stood Aunt Gizella, her face framed against the white snow. Mina shrank several inches and held me in front of her like a shield.

Aunt Gizella told Roka that Mina and I had disappeared from the yard, much to the dismay and worry of our grandmother, who'd sent her to find us. She followed our footsteps in the snow until she nearly lost all trace of us. Luckily, an old man down the street pointed her toward this house where he had seen us go in not more than an hour before.

"Why, Magda just about convinced us they were orphans," Roka said.

"Who?" Aunt Gizella asked.

"Magda."

"Uh huh." She crossed her hands angrily over her chest.

"We thought they had no living kin in the world, except for a grandmother who starved them and threw them out of the house."

"Hardly." Aunt Gizella flashed her eyes at us.

"And we were trying to decide what to do with them, whether to send them back out into the cold or let them sleep by the fire."

"Out in the cold is what they deserve. They worried us half to death."

Aunt Gizella bundled us back into our shoes and coats and thanked Roka and Yashi for taking such good care of us. My feet were heavy, and my head ached at the thought of walking all the way back to Grandma's in the snow.

"Are you sure these girls belong to you?" Roka asked. His eyes were laughing now.

Aunt Gizella's cheeks flushed bright red, and she apologized for all our trouble and promised we wouldn't bother them anymore.

"That's all right," Roka said. "I'd like seeing these girls again. They're quite entertaining."

"Please don't give them any more ideas," Aunt Gizella said. "The ones they have cause us enough worry."

All the way home she held onto my wrist until it burned and repeated over and over, "How dare you? How dare you? Now what will people think of Mama?"

But in the end, before she took us back inside to face Grandma, she hugged us close to her and made us promise to keep quiet about what had happened.

"My mother has so much to worry about without you two," she said. "If you even breathe a word of this to anyone, I'll know, and I'll find you and give such bad dreams you'll be afraid to fall asleep at night." I shivered and pressed my body against hers, certain she planned to make good on her promise.

To Grandma, she said, "I discovered these two walking up and down the streets in the center of town, having themselves a nice little holiday."

"Well, I never," Grandma said.

She shook me and Mina roughly on the shoulder and mumbled something about how Mama was raising a bunch of savages without a father to keep us in line. I wanted to shake her right back and tell her that Mama wasn't raising any savages; only she ordered us all to bed with no supper before I could say a word. That night, I was doubly grateful for the bread Roka and Yashi had given us.

The next morning Sam added his own little share of the mischief. Mina and I watched him go into the woods at the back of Grandma's house and hide behind a tree. His pockets were full of stones, though he said they were Grandma's cookies. He threw them at a little boy who was passing by and who howled like a sick dog. That brought Uncle Mihai running with us not far behind, and we giggled when he grabbed Sam by the seat of his pants and spanked him right there.

"I hate you," Sam cried. "I wish you were dead."

Uncle Mihai let go of Sam. My uncle's face was white, and his hands were trembling. "Never say such a thing," he said. "Especially to someone in your family, because the same blood flows in both our veins, and your thoughts and wishes can make the deed come true. Now look what you've done, sentenced me to die."

Sam broke away from Uncle Mihai and disappeared into the woods, but just before nightfall he tiptoed back to the house and sat quietly in a corner. He stared at a small crack in the wall and wouldn't talk to anyone.

"You see what happens when a person's mouth speaks before his mind has time to govern his words," Uncle Mihai said. "That person may be the death of us all."

It was a couple of days before Sam spoke again. Neither Mina nor I could stand his silence, so I carried in an old frog under my coat and dropped it in his lap. He glanced quickly at it and me, as if he'd forgotten I was his sister, and turned away.

"Come on, Sam," Mina said, the second day of his trance. "We need you to help us get the better of that old witch."

Sam looked at her with glazed-over eyes.

"It's no fun without you," she said.

"Yes," I said.

Later that afternoon, Mina took me aside. "We have to think of something," she said. "Isn't he starting to remind you of Grandpa, the way he sits there like a stone?"

That evening, Grandma prepared fish for dinner, and Mina turned up her nose at the smell. "I hate fish," she said. "I won't eat it."

"You will too," Grandma said.

Sam smiled a little bit and stirred in his corner.

"Don't you remember the story of Great Uncle Ziggy?" Mina asked. "He choked on a fish bone at the table and died in front of his family. What a shame it was. He had such a promising future as a doctor."

Sam put his hand over his mouth.

"So?" Grandma asked.

"Well, Mama says fish is poison for everyone in the family," Mina said. "Great Uncle Ziggy cursed it for everyone else."

"Nonsense."

"You can't make me eat it. I'll jump in the lake first."

"Stop that kind of talk!"

Grandma reached out for Mina, but she slipped away and ran out the door and stayed gone well past the dinner hour. Grandma was beginning to look quite concerned by the time she sent Sam and Uncle Mihai out to search for Mina. In a little while, they came back with only one of her shoes and a glove they found on the bank of the small lake beside Grandma's house.

"My God," Grandma said. "What kind of girl would kill herself like that over a piece of fish?" Her eyes wandered back and forth between me and Sam, and she shook her head. "Savages. Savages."

Sam laughed out loud for the first time in days and whispered in my ear, "Good girl, our Mina."

That night Grandma paced the floor and mumbled, "Poison. A family plague. Bad luck. In the blood."

It was pitch black outside when someone crawled under the covers with me and pushed me to one side. I smiled to myself.

The next morning, when Grandma set eyes on Mina, she frowned. "Returned from the dead, I see," she said. "I wish your father was here to see this."

Mina opened one eye and then the other. Aunt Gizella threw up her hands, as if to say, I can't help you now. Uncle Mihai rolled himself a cigarette. He lit it and smoked it halfway down before he lit another one. Soon, the sharp smell of tobacco filled the room. He said our hearts were made of ice and we had no love at all for our family.

The very next afternoon, only five days into the visit, we found ourselves back in Grandpa's wagon, bouncing toward Galfalva.

Mama was surprised to see us so soon. She looked tired and frayed and much thinner. Her skin seemed to hang from her face and arms. Tiny strands of hair escaped from the bun underneath her scarf and curled around her cheeks and neck. I guess Mama missed us so much that, even after Grandpa told her about the mischief we had caused, she smiled and took each of us into her arms and told us how much she loved us. When it was Mina's turn, Mama picked up something from the kitchen table. It was a bright red shawl she knitted during the nights we were gone.

"Happy birthday," she said. "Now I have two treasures born on the same day." She was talking about Kati, of course, who'd been born on Mina's birthday. "You didn't think I had forgotten, did you?"

"No, Mama," Mina said. She didn't thank Mama but gathered the shawl tightly around her shoulders and wore it to bed every night for a week.

We weren't home long before we found out why Mama seemed so worn out. My little sister Kati had a powerful set of lungs and was fond of using them, just as in my dreams.

"This baby cries all day and night to show us how unhappy she is," Mama said. "Maybe she misses her papa."

"I miss him, too," I said, amazed at how easily I was breaking my promise to Itzy.

Mama put her finger over her lips and turned away to soothe Kati.

Over the next few months, we did everything we could to make Kati happy. Mama fed her whenever she cried, and Mina and Sam and I took turns walking her at night to keep her quiet. But she was a tricky one. I held her in my arms, rocking her back and forth so that her eyes closed and her mouth relaxed from its normal pout into something that might almost have been a smile. The minute I tried to put her into bed beside Mama, she started wailing all over again. One night, as I sat in a chair rocking her gently, drifting in and out of sleep, I suddenly found myself on the main street in Marosvasarhely wearing the red shawl that was Mama's birthday present to Mina. My feet barely touched the ground, and I stopped to look in the front window of the Culture Palace that was in the middle of town. It was the place where plays and concerts were held, though we were too poor ever to go. The palace itself was crystal on the outside with dark wooden walls and a glass chandelier on the inside. Aunt Gizella looked back at me through the window with her index finger covering her lips, warning me to be silent. Uncle Mihai stood beside her. He held his right hand high in the air, and it had such a big hole in the center that I could see right through to the other side.

"Be careful not to let your mouth get too far ahead of your mind," he said. "Tell your brother." Aunt Gizella nodded and put her finger over her lips again.

The memory of that dream came back to me several times over the next few days, while I held Kati for Mama or ran to the tavern to deliver boiled eggs and lemon sugar cookies. I knew Uncle Mihai and Aunt Gizella were trying to warn Sam and me about something, but I wasn't sure how to tell my brother about my dream. He was a changed person since our visit to Grandma's and hardly ever went outdoors anymore. Instead, he stayed by himself most of the time and let his shoulders slump forward like he was carrying Uncle Mihai around on them. In between all my chores, I kept a watchful eye on Sam, waiting for my chance to tell him about Uncle Mihai's warning, hoping I might catch him before he made his daily trip to the small post office in town. He seemed to be waiting for a letter, and he usually returned home empty-handed, sullen, and angry.

One afternoon, almost two months after our visit to Grandma's, Sam made his regular trip to the post office. Mama was at the tavern, and Mina had slipped out of the house to the funeral of the baby of a family living behind the school Mina and Sam attended. Mama had told Mina she couldn't go.

"It's not natural for a girl your age to think about death so much," she said.

Mina shrugged. "I can't help it," she said. "I love the candles and the flowers and the singing and all the people, so dressed up."

Mama grabbed Mina's shoes and stuffed them under her arm before she left that morning.

Mina watched her walk through the courtyard toward the tavern and whispered, "You can't stop me, no matter what you do."

It was a cold, wet day, but she put on her best dress and coat, tied her hair back with a ribbon, and, wearing her funeral expression—shining eyes, tight mouth—went out the door barefoot, carrying dry socks in her pocket. The moment I was alone with Kati, my baby sister held her breath until her face turned blue, and I was sure she was going to choke to death. Then she let out a loud yell that went on and on. I tried rocking her and feeding her warm water with honey in it. I bundled her up with blankets and took them off again. I sponged her face and tickled her toes, but she wouldn't stop crying. Finally, I reached over and pinched her cheek so hard I left a red mark there.

"Be quiet," I said. "I hate you."

Her eyes opened wide, and her mouth clamped shut. The awful silence that followed pounded in my ears. I didn't know Sam was standing behind me until he started to laugh.

"Uh oh," he said. "You'd better hope that mark fades away before Mama gets home."

"Why?" I asked. "I'll just say you did it."

He took Kati from me and smiled and danced her around the room. "Mama will never believe it. Anyhow, if you do, I'll throw you in my underground cave and let the bats eat you alive."

I stared at him for a moment. "Bats don't like to eat people for dinner."

"Mine do. I've trained them specially with tiny morsels of your flesh."

I was so glad to have the old Sam back again that I ran forward to kiss him, but he ducked out of my reach and pulled an envelope out of his coat and waved it in front of me. It was bulging on one side.

"What's that?" I asked.

"A letter from Uncle Mihai," Sam said. "With a bullet inside."

"He's not dead, is he?" My heart raced along with fear for my uncle, who always had a kind word for me.

"No, stupid. If he was dead, how could he send me a letter? He says he shot himself in the hand, the right hand, his spanking hand, while he was cleaning his gun. He says the bullet went all the way through and left a big hole so that he won't be spanking anyone for quite a while. He says that's what came of my wishing he was dead, and he had to get a friend to write for him to tell me the news right away. Now he says I don't have to worry about killing him. He says he's the one who's sorry."

Sam passed Kati back to me and shook the bullet out of the envelope. He searched for a piece of string, wound it around the bullet, tied the string around his neck, and twirled the bullet between his fingers.

"You see what happens to anyone who raises a hand against me!" he said. He pushed out his chest and swelled up so much that his pride nearly took over the whole room.

"Wait! I don't think that's what Uncle Mihai meant," I said.

"How would you know?" He opened the door and stood there laughing, with the wind and snow at his back and the bullet glistening between his fingers.

ROSES FOR KATI

A few weeks after Uncle Mihai's letter arrived, on the first warm morning in March, Sam made a big show of putting his bullet around his neck and bragging about it to my little sister, who was just three months old.

"Be careful, my son," Mama said.

Sam cradled the bullet gently in his palm.

After he and Mina left for school, Mama took my little sister in her arms and went into the backyard to check on the patch of land where we planted our vegetables every year. I followed along, gripping the fold of Mama's skirt tightly.

"I worry about that boy," she said. She had dirt under her thumbnail and on her forehead in the place where she'd rubbed it after touching the ground, and her blouse was dusty. "I'll tell you a secret. I wish someone would steal that bullet away from him."

"Oh, Mama," I said.

Kati began to gurgle quietly and frown up at Mama, and Mama and I busied ourselves figuring out how to set up the rows of vegetables. We didn't notice when our neighbor Mrs. Davich entered the yard. She and her husband lived in a big expensive house at the end of our street, with five rooms and fireplaces upstairs and down. A few days after Kati was born, Mrs. Davich gave Mama a fancy buggy with a pink velvet ribbon on the side. Mama never used the buggy, except to push bottles of beer and cognac up the hill to our house to sell them in the tavern. About once a week, Mrs. Davich stopped by to look in on Kati and tell Mama what a beautiful child she was. Mama always mumbled a quick "thank you" and held Kati close to her, as if she were afraid Mrs. Davich might steal the baby.

"That old woman is a witch with designs on other people's children," Mama said each time Mrs. Davich went away. "Lets her evil eyes wander all over the neighborhood in search of newborn babies to snatch up in the middle of the night when their parents are asleep and can't watch out for them. I guess we should be grateful to Kati for screaming and fussing at night. At least we can be sure no one will take her away without our knowing about it."

The idea of Mrs. Davich watching and waiting all the time gave me the chills.

Our neighbor was practically on top of us that morning before she asked, "How are you, Mrs. Spirer?"

At the sound of her voice, Mama stood up straight and pressed Kati so hard against her chest the baby squealed.

"Good morning," Mama said.

"How's our lovely little girl this morning?" Mrs. Davich asked.

She glided silently toward us, and Mama flinched when Mrs. Davich reached over to brush her finger against Kati's cheek.

"Fine," Mama said. "*My* baby is fine. Healthy and happy."

At that exact moment, Kati let out a wail, as if to show Mrs. Davich that Mama was wrong. Mama always told us Kati was born unhappy with the world, as some people are, and there was nothing we could do about it.

"I'd like a word with you in private," Mrs. Davich said to Mama.

I could feel the tension inside Mama as I let go of her skirt, wrapped my arms around her elbow, and leaned my head against her waist. I held my breath and listened to hers. For that one instant, I lost the place where she began and I ended. I thought, this must be what it was like before I pushed my way out into the world. She hitched Kati high up on her shoulder and bounced me away so that I was my own separate self again.

"I have no secrets from Serene," Mama said. I could see the tiny web of lines around her eyes and the creases in her forehead that never went away anymore, even when she was sleeping. "Whatever it is you want, you can talk in front of her."

Mrs. Davich cleared her throat. "No. I don't think so."

She looked down at me with her sharp witch's eyes and twined her arm around Mama's and guided her a few feet away to the edge of the yard. After they spoke quietly for a minute, Mama shook her head "no" over and over. I couldn't be sure, but I thought she was crying. She reached for the scarf she wore whenever she went out of the house and pulled it forward until it almost touched her eyebrows. Mrs. Davich held out her hand with something shiny inside, and Mama trembled.

"Never," she said.

She backed further and further away until she practically stepped on me. I couldn't move. My feet were stuck to the ground.

"Wait," Mrs. Davich said. "We have money. We can give her the best of everything. There's talk of war now all the time. What will you do with four children and no husband? Live on the road like Gypsies?"

"That's none of your business," Mama said. "Kati is mine. I would never give her away, even if I had ten husbands and they all disappeared. You can't change that with all your gifts and your money and your black magic. Blood, Mrs. Davich. Flesh and blood bind me to this child."

Mrs. Davich wilted, and when she spoke, her voice was barely a whisper. "Promise you will think about it, at least."

"There's nothing to think about."

Mrs. Davich held her hand to her stomach and walked slowly out of the yard. Mama didn't take her eyes off the old woman's back until she was out of sight. Mama whispered that she had to watch Mrs. Davich to be certain she hadn't left any evil charms behind. By this time, Kati was screaming. I couldn't remember the last time she'd let any of us sleep through the night. Ever since she was born, Sam and Mina and I fought over who was supposed to feed or walk her. We were each sure the others schemed to miss their turns. If we accidentally fell asleep in the rocker, as I did one night, and let her slide to the floor, she would wake everyone with her howling and make Mama angry at all of us the next day. I was sick of the noise and mess and the way we couldn't play in the house because we might make Kati cry. The truth was I didn't love my little sister, though I knew I was supposed to. As Mama said, her blood ran in my veins and tied me to her forever, and even if she was mean and unhappy, she was my sister. Still, I was tired of that purple face and shrieking red mouth, and I didn't think sending Kati to live with the Daviches was such a bad idea.

My thoughts must have shown on my face because Mama shook my arm and said, "Serene! Take Kati inside. It's getting windy out here, and she might catch cold."

Kati's screams made my ears ring, and as I walked toward the house, I imagined how peaceful it would be never to hear those sounds again. I wanted to run after Mrs. Davich and beg her to take Kati with my blessing. Kati cried harder and struggled in my arms as if, like Mama, she knew what I was thinking.

I grasped her tighter and said under my breath, "I wish you were dead."

The moment those words escaped into the cool morning air, I grew dizzy and feverish. I crept inside the house and stumbled into bed, taking Kati with me. Her cries echoed in the distance. I felt as if I was on one of the trains behind our house, moving farther away toward Papa, who was waiting for me where the tracks ended and the ocean began. For a long time, I didn't know whether I was awake or asleep. Mama held my hand and told me I had the influenza, but she said I'd be all right. I closed my eyes and saw a gaping mouth that belonged to

Kati. Somehow, it belonged to me as well, and Kati and I were one. We opened our mouth wide, but no sound came out. I kicked at my blanket and jabbed my fists in the air to get away from that mouth and to wake up from my dream. I sat upright, gasping, before Mama's hand coaxed me to lie down again.

I couldn't hear Kati's cries, and when I remembered where I was, there didn't seem to be much noise in the house at all. A couple of times our village doctor's face floated in front of mine, and a hand as dry as paper rested for a minute on my forehead. Another face of a man I'd never seen before also floated by, and Mama began to sob. She was always by my side, the ends of her mouth turned down with worry and the lines in the corner of her eyes cutting deeper and deeper into the skin.

"You did this to me," I heard her say, as I drifted back to sleep.

I tried to tell her I was sorry, but I was too tired to speak. When I was strong enough to sit up on my own, Mama said I'd been in bed for over a week.

"I didn't mean it," I said.

Mama put her hand on my forehead. "You're still feverish," she said.

"Where's Kati?" My skin felt clammy, and tiny hairs prickled the back of my neck.

"Very sick," Mama replied. "Almost dead. Measured already for her coffin." She let out a single dry sob, and I saw that she had cried so much she had no more tears left.

I slid back under the covers and cried for her and for what I'd done to my baby sister. I was angry at myself for not learning anything from the hole in Uncle Mihai's hand and the bullet around Sam's neck or paying enough attention to the warnings of my aunt and uncle to love my family, no matter what. I didn't know if it was too late, but I started praying to God to undo my terrible wish. I shut my eyes so tightly my cheeks ached and pressed my fingers together in prayer until I felt sore all over. I stayed under my blankets, refusing even Mama's offer of a bowl of my very favorite bean soup. I tried hard not to fall asleep, although pictures of hands with holes in them and fingers over lips flashed before my eyes.

I buried my face in my pillow and whispered, "Please, God. I didn't mean it. If You let her live, I promise I'll never make such a terrible wish again. Kill me, not Kati."

Once I heard Sam ask, "Is she ever coming out?"

Mina giggled.

Finally, Mama pulled the blankets off my back and said, "Come on, Serene. You're fine. Stop acting this way. Did old Mrs. Davich put a spell on you? What if she crawled inside your body with you?"

"Ooh," I said. "But I can't get up."

"Why?"

"Because I'm not done with my prayers. I have to save Kati."

"Now I'm certain that woman has done something awful to you."

"No. It's true."

There was a familiar scream behind Mama. Then another, and another.

"She's not dead?" I asked.

"Does it sound that way?" Mama asked. She smiled and pulled me slowly to my feet. The room spun around, and there were black spots in front of my eyes.

"Kati's fever broke yesterday," she said. "It was a miracle. Even the doctor can't believe it. He was sure she was going to die."

That day was the first time I ever saw Kati smile. There was a light in her eyes that made them look almost green. Her skin was bright pink, and her face was full of wonder. After a few hours, though, she turned sulky and unhappy again for no reason.

Mama took extra care of me after she forced me to get out of bed. "We have to make a special effort now to stay close together," she said.

"Why, because of Papa?" I asked. I covered my mouth and made another silent apology to Itzy.

"Stop thinking about that."

"I'm sorry."

She sat down beside me and began to braid my hair absentmindedly. "There's so much evil in the world. We can't give one child away here and another there. No one can love a child like a mother can, no matter how much money that other person might have."

"You're right, Mama. You are."

Every time Mama took Kati and me into the yard, she covered my shoulders with one arm and tucked Kati to her chest with the other. She looked in front of us and over her shoulder and sucked in a deep breath, as if Mrs. Davich might have poisoned the air.

"I'll show her, that old witch," she said. "Trying to take my babies away from me."

She hardly let us out of her sight, except when she wheeled the buggy down the hill to buy beer. Then she made Sam or Mina watch us so we didn't catch a chill or a cough. Once when she returned from a trip, she brought something extra with her, a rosebush she bought from some Gypsies who told her it had special powers. She said she didn't know if that was true, but when she saw it, she knew what she wanted to do with it. We went inside the little shed next to Papa's blacksmith shop in the backyard, and she took a small wooden box from a dark corner. It was Kati's coffin, the one Mama had ordered and paid for when she had lost all hope for my baby sister. Now because God had been kind enough to listen to my prayers, Kati had lived. I tried to push away unpleasant thoughts about the awful wish that had started all the trouble, but I couldn't.

"Why so sad?" Mama asked. "No one died."

"I know," I said.

Mama removed the lid from the coffin and knocked the bottom out. Together we carried the frame to the side of the house where there was plenty of light. We filled the frame with dark, rich soil from our vegetable garden. Mama dug a hole in the soil with her fingers and put the rosebush in, covering the roots with dirt and watering it carefully so that the leaves and tiny buds began reaching immediately for the sun.

"The roses will remind us of the miracle that spared our beloved Kati," she said. "And restored the health of our beloved Serene, my own."

She bowed her head and prayed silently. She covered my hand with both of hers, and for one moment I felt safe and secure.

Mama and I fed and cared for that bush until two years later, when the Romanians started fighting with the Hungarians and drove us from our home. The first blooms were yellow like the pale sun in the early summer sky. The second blooms were the same purple as the ribbons on Uncle Mihai's uniform, and the last ones were as red as the blood that ran in our veins and bound our family together. All from that one magical bush. Kati's roses, we called these flowers, and we smiled when people from around the village came to tell us that no single plant could bring forth so many wonderful colors.

DO/\INO

$\Lambda\Lambda$iss Kovacz clapped and said "Dismissed," and the next thing I knew I was running along the dirt road that led away from school, listening to the flap-flap of my shoes and blinking at the dust they kicked up, remembering how the other children made fun of my dress. It was Mina's before it was mine, and the cotton was worn shiny in places from too many washings. Mama made the dress from bright red material when Mina was in the first grade like me. Looking at it now, you could hardly tell it was even pink anymore. I had to stop running because I was short of breath. Sometimes I couldn't catch my breath at all, and Mama said that happened because I wanted to forget how sick I'd been and God wanted to remind me how lucky I was just to be alive. I fingered the flower Mama had embroidered on the pocket of my dress to make it prettier for my first day and started to cry. I hated school, but Mama said I had to go, unless I wanted to end up washing floors in some rich woman's house.

"That's what happens to little girls who can't read and write," she said the night before school began. "There's a terrible war going on."

"Really?" I asked.

"Why, yes. They shot our poor Francis Ferdinand in the streets of Sarajevo this summer. My heart goes out to Franz Josef, losing a nephew like that." She sighed. "Who knows if Transylvania will even be a part of Hungary after all the fighting is over? Maybe one day we'll have to leave and go far away. Maybe we'll end up in America like Papa's

49

brothers. They don't let any dummies into that country. Sam and Kati and Mina and I will all get on the boat, but you'll have to stay here by yourself because you didn't want to go to school and learn how to read."

"No, I won't," I said. "Besides, you would never leave me."

Mama looked at me in that sharp-eyed way of hers that made me feel as though she could see right through my skin. "Don't be so sure. In the meantime, you're going to get an education, and that's all there is to it."

That afternoon, when the school yard was finally out of sight, I imagined Mama had opened the door of our house and pushed me into a deep hole where the steps used to be. While I was falling, people laughed and pointed at me and said I was the ugliest girl in school. When I got to the bottom, I had to crawl back out, hand over hand. The door with Mama behind it kept moving farther away.

I was so lost in my thoughts I guess I wasn't paying much attention to where I was going. I must've turned the second corner by my house instead of the first and accidentally ended up in front of the Daviches. Usually I didn't like to pass by that old witch's door because I knew she cast evil spells on children she couldn't steal. Mama said that every time Mrs. Davich came into our yard she carried along a dark shadow that covered most of the grass, and she said it was her job to be sure Kati and I didn't breathe in any more of that shadow because we might really die the next time.

As I stood in front of Mrs. Davich's house, the sky turned dark, and I got goosebumps all up and down my arms. I glanced up at the verandah, and there was old Mrs. Davich. Her gray-green eyes looked as if they belonged on the face of a dead man, and her colorless hair was pulled into a tight bun. She was skinny and wore a black dress, which only made her face and hands look whiter. She smiled at me.

"Serene," she said. She had a funny way of speaking, almost like she was biting off the ends of her words. "You've been standing there for such a long time. Is something wrong? Would you like to come inside for a glass of lemonade and cookies?"

I knew I should say "no." I tried to shake my head and walk away; honestly I did. But the cicadas were singing so loudly, and the hot, late-summer air shimmered in front of me. A strong wind at my back pushed me toward the house, except not a single branch moved on the weeping willow tree beside Mrs. Davich's verandah.

I had never been inside her house before, though Sam said he sneaked up to the window one night and saw spider webs in the doorways and bats hanging from the walls. He said the whole place glowed bright green and smelled like wet clothes left inside a dark cellar for weeks. Of course, the inside wasn't like that at all. Mrs. Davich had polished wood floors, and the whole place smelled like pine cones. She called out to a maid who came into the living room wearing a starched white apron and carrying a tray with two glasses of lemonade and a plate of cookies. The maid's cheeks were flushed pink.

The lemonade was too sour, and the cookies were hard and reminded me of the ones my grandmother made. It was best to suck on them a while before taking a bite, because that way you wouldn't break any teeth. I was glad the cookies were like rocks. I had to spend so much time working off little pieces to swallow I couldn't think about where I was sitting.

"That's a lovely flower on your pocket," Mrs. Davich said. "It reminds me of the roses that grow in your yard."

"Uh huh," I said. My mouth was too full of cookie crumbs for me to speak. The cookies themselves grew sweeter the longer I sucked on them, though after a while they turned a little bitter on my tongue.

"So, tell me. How is school? This must be your first year."

I shrugged, but not fast enough to stop one big tear from running down my cheek.

"Oh, my dear," Mrs. Davich said. She stood up and walked toward my chair and dabbed my face with a handkerchief. When she knelt down in front of me, she smelled musty. "Other children can be cruel."

"How do you know?" I asked.

"Because I was a little girl once."

"You were?" Somehow I couldn't picture her as anything but a dried-up old lady.

She took a deep breath. "I have something for you to take away the pain." She shook the sleeve of her dress, and out fell a tiny heart made of pink glass that hung on a gold chain. "If you take care of this, it will bring you good luck."

She slipped the chain around my neck before I could say "no" or duck out of the way.

"Thank you," I said.

I couldn't help liking the way the gold scratched against my skin. I wanted to touch the glass heart, but I was afraid. I'd never worn a necklace before in my life, and each time I started to reach for it I pushed my hand back down to my side.

"Touching it won't hurt it," Mrs. Davich said. "In fact, when you touch it, you should be able to pay closer attention to your wishes and read your own heart better."

I ran my index finger along the smooth edge of the glass near where it came to a point and gulped down the rest of my lemonade and sucked on another cookie before backing my way out of the house. I jumped down the steps of Mrs. Davich's verandah one at a time, look-ing back and forth to make sure no one was watching. Behind me, I could feel Mrs. Davich and her sad, dead eyes pulling me toward her. That made me jump forward with all my might.

I walked slowly toward my house, cupping the glass heart in my hand. Right before I crossed over the front yard, I took the necklace off and hid it in my pocket and didn't let go of it until it grew so hot I thought it might burn a hole in my palm. I couldn't look Mama in the eye when she asked me about my first day at school because I was sure she'd guess just what I'd been up to. She held out a plate of her own sugar cookies, which were soft and moist and had a pleasant orangey taste. Usually, she had to stop me from eating the whole batch, but on that day, I said I wasn't hungry and went to my bed at the far corner of the room and lay down with my face to the wall. I put my hand in my pocket and turned the glass heart over and over, listening to my own heart like Mrs. Davich told me I should. It said, "Liar, liar, liar."

That night I didn't eat much dinner. My secret sat like a huge stone on top of my stomach. When I got ready for bed, I worried about how I was going to sneak the heart under the pillow from the pocket of my dress. I waited until Mama and Mina and Sam and Kati were breathing heavily and not moving in their beds before reaching for that piece of glass and tucking it safely under my pillow. I fell into a deep sleep, and the next morning my head ached on the very spot where it touched the heart through my pillow.

Still, I wanted to wear the necklace because it was so pretty and because I was afraid of what Mrs. Davich might do if I didn't. Maybe Mama was right after all, and Mrs. Davich had already tried to kill me. Maybe now she might throw me down a well if I left her gift hidden away at home.

I had to be sure Mama wouldn't find out about the glass heart, so every morning I became a juggler, moving it from hand to hand until it landed in the right pocket. A couple of times, I caught Mama staring at me sideways, and once or twice she wondered out loud exactly what I was hiding from her. She didn't force me to tell her, and I went out of the house every morning with my treasure in my fist. Luckily, Sam and Mina said I was too pokey for them and hurried off ahead of me to school. They were in a separate classroom and played with their own friends, who were older and didn't want to have anything to do with me. When I got far enough away from home, I slipped the necklace on and smiled at the idea of having such a beautiful thing to wear all day long.

The mayor of Galfalva lived down the road from us and had a daughter my age named Lena. Except everyone called her Domino because she had coal black hair and eyes and white skin and because all she had to do was push a little bit and one thing after another fell over in her path until she got whatever she wanted. She was so pretty that when she stamped her foot boys would steal apples from other girls' lunches for her, fight over marbles to give to her, or throw stones at Miss Kovacz's back because she said a cross word to Domino in class. Even Sam was in love with her. He waited in a tree for her after school one afternoon, hanging upside-down in front of her face, and gave her a huge grasshopper he caught especially for her. Of course, Domino didn't pay any attention to him or me or anyone else, although I wasn't really surprised one afternoon when she started circling around me, never taking her eyes off my glass heart.

This wasn't the first time I saw the power of my strange necklace. When Mama wasn't looking, I dangled it in front of the geese in our backyard, and they sat down quietly before flopping on their sides. Afterwards, Mama stuffed them with grain so their livers would grow fat and delicious to eat. She never got over how I settled them down so they wouldn't fuss when she pried open their beaks. I could do the same thing with chickens too, make them roll over and almost offer to have their necks broken so they could be cooked for the evening meal.

That wasn't all. One day, about a week after Mrs. Davich gave me the necklace, Mama asked me to take Kati's buggy down the hill into town to the store there to fill it up with beer for Papa's tavern. Going down the hill was fun, but pushing that buggy full of bottles back up was hard work. Besides, why should I have to do everything? Why couldn't Mina or Sam help out once in a while? I held my glass heart in my hand and squeezed my eyes shut, and before I knew it, Mina, who never helped with any chores around the house, said she'd be glad to go. Mama smiled at her, the way she used to smile at me when I did things to please her. I didn't like that, so I wished Mina a little taste of bad luck on her trip home. Sure enough, her hand slipped on the way up the hill, and the buggy rolled back down before she could stop it, turning over and breaking all the bottles. Mina was in tears when she opened the front door and wheeled in the empty buggy. It was all wet inside and full of slivers of glass. Mama patted Mina on the shoulder and said it was all right. We all knew it wasn't, because she didn't give Mina that special smile she saved for the times we made her proud or did her favors.

When Sam told Mama he thought I was getting too fat and lazy, I held on to that heart and wished hard, and Mama made him sweep out the big oven in the backyard, until his face and hands were black with soot.

"You may fool Mama," he said, reaching over to pinch my arm. "But you don't fool me."

I stuck my tongue out at him, sure my magic was much stronger than his.

The afternoon Domino first noticed my necklace, I saw just how powerful my magic was. When she smiled at me, I felt the earth slide ever so slightly underneath my feet, and I was so happy I wanted to cry. I almost did cry. My eyes filled with tears, and I only stopped myself by hanging on to that glass heart and thinking about how its edges cut into my skin.

"Want to play together?" I asked.

"Yes," Domino said.

We walked to one corner of the school yard in silence and sat down in the dust where the grass had been worn away by the trampling feet of years and years of students. Domino grabbed a stick and drew a circle in the dirt. I took the stick away from her very gently, because she never gave up anything without a fight and because I was afraid to made her angry. "Dom plus S," I wrote inside the circle. She smiled at me and stood up and ran back toward school. I followed after her.

"Meet me at the corner by my house," she said. "We'll walk together tomorrow morning."

"Good," I said. Again, I tried hard not to cry, because I'd never had a friend before who wasn't in my family.

"Let me wear your necklace until we get to school," she said the next morning.

I started to shake so hard I could barely squeak out a "no."

Domino kicked her foot on the ground, and a chunk of dirt flew up and stung me on the leg. I expected her to push me into the shrubbery that lined the road, but instead she asked, "Why?"

I glanced back in the direction of Mrs. Davich's house. Although I hadn't seen her since the first day of school, I had the feeling she was always watching me, and I was afraid she'd show up one day to take my glass heart away.

"Someone gave it to me for a little while, and I promised to take care of it and not let anything happen to it," I said.

Domino frowned and ran ahead of me yelling, "Selfish! Selfish!" That didn't stop her from waiting for me every morning and trying to get me to give her the necklace for a minute or two.

In those days, back in Hungary, we only had Sundays off from school. Of course, Mama wouldn't let us go on Saturday because of the Sabbath. Instead, we went to synagogue in the morning, and on Friday nights, too. The rest of Saturday we stayed quietly inside our house, unless Sam and I managed to sneak out while Mama was busy with Kati or Mina slipped off to one of her funerals. On Mondays, when I went back to school, Miss Kovacz tested me on all the spelling words she assigned when I was absent and never took "I don't know" for an answer. More than once, she pulled me by the ear to one corner of the room and made me stand with my back to the other children after I misspelled a word. She always called on me first thing Monday, with her arms crossed over her chest and her eyebrows raised so high they looked like they might fly off her forehead. Standing in the corner early one morning, listening to the mocking laughter and whispers of my classmates, I rolled my glass heart lightly in my fingers and wondered what I ought to do about the words I missed because of the Sabbath. I knew Domino had her eye on my necklace, mainly because of its strong magic, but also because she never liked to be told she couldn't have something she wanted. An idea came to me.

The next day, when she asked to try on the glass heart, I said, "Maybe."

"Oh!" she said and danced around me.

"But first you have to do a favor for me. You have to pass a friendship test."

She stopped dancing and narrowed her eyes at me. It was a funny thing about her eyes. They were so dark you couldn't see her pupils, and that made it doubly hard to read what was going on behind them.

"What?" she asked. Her voice was low and suspicious.

"Bring me Saturday's spelling words on Sunday afternoon for three weeks, and the Monday after the third Sunday, I'll let you try on the necklace for one minute," I said.

She jumped up and down and ran ahead of me, but the mere thought of my promise frightened me so much that I didn't run after her. I was afraid to touch the glass heart because I thought it might break into a hundred pieces. I shut my eyes for a moment, and Mrs. Davich's face appeared.

"You shouldn't have given away my trust so easily," she said. "And for what? A few pathetic spelling words."

"Wait!" I said, but she vanished.

When I opened my eyes, I saw only the gray, late-September morning sky. That afternoon, I passed by Mrs. Davich's on purpose. I couldn't believe I was really looking for her. The front door was closed and the windows were shuttered, but somehow I felt those cold, dead eyes boring through me even after the house was out of sight.

Domino was true to her promise, and for the next three Sundays, she knocked on our front door and sat outside while I copied the words onto a tiny slate board that had been Mina's and Sam's and was now mine. While I was writing down the words, I glanced at her out of the corner of my eye. I wasn't sure she knew I was looking at her, but she acted as if it was the most natural thing in the world. Still, I couldn't believe she was sitting on my front steps.

Of course, Sam had to stick his nose in when Domino and I were together. He kept trying to say hello to her, and the more she pretended she didn't see him, the more he tried to get her to notice him. The first Sunday, after Mama gave each of us a piece of her delicious honey cake with raspberry jam in the middle, Sam smeared the jam on his face so that he had a dark red mustache. He hunched over and smiled at Domino, but she drew her knees up to her chest and kept her eyes glued to her cake.

"Hey, where's your necklace?" she said. She pointed at my empty neck.

"What necklace?" Sam asked. "What's she talking about?"

I shook my head "no" at Domino and turned to Sam. "Nothing, none of your business," I said. I reached inside my pocket and wrapped my hand around the glass heart and wished that Sam wouldn't say anything to Mama. He didn't.

After I finished copying words, I asked Domino if she wanted to play, and she nodded, as if she barely heard me.

"I want to show you something," I said.

She nodded again.

"No, really," I said. "It's exciting."

For the only time since we became friends, she followed me. I took her through the trees behind our house, until we came to the railroad tracks at the wood's edge.

"The train goes by here twice a week," I said. "On Tuesdays and again on Fridays. Always the same. Two o'clock in the afternoon. It's the only one around here. Mama says it goes all the way to the ocean, and one day we're going to get on it and travel far away from here."

"Why?" Domino asked. "Because of your papa? My papa says your papa's a thief, and he says your papa ran away and hid in the woods."

I reached inside my pocket and touched my necklace to keep from crying. "That's not true. Papa would never do such a thing. He's gone. Dead. And we're not allowed to talk about it."

"Why?"

"We're not. That's all."

"Why do you have to leave?"

"Because Mama says it's a big world, and we have to find important things to do in it." I smiled a little at the idea of unknown places that were far away from Galfalva.

At school, Miss Kovacz was surprised that first Monday when I knew all my words. She called on me, and I watched her fingers twitch, as if they were dying to grab hold of my ear, and slowly fold themselves back into her palm in disappointment when I spelled the words right.

"You're up to some mischief, Serene," she said. "I'll be watching you from now on, and you'll be sorry when I find out."

"Yes, ma'am," I said. Afterwards, no one laughed at me or whispered behind my back.

The next Sunday, Sam was ready for Domino with an old frog he caught in a puddle by the road on the way home from school. He tied a string around its neck to make it look like a gift.

"I'm sure she's going to love that," Mina said. The way she rolled her eyes made me laugh.

"Be quiet," Sam said.

Mina was right. Domino cringed at the sight of the frog and went right on pretending Sam was invisible.

The second Monday, when Miss Kovacz called on me again, I watched her frown settle in deeper and deeper with each word I spelled right. I was hoping she'd forget about me and my absences, but that wasn't her way. She was the kind to put a problem in her head and scratch at it until she figured out the answer or bled to death trying. She called on me on Tuesday and Wednesday too. Finally, I pressed the glass heart between my fingers and wished for her to get a real itch she couldn't scratch so she'd pick on that for a while and leave me alone. Sure enough, not a minute later, she started to break out in a rash and had to leave school and didn't come back for the rest of the week. Everyone said she must've been bitten by a spider, but I knew better.

The Sunday before I let Domino wear my necklace, she was even more quiet than usual. She handed the words over to me and rested her face in her lap while I copied them onto my slate board. Afterwards, she didn't want to go to the railroad tracks, and when I looked into her eyes, they were darker and more mysterious than ever. Before she left, she brushed against my arm, and her touch was hot and so sharp it made me jump.

"Don't forget," she said. Her black, black eyes looked just like Papa's.

The next morning she was waiting for me on the corner by her house. I slipped the necklace off and dropped it into her cupped hands.

"Only one minute," I said.

She was already running down the road, her hair blowing straight out behind her in the wind of a storm that was gathering in the dark sky. I ran after her, but she was so fast and so far ahead of me that I almost lost sight of her before I reached the schoolhouse. Groups of students parted in front of her as she ran with her head thrown back and her laughter screaming in the wind.

Miss Kovacz was inside. She had tiny red blotches all over her hands and arms, and she called on me to stand up and shouted the first word on the spelling list. I stumbled over it and the second and the third, until I realized none of the words were the same as the ones

Domino had given me the day before. I might have been able to spell one or two of them right, but each time I tried, I reached for my necklace by habit. When it wasn't there, my mind went blank. My throat was so dry it felt like tiny knives were cutting me inside. Miss Kovacz grabbed my ear and dug her nails in hard and paid no attention to my cries as she dragged me across the room to the corner, where I spent the morning. My ears were on fire, and the room spun around. Tears rolled down my cheeks and soaked the collar of my dress. I looked everywhere for Domino at lunch: in the yard, in the church across the way, and up and down the streets around school. I wandered so far I almost missed the second bell. My face was tracked with dirt, and my ears rang. I was burning up with fever. I couldn't sit still, even after I saw Domino with her head down on her desk. I couldn't tell whether she was wearing the glass heart.

She disappeared at afternoon recess, too, and by the time I caught up with her at the end of the day, she wasn't paying attention to anything but the silver buttons on the beautiful bright green sweater she'd worn to school that morning. I grabbed onto the sleeve and twisted the material hard.

"Where is it?" I asked.

The glass heart was nowhere in sight, but there was a nasty mark on her neck. I wondered whether the gold chain had started to eat through her skin.

"It stung me like a big old bee," she said. She touched the spot and winced, as if the memory of the necklace pained her. For a moment, the light went out of her eyes, and her skin was so pale I thought she looked plain, pale and dead like Mrs. Davich. "Besides, it was ugly, so I threw it away in the grass behind school."

"You . . . you," I said. I twisted her sweater harder and harder, hoping it would tear. Since it was brand new, heavy wool, all it did was give a little more each time I pulled on it.

I let go of her sweater and went out to the school yard to look for my necklace. The grass was thick and high, and I had to search for a long time before I saw something shiny hidden there. My glass heart was broken in two places. I reached over to pick it up and cut my finger on one of the sharp edges. I put my broken treasure in my pocket and wound my way slowly home, circling street after street up the long hill to the road at the top until I passed Mrs. Davich's house. It was still shut up. I arrived at our front steps, and Mama sat quietly with Kati in her arms. She asked me to charm one of the chickens into sacrificing itself for dinner, but when I went into the courtyard behind our house, the chickens scattered, and Mama herself had to run after them with Kati screaming at her hip. Later, Sam kicked me under the table at dinner, and when I cried out, Mama said I had to wash all the dishes for a week. That night, I left the necklace in the pocket of my dress and didn't worry whether Mama or anyone else would find it, since the magic was all gone out of it. The next morning I didn't go to school, either. Oh, I pretended I did. I let Mama pack me a lunch, and I washed my face and hands at the well out back and ate my breakfast as usual. When I got to the corner by the hill into town, I turned away and walked home. I went around my house to the woods behind it and rested against a tree with my broken necklace in my hand and waited for the sound of the train that passed by every Tuesday afternoon.

I must've slept most of the morning, because the train was on the tracks right below me before I heard the whistle and felt the earth beneath me rumble and shake. I reached over and dropped the pieces of my glass heart onto one of the cars on the train. They bounced along the top, and I could see them shine in the bright sunlight. I leaned forward, ready to jump onto one of the coal cars. I rocked back and forth against the tree and tried to pick up speed. Just as I was about to fly away and go wherever the train might take me, the roots of that tree twined themselves around my feet and kept me planted there, until the sound of the whistle faded into the afternoon air and the train itself narrowed down to a pinpoint in the distance.

THE FUNERAL

The first time I saw Papa again was about a year after he melted. It was at the end of the Friday service on a stuffy October evening, and I was tired from a long week under Miss Kovacz's punishing gaze and endless round of spelling words. I let the rabbi's singsong lull me into a gentle half-sleep and rested against Mama's arm, looking in a lazy kind of way for Sam and my cousin Itzy on the other side of the synagogue. I found them leaning forward with their elbows propped on their knees and their chins resting in the palms of their hands like identical twins. A man with flecks of gray hair and a pinched mouth had squeezed in between them. I stared at him for a long moment and then nearly jumped out of my seat and said, "Papa!" I closed my eyes, but when I opened them again, he was gone.

An instant later, an icy hand tickled the back of my neck. I froze, afraid to turn around and scream and make a fuss, because the service was Mama's favorite time during the week. Lately, she was always tired, and sad, too. She woke up most mornings with tears in her eyes that didn't go away by the time she fixed breakfast and sent us off to school. So I tried to be especially careful on Friday nights and Saturday mornings not to do anything that might make her angry.

"Be still, Serene," she said. She spoke out of the corner of her mouth and nudged me with her elbow. "The rabbi is almost finished."

"Yes, Mama," I replied. I hugged myself, and the ice on my neck turned into a sticky sweat.

I didn't mention anything about Papa to Mama or Mina or Sam and thought I must have been seeing things. For supper that evening, Mama had baked a wonderful sponge cake sprinkled with nutmeg, which she said would make me dizzy and cause angels to dance in front of my eyes if I ate too much. I decided it was my second piece of cake that had brought Papa back to me and vowed to take only one helping in the future. Of course, I didn't always keep my vow. Still, every time I started to reach for seconds, I saw Papa perched above the serving plate to remind me that my stomach asked for more than it really needed. Sometimes, though, I couldn't help giving in.

Later that night, Mina and I went to the shed behind the blacksmith's shop to sleep. Mama had been baking *challah* in there all day, so the shed was warm and thick with the smell of that sweet, yeasty bread. Whenever Itzy was here for his regular visit, we had to shift beds and share with one another, but if Mina and I slept in the shed, we could have a whole room to ourselves. Mama gave us a candle and some extra blankets and pillows, and we settled ourselves on the dome of the oven. The stone was still warm, and we were so close our heads touched. The candle burned steadily on the shelf below.

"Have you noticed Itzy's mustache?" Mina asked. She laughed. "Such a little man."

"So?" I said. The subject of Itzy was a sore one for me. Over the last year, he had ignored me. He didn't want to talk anymore, even after we swore a blood oath together, and he went out of his way never to be alone with me.

"Mama says Itzy's going into the Hungarian army the minute he turns seventeen. She says he's excited to fight in the war."

A cold feeling came over me, although my skin was covered with a thin layer of sweat.

"Mama says he has a girlfriend, too," Mina said. "He's going to marry her after the war."

I pulled my blanket up, until my eyes and the top of my head were the only parts of me left uncovered. The candle flickered before steadying itself again, and the air grew heavy and black. Papa appeared in the shadows, standing in front of us with a sorrowful expression on his face and dark half-circles under his hollow eyes.

"Oh, Papa!" I said. I reached out to him, but he slipped away into the corner by the oven.

"What's the matter with you?" Mina asked.

"That was Papa."

She sat straight up. "You must be mad."

"No. No. He was here this evening. At synagogue. But I thought it was because I ate too much nutmeg."

Mina frowned and scratched her head.

"Look hard," I said. "Hold my hand, and you'll be able to see him, too."

She grabbed my hand and squinted into the darkness. "Yes. That's him," she said. She dug her fingers into my skin.

"Ouch."

She jumped at the sound of my voice and practically threw my hand back in my face. "Baby, now you've ruined everything. He's gone."

"Well, I saw him first." I rubbed my fingers and thought, he came to see me and not you. "Is it really him? Or his ghost?"

"His ghost. He was too thin and gray to be our real papa."

"Don't you think we should find out if he's still here?" I asked.

"Yes," she said and slid down to the floor.

She reached for the candle and walked all around the shed. I twisted my blankets closer and closer around my neck, sure that Papa was hiding in the corner and waiting to come back and scare me, now that he'd sent Mina on a wild goose chase. She searched everywhere for him before she finally gave up and put the candle on the shelf. She climbed back on top of the oven and wrapped my blanket around her, pushing me against the wall.

"That hurts," I said. "How am I going to sleep with you on top of me?"

"Be quiet," she said. "What if he comes back for one of us and takes us away to who knows where?" Her voice trembled with excitement. "That is what I love about funerals. Feeling so close to people's ghosts you can almost touch them."

I hugged the wall and wished I still had my glass heart so I could grow myself inside the brick and no one could ever pry me loose. I drifted into a restless sleep, but Papa shook me until I woke up and held his hands out to me before folding them back into his chest. Every time I started to sleep, he nudged me awake and poked me with his finger.

"What do you think it means?" I asked Mina the next morning.

Her eyes sparkled with all kinds of wild ideas.

Over the next several days, Papa followed me everywhere. He rode on my shoulder while I was chasing down a chicken in the backyard for dinner and floated behind my ear while I rested on the hill by the train tracks at the edge of the woods behind our house. One morning when I was alone in my classroom struggling to remember my spelling words, he stood right in front of my desk and reminded me that *vadviz* ended with a "z," not an "s." That was lucky, since Miss Kovacz was still after me about my spelling words. Her rash never went completely away, and her hands were covered with blotches that itched her all the time. Whenever she started scratching herself, she called me up in front of the class and gave me one spelling word after another until I made a mistake. Then she sent me to the corner, where I shifted from one foot to the other, sure my legs would collapse under me.

One afternoon, a couple of weeks after Papa first appeared, I caught up with Mina on the way home from school. "What does he want?" I asked.

"I don't know," she said. "I wish he would follow me around like that." She tugged at her books and frowned. "Wouldn't it be fun to get

Papa inside the church? Wouldn't you just love to see the look on his face?"

"Yes." Although I didn't like the idea of Papa in church at all.

Mina laughed. "Good, because we're going to take him to a funeral at the Catholic Church this Sunday."

"What? We can't do that."

"Why not? Are you too scared?"

"No."

Though secretly I was afraid Papa might get so angry at me that he would never come back. He never set foot inside a church while he was alive, and I knew he wouldn't like to be tricked into going, now that he was a ghost. Neither would Mama. She was already worried enough about one of her daughters turning into a Catholic.

The Sunday afternoon of the funeral, I trudged behind Mina to church and broke into a sweat when she opened the door. "What if he decides to stay away?" I asked.

"He won't," Mina said. "He can't seem to get enough of you."

She grabbed my elbow and guided me into a pew at the back of the church. We sat down, and she put her hand on my shoulder, because she thought she could see Papa only when she was holding on to me. After a minute or two, he hopped into the pew in front of us, fidgeting with the buttons on his shirt and frowning at the priest and waving his hands up and down to get us out of there. Mina whispered her own special prayer for the dead—not *Kaddish*, just some dumb thing she made up. She said Papa smiled at her during her prayer, but I never saw him do any such thing.

The following Friday night after services, Mina and I went to the well behind our house.

"Papa's dead," she said, dipping the bucket into the water. "I'm sure of it. Live people can't have ghosts. The problem is he never had a funeral with a coffin and the blessing from the rabbi, and maybe that's why he came back. Maybe he wants us to give him a proper burial."

"How can we bury Papa if we don't have his body?" I asked. "Besides, what if he's not dead? Mama told me a couple of months ago that we might even get a letter from him one day."

Mina rolled her eyes. "Do dead people write letters?"

"Why not, if they can help out with spelling words?"

"What are you talking about? Listen, you didn't tell Mama you saw Papa, did you?"

"No. She gets angry whenever I talk about him."

"This evening during services, did you hear the rabbi say Mrs. Davich's brother died? It's perfect for Papa."

"What are you talking about?"

"We'll go to her brother's funeral, and so will Papa's ghost, as long as you're there. Then we'll wish Papa into that man's coffin and bury the two together. The funeral is on Sunday."

"But it's in Szereda, and that's more than halfway to Grandma's house."

"So what? It's not a school day or a market day, and we can walk there easily enough."

"But I don't want to go," I said.

"Can't you just see it? We sit behind the dead man's family, and once Papa shows himself, we make sure that he rests peacefully forever and that his soul is happy."

"I don't think Papa's going to like sharing his coffin with a man he doesn't know."

"Well, it's not really Papa. It's only his ghost, and he won't need much space."

"What will we tell Mama?"

Mina frowned. She was so used to having her own way that she never bothered with excuses.

"I don't like this at all," I said. "Papa came to me first, so I should be the one to decide what happens to him."

"All right," Mina said. "Do you want to spend the rest of your life looking for him around every corner? Do you want him always telling you what to do? Letting you know how unhappy he is with the way you wash the dishes or comb your hair?"

"No-o-o."

"Well, then, what choice do you have but to bury him once and for all?"

The more I thought about it, the more I began to like the idea of putting Papa's ghost where it belonged. I wasn't sure why he picked me of all the people in the family, because he never liked me all that much. Since he did choose me, though, I felt responsible for helping him. Mina was right. He didn't seem very happy the way he was, but I wasn't sure how willing he would be to hop into someone else's coffin. Besides, he might come back and be even more restless and unhappy if he didn't like Mrs. Davich's brother.

"I know," I said. "Let's pretend we're going on a school picnic."

"A picnic, brilliant," she said.

I was really thinking, if we tell Mama we're going on a picnic, maybe she'll pack us a lunch to take along, and that way we won't have to go hungry. Mina walked away, skipping every third step and left the water bucket for me to carry back to the house.

That night, Papa hovered over my head, teasing me and telling me to stay asleep. He spoke in a special sign language he made up as he went along and waved his hands and crinkled his nose. He translated each wink and frown and crook of his finger. He said he missed me and called me by a strange new name, Esther. It was ugly coming out of his mouth, like a dog growling after an old bone, but he was so kind to me that I didn't have the heart to tell him how much I hated the sound of the name he had given me.

"Oh," Mama said. She stepped out the front door. "Look what a beautiful day you have for a picnic. You should thank God."

She turned toward me and smiled. Small tears of happiness glistened in the corners of her eyes. I wanted to rest my head in the folds of her skirt and confess that there was really no picnic, but I couldn't bring myself to tell her the truth. It was wonderful outside, one of the very last days of summer squeezed between weeks of gray skies and hard, cold drops of rain that sting your skin. More like August than October.

The road to Szereda was dry and dirty. Mina carried the basket Mama had packed for us and shooed me away like a fly every time I tried to open the top and peek at what was inside. The funeral was to begin at one o'clock, so when the sun was directly overhead, we sat down under a tree by the side of the road and ate the lunch Mama had prepared: boiled eggs, the last of the fresh tomatoes from our garden, and sponge cake. I ate two pieces of cake, hoping the extra nutmeg would bring Papa back. Mina wanted to hide the basket so it wouldn't look like we were carrying our lunch to synagogue. Before I could stop her, she reached up and untied the purple ribbon Mama had put in my hair that morning.

"Give it back," I said.

But she held the ribbon tightly in her hand. "We'll use this to mark the place where we put the basket," she said. She gathered a fistful of grass and knotted my beautiful ribbon around it.

I ran my palm over the top of my head. It felt naked. "Someone will find it and steal it," I said. "And my ribbon, too."

Mina only tugged at me to hurry up. The rest of the way there I tried hard not to think of Papa's ghost and Mrs. Davich in the same place.

Across the street from the synagogue in Szereda was a small empty lot with a few pieces of wood sticking out of a hole in the ground. Mina said they were the beginnings of the house Papa wanted to build, and I thought if I wished hard enough he might climb out of that hole and invite us into our new home. I closed my eyes and remembered what he had looked like the last time I saw him. He was wearing his dusty work pants and a rough shirt that Mama had made for him out of muslin left over from the curtains on the back window. When I opened my eyes, the hole with the pieces of wood in it was as empty and lonesome as before, and I thought two helpings of sponge cake might not be enough to bring Papa back to me.

We walked toward the synagogue. The stained-glass picture of Moses on the wall looked a lot like Papa, except he had blue eyes and white flowing hair and he wore a red robe. Papa would never wear anything like that. His eyes were deep, like Papa's, and followed me all the way into the synagogue, waiting and watching and never missing a thing. Once I was inside, Papa's spirit was so close I could hear his voice whisper in my ear and feel the rough cloth of his coat rub against my arm.

We tiptoed into the sanctuary, a large room with an aisle down the middle and two rows of wooden benches. In front was a large shelf covered by a thick white curtain that hid the Torah in its sacred place, until the rabbi and the cantor took it out and shared little pieces of its wisdom with the congregation during Friday night and Saturday morning services. A group of people stood beside this shelf, huddled together listening to a young man in a black robe who spoke in a booming voice. Mrs. Davich worked her way free of the group and locked her eyes on mine. My knees wobbled as I moved toward her. Mina walked behind me, so close she stepped on my heel.

"Serene, you came," Mrs. Davich said. "How kind. And you brought your sister, too."

Her eyes wandered toward my empty neck, and out of habit, I reached for the glass heart that was a million miles away and crushed to pieces by now. Mrs. Davich drew back for a moment before putting one hand on my shoulder and the other on Mina's and guiding us toward the group at the front of the sanctuary. Her touch was cold and dry. Of course, the man in the robe was the rabbi. He stopped speaking when the three of us joined the group, but Mrs. Davich nodded at him, and he boomed out some more words about how sorry he was for the loss of such a young and vital man. There were tears in Mrs. Davich's eyes, not like the laughing ones that tumbled down Mama's cheek that morning. These tears were sad, and when I opened my heart to her, I saw how lonely she was for the companion of her childhood who had left her behind. I tried to shut out her sadness, but it was too strong. It started to swallow me up and made me cry.

For the first time, I noticed the coffin behind the rabbi. It was polished and new and so small I could hardly imagine one man fitting in there, let alone two. I wondered what the man inside looked like by now. Perhaps he had fallen off a horse and broken his neck so that his head was twisted around on his body, or perhaps he had died of some horrible disease that had eaten away at him until he was nothing more than a skeleton with skin stretched over his bones. Mina poked me with her elbow, and I crawled slowly out of Mrs. Davich's sadness. The rabbi gave each one of us a small piece of black lace and a pin.

"We tear this to signify the rending of our clothes in grief," he said.

No one moved. He made a small rip, holding the lace daintily between his thumbs and index fingers. His smooth, pink hands looked as though they belonged on a young girl instead of a man whose voice could rattle the candlesticks by the side of the coffin. He pinned the black material on his collar. In her excitement, Mina tore her lace in two, and that made the rabbi laugh so hard he held onto his sides. Finally he stopped, and his face turned red.

"So strong for such a delicate child," he said.

Mina smiled at him and lowered her eyes to her shoes. Her face turned red, too. I wanted to tell him that she always got carried away at funerals, lace or no lace, but she gave me such a sharp stare I decided it was best to keep quiet. After all, we'd only been invited to join the group because of Mrs. Davich.

I sat between Mrs. Davich and Mina, and Mrs. Davich took my hand and buried it gently between her own.

Mina leaned toward me and whispered in my ear, "Remember why we're here. For Papa, not that old witch."

She hooked her arm through my elbow and pressed hard. She held her breath for an instant, as if she were wishing for Papa to appear, but I knew he couldn't come unless I called him. I tried to pull my hand away from the old woman, but it was trapped beneath hers. Soon the tips of my fingers grew numb, and the numbness spread to my palm and wrist and all the way up my arm. I was afraid I might scream if I couldn't move my hand. Mrs. Davich looked at me out of the corner of her eye and read my pain perfectly before she let go of me.

Mina poked me in the side and motioned behind us. The sanctuary had begun to fill with people.

"Don't forget," she whispered.

I thought hard about Papa, but all I could see was the glass heart and, behind it, a young boy and a girl who was many years older than he. She wiped mud off his face and tempted him with a piece of candy in a bright paper wrapper.

The rabbi began to speak about the dead man. He said what a fine person he was, a beloved father and husband, son and brother. Mina pressed against my elbow again.

"Try harder," she whispered.

"I am," I said.

"Time is short, and I can't do this all by myself."

I squeezed my eyes shut and whispered, "Papa. Where are you? I need you." But everything behind my lids was still and black.

Mrs. Davich shifted so that her shoulder touched mine, and I jumped and shut my eyes even tighter. Usually, I was good at making pictures inside my head, but sitting next to Mrs. Davich, I lost the gift and saw only a gray sky that faded to white when I opened my eyes.

"This is your fault," Mina said.

"Is not," I said.

"We'll never get Papa buried this way."

The lace scratched my neck, and I wanted to cry because Papa was just as contrary as Mina. The day before he had been everywhere—at the well when I went to fetch water, on the verandah when I sat for a moment to daydream about our trip to Szereda, beside my bed when I knelt to say my prayers after everyone else had gone to sleep. I closed my eyes again and tried to imagine his face. All I could see were dark spots like tiny dead stars, and all I could hear was the small, distant sound of laughter that was hardly more than a sigh. Maybe he knew what we planned for him and stayed away because he wasn't ready yet to let us put him to rest. Maybe he was afraid that if he let us wish him into that coffin, we'd forget about him, and he didn't want to be forgotten. Not our Papa, who never liked to mix meat dishes with milk dishes and wanted things done his way and who left a big hole inside me when he vanished without saying good-bye.

The rabbi had stopped speaking, and six men picked up the coffin and carried it out of the sanctuary to the cemetery behind the synagogue. I knew it was time for me to get up, but I was pinned down by sadness. Even after Mrs. Davich herself stood and straightened her collar, I couldn't move. Mina had to grab both of my arms and lift me out of my seat, and she leaned backwards so far that her fingers left red grooves in my skin.

"You're hopeless," she said.

She led me out of the synagogue and back toward the road to Galfalva. I trailed behind her, hardly aware of where we were going. She scolded me all the way home, even after we found the picnic basket we had left earlier. My beautiful purple ribbon was covered with dust. The sight of it made me start to cry again, and I jammed it deep inside my pocket.

"Baby," she said.

I pulled away from her and said, "Leave me alone."

So what if Mrs. Davich's grief kept Papa from coming back when we called for him? It was her right to share it with everyone on the day she put her own brother in the ground. We were wrong to steal away part of his funeral for our own father who was nothing but a ghost anyway. Climbing the hill to our house, I remembered about the black lace still pinned to my collar. It didn't scratch my neck anymore, and I undid it and rolled it around in my hands for a minute and stuck my face in it. I took a deep breath and let the thin rough material tickle my nose.

"Serene," Papa's voice said. "My little Esther. What an adventure we've had for ourselves today!"

SECRETS

I held the lace in my fist so that Mama couldn't see it and tried to answer her questions about the picnic.

"Such a beautiful fall day," she said. "Where did you stop for lunch?"

"At a little park on the side of the road to Szereda," I said.

She rested her finger on her chin, trying to picture where such a park might be. "Which teacher went with you?"

"Miss Kovacz and one of her friends," Mina said. "Someone we didn't know."

"Hmm," Mama said.

"The lunch was delicious," I said. "We ate every last bite."

"I hope you shared with your classmates."

"No. It was so good we ate it all ourselves. Domino came around for some chicken."

"We didn't give her any," Mina said.

"Where's your ribbon?" Mama asked.

I glanced at Mina and back at Mama. "I was playing tag in the grass," I said. "The wind untied it."

"And carried it away before we could stop it," Mina said.

As we made up these lies—except for the part about the food—the lace scratched and bit at my palm, and I wondered if Papa was really in there, struggling to get free so he could tell Mama what a liar

I'd become. I loosened my grip but kept my hand behind my back. Luckily, Mama didn't ask me what I was hiding.

Mina pinched my arm, and later on, while Mama was humming Kati to sleep, she whispered quickly in my ear, "We have to try again. Otherwise, Papa will never find any peace."

I shook my head.

"Oh, yes," she said. "We'll have to watch carefully for another chance."

That night, I tossed on my mattress. I couldn't see Papa's face in my dreams, although I could hear his voice and Mina's, too. "Esther," he said, over and over. I covered my ears with my pillow, but that made Mina laugh. A pair of soft pink hands waved in the air, and she laughed even louder. The next day I was tired and could barely hold my head up.

"Serene," Miss Kovacz said.

I looked into her face. Her eyes were tiny slits, and her cheeks were redder than usual. When she spoke, her teeth showed, like a dog about to be hit with a stick. She was talking to me, but her words came out of her mouth backwards. All I could do was stare at her and say I was sorry. When she leaned toward me, I put my hands in front of my face, afraid she would grab me by the ear again and drag me to the corner, but instead she moved on to the next student.

That afternoon Miss Kovacz came to visit Mama. I stared at my teacher through the curtain as she crossed the front yard and stopped in front of the door to scratch her hand. I ran to the dark corner by the kitchen table and crouched down there, wishing I could melt into the floor like Papa and Grandpa before him. I wrapped my arms across my chest and tried to ignore the loud knocking at the door. Finally, Mama opened it.

"Why, Miss Kovacz," she said. She stood there silently for a long moment, as if she'd forgotten how to talk. "Please, come in."

Miss Kovacz squinted as she walked into the room, and I backed further into the corner. Mama could barely take her eyes off Miss

Kovacz, and she seemed to shrink inside herself, even though she was a head taller than my teacher.

"Serene, Sam, go back to the tavern and clean up," Mama said. "Don't forget to wipe the counter clean and spread sawdust on the floor. Sam, you watch out for your sister."

Sam laughed in that mean way of his and pulled me out of my corner. I felt torn in two. One part of me went with Sam and brushed crumbs off the counter and threw sawdust in his face when he said, "Serene is in trouble." The other part listened to the wind blowing against the windows and, in that hollow sound, heard Mama's voice asking Miss Kovacz about the picnic and Miss Kovacz's reply.

"Lies," the wind said, as it rattled against the glass. "Slow. Lazy."

"No I'm not," I said. "My tongue gets stuck. That's all. And the words jump off the page."

"Who are you talking to now?" Sam asked. "Serene is crazy! That's what Miss Kovacz is telling Mama."

"She is not."

"Is too." He picked an egg shell from off the floor and threw it at me and ran out the door.

I swept the floor three times, piling egg shells in a corner and stomping them into tiny flakes, listening with most of my mind for Miss Kovacz's words, or Mama's, being carried by the wind. I couldn't stop dusting and wiping. The sky was dark by the time I returned home, and I was hungry, though I peeked through the window to be sure Miss Kovacz was gone before I went inside. Only Mama and Sam and Kati were there. I thought maybe I should be like Mina and slip away for a while, but the only place I could go was Mrs. Davich's house, and Mama had forbidden that. Besides, I didn't like the food there.

Mama was busy setting the table when I opened the door. I slipped in quietly behind her, picked up some forks, and placed them on the table. She jumped when she saw me.

"Oh," she said. "Don't sneak up on me like that."

"Why?" I asked.

"You scared me half to death. I thought you were a ghost."

Now it was my turn to jump.

Mama glanced at me sideways. "What Miss Kovacz tells me isn't good," she said.

"She hates me, Mama," I said.

"No. Now you listen to me. Where were you girls on Sunday?"

Sam laughed out loud from his bed at the other side of the room.

"Be quiet," I said.

Kati had been napping, and she kicked off her blankets and started to whimper.

"I expect this from Mina but not you," Mama said.

"Yes, Mama," I said.

"Well, where were you?"

"The truth!" Sam said.

He laughed again. I raised my fist and could almost feel the way his skin would sag against my knuckles when I punched him in the nose.

"Stop that, Serene," Mama said. Her voice was so sharp it cut through me like a knife.

I dropped my hand into the pocket of my dress.

"Go on," she said.

"We were sorry for Mrs. Davich," I said. "She was so unhappy in synagogue because her brother died young. And we wanted to see the house."

"Which house?"

"The one Papa was building for us in Szereda. Will he ever come back?"

Mama put her hands on my shoulders and looked me squarely in the eye. I was uneasy beneath her steady gaze.

"Stay away from that woman," she said. "Isn't it enough that she almost killed you? She's dangerous, and I don't want you to have anything more to do with her." She poked me hard with her finger.

"Ouch," I said.

"Leave her alone, and as for the house, it is only a hole in the ground. You girls and your silly ideas."

She released me from her grip and pushed me gently away when I tried to hug her. "Mrs. Davich would take you away from me, if she could. And forget that nonsense about Papa. He's gone, and that's all you need to know."

"Yes, Mama."

"Right now, your job is to learn how to read and write."

"But Miss Kovacz is a witch."

"No she's not. She's a fine teacher who's only looking out for your welfare. Why she even walked all the way up the hill just to ask if she could tutor you an extra hour after school each day. Until you catch up with the other children."

I put my hands over my ears. "I won't do it! It's her fault I can't read."

"You have no choice. I won't raise a pack of ignorant children."

I ran out the door into that cold October night with no hat or gloves and circled around the house to the edge of the woods. At first, I wished Papa would come and take me away. Later, I imagined I would lose myself among the trees, and no one would be able to find me until the following spring, when nothing would be left but a pile of bones. The sky grew darker, and a sharp rain began to fall, pricking my skin like tiny pins. I turned back toward the house because I didn't have anywhere else to go.

The words danced across the page, turning somersaults and cartwheels, mocking me. A long bony finger pinned an "A" down on the paper. The edges of the letter wiggled and squirmed to get free.

"Look again," said the scratchy voice attached to the finger.

I glanced up into Miss Kovacz's yellow eyes, all rimmed in red and impatient. She stabbed the page with her finger. "Start here," she said. "Slowly. Don't skip any letters, and don't put in anything extra."

"*Kadar* . . . years . . . *Arpad* . . . ," I read.

"No! No! Where do you see that? 'Years ago, *Arpad* made a new law.'"

"Oh." I lowered my eyes.

"Do you do that on purpose? Don't you stop to think about the sense of the words?"

I shook my head.

"I don't know what to do with you," she said. "You can barely read at all."

"I can too," I whispered to the page. I thought, Miss Kovacz hates me so much, and that's why I can't read while she's around.

"Try again," she said, her hot breath on my cheek.

I was crying, and I rested my face on top of my desk so that the words in the book marched away from me like straight lines of tiny bugs for as far as I could see.

"That's all for today," she said. She turned away.

I wanted to tell her how, before I ever started school, I watched while Sam studied with Mama and learned his lessons better than he had. How I kept track of the money in the tavern and could figure the cost of a whole table's worth of drinks and make change without ever having to write down anything.

"Be careful of Serene," Sandor, one of our craftiest patrons, always said. He never looked anyone straight in the eye. "You can't slip a free drink by her and hope for an extra penny in change, like you could with her papa."

The next afternoon, Miss Kovacz didn't make me stay after school. Instead, she walked back up the hill to our house to talk to Mama, and when she was finished, Mama called me in from the yard.

"Do you want to repeat the first grade?" she asked. She took my arms in her hands. They were so hot they made me sweat and nearly burned my flesh, though our house was always drafty in the autumn.

"No," I said.

"I'm sure you can do your reading. I've watched you around here."

"Miss Kovacz makes the letters slip and slide until I can't see them at all."

"How?"

I swallowed hard. "I don't know."

"I'm sure I don't either."

That evening, I found the piece of black lace hidden in the pocket of the dress I wore to the funeral in Szereda, and after I folded the lace under my pillow and fell asleep, Papa stood on my stomach and explained why he had melted. I didn't understand most of what he said, because he spoke in his new language. He told me it was called English, and it made him sound as if he had a bone stuck in his throat. He drew a couple of letters of the English alphabet on a piece of paper he carried with him. The letters were odd, boxy-looking things that made my eyes water. He said this was how everyone spoke and wrote in the place where he lived. He said he was trying hard to learn his new language, but his words came out so slowly most people lost patience with him and walked away before he could finish. He said he was talking less and less now, losing his Hungarian much faster than he was gaining his English. That must have been hard for him, because I'd never met anyone who liked to talk as much as Papa. Finally, he grew so heavy I couldn't breathe.

"Let me go," I screamed. "You're choking me. It is all your fault. You left us, and Mama doesn't love me anymore!"

I reached up to knock him off my stomach, and Mama grabbed my hands. "Be still, Serene," she said. "You're having a bad dream. That's all. It can't hurt you." She put my hands down at my sides and rubbed my forehead gently. "Shh. Go back to sleep now."

"I'm sorry, Mama," I said.

"That's all right. Be quiet. You don't want to disturb the others."

Mina was waiting for me at the corner so we could walk to school together the next morning, something she hardly ever did before I started seeing Papa's ghost. "You yelled so loud last night," she said. "Were you trying to wake the dead? What did you dream about anyway?"

"Nothing," I said. "Well, almost nothing. I mean, Papa was there, and I couldn't breathe. I asked him to go away. That's all."

"Why? We haven't seen him at all lately. Why did you chase him away again? How will we ever talk to him? You always ruin everything."

"Do not."

She whispered Papa's name over and over, but it didn't work. He didn't come back to us. He had already showed us what he thought about funerals, and all her wishes did was deliver the young rabbi from Szereda to our front door late that very afternoon. He told Mama he was worried when he didn't see us at the *shiva* for Mrs. Davich's brother. Since we'd come to the funeral, he was certain we were great friends of Mrs. Davich's and would want to visit with her and her family afterwards to talk about our memories of the dead man.

"I asked Mrs. Davich whether your girls had arrived home safely," he said to Mama. "She didn't seem to know, so I decided I'd better come and check for myself."

"Well, as you can see, they're both here in one piece," Mama said.

Mina slipped off into a corner, while Mama offered the rabbi some tea. His eyes kept wandering toward my sister, and Mama frowned and said she was sorry she didn't have time to visit because she had to fix dinner. The rabbi thanked her for the tea and backed toward the door, knocking over Mama's broom on his way out.

"Up to no good, that one," Mama said. "Barely old enough to shave. Your grandma married a holy man, and look how much happiness that brought her."

"Oh, Mama," Mina said, smiling.

The next afternoon, Miss Kovacz paced back and forth, jabbing the air with her fingers and saying how she'd never had a student as impossible as I was. She wrapped her claw around my head and pushed my nose just inches above a page I was supposed to read.

"Read only what you see," she said. "No more."

I tried, but the words at the beginning of one sentence hopped to the end of another, and the last sentence slithered off the page onto my lap where it broke into a hundred pieces.

"I give up," she said. "Go home."

"Thank you," I said and tiptoed out of the room.

I ran up the hill to our house and opened the front door. Mama looked up from the stove for a moment and went right back to stirring the chicken soup she was preparing for dinner. She didn't tell me what she did while I was in school or say how much she missed me and how she stopped every few minutes in the afternoon to glance out the window and see if I was coming. She didn't even answer me when I whispered about the hole in Domino's new sweater and the spot of blood on her handkerchief. Kati was screaming, and Mina was nowhere to be found, and Sam came home with a hole in his pants and a coin someone in his class had given him. For the first time, I saw that Mama's hair was turning gray, and she didn't have many kind words for us that day, even after I sliced potatoes for the soup and set the table.

"What's wrong, Mama?" Sam asked.

"You children will send me to an early grave," Mama said.

"No!" I said.

I ran to my bed and hid under the covers, wondering what had become of my kind, loving Mama. Perhaps Papa stole her away in the middle of the night and left us with her empty shell in this dark, lonely place.

LEAVE TAKING

Heavy snow bent the branches of the tree that scratched against my window. It was so cold the first December morning of school vacation that I didn't want to leave my bed, even though I had a plan to make everything right with Mama again. I would get up every morning, before the others, fetch water for her coffee, and prepare breakfast. After we were finished eating, I would take Kati outside and run her around in the yard until she was too tired to stand and she would have to sleep most of the rest of the morning.

I had already made Mina swear to stay home these next two weeks. I told her how hard I was wishing for Papa's ghost and lied about a dream I had where he promised to visit after she stopped going to church and started falling in love with the rabbi from Szereda. I gave my last three copper coins to Sam so that he would quit dropping out of trees on top of people and hinted at more money hidden in a secret place by the railroad tracks, if he would behave himself. At night, I prayed to God that my brother and sister wouldn't find out about my lies and worried that my magic wasn't strong enough to keep them home. As for me, I decided to show Mama how serious I was about school by studying every day of the vacation. I would recite the poems in my reader and copy lists of spelling words over and over so she would see we didn't need any Miss Kovacz. I could never forgive my teacher for making Mama lose faith in me, but I would work hard to show Mama I cared about learning.

I slipped out of bed the first morning of my vacation and dressed quickly. The air was freezing when I opened the front door just a crack and squeezed through so that I wouldn't disturb the others. I ran to the well and got a bucket of fresh water. I put a kettle on the stove and stuffed logs inside it to heat it back up from when it had died down overnight. My fingers were like ice. I set out the breakfast dishes and warmed up the mush that was left over from dinner the evening before. Pretty soon, the house was full of the sweet smell of that mush and the sharp smell of Mama's coffee. Kati started to cry, and I rushed to pick her up, but I was too late. Mama sat up with the sleep still in her eyes.

"Why don't you rest some more?" I asked. "I'll take care of Kati."

"There's no sense in that now," she said. "Once I'm up, I can't go back to sleep."

"Well, why don't you sit there and let me bring you coffee in bed?"

"I've never heard of such foolishness."

"Come on, Mama. Why don't you try it?"

She sighed. "All right. Just this once."

Kati kept on screaming, so Mama had to get out of bed anyway and rock her in front of the stove. Mina was cross because she said Kati woke her up too early, and she got dressed and told Mama she didn't want any breakfast. I grabbed her arm and whispered that I'd never bring Papa back if she left.

"So what?" she asked. "All you ever do is talk about him, but I haven't seen him since the funeral. I have better things to do than wait around all day for a ghost."

"Like what?" I asked. She pushed me aside and ran out the door before I could stop her.

Kati yelled louder and louder. After breakfast, Sam twirled his bullet in his hand and crawled out the window, taking his slingshot with him. Only Mama and Kati and I were left, huddled together around the stove.

"I don't suppose many people will come out for a drink at the tavern on a day like today," Mama said. "I don't know how I'll ever make enough money to feed this family."

That afternoon, while I was watching Kati in the yard, Sam zig-zagged between the trees behind our house.

"What are you doing?" I asked.

He held a tiny chain with something attached to it. For a moment, I thought it was my glass heart and forgot all about Kati. I followed Sam into the woods, running so hard the cold wind burned my throat.

"What's that?" I asked, when I finally caught up with him.

He dangled the chain in front of my eyes. "A gold coin," he said.

"Oh."

The ends of my mouth turned down. The coin wasn't at all what I was hoping for. Still, it was bright and new. I'd never seen one quite so big before, and I wondered what the scratch on his cheek and the bruise on his forehead had to do with the coin.

"Where did you get it?" I asked.

"From fat old Sollie," he said.

"Domino's brother? The mayor won't be happy about that. You're in big trouble now." I remembered how Mama threw up her hands whenever he came home with torn pants or a black eye and warned him to behave or she would send him to live with the Gypsies.

"I'm not in trouble. Mama won't ever find out, unless you tell her. So you have to hide the coin with the rest of your money."

"Oh, no. No. I already gave you my pennies. That's enough."

"It's mine. I earned it. I fought him for it and won."

"Mama won't see it that way. She'll make you give it back."

"That's why you have to hide it for me."

He slid the coin off the chain, dropped the gold piece in my pocket, and ran away before I could make him take it back. I wanted to throw it as far as I could into the trees, but it felt cool and shiny in my hand, and its rough edges tickled my skin through the hole in my mitten.

Besides, I'd never touched anything quite so valuable before, and I hoped the coin had a magic of its own that might help me keep my brother and sister out of mischief and in Mama's good graces. I went back to the yard to look for Kati, but she was gone. She was almost a year old and wandered off all the time, now that she had learned to walk. She especially liked to stand in the middle of the street, although she wasn't there when I went to look for her. I called her name, but she didn't answer.

I didn't hear Mama come up behind me, and I jumped when she asked, "What's going on here?"

"I lost Kati," I replied. "She was in the yard a second ago."

I ran toward Mrs. Davich's house without stopping to think about where I was going. When I got there, Kati was crawling up the steps to the verandah. The air was a little warmer than it had been in the morning, and since the snow was starting to melt, Kati took off her mittens and threw them on the ground. Her tongue stuck out the edge of her mouth. Mrs. Davich scooped my baby sister into her arms and brushed her hand across Kati's face.

"Kati!" Mama yelled from behind me. "Come away from there this instant! You're in danger."

Mrs. Davich hugged Kati before putting her back down, and Kati started to cry. She stumbled toward the steps, and the instant Mama reached her, she lifted Kati high in the air and settled her on her hip.

"Leave my children alone," Mama said to Mrs. Davich.

The old woman shrank back, and Mama turned toward me, grabbing my elbow and holding it high above my head. Her grip was tight, and the muscles in my arm began to burn.

"This is your fault," she said. "Who knows what might have happened to this poor child if we hadn't found her in time. Kati watches you two girls, and if you can't leave that old woman alone, how do you expect your poor little sister to stay away from her?"

The mayor was standing in front of the stove when we got home. "Mrs. Spirer, your son is following in his father's footsteps," he said.

"What do you mean?" Mama asked.

"He is turning into a bully and a thief."

"My husband isn't a thief, and neither is my Sam."

"Oh? He blackened Sollie's eye and stole his gold coin."

Mama turned toward Sam, who was leaning against the wall. "Is this true?"

"Of course not, Mama," he said.

"Would you like for me to get Sollie?" the mayor asked. "Would you like to see your son's handiwork for yourself?"

"That won't be necessary," Mama said. She held her hand out to Sam. "Give me the coin."

Sam hung his head. "I don't have it," he said. "Honestly." He shrank back against the wall.

"Listen here, young man, you will have to repay Sollie, although God knows where you'll get the money."

"Yes, Mama."

After the mayor left, Mama sent me and Sam to bed without any dinner. Mina came home sometime later, but I was asleep and didn't hear her get into bed beside me.

The next morning, Mama gathered us around the stove. "I have to do something about you children before it's too late," she said. "You children are getting too wild. Stealing things, failing at school, turning into Catholics. For all I know, the mayor tells everyone I'm an unfit mother. What if he tries to take you away from me for good?"

She frowned and flattened her skirt with her hand. Then she looked at each one of us for a moment and shook her head. "Before that happens, I have to do something," she said. "Sam, I'm sending you to live with Uncle Herman and Aunt Regina." She was talking about her sister and her husband. They lived a few miles outside Szereda and didn't have any children of their own.

Sam's face turned white. "But I hate Uncle Herman," he said. "He's ugly. Besides, he stinks."

That was true. Uncle Herman did smell of stale tobacco, and sometimes he ate so much he popped the buttons on his shirt and got red spots on his cheeks and nose.

"Even so," Mama said. "You're going to live with them for a while until I can straighten things out. You'll be on your best behavior. No more fighting and no more stealing. Aunt Regina will see to that."

I was shocked by Mama's news, afraid I might never see my brother again. I could just imagine old Aunt Regina sitting on top of Sam every time he had a fight, squashing him flat. After I let the idea settle in for a minute or two, though, I decided it wouldn't be so terrible without him. Mama was right. She did have to do something about him, and the rest of us, too. Of course, it would have been best if she had sent Kati away, but still it would be nice with only my two sisters and no more dead bugs on my pillow or scary stories about bats.

"And one more thing," Mama said. "Serene, you will go to Grandma's for the rest of the school year."

"What?" I asked. "No. I won't do it."

"Yes you will. It's a bigger village. The schools are better there. I wrote to Grandma, and she wrote back to tell me she would be glad to have you."

I knew Mama had received a letter from Grandma a few days before, but she'd read it quickly and stuffed it into her apron pocket without telling me what news it contained. I was sure Grandma hadn't written to say she wanted me to come. Whenever I was around, she watched me as if she thought I might steal something. She wasn't kind, and she cooked food for so long she drained away most of the flavor. I wanted to ask Mama how she thought I could live with a grandmother who hated the very sight of me. I wanted to tell her that I wouldn't go, that I'd run off and find Papa someplace where she'd never hear from me again for as long as she lived. Instead, I sat there like the stone statue of Emperor Franz Josef in the middle of our village square that never moved, no matter how many rocks or old pieces of fruit you threw at it.

I didn't eat much for the next couple of days and slept most of the time. During my waking hours, Sam sat in a corner, staring out the window. Once, I tiptoed behind him and tried to put my arms around his waist. I wanted say I was sorry, but he pushed me down on the floor and wouldn't speak to me, as if I were to blame because Mama was sending him away.

"I have to go, too," I said.

He shrugged and kept looking out the window.

The night before Sam left Mina shook me awake. "Don't forget about Papa," she said. "Don't let him get too far away, or we may never find him again."

"I won't," I whispered.

The next day, I said good-bye to Sam, but he looked straight through me. I watched him disappear into the distance, sitting stiff and as far away as possible from Uncle Herman in the front seat of his wagon. He didn't ask for his gold coin. He might have forgotten about it, but I didn't offer to give it to him. I didn't cry either.

On my last night at home, I slept in Sam's bed. The pillow still held the shape of his head, and when I crawled inside the covers, I thought he was there with me. Early the next morning, Grandpa knocked on our door and took my little pack and lifted it silently into his wagon.

"Don't you want to sit in front?" Mama asked. "Miss Sleepy head."

"I like it better in the back," I said.

She helped me on with my coat, and I was so tired I could hardly lift my arm. I hid Sam's gold coin in my pocket and fingered it, while Mama kissed my forehead and cried over me. I wanted to shove her away and make her stop, but I couldn't seem to let go of her.

Mina stood by the door and gave me a hug. When Mama wasn't looking, she slipped her two pieces of black lace into my other coat pocket.

"For luck and for getting Papa's ghost back" she said. She smiled, but her face was wet with tears. I wondered if she missed me already.

Kati watched me with wide eyes, sucking her thumb, quiet for one of the few times since she'd been born.

Mama gave me a basket of food for the trip. Secretly, I decided to throw it away before I arrived at Grandma's, but once I was underneath the scratchy blanket in Grandpa's wagon, alone this time without my brother and sister, I reached inside the basket and found one of Mama's very best linen napkins. I was filled with love for her and wished I could keep the food she packed forever. I slipped the napkin in the front of my coat and, with Sam's gold coin in one hand and Mina's lace in the other, watched Mama and our house and my sisters grow smaller and smaller, until we passed the bend in the road and I couldn't see them at all.

MOVING PICTURES

I had trouble sleeping at Grandma's. The smells were all wrong. In Galfalva, the house was always full of the smell of chicken or whatever wonderful soup Mama happened to be making, but Grandma's house was sour from too much vinegar in the cucumber salad and musty from wet scarves and gloves that never dried out before someone put them back on. The sounds were wrong, too. Mama and my sisters and brother were silent sleepers, but Grandma snored in a loud buzz that started the minute she closed her eyes and didn't stop until the next morning. Grandpa was quiet, but every once in a while, he'd snort out loud. Aunt Gizella made the strangest noises of anyone, a soft weeping that went on all night long.

I was so tired my eyes ached, and I kept seeing dark spots in front of me. My stomach hurt from the lack of sleep and growled in the middle of the night, though I wasn't hungry. I dreaded those endless hours of darkness, twisting beneath my sheets, begging silently for sleep. My third evening there, I dozed in a soft fog, when Grandpa cried out, "Shumi! Shumi!"

I sat up, sweating and angry at Papa for visiting Grandpa instead of me. I choked back my tears to keep from waking the others. A gentle pair of hands picked me up from behind, put me down again on the straw mattress closest to the stove, and covered me with a soft wool blanket. Early the next morning, I awoke beside Aunt Gizella. She was still sleeping, and there were tears on her cheek. I reached over to brush them off, and she blinked.

"Why are you crying?" I asked.

"Because it's a sad time of the year," she said.

"Why?"

"It's always so gray outside, and sometimes snow piles up so high in front of the door we can't open it. Once or twice every winter, our cow gets stuck inside with us." She wrinkled her nose, and I laughed.

"Rest now," she said. "Enjoy the warmth while you can."

I smiled at her and tumbled down a long dark well with Papa at the bottom. He floated on top of the water as I splashed down beside him, and I gasped for air because I couldn't swim. Someone shook me roughly on the shoulder. Only it wasn't Papa; it was Grandma. Her face was so close to mine that I felt naked under the blankets.

"Honestly, child," she said. "Must you thrash around so at night? Isn't it enough that you don't give us a moment's peace during the day? It's time to get up."

"I'm sorry," I said. I dragged myself out of bed into the icy room, ate a quick breakfast, and started my morning chores.

I arrived at Grandma's a week before the winter session of school began. During that time, I helped her in the small general store she had opened in front of the house. Uncle Mihai built it for her shortly after she had sent us home the year before as punishment for all our misdeeds. The store was tiny and had only one window, but it was busy most of the time. Grandma enjoyed counting her money at the end of the day and complaining about how the rest of us thought it grew on trees.

In spite of everything, I liked Grandma's store. She sold buttons and thread, hunks of rock candy that were pure sugar, and little bottles of headache medicine that smelled like wine and made me dizzy when I sneaked a spoonful behind her back. Grandma didn't like it when I walked up and down the aisles, reading the labels on all the bottles and twirling the little spools of thread around and around in my hands, so she would dream up an errand and send me to the storage shed where she kept her supplies. It was at the far end of the yard. I hated that shed because it was damp and full of cobwebs and old barrels and dusty jars with funny-looking leaves inside them. It smelled strange too, like fruit that had been left too long on the vine. I was always afraid I'd find something dead in there, maybe a bird that accidentally got trapped when the door was locked, a squirrel, or even Papa. Not his ghost, but his earthly skeleton with the flesh peeling off his bones.

Whenever Grandma sent me to the shed, I hung back for a while and dusted the shelves or rearranged some bottles on the counter, hoping she'd make Karl go instead. He was a young man from the neighborhood, not much older than Papa had been when the photograph on Grandma's mantle was taken. Except Papa wore an army uniform and stared proudly into the distance, while Karl could never look me straight in the eye and usually acted as though he was about to take something. One morning, I caught Aunt Gizella smiling at him the same way Mina had smiled at the young rabbi. He smiled back. Then he saw me watching, and afterwards, if he was in the shed, he let me wait outside while he found things for me. He never gave them to me right away. Instead, he made a game of it, dangling the jar I needed above my head or standing at the door and putting both hands behind his back.

"Guess which one," he said.

Of course, I always guessed wrong, and the only way I could get him to give up the jar or bottle was to cry.

"Lazy child," Grandma said one afternoon. "Didn't I ask you to bring me vanilla from the shed?"

"Yes, Grandma," I said. I ran a cloth over some bottles of cough medicine that had a picture of an old man with a white beard and glasses on the front.

"Well, what's keeping you?"

"I'm dusting."

"It's perfectly clean in here. Go on now."

No one was in the store or likely to come for the rest of the day, since it was cold and snowy outside, so I couldn't see why she had to have that vanilla. But there was no arguing with her and no sense in trying to explain my fear of dead bodies in her shed. I reached for my coat without another word. I wandered slowly across the yard and opened the shed door. It was darker than usual inside, and although I'd forgotten to bring a candle with me, I was sure I saw something that shouldn't be there propped against the far wall, something stiff and rotting.

"Karl?" I asked. I heard a groan. "Please don't tease me."

I stumbled toward where the vanilla barrel should have been, dropping the glass jar Grandma gave me to carry the vanilla back to the store. It crashed to the floor and broke into a thousand pieces. I bumped my knee hard against the barrel. It wobbled, and the lid flew off, and the next thing I knew, my hands and feet were covered with a sweet, sticky liquid. I screamed and ran out into the yard and toward the house, not locking the door behind me. Grandma was waiting for me in front of the store.

"Where's the vanilla?" she asked. "And the glass jar?"

I was trying to catch my breath and couldn't speak.

"What's the matter with you?" she asked.

"There's . . . There's a dead body in the shed," I replied. "It might be Papa."

"What?" She wrapped her shawl around her shoulders and dashed outside without a hat or gloves.

I paced up and down, wondering how Papa's body had ended up in Grandma's shed. A few minutes later, she returned with a piece of the broken jar in her hand.

"Let me tell you something," she said. Her voice was low and icy. "There's no dead body in that shed. Foolish girl. Only broken bottles everywhere and my barrel of vanilla tipped over. Do you know how much it will cost to replace it?"

I shook my head.

"You'll be an old woman by the time you pay me off," she said.

That evening at dinner, she mumbled, "Savages. Worshippers of the dead. My poor Shumi. Married to an evil woman who teaches her children such things. Dead bodies! An insult to God and a lie to make up for spilled barrels of vanilla and everything broken."

"But I didn't do it on purpose," I said.

"Be quiet."

"Stop it, Mama," Aunt Gizella said.

"You're a fine one to talk," Grandma said. "She's family, and that's the only reason she's here. But family or no family, she has to pay for the food she eats and the bed she sleeps in. That's a fact. Nothing around here is free, no matter what you may think."

"It's not right to treat her like a servant."

"We'll do things my way, and when and if you ever find a husband and have a home of your own, you can do as you please."

Aunt Gizella stared at Grandma. "You always have to bring that up, don't you? You'll never let me forget about Jacob."

She stood up. Her whole body shook, and she leaned forward so that her eyes were level with Grandma's. Grandpa, who was settled comfortably into his chair, put his hand between the two of them, and Aunt Gizella sat back down again. We finished our dinner in silence, and none of us dared to look at the others.

A couple of mornings later, on the very last day of the year, I gazed out the window, remembering the exact color of Mama's hair and the way Mina tossed her head back when she laughed. I longed for one of Sam's stories about bats and spiders and would even have welcomed the sound of Kati's screaming because I was so homesick. I missed the yellow birthday cake Mama always baked this time of year and the knitted scarves and sweaters she gave us in December to keep us warm during the winter ahead. I didn't come to the table when Grandma called me for lunch, and I wouldn't talk to Aunt Gizella either, until she grabbed my elbow and announced to Grandma and

Grandpa that she was taking me into town for the entire afternoon. Grandma dropped a dish on the table, but luckily it didn't break. Afterwards, she walked around muttering about what ungrateful children we were. Aunt Gizella pulled me close to her and said she had a big surprise for me.

"What is it?" I asked. "Tell me. Please. What is it?"

"My, my, I thought you'd forgotten how to talk at all, but I see you just needed an excuse," she said.

After we cleared the dishes and washed and dried them, we set off for town. We passed by Roka's house, and I looked for him out of the corner of my eye, hoping he would invite us in for another piece of his wife's wonderful bread. But his windows were dark. Aunt Gizella pretended not to recognize the house and hurried me away.

We arrived at the center of Marosvasarhely, a big square with many shops and gas lights everywhere that were lit early in the day this time of year. We walked past the Crystal Palace, with its huge windows and sparkling glass chandelier. The building next to it had no windows, and there was a sign on the door that said, "Moving Pictures."

"Here we are," Aunt Gizella said.

"How can pictures move?" I asked.

"You'll find out."

She paid a man who sat inside the door two pennies, and he led us to a darkened room where people sat in rows of wooden chairs. A tall man with a big hat leaned over a piano. The front wall of the room was partly covered with a sheet, and soon someone at the back turned on a magical machine that cast pictures on the wall. The first one said, "Young Lovers." The man at the piano began to play soft, quiet music, and the most wonderful things started to happen on that wall. A beautiful young girl appeared and wiped her eyes and opened her mouth into a huge "O." An older man paced back and forth behind her and shook his head and then made a fist in the air.

"What does it mean?" I asked. "Who is he, and why is he angry with her?"

"Shh," Aunt Gizella said. "Be quiet." She never took her eyes off the man and woman.

The music grew louder, and a black piece of paper with some words flickered on the wall. "You may never see him again," the first line said. "But why? I love him," the second line said.

Next, the woman was by herself in the snow. She walked fast, but she stopped to glance behind her every few steps. There were tears on her cheek, and she kept blowing on her hands because she'd gone out without any mittens. After a while, she came to a building with a sign that said, "Train Station." She went in and, digging deep inside her pocket, pulled out a coin. She gave it to a man behind some bars and moved her lips. He studied her face for a minute and looked at the clock on the wall. She frowned, blew on her hands some more, and went outside where she sat on a bench for a moment. She stood up again, stomping her feet and jamming her hands into her pockets.

"Why doesn't she go inside where it's warm?" I asked.

"Maybe she's waiting for someone," Aunt Gizella said.

I wanted to tell Aunt Gizella she should wait inside where it was warm. But my aunt's whole body was tense, and her eyes never strayed from the woman on the screen. I hoped something exciting would happen, because I was tired of this stupid woman who didn't do anything except act unhappy and stay out in the cold. Just then, a train rolled onto the tracks. The woman glanced behind her and allowed herself to be helped up some steps to a car by a man in a uniform who stood beside the train. She sat down and stared out the window, wiping her cheeks with a handkerchief. As the train began to roll forward, the woman's eyes opened wide, and she smiled and waved at someone we couldn't see. Another black piece of paper flickered on the wall.

"Lazlo, my love!" it said. "You're here at last."

A young man appeared on the wall. He ran toward the train until he was right beside it and searched the car windows. He didn't get to the woman's window before the train pulled out of the station. Now the man at the piano played louder, and all sorts of amazing things happened. The train began to go very fast, and I ducked down, afraid it would run me over.

"Sit up, silly," Aunt Gizella said. "It can't hurt you."

The man on the wall ran faster than anyone I'd ever seen before and caught up with the train. He grabbed onto the last car, climbing hand-over-hand until he was on the roof. Slowly, he stood up and side-stepped to the end of the moving car.

"Be careful!" I shouted. "You'll fall."

He swung down the side of the car. His mouth was open in a silent scream. Aunt Gizella held her breath and covered her eyes for a moment, and a woman in front of me said, "My God!" The woman beside her gasped out loud. All we could see on the wall was the young man's hand. It held on to the narrow ledge of the car, but the fingers grew whiter and whiter as they dropped away, one at a time. After the last one let go, the young man somersaulted into the picture and fell to the ground.

"Oh, no!" I said. "He can't die."

He jumped right back up and started running after the train again. This time when he caught up with it, he climbed onto the steps leading to one of the passenger cars. He hung over the railing for a moment, and we watched the tracks going by so fast beneath him that they were almost a blur. He stood up and opened a door to the last passenger car. Inside, he had to squeeze around a fat woman, three of her children, and several men in uniforms. He covered his face so no one would recognize him and throw him off the train for not paying his fare. The music got very quiet again, as Lazlo walked up and down the aisles of each car, cupping his hand to his mouth and moving his lips. Another black piece of paper appeared on the wall.

"Emilie!" it said. "Where are you?"

The young man kept walking, until he saw the young woman sitting quietly by herself, looking out the window with tears in her eyes. He slid into the seat next to her and waited for her to notice him. After a couple of seconds, she turned toward him and drew back with her hands up at her shoulders. The two of them fell into one another's arms and kissed. A black circle enclosed them and grew smaller, until it disappeared and the wall said, "The End."

The man at the piano kept on playing the same kind of music he'd played when the young man was chasing the train.

"I think that means we're supposed to leave," Aunt Gizella said.

"Can't we stay and see it again?" I asked. "I want to see Lazlo fall off the train."

"No. I don't think so. Maybe some other time."

I stood up slowly and put on my coat, imagining what I might look like if someone made a moving picture of me on the wall. My arms would circle in front of my face before they slid into my sleeves, and my lips would move up and down. I'd blink five or six times and look straight ahead. I laughed.

On the way home, we stopped at a general store that was like Grandma's, except with a lot more aisles. In the back was a bar, and Aunt Gizella ordered me a drink of fizzy water mixed with red syrup that tasted like raspberries. A man behind the bar sprayed the water from a bottle into my glass, and Aunt Gizella ordered green water for herself.

"Moving pictures," she said. "Have you ever seen anything like them?"

"No," I said. "Lazlo kept running after the train and never got hurt. Wouldn't he at least have broken his arm?"

"He certainly did love Emilie, don't you think?"

"I guess so."

"It was beautiful to see two young people find each other like that."

"I thought Emilie was stupid."

"No, she wasn't. You're just too young to appreciate these things."

I nodded and took another sip of my drink.

"One day you will grow up and find out how important the love between a man and a woman is," she said.

When I reached the bottom of my glass, my drink was thick with the syrup and sweeter than before. "I wish Grandma had these in her store," I said.

Aunt Gizella laughed under her breath.

"If you think love is so special, why didn't you ever marry?" I asked.

She sighed. "It's a long story to tell such a little girl," she said.

"Who's Jacob?"

She took a deep breath and folded her hands in her lap. "Many years ago, before you were born, right after your parents got married, I was like Emilie, in love with a man. Only his name was Jacob, not Lazlo. Do you know what a *nadan*, a dowry, is?"

"Mama told me about that once. Isn't it money that the wife gives to her husband so he'll marry her?"

"Something like that, but I didn't have a *nadan*."

"Why?"

"Mama and Papa don't have any money."

"They couldn't buy Jacob for you?"

"That's right, and one morning, he disappeared. Gone, like that." She snapped her fingers. "I waited for him for a long time. I thought he was dead, until a friend of Mama's told us she saw him at a hotel in the next village over with his new *shiksa* wife. You've heard of a *shiksa* before, haven't you?"

"Yes, a non-Jew."

"Right. Well, his wife was blond-haired and blue-eyed and as big as a house with his baby inside her."

"Did you ever see him again?"

"No. Afterwards Mama said she should never have let Shumi marry Rosa. Your grandma tried to get Shumi to give us his dowry, but Rosa wouldn't let him. At least, that's what Shumi told Mama. But with your papa, who knows what the real truth is?"

"What do you mean? Don't you like Papa?"

"Of course I do. He's my brother. It's just that sometimes he stretches the truth a little. I don't know what happened to Rosa's *nadan*. The point is Mama says Rosa is tight-fisted, and that's why I don't have a husband."

"That's not true, is it?"

"No, but Mama has a memory like an elephant. She blames you because I'm not married."

"But I wasn't even born yet."

"That doesn't matter to Mama. You're Rosa's daughter."

"I guess you couldn't buy another husband."

"With what? Besides, Mama told me no Jewish man would want anything to do with a woman whose fiancé left her for a *shiksa*."

"Sam says I'm a *shiksa*. He says Mr. Kosich is really my papa, and that's why I'm not dark like everyone else in the family."

"Nonsense. My brother is your papa, no doubt about that. You two are so much alike. Both of you always say what's on your minds, even when that gets you into trouble. You look like him, too. Not your coloring, but the rest of you, especially your eyes. You're your father all over again."

"Oh." My father all over again. I took one long last swallow of that delicious drink and let the bubbles tickle the inside of my nose.

"Anyway, I'm well past the marrying age now."

"What about Karl?"

"Don't be ridiculous."

"Good. I don't like him either."

She frowned.

"You're not that old," I said. "Not like Grandma."

"Well, now," she said. "There's a wonder, though I'm afraid at thirty-two my only hope for a husband is some old goat whose first wife is dead and who needs a maid to look after his children."

I closed my eyes and imagined a moving picture of Aunt Gizella and Jacob. She was a young girl with rosy cheeks and dark hair and was much too shy to kiss her lover in front of other people. Jacob ran his finger along her cheek and said good-bye, glancing quickly at her under his eyelids so you could tell he had other things on his mind. Aunt Gizella sat by the window waiting for him, as the weeks flew by. Every once in a while, Grandma walked by, and the two of them moved their lips. A black piece of paper appeared on the wall behind them.

The first line said, "Where is he? It's not like him to stay away so long." The second line said, "Men are like that. You can't trust them." The third line said, "He'll come back. I know he will."

Grandma smiled and had a wicked look in her eyes. A little while later, Grandma stood beside Aunt Gizella, shaking her fist, and Aunt Gizella looked up at her and straightened the front of her dress to show Grandma she hadn't given up yet. The black piece of paper said, "It's over. He's run away with a Gentile. No one will ever have you now." Aunt Gizella put her head in her lap, and the black circle closed around her until it was covered by the words, "The End."

Suddenly I remembered about the gold coin Sam gave me. It was hidden deep inside my coat pocket, safe from Grandma's prying eyes and Karl's greasy fingers. I reached around and pulled it out and put it on the bar in front of us.

"What's that?" Aunt Gizella asked.

"A coin I got from Sam," I replied. "I want you to take it."

"Why?"

"It's your *nadan*. Now you can buy Jacob or anyone else you want."

She tossed her head back and laughed, sounding for all the world just like Papa. She wrapped her arms around me and hugged me so close she raised me right out of my chair. She smelled fresh, like Mama, and for that one moment I thought I was home again.

CAT'S EYE

I stood alone in the school yard while Sophia circled around me.

"Screne," she said. "I've never heard of anyone with a name like that. Serene. Serene."

She rolled my name off the end of her tongue, trilling the "R" just to make fun of me. I wanted to kick her, but she was a head taller than me, so I watched and listened and didn't move.

I spotted Sophia that first morning, right after Aunt Gizella walked me to the front door of the school house and introduced me to my new teacher, Miss Zora, who took my hand and led me into the classroom. Her palm was as soft as Kati's cheek. Sophia sat in a corner, her dark curls flying in all directions, her head high above the heads of the other students. Miss Zora told everyone that I had come to spend the winter with my grandparents. She gave me the desk closest to the stove. "To make our newcomer warm and welcome," she said.

At lunch, she asked me to sit in the front of the room with her. "Soon you'll have a special friend or two who you'll want to eat with," she said. "For today, we'll sit together so you won't feel too lonely or miss your old school."

I wanted to laugh and tell her how much I hated that school, especially Miss Kovacz. Miss Zora was young, not much older than Mina, and she was pretty, too. A silver barrette swept her bangs off her forehead, and her frilly collar lay perfectly around her neck. I kept quiet and ate the two boiled eggs and the piece of cheese Aunt Gizella had packed for my lunch and watched Miss Zora out of the corner of my eye. She poured me some tea that smelled like mint and was flavored with honey. I smiled.

"You'll like it here," she said. "I'm certain of that."

"Thank you," I said.

"For what?"

She rested her hand on top of mine for a moment and told me to go outside with the other children for a breath of fresh air. I fell in love with her and wanted to stay inside with her for the rest of the lunch hour, but I was afraid to make her angry. So I jumped up and acted as though I was happy to get away.

Sophia pounced on me the minute I opened the schoolhouse door and followed me into the yard, singing out my name in that funny way of hers.

"Serene was my grandmother's name," I said. "It belonged to someone else before that, So-fee-a." I hissed the "FEE" to show her I didn't like her name any more than she liked mine and bit down on my lip, tasting a drop of my own blood.

That afternoon, I caught her looking at me once or twice. She mouthed "Serene," pausing again over the "R." Even when I couldn't see her face, I could feel her eyes burning holes in the back of my head.

Aunt Gizella was waiting for me in the school yard when Miss Zora rang the bell and dismissed us. We walked slowly toward home. The day was mild for early January, and some of the snow had begun to melt, leaving an icy brown slush that tickled our toes through our shoes.

"How was your first day of school?" she asked.

"Everyone was very nice, except for this one girl, Sophia," I said.

Aunt Gizella frowned. "She's a bad one, or so I've heard. Her father deserted the family long ago and ran off with a band of thieves. Her mother lives in town with Sophia's grandparents. They are awful. They put spells on people."

"How?"

"They sneak into your house at night and steal a piece of clothing or jewelry. Then they rub it with an evil charm." She brushed her free hand across her lips. "That's what your grandma tells me, anyhow."

"I don't think Sophia likes me."

"Good. I'd stay far away from her, if I were you. Always count the buttons on your dress, and be sure you have your mittens before you leave school every day."

"Yes, Aunt Gizella." I laughed a little.

"You make fun now, but you may be sorry later."

I wondered whether Sophia and her family could really harm people or even kill someone, and I thought I might not sleep so easily at night anymore, knowing they might hurt me. I hoped Papa's ghost could protect me from them.

"Why are you so quiet?" Aunt Gizella asked.

"I'm thinking, I guess," I replied.

"About what?"

"My teacher. She's nice."

Aunt Gizella raised one eyebrow. "Is that right?"

"Yes, Mama." I clamped my hand over my mouth. "I mean Aunt Gizella."

She poked me in the arm. "I'll race you to the edge of the yard."

She started running so fast her braid flew out of the scarf that covered her hair. I slid in the snow a couple of times before I finally caught up with her. She tucked her braid back into her scarf.

"I hope no one saw that," she said.

"What?" I asked.

"The way my hair fell down."

"Oh, yes. Mama told me Jewish women aren't supposed to show their hair outside the house. She tried to make Mina cover her head after her twelfth birthday in December."

"What happened?"

"You know Mina. She won't even wear a hat in winter. Mama says she's contrary. She came out feet first and hasn't been right since."

Aunt Gizella laughed out loud before her expression grew serious. "It's not good for a woman to be too proud of her hair."

I reached up and fingered the fringes of her scarf. "But your braid is beautiful."

She smiled shyly. "Thank you."

The next day, after lunch, Sophia circled around me again. "No one but me will play with you," she said.

"No one likes you either," I said.

"That's why we should be friends." She grabbed my arm and dragged me to the edge of the yard.

"My aunt told me to stay away from you." I gasped, knowing I shouldn't have said that.

"How come?"

"She didn't mean anything by it. Really."

Sophia shrugged. "Where are your mother and father?"

"I'm not going to tell you."

"Why?"

I pulled away from her and ran back toward the schoolhouse, afraid of what Sophia or her family might do to my aunt.

A few days later, while I was busy reading with Miss Zora, Sophia took my lunch basket, sliding it from under my desk and pushing it back and forth between her feet. I froze after I swiveled around to look at her, and her lips curled into a tight smirk.

"What is the matter, Serene?" Miss Zora asked.

I turned back toward my teacher. "Nothing, Miss Zora," I said.

At lunch, Sophia put her foot on top of my basket. "You have to eat with me now, or you'll go hungry" she said.

I sat down at the desk beside her, and she slid my basket toward me. "Aren't you scared to be so far from home with the war going on?" she asked.

"Leave me alone," I said.

She leaned toward me and put her face so close to mine I could smell the apple she had just eaten on her breath. "My papa's in the Hungarian Army. The reason he's in there is that he owed money from a card game. The mayor of our town told him he could either go into the army or to jail."

"Well, my papa's dead, so you can't hurt him."

She narrowed her eyes and glanced quickly out the window. "Where's your mama? Dead, too?"

"No. Just far away."

"Where?"

"At home. Somewhere. Grandpa always comes to pick me up, so he knows how to get there."

"Oh."

She dug into her own basket and brought out a piece of candy wrapped in green paper and dropped it on my desk. I pushed it away.

"Take it," she said, her voice hard.

I put it in my pocket.

"Why don't you eat it now?" she asked. "Don't you like candy?"

"I'm not hungry," I said, though the truth was I didn't want something that belonged to Sophia inside my body.

"My mama reads palms. She can tell the future. Has anyone ever read your palm?"

"No." I made a fist and jammed it into my pocket, where it bumped against Sophia's candy.

"Maybe you could meet Mama. I know she'd like that. She talks about you all the time. I told her you and I were best friends."

I shivered.

After that, even though I tossed the candy in the grass beside the road, it was almost as if Sophia had planted her mother inside my head. I looked for her everywhere and imagined she was a tall woman who wore beads and smelled like the rose water that came in little bottles in Grandma's store. Sometimes I held my palm out and saw her long fingers entwined with mine, her nails painted, moving slowly along the lines in my hand, reading every twist and turn of my life.

"Why doesn't your mama walk you to school?" I asked Sophia one day after lunch.

"She's too busy," she said. "Come here. I want to show you something."

I followed her to the back of the schoolhouse She reached so far into her pocket I thought she might tear her coat, and when she pulled her hand out and opened it, a tiny glass ball rested on her palm. She held it up in the sunlight and rolled it carefully between her index finger and thumb. It was yellowish-green with a black dot in the center. I couldn't take my eyes off it. I tried to grab it away from her, but she straightened her arm out so that the glass ball hung just out of my reach.

"It's a cat's eye," she said.

"A real one?" I asked.

She nodded. "Mama cut it out of my cat the day he died—a big black cat with huge ears and long white whiskers."

"How did he die?"

"Mama said he was old and tired and ready to leave this world. She cut out the eye while I was at school, and I've had it ever since."

I felt a little sick at the idea of carving an eye out of a dead animal.

"The cat is dead, but the eye is still alive," Sophia said. "Look at what happens when I cover it with my hand. Watch how the dark part gets bigger like a real eye."

She shielded the eye from the sun, and the spot in the center grew much larger. When she held the cat's eye up to the light, the black dot almost disappeared.

"It's magic," she said. "I use it almost every day to make wishes."

For the first time in months, I reached for my neck and the glass heart I'd thrown away so carelessly. I stared at the eye and heard the soft voice of Sophia's mother trilling the "R" in my name. "Can I make a wish on it?" I asked.

Sophia tightened her fist around the eye. "Only one. And only if you're nice to me."

"When can I make it?"

"When I say so, and it has to be a good one. I'll let you know when I'm ready."

I made list after list of possible wishes and coveted that cat's eye. I had so many wishes it was hard to choose just one. First of all, I wanted Papa to come back, and I wanted to go home to Mama and make her happy again, the way she was before Mina started going to funerals, Sam began to run wild, and Miss Kovacz scrambled the letters on the page so I couldn't read them anymore. I wanted Jacob to give up the *shiksa* and marry Aunt Gizella and Grandma to be nice to me and stop hating Mama.

"*M*iss Spirer!" Miss Zora called. "Wait."

She walked toward Aunt Gizella and me as we stood at the edge of the school yard. I watched her approach, and my heart was filled with love for her once again. I thought she was beautiful. Her soft hair fell just below her shoulders, and when she smiled, you could see that one of her front teeth bent slightly over the other.

"I need Serene's help," she said, "and I'm hoping you will agree to lend her to me for a little while."

Aunt Gizella stared at her from beneath her thick eyelashes. "Go on," she said.

I could hardly breathe.

"You've probably seen the Russian soldiers, our prisoners of war," Miss Zora said. "They're everywhere."

"Poor souls," Aunt Gizella said. "They're stuck here, mending our fences instead of fighting battles, but at least that way they aren't killing our countrymen."

Miss Zora sighed. "True enough. What I propose is an errand of mercy. I would like to take Serene with me two afternoons a week to distribute food and extra clothing to these men."

Aunt Gizella pursed her lips. "Her grandmother needs her after school."

"But—" I said.

Aunt Gizella pushed me gently aside, as Miss Zora moved closer and whispered something in her ear.

"Well, all right," Aunt Gizella said.

"Thank you, Miss Spirer," Miss Zora said. "The soldiers will love Serene, and it will be a good experience for her to learn about helping others."

Aunt Gizella nodded. "True enough. A valuable lesson for a young girl."

"Can we go today?" I asked.

"That is up to your Aunt," Miss Zora said.

I grabbed Aunt Gizella's hand and squeezed it as hard as I could.

"I can see she has already made up her mind to go with you," Aunt Gizella said. She knelt down and kissed my cheek. "Have a good time, little one, and be careful."

"I will," I said.

"She won't be late for dinner," Miss Zora said. "I promise."

That first afternoon was so exciting I almost forgot about the cat's eye. I had Miss Zora all to myself, and it was like a dream. We crossed through the center of town together, past the building with the sign that said "Moving Pictures" on the door, and turned down one of the side streets. I was so proud to be with her. Lines of soldiers banged their shovels against the hard ground and blew on their uncovered hands to stay warm. Several of the soldiers knew Miss Zora, and when she stopped to talk to two of them, she spoke slowly and drew pictures in the air. She asked me to give them each an apple from the bag I was carrying, and they both smiled at me and wrapped their icy fingers around mine for a brief instant.

"Dmitri?" Miss Zora asked the two soldiers.

The younger one pointed behind us and waved his arm, as if to say, "Far away down that road."

"Thank you," Miss Zora said.

We wound around the back streets, and I forgot about how numb my toes were and how tired and hungry I was. Finally, we found Dmitri, a tall blond soldier leaning against the trunk of a barren tree. He smoked a cigarette, which he dropped the minute he saw us and crushed under his boot. He stood up and buttoned his collar.

"Dmitri," Miss Zora said. She pushed me toward the soldier. "This is my student, Serene."

He smiled and swept his arm up in the air and bowed. I giggled.

"Why don't you give him an apple?" Miss Zora asked.

I held one out to him. He bowed again, and I dropped it into his large, rough hands. Miss Zora reached forward but stopped before she touched him. His uniform was torn and splattered with mud. He leaned toward her, and she whispered something in his ear. Afterwards, she took my hand and led me quickly away. At the front door of Grandma's house, she bent down to straighten the collar of my coat.

"Let's make our visit to Dmitri our secret," she said, smiling.

I was thrilled and hugged our secret to my chest.

Over the next two weeks, we went to see Dmitri several times. Once, when Miss Zora was bandaging the hand of another soldier, I told him about Sophia and her mother and the cat's eye, and I asked him what I should wish for. He studied my face carefully, as if he understood every word, and when I was finished, he said "Serene" very slowly, trilling the "R" exactly the way Sophia did.

A few days later, after lunch, Sophia stopped me in the school yard and said that if I still wanted to make a wish I had better do it soon, before her mother decided to take the cat's eye away. That afternoon, I followed Miss Zora carrying a bag full of special clothes she gave me. She told me Dmitri's uniform was so worn out that it was time for him to have a new suit. Her face was flushed, and she ran rather than walked through town. She didn't take my hand the way she usually did or stop to talk to any of the other soldiers. I gave the bag of clothing to Dmitri, and he looked inside, his eyes wide. When Miss Zora stood on her tiptoes and kissed him on the cheek, she reminded me of Emilie in the moving picture I had seen with Aunt Gizella, and from somewhere deep inside me, before I could stop it, my wish took shape. I wanted Miss Zora and Dmitri to run away together and live happily ever after like Lazlo and Emilie. Emilie didn't seem stupid to me anymore, and I thought I understood now why the love between the two of them made Aunt Gizella so sad and dreamy.

I don't know what I thought might happen—a bright light across the gray sky, a sad waltz played on an old piano, a passionate embrace with me in the middle. Everything was quiet, and Miss Zora and Dmitri stood perfectly still in front of me. She seemed to have forgotten all about me, and the two of them turned and disappeared around a corner at the far end of the street. I waited until it was almost dark, and when she didn't return, I retraced our steps through town and walked home alone. I didn't tell anyone what had happened, ate my supper in silence, and went to bed without doing my lessons.

The next day, Miss Zora wasn't at school. An older woman, Mrs. Schwarcz, whose husband was in the army, came in her place and told us Miss Zora was ill. I wanted to believe her, and at lunch, I asked her when Miss Zora would be back.

"Soon," she said. "Very soon."

But I knew I would never see her again. Sophia and I huddled together behind the school house, and she showed me the cat's eye. It glowed bright green, and the pupil was only a black speck in the middle.

"It has been busy," Sophia said, smiling her hard smile. "I can tell."

About a week after my teacher disappeared, I asked Aunt Gizella, "Do you think Miss Zora is happy?"

"My dear," she said. "I certainly hope so, but times are hard. Money is scarce. People in town are talking. They say Zora is carrying that man's baby. I don't know how the two of them will survive or where they will go."

"Won't they be like Lazlo and Emilie?"

"Who?"

"You remember. In the moving picture."

"Oh, that. It's only make-believe."

"What do you mean?" I covered my face with my hands and started to cry.

"It must have been terrible for you. I never dreamed Zora would expose you to such a thing. Mama is beside herself. She blames me for letting you go with her. It will be months before she gets over it, if I know her."

"I miss her. I want her back."

She wrapped me in her arms. "I know you do, but you mustn't worry about Miss Zora now. You have yourself to take care of."

But I dreamed about her for months after she disappeared. At first, she looked happy. Later, though, her cheekbones stuck out of her face. I tried to tell her I was sorry for my wish, but she never seemed to hear me.

KARL

Grandma told us Karl was sneaky. "All dark and hunched over and with sharp eyes like a Gypsy," she said. "You'd better count all your fingers and toes after he's been here. I wish I wasn't such an old woman. Then I wouldn't need him to carry things for me."

Grandma was right about Karl. I didn't like the way he stared at my aunt with his greedy eyes. She thought he was handsome and sneaked him extra pieces of fruit and extra helpings of potatoes on the days he worked for Grandma.

One afternoon, while Aunt Gizella and I sat alone by the kitchen stove, I said, "I think Karl is mean."

"Why?" Aunt Gizella asked.

"He steals things."

"No, he doesn't. His family is poor, poorer than we are. And his mother is sick. So that's just your grandma talking, looking down her nose at people who are worse off than we are. I'll tell you a secret. Not long ago, I gave him an honesty test."

"How did you do that?"

"I put some coins on the table by the inside door, and guess what? No one touched the money the entire day."

In spite of Aunt Gizella's honesty test, I still didn't like Karl. He usually helped out during the week, while I was in school. One Tuesday morning, he came early and walked me to school because Aunt Gizella had a cold. He didn't try to hold my hand, but I wouldn't have let him anyway.

"My aunt's pretty, isn't she?" I asked.

He pulled at his collar and scratched his neck. "Yes, very pretty," he said.

"Grandma says all you care about is our money."

He jammed his hands in his pockets and lowered his head against the wind, looking for all the world just like Papa. I crossed over to the other side of the road, wondering how I could get Sophia to give me another wish on the cat's eye so I could get rid of Karl.

Ever since Miss Zora ran off with the Russian soldier, Grandma wouldn't allow me to go anywhere by myself. When Aunt Gizella's cold grew worse, I told Grandma I knew the way to school, but she said, "You have worse judgment than a chicken. First you take up with a Russian sympathizer. God knows who you'll take up with next if I turn you loose."

She sent Karl with me every single day for a week. He and I both disliked these walks, and I stayed on my side of the road and wouldn't let him cross over. Finally, Aunt Gizella's cold got better, and she regained her spirits.

Early one February morning, I stood in the front yard, shuffling my feet on the hard ground. The door to Grandma's shed opened, and Karl came out. My aunt dashed across the frozen grass and reached out to him, brushing his coat with her glove. They leaned into one another, their heads down. I ran to her and pushed myself between them. I took her hand and dragged her away from him, and he turned toward Grandma's store and didn't wave or say good-bye.

That afternoon, my aunt wasn't waiting for me. I searched every inch of the yard, but she was nowhere in sight. The sky was light gray and dotted with clouds, and the air was so misty it made my skin wet and my hair soggy. I stood in front of the schoolhouse, stamping my feet and wiggling my fingers inside my mittens to keep out the wet ache. After the last child and teacher had left, I began to get angry at Aunt Gizella. If I came home alone, Grandma might throw a dishrag at me or make me sleep in the barn with the cow, so I knew I had to wait for my aunt. Now it was beginning to rain hard and get dark. School was more than a mile away from Grandma's, and at this time of day, hardly anyone would be on the road. Someone might sneak up on me and stab me with a knife and leave me in a ditch to die.

"Papa, where are you?" I asked. Rain beat against the schoolhouse windows. "This is your home. You went to this school. Don't you like it here? Why won't you help me?"

The sky grew darker, and I bent my head into the wind, putting one foot down in front of the other until I ran smack into someone.

"Papa?" I asked.

"I'm not your papa, you silly brat," a voice said.

"Karl? What are you doing here? Where's my aunt?"

I yanked at his coat and started hitting him. He grabbed my shoulders and wrapped me in the crook of his arm and dragged me home beside him. He let go of me in front of the door to Grandma's house.

"Next time they can find someone else to do their dirty work," he said, before he vanished into the rainy night.

No one looked up when I came in, not Grandpa, who was staring at a book on his lap and turning the pages so fast he couldn't have been reading them, or Grandma, who was stirring a sour-smelling soup on the stove, or Aunt Gizella, who sat at the far end of the dinner table, her face lost in the darkness.

Finally, Grandma turned to me. "Child," she said.

Grandpa trembled a little in his chair, and Aunt Gizella jumped slightly. Grandma's voice stung my ears.

"I'm fine, really I am," I said.

"Well, change out of those wet clothes before you catch pneumonia," she said. "You think you can get away with staying out by yourself until all hours, doing God knows what, and come home soaked through and dripping everywhere. I suppose now you'll take it into your head to get sick and die on me." She threw up her hands in disgust.

"I already almost died once, so it won't happen again."

"What?" Aunt Gizella whispered from her place in the darkness.

I ran to her and buried my head in her lap and let her take off my wet clothes and put me to bed. She washed my face and hands with hot water and covered me with a warm blanket and watched over me until I fell asleep.

The next day she walked me to school, as usual, and when we arrived at the front door, she noticed I was missing a mitten.

"I'm sure I left it at home," I said.

"As long as Sophia doesn't have it," my aunt said. "Take care to keep your hand inside your coat pocket when you're outside. I've heard stories of little girls who lost fingers and entire hands by forgetting to wear their gloves in the cold. It's not pretty either. Your skin turns blue and black and starts to swell."

I stuck my bare hand in my pocket. "I promise I won't let it out."

"Good."

"Are you in love with Karl? Is that where you were yesterday?"

She smiled a sad smile and looked down at the step below her. "Don't let your imagination run wild."

She gave me a gentle nudge toward the door, and I realized she hadn't answered my question. I was afraid to turn around and ask her again, because I thought she'd have to tell me the truth the second time. And I knew I wouldn't like the answer.

That morning, Sophia sat next to me. Each of the first-year students read out loud a paragraph from a book we'd been assigned about the Magyars and how they came all the way from someplace called Estonia to settle here and take over the land. The book said they rode tall horses and wore jackets braided with gold and fought with huge swords. After both Sophia and I took our turns, she slipped a note into my hand. Luckily, one of the boys stumbled over the name of a man, Verboczy, who made a record of Magyar law almost four hundred years ago. We all began to laugh and point at the boy and bounce around, until Mrs. Schwarcz clapped her hands and yelled at us to sit back down in our seats. While she was busy with the troublemakers, I opened

Sophia's note, and for the first time since I left Galfalva and Miss Kovacz, words started playing tricks on me. They slid to the edge of the page and crawled back and forth. I wanted to throw the note on the floor and stamp it under my feet to make the words behave, but it stuck to my fingers like glue. So I hid it in my lap and took a deep breath and looked again at the open book on my desk. The words there stayed in place, and I read a sentence about how the Magyars lived in tribes and made their own laws. When I peeked down at the note resting in the fold of my skirt, the handwriting was thin and spidery and had legs going in all directions.

The note still clung to my hand during morning recess, and I had to crumble the paper to fit it into my coat pocket. I went out the front door and around the corner to the back of the building so that I could try to read the note one more time. I leaned against the wall to block out the cold morning wind, and the words danced around the way they had inside. Sophia crept up behind me and touched my shoulder.

"What's wrong with your writing?" I asked. "These words don't look anything like the ones we study in school."

"That's from Mama," Sophia said. "Her family came here from Russia when she was ten years old, and she never learned how to write in Hungarian. She can speak it well enough, though."

"So, what does it say?"

"Last night, we were talking about you. Mama stirred the tea leaves in the bottom of our pot after dinner and sat down to write you this note. She said, 'A young man with fear in his heart will bring big trouble to Serene.'"

"How did your mother know that?"

Sophia sighed. "Mama wants you to give her something special of yours so she can put a spell on it and get rid of him for you."

"Can't I use the cat's eye again?"

"No. Mama took it away. You'd better do exactly what she says, unless you want to get into trouble."

I held the note up, and the wind lifted it from my fingers and sent it high up in the sky. My thumb began to ache, as if it had been left uncovered in the cold for too long, and I could have sworn it was starting to turn blue at the tip, even though I had kept my hand in my pocket. I had the sudden feeling that something terrible was about to happen to my aunt.

I left Sophia at the back of the school house and ran all the way to Grandma's, not thinking about how angry she might be when I came home by myself in the middle of the day. I had to be certain my aunt was all right. The house was empty, except for Grandpa, who sat with his nose buried so deeply in his book that he didn't seem to notice when I came in. I went back outside and peeked into the window of Grandma's store. She was busy dusting shelves and rearranging bottles. Then I went to the shed.

The door was ajar, and I slipped inside and inched my way forward, in spite of my fear of the place. A candle flickered in the distance, and I heard the sound of whispering. I wound my way through the rows of shelves and stacks of barrels, miraculously failing to upset any crates or knock any bottles to the floor. As I approached the light, I saw two shadows on the wall. I knelt behind a barrel and raised my head slowly. There, in the far corner of the shed, Aunt Gizella and Karl were joined together in a clumsy embrace. The top buttons of her coat were open, and her scarf had fallen to the floor. Karl groped at her and grunted like an ape. I froze and jammed my fist into my mouth to keep from screaming. Karl and my aunt were not beautiful together, like Lazlo and Emilie or Miss Zora and Dmitri. Karl was awkward and pawed at my aunt, while she ducked and wove about as if she might fall on the floor. The two of them bumped up against one another and crashed against the wall. My aunt's eyes were closed, and her fists were clenched. I wanted her to make him stop, but she kept right on kissing Karl. I fell to my knees panting and crawled silently out of the shed.

I circled back around the house and slipped into the front door. Grandpa glanced up at me, almost without recognizing me, and returned to the book he was reading. I tiptoed to the dresser where Aunt Gizella kept her scarves and pushed aside several handkerchiefs before I found what I was looking for: her cotton scarf with gold tassels and a Star of David embroidered on one edge. It was her favorite, and she wore it to synagogue only on the most special occasions. I stuffed the scarf into my pocket and ran outside.

Somehow my feet took me toward Sophia's house instead of back to school where I belonged. She had told me many times where she lived, and when I knocked on the door, a thin blond woman with tiny wrinkles around her eyes opened it. Her hands were small, and the fingernails were bitten-back and jagged. She led me to a chair by the stove.

"You must be Serene," she said, rolling over the "R" in my name. "You have difficulty at home."

I knew I had met her somewhere before. "And you're Mrs. Gorgei," I said.

"Who else? Now, tell me about this trouble."

"Karl—the man who works in Grandma's store. I saw him kissing my aunt. He has put her under a spell and made her think she is in love with him."

"I see." She slid a handkerchief out of her cuff and gave it to me. It smelled of nutmeg and Mama's honey cake. Sophia's mother rose from her chair and stood behind me and rubbed my shoulders until all the pain was gone.

"You have something for me."

I gave her my aunt's scarf. She took it gently from me and held it up to the light, feeling the material and flicking the tassels against her cheek.

"Very good," she said. "Excellent craftsmanship."

"My aunt embroidered it herself," I said.

"Leave everything to me. Go back to school. Go home afterwards. Act like nothing happened, and I will free your household from this menace."

I knew I should be relieved, but I wasn't. I did what Mrs. Gorgei said and went through the next two days trying hard not to worry. My aunt watched me with concern.

"Are you ill?" she asked, after dinner one evening. She touched my forehead. "You've hardly eaten anything these last two days, and you have dark circles under your eyes. Perhaps I should go for the doctor."

"No," I said. "I feel fine."

Early one morning, a few days after I had visited Sophia's mother, Grandma sent me to the shed for several bottles of cough syrup. The door creaked when I opened it, and I knew immediately that someone else was in there. I pressed myself against the wall and sidestepped forward.

"Who's there?" I asked.

Someone hissed and clamped a hand on my shoulder. I turned around, and a man stood in the shadows in front of me.

"Karl?" I asked.

"How did you do it?" he asked. "She liked me well enough until you came around, poking your nose in where it didn't belong."

"You shouldn't have kissed her. Did Grandma catch you?"

"What business is that of yours? I've done it lots of times."

He pinched my nose and shook me so hard my teeth rattled. Then he shoved me against the wall. I started to cry.

"Go ahead," he said. "Cry all you want. No one will hear you, and if they do, they won't come to help you. They don't care about you. They don't care about anyone."

He grabbed my arm and squeezed.

"Ouch," I said. "Stop it."

"Good," he said. "Now you know how it feels. She had no right to fire me, the old witch, and she wouldn't have, if you hadn't put the wrong ideas into her head. How am I going to eat?" He punched me, but not hard, in the stomach. "Not that it makes any difference to you, as long as your own belly is full."

He lurched forward and spun around on his heel, like the men at Papa's tavern who had had too much to drink. He crashed through the door and disappeared into the early morning fog.

I brushed the dirt off my coat, wiped the tears from my cheek, and poked my head out the door. "Karl?" I whispered.

The yard was empty.

I walked slowly past the store and into the house. I stopped at the door to watch Aunt Gizella dry the last of the breakfast dishes and put them away. When she was finished, I came up behind her and threw my arms around her waist.

"Do you love me?" I asked. "Tell me the truth."

She turned around and knelt down in front of me, rubbing her palm against my cheek. Her face was flushed from the steamy dish water, and she smiled at my sudden display of affection.

"Of course I love you," she said. "What kind of question is that?"

TIBOR

Aunt Gizella needed a husband. Not someone like Karl, who was much too young for her and had no money to give her the kind of life she deserved. As far as anyone knew, Jacob was still married to the *shiksa*, so I set my sights on Tibor, a rich merchant just past his fiftieth birthday who showed up early one warm Sunday afternoon in March. The trees were starting to turn green and the wildflowers poked their leaves through the ground. Tibor drove his wagon to the front of Grandma's store and climbed down, offering to sell her fabric, ribbons, and rose water. Aunt Gizella and I watched from the store window.

"Why haven't I seen him before?" I asked Aunt Gizella, after Tibor finished haggling with Grandma and drove away.

"That old goat," Aunt Gizella said. "He has eyes in back of his head and only comes out when the weather is warm. He's as homely as a wart, isn't he?"

I slipped my hand inside my aunt's. "He's not so ugly."

"If you don't mind sunken-chested, gap-toothed old men in baggy pants."

"Did he see us at the window? I thought he was looking at you."

"He was not."

"Was too!"

The next Sunday, Tibor drove his wagon to the front door and spoke briefly with Grandma, while Aunt Gizella and I watched from the window again. Grandma invited him inside. I grabbed my aunt's arm, my fingers hot and tense on her skin. I let the excitement from my body pass into hers. The two of us sat at the table and composed ourselves. Aunt Gizella's eyes were shining, and I kept my head down, hoping Grandma wouldn't scold me for acting silly in front of Tibor.

"Look who I found," Grandma said in a loud voice as she came through the door.

"Good afternoon," I said.

Aunt Gizella poked me with her elbow.

"Humph," Grandpa said. He didn't even bother to raise an eyebrow.

Tibor sat at the opposite end of the table from my aunt, lowering himself carefully into the chair so that the legs wouldn't squeak. "How did the winter treat you, Miss Spirer?" he asked.

"Well enough, thank you" Aunt Gizella said curtly.

He turned toward me. "Who might this be?" He smiled slightly.

I saw the gap between his teeth and decided it wasn't so bad. Tibor noticed me staring at his mouth and clamped it shut. His cheeks flushed pink.

"Serene," I said. I coughed and folded my hands in my lap.

"My granddaughter," Grandma said, nodding at me with disapproval.

"I'll make us some tea," Aunt Gizella said. She rose quickly and banged the kettle on the stove.

"That would be lovely," Tibor said. "It's still too cold outside for me. I don't really feel right until the last frost of the year is over."

He took off his hat and glanced at Grandpa and Grandma and me, before letting his eyes come to rest on Aunt Gizella's back. His skin was pale after the flush on his cheeks faded, and his eyes were dark brown, buried deep in their sockets and surrounded by thick folds of skin that had tiny lines everywhere. He bowed his head, and I could see a bald spot at the very top. His thinning hair was gray and fell over his eyes. When he looked back up, his eyebrows were arched high, and his mouth was only slightly open. I put my hand on top of his. I felt sorry that the hole between his teeth and his bald spot seemed to get in the way, when all he wanted to do was sit in his chair and watch my aunt for a little while. He leaned back, and this time the chair legs squeaked on the floor. Grandpa sighed deeply.

We finished our tea, and Grandma and Tibor went to the store to discuss business. Aunt Gizella moved slower now, and the vein in her temple had stopped throbbing.

"Traitor," she said. "Why did you hold hands with him?"

"He's nice," I said.

"That's easy for you to say."

After Tibor left, I held a basket of thread for my aunt and picked out the different colors she needed to embroider a handkerchief.

"He's not a handsome man," she said.

"He's much nicer than Karl," I said.

She gave me a sharp look. "When I was younger, I wouldn't have paid any attention to him. He would've been too old. Besides, he's second-hand goods." She set down her embroidering and put her hand on her forehead. "His first wife died a year ago. They had two daughters."

"I hope they look like her."

"Me too." She began to hum quietly and picked up her embroidery again.

"He wants to marry you."

"What are you now, a matchmaker?"

I pinched my lips together and hunched my shoulders like Tibor and made my voice scratchy. "How did the winter treat you, Miss Spirer?"

"That doesn't mean a thing. It's a polite form of speech."

"I love you, Miss Spirer. And what about your *nadan*?"

"First of all, I don't have a *nadan*."

"What about your gold coin, a gift from your niece?"

"All right, except for the gold coin, I have no money. Besides, he's a rich man already. That's the only reason Mama gives him the time of day, certainly not for his looks or charm." She jabbed her needle in and out of her handkerchief. "Anyhow, I'm not interested in him." She stopped embroidering again. "Can you imagine what it would be like to kiss him? You'd press your lips next to his, and he'd suck them into that hole between his teeth."

I thought kissing Tibor was much better than kissing Karl, but I didn't say so.

A couple of days after Tibor's second visit, Aunt Gizella and I were walking home together from school. She was more quiet than usual, and I thought I knew why. The blue sky and the smell of fresh grass made me lonely for Mama, the way spring afternoons will, and I imagined my aunt was missing Karl. So I was grateful when we turned onto Grandma's street and saw Tibor's wagon standing in front of the house.

"You have a visitor," I said.

She stopped short at the sight of the wagon, pushed a few strands of hair back under her scarf, and straightened the buttons on her dress. She took a deep breath.

"I thought you didn't like him," I said.

"I don't, but that doesn't mean I want him to see me with my hair flying every which way and dust on my skirt," she said. She pushed me in front of her so that I walked through the door first like a shield. "Protect me."

Tibor sat at the table with Grandma, drinking a cup of tea. He stood up when he saw my aunt and pulled out a chair for her to sit next to him. Aunt Gizella guided me into that chair and took another at the other end of the table.

"Good afternoon, Miss Spirer," he said. "Good afternoon to you, Serene. You're looking quite well today."

"Thank you," I said. "So are you."

He smiled. Aunt Gizella sneezed and coughed into her handkerchief. Tibor's arm was resting on top of a package wrapped in brown paper, and he slid it toward my aunt.

"When this came my way, I was reminded of you," he said.

My aunt stared at it but didn't move.

"Please, take it," Tibor said.

She reached for the package and opened it slowly. "Ivory lace," she said. "It's lovely, but it's so expensive. I couldn't possibly accept it."

"No, please. I paid a good price for it." His eyes were moist, and his mouth narrowed down to a thin line. He leaned forward in his chair.

My aunt sighed. "Thank you."

She excused herself to make some fresh tea and moved quickly around the stove, almost letting a cup slip between her fingers. Luckily, Tibor jumped up and saved it. She glanced at him sideways and pulled the cup away from him before he had a chance to let his hand linger on hers.

After we were finished drinking our tea and eating Grandma's stale cookies, Tibor asked my aunt and me to go for a walk in the neighborhood. The afternoon sun was shining brightly through the window, and I was glad for any excuse to get away from Grandma. I stood up right away and said we wanted to go, but Aunt Gizella hung back. When Tibor held out his arm to her, she lowered her head and didn't move from her chair.

"Come on," I said.

I ran to her side and tugged at her elbow until she finally stood up. Her face and neck were bright pink, and her temple throbbed. She reached forward and took Tibor's arm, and the three of us walked out the door. As we turned the corner at the end of Grandma's street, I noticed Tibor was dragging his right leg.

"What happened to your leg?" I asked.

Aunt Gizella poked me. "Excuse my niece," she said. "She seems to have lost her manners."

"Nonsense," Tibor said. "I like a person who speaks her mind."

"Well, what happened?" I said.

Aunt Gizella flashed her eyes at me, and I took a step back.

"Right before the war started, we heard rumors of a wandering band of Romanians," Tibor said. "They were supposed to be murdering our chickens for their blood and God knows what else. The Romanians say they hate Hungarians because we stole their land and because we're too proud, but I think it's because our two peoples are so different. They're Romans, and we're Magyars, and we have to live so close together."

I turned to Aunt Gizella. "Do you remember Mama's brother, Mishi?" I asked.

"The traveling musician," she said. "Yes, God rest his soul. They found him in a ditch by the side of the road a year ago last autumn, wasn't it? He was a wonderful man, so full of life."

"Mama still cries every time she talks about him because he was her favorite brother. She says he was murdered by a Romanian. She says all Romanians hate us. Is that true?"

"Possibly."

"If your uncle died such a horrible death, perhaps you don't want to hear the rest of the story," Tibor said.

"Please, I do," I said.

"She likes blood and gore," Aunt Gizella said.

"I do not!" But the truth was I missed the stories Sam always told me about bats who feasted on people's livers.

"One of these Romanians stood right under the gateway I built in my yard after my wife died," Tibor said. He glanced quickly at my aunt, who looked down at the ground. "It's a tradition to build such a gate for the dead to ease their passage from this world into the next. I don't speak Romanian, but I had the impression this man was calling me a dirty Jew and a Hungarian son of a dog. I couldn't let him get away with that, could I? Normally, I'm a peaceful man, but the idea of him standing underneath my wife's gateway cursing me like that was too much for me, so I ran after him with an axe. I lifted it high over my head and hit him a good one. The next thing I remember was falling over a tree stump. The axe bit into my leg, and the doctor who took care of me said I was lucky to have this thing at all." He patted his poor leg in satisfaction. "Well, at least all our chickens stay home these days. When you come to my house, I'll show you the gate with the man's footprint. It's still there in the mud after a whole year. No rain or snow will ever wash it away."

"I'd like to see it," I said.

My aunt cleared her throat loudly.

After that day, Tibor became a regular visitor at Grandma's, and he almost always brought wonderful gifts, purple and red ribbons for my hair, lavender water, candy that tasted like the mint leaves that grew wild in our backyard at home. Each time he came, I made sure Aunt Gizella sat next to him and walked beside him. Once or twice, I even hooked her arm through his, until the magic began to take hold and the sound of his foot dragging on the front porch made her bounce out of her chair.

One afternoon, Tibor drove me to the edge of town to show me something special there.

"Are you going to marry my aunt?" I asked.

"My favorite thing about you, Serene, is that you don't mince words," he said.

"You should ask her."

"I love your aunt. I have for some time, and I want her to be my wife. But does she love me?"

"She doesn't know it yet, but she does. Besides, Grandma likes you."

"I worry about taking Gizella away from her family, taking her away from you. She loves you very much. If we marry, maybe you could come and live with us. Would you like that?"

"Oh, but I'm going back to Mama at the end of the school year. I could visit you in the summer."

He took my hand and pointed to the mountains far away in the distance. "Almost five hundred years ago, an evil prince, Vladimir Tepes, built tunnels and caves in those mountains. He held thousands of prisoners inside and tortured them until they died. He drove stakes into their hearts and dipped his bread in their blood."

I clung to him.

"He killed for the sheer joy of it," Tibor said. "Everyone says he was the son of the devil, and the ghosts of his victims are still inside those mountains."

"I believe in ghosts," I said.

Tibor knelt down in front of me. "I can tell. You're very brave."

"I used to see my papa's ghost all the time. Papa left us and then died on a boat to America. His ghost used to follow me around in Galfalva and sit on my shoulder and whisper in my ear. Only mine. No one else's. But since I've been living at Grandma's, he doesn't come to me very often. I don't know why."

"Your grandmother is a powerful woman. Perhaps your papa is frightened of her. She may hold a grudge over something that happened years ago."

"I saw Papa's body once inside Grandma's shed. Not his ghost. His real body."

"It sounds to me like your papa hasn't passed over to the other side yet. He hasn't found his final resting place."

"That's what my sister Mina says." I stared at those distant blue-green mountains, shimmering in the afternoon sun. "We even tried to bury his ghost once in a coffin with another dead man, but it didn't work."

"Hmm. I'm not surprised. Who wants to share a coffin? Besides, what if he wasn't ready for you to put him in the ground yet?"

"Maybe he thinks I'll forget him, but I never will."

"It sounds to me like you miss him very much."

"I do."

One Sunday, a few weeks later, Tibor told us he would be alone
for the Passover holiday and the *seder*. The ritual dinner was usually a
family celebration, but since his two daughters were going to visit relatives, he planned to have a quiet dinner on his own.

"You could come to our *seder*," I said.

"Serene!" Aunt Gizella said.

"I suppose," Grandma said. "Yes, indeed. That's a fine idea. Isn't
it just like children to be so ungrateful and forget about their parents on
such an important occasion?"

"Good," I said and rested my head against Tibor's shoulder.

Until the afternoon Grandma and I invited Tibor for the Passover
seder, Aunt Gizella hadn't missed the scarf I gave to Sophia's mother,
but as we stood at the front door and watched Tibor's wagon disappear
around the corner, Aunt Gizella touched the everyday scarf she was
wearing and frowned.

"I haven't seen my favorite scarf for weeks," she said. "I wonder
where it could be. I'd like to wear it for the *seder*. It's pretty, don't you
think?"

I shrugged, and the palms of my hands started to sweat.

The next morning during recess, I dragged Sophia to the back of
the school yard.

"Where is my aunt's scarf?" I asked. "Your mother promised to
give it right back to me."

"That's not what she told me," Sophia said.

"My aunt will be angry if it's lost, and I'll be in trouble. I'll give
you two pieces of lace that I got from a rabbi at a funeral in exchange
for it."

"Why would I want some dumb old lace? I'll have to talk to
Mama."

"Promise?"

She made the sign of a cross over her heart, but I should have
remembered how many times I'd seen Sophia swear on her mother's

grave that she would give back an apple or replace a button and forget about it the very next minute.

Three mornings later, Sophia said, "Mama doesn't have the scarf."

"Where is it?" I asked.

"She wouldn't say."

"Why won't you give it back?"

She stuck her tongue out at me.

"You didn't even ask your mama at all," I said.

Sophia pushed me so hard that I fell onto the ground. "I did so," she said. "She thinks it is better that you don't know who has the scarf now. Ask her yourself, if you don't believe me." She turned on her heel and walked away.

"I will!" I shouted after her.

I brushed the dust off my dress, and the morning breeze raised goosebumps on my arms and neck. I pressed my back against the school wall. I rested my head between my knees, and every time I breathed, someone touched my elbow. When I looked up, I saw a wisp of blond hair out of the corner of my eye. I shook my head and stood up slowly and walked to the front of the school house, but later someone began rubbing my shoulders as I labored over my spelling. At first, I thought it was Papa, and for the second time that day, I saw that same wisp of blond hair. While I was eating my lunch, someone put a hand on top of my head and told me to calm myself and filled my mind with the idea of my aunt's treasured scarf. I was sure now it was Sophia's mother, and at afternoon recess, I looked for her everywhere until I saw her waving at me from the edge of the school yard. I ran to her.

"Please, Mrs. Gorgei," I said.

"I sold the scarf," she said.

"But it wasn't yours to sell. Who bought it?"

"I can't say."

"Why not?"

"I don't want to hurt you."

"But I have to get it back for my aunt." I grabbed a fold in my skirt and twisted it between my fingers. "She is thinking of marrying a man, and she keeps looking for the scarf because she says it makes her beautiful."

"If she marries this man, she'll need more help than a scarf can give her."

I tried to look her straight in the eye, but the bright sun blinded me.

"I lied," she said. "I still have the scarf, but I'm saving it for someone. An older man. A rich merchant, I think, who lives outside of town with his two daughters. He has a gap between his teeth."

"I don't believe you," I said.

"Suit yourself."

"Why are you saving it for him?"

She laughed. The sun was hot on my shoulders, and my legs buckled underneath me. I tried to grab on to her to keep from falling, but her arms turned into branches, and her skin turned into leaves. A group of boys from my class came up behind me and formed a circle around me.

"Serene is crazy," they sang. "She talks to bushes. Serene is crazy."

I fainted.

The insides of my eyelids were bright yellow, and when I opened my eyes, the boys drifted out of sight. I was breathing hard, holding onto the bush that used to be Sophia's mother.

"Where are you, Mrs. Gorgei?" I said. "I have so many more questions to ask you." She didn't come back, of course.

That evening, as Aunt Gizella tucked me into bed, I wrapped my arms around her neck. "I know where your scarf is," I said. "I gave it to Mrs. Gorgei."

"Why on earth did you do that?" she asked. "You know exactly what that woman is capable of."

"I was afraid of Karl. I wanted to make him go away so you wouldn't end up marrying a poor man, and Mrs. Gorgei said she could

help. She took the scarf, and now she's says she's promised it to someone else, and it isn't hers to give anymore."

Aunt Gizella pulled me close to her.

"You don't love Karl, do you?" I asked.

"I suppose not," she said. There were tears in her eyes. "I wonder
if Sophia's mother put him in my path in the first place just to cause me
pain."

"But now you have Tibor."

"Now I have Tibor."

"I like him."

"I'm glad. I can't bear to think what might happen if you didn't,
my little matchmaker. Ah, well. If nothing else comes of this attach-
ment, I believe you've found your calling in life."

PROPOSAL

"What are your daughters' names?" I asked Tibor, after we finished the *seder*.

"Ruth and Anna," he replied.

"I would like to meet them."

My aunt kicked me under the table and patted my wrist sharply.

"You should bring them for a visit," Grandma said.

Tibor reached into his vest pocket and pulled out a copper coin. He dropped it into my palm, and I held it in my hand, feeling rich and happy.

"For you," he said. "A Passover gift."

"Thank you for the penny," I said.

"I know," Grandma said. "Why don't you bring your daughters to dinner on the last night of Passover? That way we can all break bread together."

"No more *matzo*," I said. "Thank God."

"I agree," Tibor said. "It's too dry. It has no taste, and I, for one, have never cared for it."

Aunt Gizella looked at him. He smiled with his mouth closed, and Grandpa lowered his eyes to the table and let the steam from his hot tea fog his glasses.

"What difference does it make whether we liked the taste of *matzo* or not?" he asked. "We eat it to remind us of the exile of the Jews from Egypt, and that is all there is to say about it."

"You are right," Tibor said. "I spoke out of turn." He winked at me.

The following Tuesday, at the end of Passover week, Tibor arrived with his two daughters.

"Ruth, Anna, this is Serene," he said.

Ruth, who was a head taller than her father, smiled and nodded politely so that her dark curls fell forward on her cheeks. Anna peered around Ruth's waist. Her frizzy blond hair looked as if it hadn't been combed in days, and her collar was crooked. She stuck her tongue out at me.

At dinner that night, I couldn't take my eyes off Ruth. She looked a lot like her father, dark hair and eyes, pale skin, a gap between her front teeth, though hers was so small you could barely see it. Where Tibor's face was too long and his features were crooked, her nose was well placed between her eyes, and her mouth was thin and delicate. When she stood beside her father, their faces were almost identical, yet she was beautiful, and Tibor was plain at best.

After dinner, she rose immediately to help Aunt Gizella clear the table. Anna played with her cake crumbs and took tiny sips of milk. Ruth never said a word but stacked the dishes quietly. She didn't laugh out loud when Tibor told a joke or Anna spilled her milk, but she always seemed to be smiling. She reminded me of Miss Zora, and I let myself fall a little bit in love with her.

After Tibor and his daughters left, I practiced sitting still with my hands resting in my lap and a quiet smile pasted on my lips, imitating Ruth.

"What is the matter with you?" Grandma asked. "Did you eat something that didn't agree with you? You look sick."

"I'm just resting," I said softly.

She turned to my aunt. "This child is a burden to me. I never know what to expect from her."

Aunt Gizella glanced at me sideways, as if she understood exactly what I was doing.

Tibor, Ruth, and Anna returned the Sunday after their first visit. It was the middle of April, and Anna soon grew restless and bored. Tibor began to lose patience with her and ordered her to go outdoors. Aunt Gizella was embroidering a tablecloth, and Ruth took up one end, pulled a needle from my aunt's pin cushion, threaded it, and began hemming the edges. Grandma and Tibor disappeared into the store to talk business, and after a few minutes, my aunt looked up from her embroidering and frowned.

"Where's Anna, I wonder?" she said. "Serene, why don't you go outside and play with her? Aren't there some things around here you'd like to show her?"

"Like what?" I asked. I was busy studying the way Ruth held the needle between her index finger and thumb.

"I don't know. How about the woods in back of the house? Go on now, and find her."

I stood up slowly and shuffled out the door. Anna sat at the edge of the woods behind Grandma's house and stirred the dirt with a stick.

"There's nothing to do around here," she said. "How can you stand it?"

"Let's go back into the house," I said. I didn't like the idea of Aunt Gizella and Ruth sitting so peacefully together.

Anna jumped up. "I have an idea. Let's hike over toward the mountains with ghosts inside." She put her hand around her neck and pretended she was choking herself. "Help! Let me out."

"I'm not allowed to walk that far without an adult."

She threw down her stick. "Baby!"

She ran into the woods, and I ran after her. After all, I was supposed to look after her, even though she was two years older than me. I liked Tibor, and I thought he would make a good husband for my aunt. But I wasn't so sure about his daughters, and I wondered whether I'd made a mistake in encouraging him and whether I would have to pay Mrs. Gorgei another visit so she could put a spell on us to get rid of all of them.

"Hurry up," Anna called from deep within the woods.

I followed the sound of her voice, and soon the branches of the trees were so thick with leaves that no sunlight could shine through.

"Anna!" I shouted. "Come back. Aunt Gizella will never forgive me if I lose you."

She sneaked up behind me and laughed in my ear, nudging my shoulder. I almost fell forward and cut myself in two on a sharp tree trunk.

"This is fun, isn't it?" she said.

"No," I said.

"Want to hear something strange? We studied about it in school. Have you ever been to Budapest?"

I shook my head.

"Well, in a church there, locked in a vault, is a mummified hand of one of our kings, Stefan, who became a saint," she said. "The hand is about eight hundred years old."

"Can you really see it?" I asked. "What does it look like?"

"I don't know, but I'm going to Budapest to find it one day and bring it back here." She circled behind me and clamped her hand down on my shoulder. "I'm the mummy of Stefan of the Arpad dynasty."

Her voice was so low, almost as if St. Stefan's spirit had taken over her body for a moment. The sky looked black. The wind whistled through the leaves, and the air was as cold as a December afternoon. Then the sun pushed through the clouds, and the leaves grew still. Anna laughed in that high, squeaky way of hers.

"I'm hungry," I said. "I'm going back. You'd better come too."

She rushed ahead of me, tearing the hem of her skirt on a branch. That made her laugh even more. I saw the tips of her blond curls as she wove in and out of the trees. When we came to the end of the woods, Aunt Gizella was waiting for us with a worried look on her face.

"Goodness," she said. "You two girls were gone so long we were afraid you were lost or kidnapped."

Anna rolled her eyes up until only the whites showed.

"Oh, my God," Aunt Gizella said. "This child is having a fit."

Anna rolled her eyes back down and laughed.

"I'm sorry, Aunt Gizella," I said. "We'll be more careful next time."

Of course, Anna wouldn't touch the delicious cabbage rolls my aunt had prepared for dinner. They were sweet, but with a taste of vinegar that made my eyes water after each mouthful. Ruth picked daintily at hers, chewing each tiny bite many times more than she really had to. Finally, Tibor dug his fork into a roll on Anna's plate.

"Pa!" she said.

"What?" he asked.

"That was mine."

"You weren't eating it, and there's no sense in wasting perfectly good food."

"Pa is right," Ruth said.

Anna reached over and pinched her sister on the arm. Ruth didn't cry out, though there were tears in her eyes.

"Look what you've done," Tibor said. "You've made your sister cry."

Anna made a mean face at Ruth. "You're not my mother," she said.

Tibor turned to Grandma and Grandpa. "Please excuse my younger daughter," he said. "She hasn't been herself since her mother died." He glanced quickly at Aunt Gizella, who patted his hand.

Later, after Tibor and his daughters were gone, Grandma said to Aunt Gizella, "I'm not so certain about Tibor anymore. What will you do with that child of his?"

"Don't worry," Aunt Gizella said. "He hasn't asked me to marry him yet."

"He wants to," I said.

"Shh."

"He's certainly rich enough," Grandma said. "But raising another woman's child, especially one like that, can poison even the happiest marriage."

"For once," Grandpa said, lifting his eyes from his book and squinting at my aunt, "you should listen to your mother."

I crossed my fingers behind my back and wondered whether Mrs. Gorgei was already at work on Tibor without my even having to ask.

The following Sunday, Tibor brought Ruth and Anna for another visit. "Anna has something she wants to tell everyone," he said.

She stood up and took a deep breath. "I'm sorry I was so impolite the last time I was here," she said. She didn't sound the least bit sorry.

She pulled out two tiny glass candle holders from a cloth sack she was carrying and handed them to Grandma, who went to the window and turned them around in the light before setting them down on the table. Anna gave a leather bookmark to Grandpa, who stuffed it in his shirt pocket without looking at it, and a lace handkerchief to Aunt Gizella. My aunt tried to hug Anna, but she twisted away.

"Anna," Tibor said.

"All right," she said. She stood perfectly still with her arms at her sides, while my aunt kissed her on the cheek.

"What about Serene?" Tibor said.

"Oh, yes," Anna said.

She dug around in her sack for a minute and pulled out a pin in the shape of a tiny gold star of David. Tibor helped me fasten it to the collar of my dress, and Aunt Gizella bent down to examine my pin.

"It's beautiful," she said.

"Thank you," I said. I was trembling with happiness.

Anna and I went out to the yard, and I fingered my gold star.

"The mummy's hand," she said, pointing at my fingers.

I looked straight at her and thought about that dead claw, separated from its owner and wrapped in layers of gray bandages, locked away in a dark church in Budapest. I was dying of curiosity to see it.

At supper, Tibor tapped his fork on his glass. "We have something to tell you," he said.

Grandpa raised his head up from his bowl of potato soup, and Grandma frowned. My hand shook as I reached for a glass of water.

"Tibor has proposed," Aunt Gizella said. "We are going to be married."

Grandma pushed her chair away from the table. "What's your hurry?" she asked.

"Mama. Be happy for me."

Grandma stood up and walked away from the table. Aunt Gizella was at her heels. Anna smiled a wicked smile, and Ruth busied herself clearing the table. Tibor buried his face in his hands, and I ran to my aunt's side and slipped my hand into hers.

"I'm sorry for bringing you so much pain," I said.

Aunt Gizella let go of my hand and took a step toward Grandma. "For years, all I ever heard from you was how much money it cost to feed me and how I let Jacob run off with a *shiksa*," she said.

"Be quiet," Grandma said sharply.

"Why? He knows all about it, and so does the entire town. How could they not know about it, when you announce it to the whole world every chance you get?"

Grandma spun around and grabbed Aunt Gizella by the shoulders. "The second daughter is a terror. Marry into that family with that girl if you want to be unhappy for the rest of your life."

Grandpa rose slowly from his chair and cleared his throat. The room was silent.

"Tell me, my child," he said.

Aunt Gizella turned toward him.

"Is this what you want to do?" he asked. "Are you absolutely certain?"

She nodded.

"You should marry him only if it will make you happy, not for money or a nice place to live," Grandpa said. "There are worse things than being poor."

"I'm an old maid, Papa," she said. Tibor came up behind her, and she leaned into him and closed her eyes.

Later that night, Tibor and his daughters left, and Grandma went to the store to count the bottles of cough medicine on her shelves. Aunt Gizella and I sat together at the table, and I touched my gold star.

"It's lovely," my aunt said.

"I know," I said. "I'm only going to wear it to synagogue, not to school. I don't want Sophia to see it."

"That's wise. Tibor is such a thoughtful man."

"Do you love him the way Emilie loved Lazlo?"

"I think some people are born to find love and keep it, and others aren't. Some of us are like Lazlo. We miss the train carrying the one we are supposed to love forever, but we can't run as fast as Lazlo or hang on long enough. We let go, and we fall off, and the train keeps on going without us."

"What do you do then?"

"Wait and see what the next train brings, and if it's good enough, we climb on board and ride away."

"I wish . . ."

"What?"

"That Papa never left home and Mama didn't have to raise the family by herself. That you married Jacob and had six children by now."

"Oh, my dear Serene. Why wish for what will never come true?"

)

MARRIAGE

Aunt Gizella and Grandma argued endlessly about when the wedding should take place. Aunt Gizella said she wanted to get married the last Sunday in May, just in time for Tibor's daughters to finish school and pack for a trip to Debrecen to visit Tibor's brother. That was to be my aunt's honeymoon. Grandma said that, as the mother of the bride, she hadn't been properly consulted and that she needed more time. She had to speak to the rabbi, notify the family, and make sure everyone else in town knew about the marriage. She wanted Aunt Gizella to wait until the end of the summer, and perhaps longer.

"Why?" Aunt Gizella asked.

"It's not customary to hurry things like that," Grandma said. "Unless there's a reason." She eyed my aunt sharply.

Aunt Gizella laughed. "Oh, Mama. I'm not fifteen years old anymore."

Finally, they agreed on the second Sunday in June, and Grandma's mood swung from joy over the prospect of such a wealthy son-in-law to anger over her daughter's ingratitude. When she was feeling unhappy, she shuffled around the house and muttered under her breath or sent me to the shed on a meaningless errand.

One afternoon, while Aunt Gizella and I were dusting the shelves in the store, Grandma said, "Well, I guess the mother is always the last to know in such matters."

"Honestly, Mama," Aunt Gizella said.

"Thank goodness I'll have Serene to help out, once you're gone."

"But I'm—" I said.

My aunt stepped in front of me and motioned me to be quiet. That evening I wrote a letter to Mama and asked if I could come home right after Aunt Gizella's wedding. It was three weeks before I received a reply.

In the meantime, Ruth and Tibor and Anna continued their regular Sunday visits. Ruth and my aunt sat together, sewing the wedding dress and veil and other clothes Aunt Gizella needed for her new life, and I watched them for as long as I could, until Grandma or Tibor sent me outside to play with Anna. Sometimes, I knelt at Ruth's feet and handed her pins and thread and studied the tilt of her head. I loved the way the tip of her tongue poked out the edge of her mouth. She rested her cheek on my aunt's shoulder, and once, she even called my aunt her "beloved mother."

"She's not your mother," I whispered. "She's my aunt."

No one seemed to hear me.

The Friday before my aunt's wedding, I finally received a letter from Mama. It was full of news about the family, but none of it was good. Mina had run away to Szereda to visit the rabbi there. When he brought her safely home again, she told Mama she was in love with him and planned to marry him the following summer when she was thirteen. Mama was beside herself with worry. On top of that, Kati was sick all spring with a cold and was even sulkier than usual. She kept Mama and Mina up all night. As for Sam, Mama hadn't heard from him in months. She supposed the war held up the mail, but she was expecting him home shortly. Of course, there had been no word from Papa.

"As for you, my dear Serene," she wrote. "I miss your gentle presence. The reports from your new school are excellent, as I was certain they would be, and your grandmother tells me you are a great comfort to her. In fact, she has asked if you can remain there for the rest of the summer. I know you want to come home, but you are so kind. You won't mind staying with her for a little while longer, will you? You seem to be the only person in our family who can get along with her."

I crumpled the letter in my fist, stuffed it into my pocket, and went back to helping my aunt prepare a Sabbath lunch for Grandpa's two brothers and their wives and three of our cousins who were coming Saturday afternoon. Grandma didn't invite anyone to the wedding, since she had no brothers and sisters and her cousins all lived far away in the north. My aunt saw the look on my face and gave me a quick hug.

"What is the matter, little one?" she asked. "Bad news?"

"Mama says Mina tried to run away," I said. "She wants to marry the rabbi in Szereda, but Mama thinks it's an awful idea."

"It looks as though everyone is deserting you. I want you to visit us as soon as we get back from Debrecen. I'd love to take you with us, but the wagon is too crowded as it is. Besides, you know Anna."

"She hates me."

"She hates everyone. That's just her way." She laughed a little under her breath.

"I want to go home."

"I know you do."

We sat down at the table, and she fingered one of the napkins we had set out there.

"Tell me about Papa," I said. "What was he like as a little boy?"

"Well, you must remember he is twelve years older than me, and I was a very small child when he left home."

"How old were you?"

"Three. So you see, I had to rely on other people's memories of him. Mainly Mama's."

"Did she like him?"

"Oh, my. Yes she did. To hear her side of the story, the sun rose and fell around your papa. She had great plans for him."

"What kinds of plans?"

"She wanted him to stay in school, become a learned man, a rabbi."

"What happened?"

"Your papa had other ideas. First of all, she could never really interest him in reading and writing. All he cared about was making money. So he'd pretend to go to school and then sneak away and do field work or whatever jobs he could get his hands on. Your papa was very good with animals. Not always so good with people. He had quite a temper."

I nodded.

"But animals loved him," she said. "Anyway, after a while, Mama gave up on sending him to school. He's the only member of the family who is more stubborn than she is. When he was fifteen, he joined the army. They needed men to care for their horses, and Shumi was husky and lied about his age. So they let him in."

"What did Grandma do?" I asked.

"What else? She yelled at him and begged him to change his mind. But he wouldn't, and stayed in the army ten years before marrying your mother. In the end, she forgave him as best she could. He was her favorite child. The one most like her, I think. Most like your Mina, too. What did you call her that time?"

"Contrary."

"Yes. Mama loved that contrariness in him. It bedeviled her, I think, and he always felt guilty about not living up to her dreams for him. He sent her money every month while he was in the army and brought her gifts that she ignored while he was home and fussed over after he was gone. Even after he married your mama, he still sent money."

"What about Mama's *nadan*?"

"Maybe your grandmother asked for a little too much that time. Pushed too hard. You never want to do that with Shumi. Best to let him think it's his own idea. I'll tell you a secret. He still sends her money. Not every month, but a little bit maybe once or twice since he's been gone."

"Papa! But what about Mama and the rest of us?"

"I don't know. Shumi has a debt to repay to your grandma, a tie that goes deeper than with anyone else, a tie that can never be mended with envelopes full of money."

The next day, right after the morning service, Grandma's rabbi and Tibor came to the house to inspect my aunt's wedding clothes. Tibor brought her lace and gave her several gold crowns to buy silk cloth, and he was supposed to let the rabbi know he was satisfied with the way his money had been spent. When the rabbi asked about the *nadan*, Tibor took him aside and whispered in his ear. Grandma studied the rabbi's face, while Grandpa and Aunt Gizella stood in one corner with their heads down.

"Everything is in good order now," the rabbi said. "We have erected a *huppah* in the synagogue courtyard, and we are ready for the wedding."

"Good," Grandma said. There was an edge to her voice.

A little while later, the rabbi said his good-byes, and Tibor left, too, kissing my aunt gently on the cheek.

"Enjoy the day," he said. "This is your last chance to be alone with your family."

"I will try," she said.

Grandpa's relatives arrived at one o'clock for a bridal lunch of cucumbers in vinegar, paprika chicken, potatoes, and sponge cake with fresh raspberries.

"I'm much too nervous to eat," Grandma said. She swallowed hard and folded her hands over her empty plate. "Tibor is a good man."

Great Aunt Minnie, who was married to Grandpa's older brother, poked her fork into her cake and sighed. "How do you know?" she asked.

"He's rich and has promised to take care of Gizella for the rest of her life—and to throw a few pennies our way, as well."

Great Aunt Minnie stared down the length of her rather long nose across the table at Grandma. Grandpa's face turned bright red, and he brought his wine glass to his lips and let it linger there a while. His eyes were dark, and he looked just like Papa.

"Mama!" Aunt Gizella said.

She banged her fork on the table, and Grandma dabbed her lips with her napkin to hide her sly smile.

Early on the morning of the wedding, Tibor helped Ruth and Anna down from his wagon and left them in front of Grandma's house without a word. Then he drove off toward the synagogue. Aunt Gizella and I watched him through the curtains.

Ruth and Anna knocked on the door, and I let them in. Grandma and Grandpa were dressed in everyday clothes, since they wouldn't be going to the wedding, as was the custom in those days. Instead, they would stay home together to talk about their memories of their daughter.

"It's almost like sitting *shiva*, except no one has actually died," Aunt Gizella said.

Ruth, Anna, and I were to walk my aunt to the synagogue. She looked beautiful in her white silk dress with short sleeves and a high collar. She borrowed a wig from Grandma to cover her hair, and a thin veil of white lace hung over her face. It rustled slightly every time she blinked or smiled. When it came time to leave, Aunt Gizella trembled. Grandma busied herself at the stove and pretended not to notice us, and Grandpa sat very still in his chair, holding a book to his chest, nodding slightly as we moved across the room.

Outside, Anna stopped by the side of the road. She kicked up dust with her shoes and hummed the same two notes over and over. Tibor waited for us in front of the synagogue. He put his arm around Aunt Gizella's waist and led her to the small courtyard in the back that was little more than a square of dirt with no trees to shade us from the hot summer sun. Ruth and Anna and I followed close behind.

The rabbi waved my aunt and Tibor forward. He sat underneath the *huppah*, a canopy with white silk stretched over the top and tiny fringes falling over the sides. It was barely large enough to cover the rabbi and my aunt and Tibor. Behind the rabbi were two of his pupils, not much older than my brother Sam. Aunt Gizella and Tibor stood in front of the rabbi, and one of his pupils rose and took my aunt's hand and led her around and around Tibor. The rabbi gave Tibor a glass of wine and took another for himself. Whenever he said something in Hebrew, the two of them lowered their heads and drank a sip. Aunt Gizella began trembling again, and her veil shook. Tibor hooked his arm through hers. Ruth stood quietly at my side, while Anna raced back and forth between the synagogue wall and the courtyard and got dirt all over the hem of her dress and tore the buckle off one of her shoes.

The sun beat down hard on my shoulders, and before I knew it, the rabbi said the first words of the *Alenu*, the final prayer. The rabbi blessed my aunt and Tibor, and the two of them leaned into the sunlight and marched toward Tibor's wagon. Ruth and I trailed behind them, but Anna ran ahead to the wagon. One of my great-uncles stopped us on the way and pressed a tiny cloth purse into Aunt Gizella's hand. A cousin kissed my aunt on the cheek and wished her well. We all climbed into the wagon, and Ruth and Anna and I crowded together in the back.

"Well, now that the wedding is over, how does everyone feel?" Tibor asked.

"Wonderful, Pa," Ruth said. She smiled.

"Fine, Pa," Anna said in a mean voice.

Tibor pretended not to notice Anna and put his arm around my aunt. Anna scowled.

"What about Ma?" she whispered.

"Shh, Ma is dead," Ruth said softly. "Don't you think Pa deserves to be happy?" She patted my hand. "Besides, now we have a new sister."

"No, *I* don't."

When we arrived back home, Grandma had smeared the doorposts with honey, as Jewish families did when someone got married.

"They want us to be happy and have all the sweet things in life," Tibor said.

"I hope so," Aunt Gizella said.

Grandma and Grandpa greeted us in silence, and we sat at the table and didn't say anything to one another while we ate our meal. Tibor shifted uncomfortably in his chair before he finally rose to go, and Ruth rose along with him, grabbing onto Anna's arm. Aunt Gizella reached across the table and squeezed my hand.

"We'll see you soon," she whispered.

"I'm lonely for you already," I said.

"And I am for you, as well."

She smiled, but there were tears in her eyes. Grandpa got up from his chair and stood behind Aunt Gizella and touched her shoulder.

"It is time for you to go," he said softly.

"I know," she said. She leaned back in her chair so that the top of her head rested against Grandpa's chest.

"You are my favorite child."

She took his hand in hers and rubbed it against her cheek..

We gathered in the front yard and watched the wagon pull away. Aunt Gizella turned toward me and waved until she was out of sight. Grandpa's face was ashy gray as he shuffled into the house. Grandma pulled me inside.

"You can't stand here all day," she said.

"Why not?" I asked, not wishing to take my eyes off the empty place in the road where my aunt had sat the moment before.

The next day, Grandma stomped around the house. "They always leave," she said. "Lazy child. You were the one who convinced her to marry that man, and since you're to blame for her leaving, you have no right to mope around here."

We went to the store, and I had to sweep the floor from corner to corner three times before she was satisfied.

"This will do for now," she said. "I saw how you and Gizella always whispered secrets to one another. She couldn't stand Tibor until you came around. You'll have to do your aunt's work as well as your own from now on. The two of us will have ourselves quite a busy summer. You have a debt to pay, or have you forgotten about my broken barrel of vanilla?"

That afternoon, she sent me to the shed for rose water, and I dragged my feet across the yard and opened the shed door. A gust of hot air slapped me in the face. The shed was full of spider webs and moist dirt smells, and I had to feel my way along the damp walls until I found the bottles of rose water. I lit a candle, and suddenly someone began breathing down my neck.

"Karl!" I shouted. "Aunt Gizella's gone. Now get out of here before Grandma sees you."

"She can't hurt me anymore," a muffled voice said.

The candle flickered and fell to the ground, and the air in front of me was filled with smoke. Flames licked at my toes, and I stumbled out the door and into Grandma's arms.

"There's a fire!" I shouted.

Grandma shoved me to the ground and moved with a quickness I'd never seen before to the well in the yard. She started pumping. The pump jerked Grandma off the ground, but she wrapped her thin arms around the handle all the way up to her shoulders and hung on. When the bucket was full, I helped her carry it to the shed. The candle burned a small hole in the dirt floor, and the fire was more smoke than anything else. We poured water on it, and it hissed and turned the smoke black.

That night I went to bed without any supper and the next morning, right after breakfast, Grandma made me go to the shed four times. Each time I thought I saw Karl standing in the corner, laughing at me. Later, she made me move all the bottles from one side of the store to the other, until my arms ached and my legs were so sore I could barely stand. I knew I had to leave soon. I couldn't stay any longer without my aunt to protect me from my grandmother and her endless scolding. I took a pillowcase from my aunt's empty bed and pretended to put it on my pillow. But I really hid it underneath my bed covers and, when no one was watching, jammed my coat, two extra dresses, my socks and underwear, and Mama's linen napkin inside. It was dusk, and Grandma was still in the store, since she liked to stay late each night and count her money. Grandpa dozed in his chair. I decided to carry Papa's funeral lace and my two coins—one from Sam and the other from Tibor—in my pocket and to pin the gold Star of David under my collar.

When Grandma returned from the store that night, she and Grandpa climbed into bed. I put my nightgown on over my dress and slipped under my covers and said good night. Then I waited, and sure enough, in a few minutes, the sound of Grandma's snores filled the room. Grandpa moaned several times in his sleep. With my pillowcase in my hand, I tiptoed out the front door, opening and closing it carefully, grateful when it didn't squeak and wake everyone up. I never looked back, and I never said good-bye. Instead, I took a deep breath of the fresh night air—it smelled of freedom—and ran across the yard and around the corner and down the road toward home.

THE ROAD TO GALFALVA

The spire of the Catholic church in the town square cut through the night sky like a sword. The leaden domes of the heavy buildings around it shone dully in the light of the half moon. It was so dark I could barely make out the road in front of me. I was worried that Mama might not let me stay once I arrived in Galfalva, but I was too frightened of being alone on that deserted road to make up a lie about why I came home before I was supposed to. A gentle breeze blew, and I leaned into it, forcing one foot down in front of the other. After a while, I couldn't see Marosvasarhely at all.

From time to time, clouds covered the moon so that there was no light. Once, I nearly lost my balance and slipped into the ditch at the side of the road. I twisted my ankle and cried out as I grabbed on to a tree.

"Papa, help me," I whispered.

"My little one," Papa sighed in the wind. "I'll do what I can, but you have no one else to protect you."

The tree bark dug into my palms. "I may die here tonight."

"I'll try to save you because I want to see you very soon."

"You do?"

The moon pushed through the clouds, and I rubbed my ankle and started walking again. In a little while, I grew tired and leaned against a shrub to rest for a few minutes. Something bumped me on the head, and in the instant before I fell to the ground, I thought I saw Mrs. Gorgei.

"What are you doing here?" I asked. "Why aren't you at home with Sophia?"

"Shh," she said.

My head ached, and she stood over me in the dim moonlight.

"Mrs. Gorgei?" I asked.

"Be quiet," she replied. She kicked me in the ribs.

"Don't hit me again, Mrs. Gorgei. Please."

"Then let go of your sack."

Her voice sounded different, lower and rougher. The pillow case was still in my hand, and I clutched it closer to my chest.

"Give me that," she said. She scratched my arm as she grabbed my pillowcase away.

"Why are you doing this, Mrs. Gorgei?" I asked.

"Who's Mrs. Gorgei?" She reached down and slapped my cheek. "Shut up, or I'll cut your throat out." She drew a knife from her sash and shook my clothes out of the pillow case. "Not one thing of value." She stood over me and ran her knife across the tips of her fingers.

I wrapped my arms around myself. "Get away from me."

She laughed and knelt down, yanking my arms and holding both of my hands against her side. She went through my pockets and found the coins hidden there. Then she patted my dress and lifted up my collar and ripped off my gold Star of David. The harder I fought to free my hands the harder she held onto me. She drove her knee into my chest.

"You're hurting me," I said.

"For the last time, be quiet unless you want me to slice you into a thousand pieces and feed you to the wolves," she said.

She held my pin up to the light. For a moment, she didn't look like herself at all but like a boy with blond hair, skinny arms, ragged pants, and a mean mouth.

"Pure gold," she said. "That should be worth something."

She slapped me twice more, and her knife gleamed in the dim moonlight. I closed my eyes and bade my last farewell to this earth, and everything around me went black.

The next morning, I woke up with the first light and brushed the dirt off my dress. At first, I was sure I was dead, but heaven looked too much like the road to Galfalva. Besides, my head and shoulders ached, as if someone had tried to pull my arms out of their sockets. I thought, I must still be on this earth. Otherwise, I wouldn't hurt so much. There were bruises on my arms and bumps on my head and cheeks. I couldn't open my eyes all the way. When I rolled over on my side, my ribs hurt, and I saw my extra dresses and coat scattered by the side of the road. I reached inside my pocket, and my coins were gone. I turned up my collar, and my pin was gone too.

"Sophia," I said. "Your mother took everything. Why?"

I wondered if Grandma missed me yet and whether she would send Grandpa to find me. The idea of seeing her again frightened me enough to make me crawl around on the ground and gather together my belongings. After everything was safely back in my pillowcase, I steadied myself against a tree and stood up. The road spun beneath my feet, and I had to sit back down. I took a deep breath and tried standing again, slower this time so that everything stayed where it was supposed to be.

"Be thankful you escaped with your life," Papa whispered in my ear. "Not everyone is so lucky."

"Papa," I said. I couldn't see him.

I rubbed away the dirt on my cheeks with my collar and began walking slowly toward home. Every step hurt. After what seemed like hours, a sign on the road said that Galfalva was only ten kilometers away. So close. The sun was low in the morning sky, and the air wasn't warm yet. A fine layer of dew covered the grass by the side of the road, and I knelt down and wetted my lips on it. My throat was parched, and that tiny bit of moisture only made me crave more water. There were no wells and no other soul in sight, so I made myself keep moving. I knew the sooner I got home, the sooner I'd be able to drink and eat and sleep. That is, if Mama didn't turn me around and put me right back on the road.

I dragged my feet along the dirt and was almost ready to drop my pillow case, when I decided to play a game to take my mind off my aches and pains. I would pretend I was eating a bowl of Mama's bean soup. I would take one tiny spoonful and then another, careful not to eat too much at once. I had to make that wonderful soup last my entire journey. After each taste, I could feel the soggy beans in my mouth as they melted to paste and slid down my throat. The game worked, because my eyelids grew heavy as they always did after a big meal, and my stomach felt full of that make-believe bean soup.

"Serene!" someone shouted from behind me.

I tried to run, but everything went black again. When I awoke, a man was bent over me, brushing my face with a wet cloth. He helped me sit up and gave me a ladle filled with water. I started to gulp the water, and he pulled the ladle away.

"Slow down," he said. "You'll make yourself sick."

I stared at him for a long moment, while his eyes and nose and mouth arranged themselves into a face. I had seen those eyes before. They always looked to the left, when they meant to stare right at me. Then I remembered they belonged to Shifty. At least, that's what Sam and I called him behind his back.

"Never trust a person who can't look you straight in the eye," Sam said.

He was right. Shifty was a traveling salesman of small trinkets and pots and pans, who came through Galfalva five or six times a year and stopped in Papa's tavern. He was always trying to secure himself an extra drink without paying for it, and whenever he asked for a third or fourth, he pretended he had already given me a gold crown to cover the entire bill, though he had done no such thing.

"Check your pockets," he said. "You're a small girl, and it's easy for small girls to forget."

"I didn't forget," I said. I held my hand out for payment, while everyone at his table laughed.

"My credit was always good with your papa."

"Papa's not here now. Mama only does business in cash."

After a night on the road with no food and water, I was glad enough to drink Shifty's water and eat the small piece of stale bread he offered me, in spite of all the times he had tried to steal from me in the past.

"You look like you just escaped from the war," he said. "I know our side is doing poorly, but I didn't think the Hungarian army had stooped to recruiting little girls." He rubbed his chin. "Are you lost?"

"No, " I said. "Please take me back to Mama's."

He helped me stand, lifted me up onto the front of his wagon, and threw my pillow case in after me. Once the wagon started to move, all the pots and pans and trinkets inside began to chime, and their quiet singsong put me to sleep. After what seemed like only an instant, Shifty gently shook my shoulder.

"Here we are," he said.

I stretched my arms and legs and twisted slowly in my seat to get my first glimpse of the front yard. I knew every blade of that grass and every piece of wood in our old white house with the verandah. Kati's roses were still blooming on one side of the house. I rubbed my eyes, afraid everything would disappear. But it didn't. I reached over and kissed Shifty on the cheek.

"Thank you so much for bringing me home," I said.

"Can I count on you for a free drink this evening?" he asked. His eyes were glued to a pot that hung above my shoulder.

"I'm sure Mama will be happy to give you one."

I grabbed my pillowcase and jumped down from the wagon, and he drove quickly away. The front door was open, and I stood in the doorway, breathing in the smell of fresh bread and listening to the sound of crickets outside the window. I could see the top of Mina's head poking out from beneath her covers. Kati was sitting in a small raised chair at the table, chewing on a cookie. She was much bigger than when I left, and her hair was thick and brown. Her eyes opened wide when she saw me, and she dropped her cookie and pointed at me.

"Mama! Mama!" she cried.

Mama stood at the stove, stirring something. She looked at Kati and then turned toward me and shook her head and squinted. She dropped her spoon.

"Serene, is that really you?" she asked. "You've grown so tall. You hardly look like yourself anymore. What are you doing here? My goodness. We weren't expecting you until August."

I ran to her. "I've missed you so much," I said. "Please don't make me go back to Grandma's."

She wrapped her arms around me, and I remembered that Mama was big and strong, not like Grandma, and that her bones were solid.

I heard giggling behind me, and Mina grabbed me around the waist. I turned to hug my sister, and the two of us danced around the room. Kati wailed. Mina smiled, but her eyes had a new look of sadness, put there, I was sure, by the rabbi from Szereda. In that instant, I decided that men were nothing but trouble and that I'd never have anything to do with them, if I could help it.

Mama sat me down at the table. "My God," she said. "You look awful. Let me wash off those cuts and bruises."

"I'm hungry," I said.

"Of course. You couldn't be otherwise and be my Serene." She fed me some leftover corn mush and cheese. "Eat slowly so you don't get sick."

She hovered around me and dabbed my face and hands with a towel whenever I set down my spoon.

"How did such a thing happen?" she asked. "Did you walk all the way home by yourself? Does your grandmother know where you are?"

"Please," I said. "Can I stay? Grandma hates me."

"Why I've never heard such a thing. Her letters were always full of such glowing praise."

"I'm so tired. May I go to bed now?"

"You should clean up first. Those cuts might get infected."

"I'm fine."

I shuffled over to my mattress and fell down on top of it, hugging it like an old friend I hadn't seen in a very long time. I fell instantly asleep and awoke to the sound of familiar voices. The sun was bright in the afternoon sky, and Grandpa stood stoop-shouldered in the doorway, talking to Mama.

"I'm afraid things got out of hand, with all the commotion about Gizella and her new husband," he said. "You know how hard-headed Irena can be."

Mama patted his arm. "Serene is here, bruised, scratched, and beaten, but thankfully in one piece," she said.

I buried myself in my bedclothes. Mama invited Grandpa in for some tea, and the two of them talked quietly together at one end of the table. Kati sat in her chair at the other end with Mina opposite her. Mina leaned forward, trying to catch every word that passed between Mama and Grandpa. Finally, Mama ordered me to get out of bed.

"Give your grandfather a kiss," she said. "He's been on the road most of the night looking for you."

I pecked Grandpa on the cheek. "I'm sorry," I said.

He took my hand and squeezed it. "You look like you've been in a fight," he said, studying my face with concern. "I'm glad you're safe. I was afraid for you. You may not believe this, but your grandma is sick with worry and wants to make things up to you when she sees you again."

"She does?"

"Come here," Mama said.

I sat down in the chair next to her.

She looked at Grandpa. "Well, what should we do with this child?" she asked.

"Please don't make me go back," I said.

"Shh. I want to hear what Grandpa has to say."

"My head tells me she should come with me to Marosvasarhely and patch things up with her grandma," he said. "Although I'd like to have her back to help soothe her lonely old grandma, my heart tells me she should stay here with you. In the end, it's up to you, Rosa."

I slid into the chair beside Mama, trying hard to read her expression, but I was out of practice, after all those months away. My knees began to wobble, and I drummed my fingers nervously on the table.

"Be quiet," Mama said. "You children certainly are a trial." She rose swiftly from her chair. "Mina, help me make lunch for Grandpa. No arguments now. Serene, you stay where you are and don't move. After we've all had enough to eat and our minds are clear, we'll decide what to do about our little runaway."

FAMILY STORIES

I was sure Mama had decided to send me away for good, because she wouldn't look at me when I helped her wash the lunch dishes.

After I put the last one away, she said, "Our Serene has been quite a handful."

Grandpa nodded.

"In that case, I think I'll keep her here and spare you further trouble," she said.

"It will be awfully quiet at home," Grandpa said. "But I'm certain it's for the best."

I stood up and slipped behind his chair. I threw my arms around him, almost knocking the wind out of him. He drew his hands into his chest and leaned forward, as if he wasn't used to being touched. I felt foolish and let go. A little while later, Mama, Mina, and I gathered in front of the house to wave good-bye to Grandpa. All I wanted to do after he was gone was roll around in the grass and rub my face in the heavenly dirt of my own front yard. Mama went inside to tend to Kati and left Mina and me on the verandah.

"You're such a ninny," my sister said.

"Why?" I asked.

"Mama was never going to send you back there."

"How do you know?"

"I know."

That evening, Shifty came to the tavern. While Mama was busy pouring beer for some patrons at the bar, I sneaked an extra glass of *slivovitz* to him. It had been many months since I had smelled that tart plum brandy, and I had forgotten how it made my eyes water. I kept my head down and covered the glass with my hand. I hadn't spoken to Mama about my promise to Shifty because I didn't want to do anything to remind her about my running away.

"Shh," I said. I slid the glass onto the table in front of him. "Only this once, and don't you ever breathe a word to Mama or ask for another without paying for it."

"Thank you," he said. His eyes stared at the wall behind me as he lifted his glass to me. "To Serene." He bent his head back and swallowed his drink in one gulp. His eyes were red when they came to rest again on the wall.

Just before bedtime, Mina asked, "Mama, can Serene and I spend the night in the shed? You know how much we love to sleep on top of the oven, especially on a night after you've baked bread in there."

"That's not such a good idea," Mama said. "This is Serene's first evening back, and I'm worried about those bruises on her face."

"I feel fine, Mama," I said. "Can we go, please? Can we?"

"You'll stay up talking and laughing all night, and you need your rest, after what you've been through."

"We'll go to sleep right away. I promise."

"All right, but I don't want to see any tired faces in the morning."

Mina and I lit a candle and walked slowly across the cool grass to the shed behind the tavern, carrying our pillows and blankets over our shoulders. There was no moon, and it was pitch black outside. So we had to step carefully and hold out one hand in front of us to keep from running into anything. She patted the brick wall of the shed, until she found the door. We went inside and put the candle on the shelf below us, settling ourselves on top of the oven the way we had done in the old days, before I went to live with Grandma. I was closest to the wall, and Mina stretched out beside me.

"Do you think Papa will come to us like he did the last time we spent the night here?" she asked.

I shrugged.

"Do you still see his ghost?" she asked.

"Sometimes," I said. "Not very often."

"Really? Where?"

"I don't exactly see it anymore. But he still talks to me like he did last night when I was on the road, and I called out to him."

"Then he's not at rest yet, the poor dear."

Mina was silent for a moment, and I wondered if she was busy hatching a new plan to bury Papa.

"Aunt Gizella's husband told me he built a gateway in front of his house to ease his first wife's passage from this world into the next," I said.

"What's he like?" she asked.

"Funny looking. Old. Stooped over and with a big black hole between his front teeth." I turned to the wall behind the oven and scratched off a piece of dirt that had settled there and jammed it between my teeth and spread my arms out and opened my mouth wide.

"Oh! I hope he doesn't look like that. Poor Aunt Gizella."

"No. He's very nice." I spat out the dirt.

"Why did he build a gate for his first wife? Didn't she have a proper Jewish funeral?"

"Yes."

"Well, in that case, a gateway won't do for Papa, because he would have to have a funeral first."

The candle flickered on the shelf below us and went out, and Mina and I screamed and held onto one another.

"Papa," she whispered.

A branch thumped hard against the outside of the shed, and the sound made us hold onto one another ever tighter than before.

After a little while, I asked, "Do you love the rabbi from Szereda?"

She slid down from the oven and fumbled around in the dark. She lit the candle again, and the light made her shadow stretch over the entire wall.

"You're a giant," I said.

"Yes, I am," she said. She pulled herself back up onto the oven and faced toward me. "I want to marry Aaron. Did I ever tell you that's his name?"

"What about church? Will you still go?"

"No." She pinched me. "Unless I can sneak out when no one will find out." She rolled over on her back. "Mama says I'm too young and have to get educated before I marry. She says he doesn't have any money."

"My teacher in Marosvasarhely fell in love with a Russian soldier."

"So?"

"He didn't have any money either, but she ran off with him anyway. Afterwards, Aunt Gizella said they might starve to death."

"Aaron's not a Russian soldier, and he has a home. Besides, we're already poor, so I don't see what difference that makes. Mama spies on me all the time. She even makes my teacher tell her right away if I don't arrive in my classroom on time. But I'll show her. I'll leave for good one day. I will, and you'll never see me again."

I wrapped my blanket around my shoulders. "Don't talk like that."

Late one hot June morning, about a week after I got home, a wagon turned the corner and stopped beside our house. At first I didn't recognize the two people sitting in the front of it. One was a fat man in a beige cotton suit, and the other was a boy in a suit identical to the man's. The two of them stared straight ahead and didn't move. Finally, Mama went to the door and looked out.

"Sam!" she said. "My God! You weren't supposed to come until early next week."

At the sound of her voice, the boy turned his head slightly, and I could see that he was my brother and that the man next to him was my poor fat Uncle Herman. Sam jumped down from the wagon. He walked toward Mama like a man used to carrying a large belly in front of him, except he was as thin as a reed. When Mama hugged him, his hands hung limp at his sides.

"I'm so glad to see you," she said. She pushed back from him. "How you've grown. You're a regular young man now."

Sam reached into his jacket pocket and pulled out a piece of straw. He bit down on it and let it hang on his lips, exactly the way Uncle Herman did when he dangled a cigarette from his mouth.

"Yes I am a young man," Sam said.

"I'm happy to see you learned such good manners from your aunt and uncle," Mama said.

Uncle Herman stepped down carefully from his wagon and waddled toward Mama. If anything, he was fatter than when he had come to take Sam away. He took his hat off and fanned his face with it.

"Weren't you expecting us today?" he said. "I thought Regina wrote to tell you we were coming. Could we have mixed up the date?"

"No matter," Mama said.

"Our Sam here is quite a boy. If you'd like to fix us something to eat, I'm sure I can fill you in on all his comings and goings over these last several months."

Mama had prepared a chicken for dinner the night before, so she put the leftovers on the table, along with fresh bread and some cooked potatoes. We all sat down. Uncle Herman eyed the food hungrily and breathed in the aroma of that yeasty bread, but after Sam cleared his throat, my uncle shook his head.

"No, dear sister," he said.

"What's wrong?" Mama asked. "Are you ill?"

"No. But as my physician over here reminds me, I have to watch my diet. I have gout, don't you know, and until my young nephew here took me under his care, I suffered awfully from it. No more, though, because he keeps track of everything I put into my mouth." He groaned a little.

"I must say I'm surprised. I've never known my son to pay attention to what other people eat. He only thinks about what goes into his own mouth."

"Not anymore. He's become a real little doctor, our Sam. He makes me eat raw fruits, vegetables, and crushed juniper berries steeped in cherry juice like a tea—horrible and really bitter. I hope I die before I see another glass. No fish or fowl or beef." He licked his lips, and his eyes began to water. "No gravy. No bread." He started to reach for some bread and, thinking better of it, let his hand drop into his lap. "I shouldn't."

Sam lowered his eyelids in satisfaction, and I wondered if some other boy had crawled inside my brother's skin.

"How did Sam become so interested in doctoring?" Mama asked.

"It was quite by accident," Uncle Herman said. "The people in the house next to us have a baby who was down with a high fever. The mother was very distraught, and while we were visiting, the baby choked and stopped moving and turned pale."

"How awful. I know what it means to have little ones that sick. I almost lost two of mine."

My uncle nodded sympathetically and mopped his brow with a big white handkerchief he shook out of his shirt pocket. "That must have been a terrible time for everyone."

"It was."

"Anyhow, the mother, our neighbor, was certain her baby was dead, but our Sam plucked a goose feather from a pillow and held it under the baby's nose. The baby breathed on it, and it fluttered a little bit. Sam told us she was alive, and he was right. He washed her forehead with a cool cloth and loosened her swaddling, and by the next day, she was practically well again."

"Bravo, Sam!"

Mama clapped her hands, and so did the rest of us. Even Sam joined in.

"There's more," Uncle Herman said.

"Oh?" Mama asked.

"Word spread around the village about this nine-year-old medical prodigy, and as you can imagine, the lines started forming at our front door. As luck would have it, a friend of mine lent us a couple of books on medicines and herbs, and Sam pored over them. So here's our Sam. 'Try some mint and rosemary for that headache and eliminate cheese and herring from your dinner.' Or, 'Drink apple vinegar mixed with water with your meal to get rid of that heartburn.' People did what he told them to do, and they got better."

Right before Uncle Herman left, he wrapped his arm around Sam's shoulder. "I've memorized all of your suggestions, and I'll try to follow them to the letter," he said.

"Good, Uncle," Sam said. The two of them shook hands.

My brother looked very pleased with himself, but I knew that my uncle would go to his grave with his knees and ankles swollen by gout and that he would probably help things along that very evening by dining on roast goose, herring, and asparagus.

For the next few days, Sam sat in the chair by the stove or wandered lazily around the house. He didn't say much and didn't want to come outside and play with me. He ignored Kati when she tried to crawl onto his lap, even though she adored him. At first, Mama didn't pay much attention to the change in Sam. She probably thought it was a passing mood and told us not to worry ourselves over him.

"I guess the boy doctor is too good for us these days," Mina said to Mama one afternoon.

Mama grabbed Sam by the elbow and made him sit down at the table. "Are you sick, my son?" she asked. "Perhaps *you* need a doctor."

"I'm not sick," he replied.

"Why are you so unhappy?"

"At Uncle Herman's, people listened to me. No one listens to me here."

"I'm not going to listen to him," Mina said. "He's just my brother. Why should I bother with what he has to say?"

"You see what I mean," Sam said. "I'm going to be a famous doctor one day, and no one around here cares."

"Aunt Gizella told me I'm going to be a matchmaker when I grow up," I said.

Mama laughed.

"I never want to marry, myself," I said. "But Aunt Gizella said I have a gift for bringing men and women together."

"And why have you decided not to marry?" Mama asked. "My children are so grown up all of a sudden."

"Because men and women make each other too unhappy."

"I see."

"What has that got to do with me?" Sam asked.

I shrugged.

"Medicine is a noble calling," Mama said. "As is matchmaking. But you are many, many years away from becoming a doctor. In the meantime, you should enjoy your life."

"I don't want to do anything else."

"Give yourself time, my son. You will grow up soon enough and inherit all the cares of adulthood. But you will only be a young boy once, and when your childhood is gone, it's gone forever."

"I don't care."

Mama and I stood beside the vegetable garden she had started that year without my help. Her tomatoes hadn't grown very big yet, and delicate, fern-like carrot leaves had just begun to poke through the soil. Kati was playing in the dirt, pulling up Mama's plants and pretending to stick them in her mouth.

"You stop that!" Mama shouted playfully.

Kati laughed and threw dirt in the air. Mama chased after her, and my sister ran away as fast as her fat little legs would carry her.

"So, what do you think of this little one?" Mama asked. She came up behind me gripping Kati's hand firmly in her own. "She's one and a half years old already."

I still didn't like Kati, because she cried and stuck her tongue out at me if she thought Mama wasn't looking. But I didn't want to hurt Mama's feelings.

"Kati's fine, Mama," I replied.

"She's the exact image of your papa, don't you think?" she asked. She let go of Kati's hand, and Kati began to dig in the dirt at her feet.

"Yes."

That was true, especially around the eyes. They were pitch black, and when they followed me around the house, I thought Papa himself was home again.

"Do you think he'll ever come back?" I asked.

"I don't know," Mama said. "His spirit is here with us all the time. Can't you feel him? I see him in all of you children."

"Even me."

"Especially you. The shape of your face. The set of your mouth."

"But I'm blonde."

"The resemblance goes much deeper than hair color."

Mama reached down to tickle Kati and wipe the dirt off her hands. Kati thought Mama was playing a game and stumbled off to the edge of the garden, where she began pulling the leaves off the marigolds Mama had planted there. Mama wagged her finger at my little sister, and Kati shrieked.

"Why don't you ever want to talk about Papa?" I asked.

"I want to tell you a story about the time I was your age and my own papa left home," Mama said. "I was like you. I asked my mama about him day and night. 'Would he come home? When? Where did he go?'"

"Oh, Mama. I don't ask you about him all the time."

"That's a matter of opinion."

"Mama!" Kati called.

Mama waved at her. "In a minute, little one," Mama said. "I have to talk to Serene right now."

Kati pouted.

"Now, let's see," Mama said. "Where was I? Oh, yes. Too many questions. One day, Mama said she didn't want to talk about Papa anymore, so she told me about a rabbi everyone called the Ba'al Shem Tov. He was born with the name Israel ben Eliezer. Ba'al Shem Tov means 'Master of the Divine Name.' Israel ben Eliezer was the first rabbi to take this title, but others came after him, and altogether they were known as the Ba'al Shem Tov."

"Only one name for so many men?"

"Yes. It's strange, isn't it? The first Ba'al Shem Tov was born in Russia a little over two hundred years ago. He was supposed to be able to talk directly to God, and he brought about many miracles."

"Like what?"

"Once when a young child in his village was very ill and about to die, this rabbi asked God not to send the Angel of Death. The Ba'al Shem Tov became quite angry with God and reminded Him that for a child to die before the parent upset the natural order of things."

"Is that what you said to God when Kati and I were sick?"

"I tried to honor Him because I wanted Him to do what I asked. I begged Him not to take you away from me. I'm not the Ba'al Shem Tov. God never talked to me, but He must have heard me because you're still here."

I smiled at her.

"In the story, the rabbi petitioned God in behalf of the child, and He relented," she said. "The child lived a long life. After that, whenever the rabbi needed to ask God for a favor, he would go into the forest by his house and stand underneath the branches of a walnut tree that had been planted in the year of his birth to offer a special prayer."

"Did God answer?" I asked.

"Yes, He did. He helped the Ba'al Shem Tov perform many miracles."

"I'd like to meet the Ba'al Shem Tov."

"I would too." She sighed. "Anyhow, when I was your age, I tried to act like the Ba'al Shem Tov and talk to God to make Him bring my papa home again. One night, after everyone else was asleep, I sneaked out into the woods behind our house."

"By yourself? Were you afraid?"

"Of course I was. It was a bitter cold night in October. I forgot my shoes and had nothing on but a nightgown. I brought a small blanket with me and wrapped it around my shoulders. I sat down under one of the tallest trees in the woods and leaned against the trunk. I told God over and over that I was a follower of the Ba'al Shem Tov and asked Him to send my father back to me. I reminded Him that a little girl like myself needed a father."

"Did God answer you?"

"Not in so many words, but I fell into a light sleep and saw my grandfather and my great-grandfather."

"So? You just had a dream in the woods."

"No. It was more than that. I had never met either my grandfather or my great-grandfather and only heard of them through the stories my mama told me. We had no photographs. Yet after that night, I could describe each of them perfectly down to the bald spot at the very tip of my great-grandfather's forehead and the crook in my grandfather's bottom teeth. They died before I was born, but God put their pictures inside my head."

"Did your prayers bring your papa home?"

"That depends on who you ask. The next morning, Mama was waiting for me in front of the house. Your Aunt Regina was running all over the village looking for me. Everyone was sure I was dead. The very same afternoon Papa came home. He strolled down the middle of the main road into town, as big as life, as if he'd never been gone, and stayed home from that day until the morning he died."

"You made a miracle."

"I thought so at the time. The funny thing was that when I told the story a few years later, Regina said I'd gotten it all wrong. She said Papa returned in December, but everyone knew I went into the woods in October. According to her, that was the truth, and my night in the woods had nothing to do with bringing Papa home."

"When did he come home?"

"Who can say? Mama sided with Regina, and Papa said he couldn't remember. So I decided then and there that facts are slippery. They change with the teller. Finally, after lots of family arguments, my mama said it didn't make any difference when Papa returned. He was back now, and that was all that mattered. That and my belief in the power of my own prayers."

"Was she right?"

"I don't know. I've wondered about that a lot over the years." She glanced across the yard at Kati. "I hope she was."

Part Two
EXILE, 1916-1917

PRESERVES

The war had been going on for two years, and although there was no
fighting in our village, soldiers in the Hungarian army often stopped
by our tavern. As 1916 wore on, everyone began to talk about the Romanians, who were about to enter the war on the other side and who
had their greedy eyes on our land. That summer, business in the tavern
was slow, and Mama worried endlessly about how she would be able
to keep all of us fed. She made sugar cookies that tasted of fresh oranges and put them in the tavern, but most days Sam and I were the
only ones who ate them. Once in a while, my brother even took a sip of
beer, when he thought Mama wasn't looking.

Mina was still in love with the rabbi from Szereda, and although I
had given up matchmaking in favor of more childish pursuits, I sneaked
the letters Mina wrote to him every week out of the house and to the
post office. If Mama knew what I was doing, she never said a word
about it. I wondered what was in those letters, and once I opened one
and read a paragraph or two before stuffing it back in the envelope.
Mina wrote about how much she missed the rabbi and asked why he
didn't visit more often. She called Mama her jailer and threatened to
run away, but I'd heard the threat so many times before that I didn't
think she would ever carry through with it.

Mama watched Mina like a hawk. It was Mama's greatest wish
that all of us should be educated, not just her son. We were supposed to
make something of ourselves in the world, although Mina and I weren't

quite sure what that should be. Sam already knew he was going to become a doctor. People in our village, too, came to recognize his gift for healing. They lined up at our front door with their ailments, and most of the time, since these ailments were sore throats and stomachaches, Sam was able to make his patients feel better. But Mina only wanted to become a rabbi's wife, and I wasn't certain what talents I possessed, other than bringing men and women together who were sometimes happy and sometimes not. Mama said she doubted that talent would keep food on my table and a roof over my head.

One hot day in early July, Rabbi Aaron came to talk to Mama. It was late in the afternoon, and his dark hair was so damp it stuck to his forehead. He had walked all the way from Szereda because he was too poor to afford a horse and wagon. He slid quietly into the room and sat down at the table. His hands were no longer pink and smooth. Now whenever he came to see us, there was dirt under his fingernails, and this time he also had a callous on his thumb. Tiny lines had sprouted around his black eyes, and he didn't smile much and spoke so softly I had to lean forward to hear him. I wondered what had happened to his loud voice. Mina poured him a glass of tea and put a huge piece of Mama's honey cake on a plate. When she set the cake down in front of him, he let his hand rest on hers for a long moment and leaned his head to one side so that the whiskers of his mustache brushed against her arm.

After he finished his tea, Mama stopped sweeping the floor and sat down at the table next to him. She shooed Mina and me away, and we hovered at the far end of the room.

"I've invited him to stay for dinner," Mina said.

"We'll see," Mama said. She turned toward the rabbi. "So, you think you love my daughter."

"Yes, Mrs. Spirer," Rabbi Aaron said. "I do."

"And you want to marry her."

"Yes."

"How old are you?"

"I'll be twenty-three in October. That's a good marriageable age for a man in my position."

"Have you saved any money? How do you plan to support my daughter? As you can see, we have no money, so she will bring nothing to the marriage."

"Mama!" Mina shouted.

"Hush," Mama said. "You are young and have no idea what it means to earn a living for yourself." She folded her hands on the table. "Do you own a house, Rabbi?"

"No," he said. "I rent a small room in the home of a member of our congregation. Mrs. Davich's cousin."

"I see. Are you planning to buy a house, if you and Mina get married?"

"With what?"

"Exactly. Is your room big enough for two people?"

He shook his head.

"It seems to me you have a lot of thinking to do before you go filling young girls' heads with big ideas about marriage," Mama said.

She stood up, and Mina dashed across the room. She was crying, and she put her head in the rabbi's lap. Mama pushed Kati and me out the door, and the two of us went to the garden to pick vegetables for dinner. When we returned, Aaron was gone.

"What happened?" I asked.

"He said Mama was right," Mina replied. "He said he couldn't afford to marry a girl with no money, no matter how much he loves me. And I know he loves me. I'll never see him again." She stared at Mama. "This is all your fault. I hate you!"

Mama turned pale.

One night in early August, two soldiers stopped by the tavern. They had dark circles under their eyes and dust all over their uniforms. They tossed their silver helmets, scraped and covered with dirt, on the table and propped their guns in a corner. Sam wandered over to the corner and ran his hand up and down the barrels and slipped his finger into one of the triggers.

"Sam!" Mama said. "Come away from there this instant."

Sam pulled his finger slowly out of the trigger.

"He'll be all right," the first soldier said. "It isn't loaded."

"I won't have my children touching guns," Mama said.

"Sam?" the second soldier asked. "Do you like rifles?"

"Oh, yes," Sam said.

"Would you like to join the army and fight in the war?" the first soldier said.

"Could I? I mean, would they let me?"

The two soldiers laughed and slapped each other on the back. "Why don't we sign him up right now?" the second soldier said. "We can take him with us to help us chase those Romanians back to where they belong. Whores. They sold themselves to the highest bidder."

"What kind of army wants ten-year-old boys?" Mama asked. "My son isn't going to fight in any war. He's going to stay here and go to school so that one day he'll become a great doctor."

"A great doctor, is it?" the second soldier said and poked his friend. "We'll need a steady pair of hands to sew us back together after those Romanian bayonets tear us apart."

Mama poured them the last of our beer. "This is all we have. Now drink this up and be off. We don't want to listen to anymore of your talk."

The soldiers finished their beers and bade Sam a mock-tearful good-bye. He stood at the door of the tavern and waved at them until they were out of sight. A few minutes later, the mayor came rushing in. His face was red, and his hands were trembling. We all gathered around a table in the middle of the tavern.

"I need to talk to you, Mrs. Spirer," he said. "All of you. The Hungarian Army is coming. The Austrians, too." He sneezed loudly and looked as though he was about to burst into tears.

"Calm yourself," Mama said. "Sam, bring the mayor a glass of water."

Sam made a face, as he took a glass from a shelf and dipped it into the bucket Mama kept behind the bar. After a couple of sips, the mayor was breathing normally again, but his face was still beet red.

"The Romanians have entered the war," he said. "It's official. We have to leave Galfalva now, because there will be fighting right here in our streets. The Hungarian army will use our homes to shelter our soldiers."

"Why do they have to take our homes?" I asked.

"They need a place to live. Don't you want to help out your countrymen, after all they have done for you? Do you want to be a Romanian for the rest of your life?"

"No."

"Where will we go, and what will we do?" Mama asked.

"You'll be safe," the mayor said. "That much is certain. The Army has arranged everything with people up north. They'll make room for us in their homes and let us send our children to their schools."

"Why would they do that?"

He shrugged. "Because we are all Hungarians."

"What if these people don't really want us?" I asked.

"Yes," Mina said. "What if we don't like them?"

"I'm afraid we have no choice," the mayor said.

"But I don't want to go," Mina said.

"Neither do I," I said. "This is our home."

Kati sucked her thumb.

"I want to go," Sam said. "I can't wait to leave."

"Listen carefully," the mayor said. "Pack everything you can carry and be at the train stop at the edge of town on Friday at one o'clock."

"That's just two days from now," Mama said. "We need more time."

"As I said before, we have no choice. Take as much as you can, and don't forget to leave a little something behind for the soldiers to help them in their fight."

"Yes. You're right. We should do that." Mama's eyes lingered on each of our faces for a moment. Her voice was low and resigned.

Sam sat down and tilted his chair back on two legs and smiled to himself. Mina crossed her arms on the table and rested her cheek on top of them, and Kati stood and walked unsteadily to Mama and grabbed onto her skirt. I took a deep breath and wondered whether Papa would come with us on our long journey to the north.

I crammed my clothes into a pillowcase and started throwing in gloves and combs and scarves. Mama said I should put everything I needed inside but not fill it completely. Pretty soon, though, I had jammed so many things inside that I almost couldn't knot it.

"You'll have to carry it a long way down the hill to the train stop," Mama said. "Your arms will ache, and you'll wish you hadn't tried to bring everything. It's better to take less and leave some nice dishes for our soldiers and candles so they can see when it gets dark."

"Yes, Mama," I said.

But that didn't stop me from picking up a knife off the table and a soup ladle off the stove and Kati's old ball from between my mattress and the wall and stuffing them into my pillowcase. I wanted to save as many of my own things as possible. Strange people would be living here once we were gone. They might break the dishes I left behind and tear the straw out of my mattress or burn our table and chairs to keep warm in the winter and rip apart the napkins Mama had embroidered with so much love and care for our holiday meals.

Friday came much too quickly, and that morning, Mina remained in bed staring at the ceiling, while Mama prepared an early lunch for us. My sister had barely spoken to us over the last few weeks, since Rabbi Aaron's visit.

"Eat as much as you can," Mama said. "We'll be on the train until this evening."

"I'm not hungry," Mina said. "I'm not going with you. I'm staying here."

"That's what you think."

Mina shrugged.

Mama turned away from her. "Leave her alone," she said to Sam, Kati, and me. "She'll come to her senses."

We searched under tables and in corners for the things we wanted to take with us. Sam was so busy packing he ate his lunch standing up, though Mama tried to warn him about how terrible that was for his digestion.

"You, of all people, should know that," she said. "My son, the doctor."

After we cleared the table, Mama sat down on the bed with Mina. "You can't stay," Mama said.

"I would rather die here alone than go so far away," Mina said. "With no hope of ever seeing Aaron again."

"There are so many things in the world a young girl like yourself can do," Mama said. "Why would you want to die before you have the chance to do them?"

Mama straightened the front of her dress and drew herself up tall, suddenly angry instead of understanding. Beads of sweat rolled down her cheek, and her upper lip quivered a little. She gripped Mina's arm.

"I don't have time to argue with you," she said. "You will not break this family apart. That's all there is to it."

She pulled my sister out of bed. Mina held back a little before she finally gave in and stood upright.

"I knew it," Sam said. "I knew you were afraid to die."

"Be quiet," Mama said sharply. "No arguments. Finish your packing, Mina."

Just as we were ready to leave, Mama stood by the door post and loosened the nails holding up our *mezuzah*, the tiny container with Hebrew letters on it that marked ours as a good Jewish home. She pulled the little container down and turned it around between her fingers.

"Do you know what's inside?" she asked.

"No," I said.

"A scroll of paper with a saying by the great holy man Rabbi Akiva. 'Whatever measure God metes out to you, whether of good or of punishment—love Him.'"

"Is God punishing us now?"

"Certainly not. He is saving our lives."

"But I don't want to go."

"I know." She tapped the *mezuzah* on the palm of her hand. Then she reached for a string inside her pocket and hung the *mezuzah* on it and tied the string around my neck. "You wear this and watch over it for us. Remember, we'll never be able to have a proper home without it."

I held the *mezuzah* close to my chest, proud to be in charge of the part of our home we would always take with us, no matter where we went. Mama went back inside and began looking through all our half-empty drawers. On her last trip past the stove, she opened a cupboard and found several jars of raspberry preserves she had canned the previous fall. Mina and I had picked the raspberries from bushes that grew wild in the woods behind our house and watched Mama stand over the stove, while the steam from the boiling raspberries misted the air. She had poured the raspberries into eight jars and sealed them.

"I love to do this, because it reminds me of the first year Papa and I lived in this house," she had said. "We went into the woods and found raspberries there. Red gold, your papa called them, and patted my stomach where Mina was growing inside."

Mama touched the tops of the jars lightly with her fingers. "We should take most of these but leave two or three behind for the soldiers," she said. "I'm not sure how we will we carry them."

"I know," I said.

I pulled the cloth off the table and spread it on the floor. I slipped the cases off our pillows, found an extra towel near the stove, and wrapped each jar before placing it on top of the tablecloth. When I was finished, I twisted the ends of the tablecloth in my hand and tried to lift it, but it was too heavy for me.

"That's an awfully large bundle for someone your size," Mama said. "Mina, you carry it."

"I don't want to," Mina said. "It's too far."

"Do as you are told," Mama said. "We have no time for your temper."

Mina frowned at Mama.

By noon, we were all packed. I walked around the house, surprised at how empty it was even though we were leaving so much behind. I stopped at a chair by the fireplace and thought of how I had rocked Kati to sleep in it. I rested my cheek on the table and could almost smell the fresh bread and chicken and wonderful bowls of soup I had eaten there. I leaned on the stove and remembered the many times I had boiled water for tea and watched Mama cook dinner there. I sat down on my mattress and closed my eyes and thought of all the nights I had fallen asleep to the sounds of my family coughing or sneezing or sighing in the middle of a dream. I stood and picked up my pillowcase and walked to the door. I took one last look around my house. Except it wasn't really mine any more. If I ever saw it again, it would be different because someone else would have lived here while I was gone. Eaten meals at my table, put scratches on the wall, slept in my bed. A pair of invisible hands held me in the doorway for a long moment.

"Papa," I said and glanced at the tiny nail holes where the *mezuzah* used to be.

"It was supposed to bring us luck and many, many children," he whispered.

"Will you come with us?"

He pushed me outside into the blinding sunlight.

We saw lots of people on our way to the train stop. Some of them carried bedding and suitcases with shirt sleeves hanging out the sides. A few of them talked excitedly among themselves, but most were quiet and kept their eyes fixed on the road. To pass the time, Mama filled our ears with stories of the new people we were going to live with. They were a rich Jewish family named Kaufman, and she said their house had wooden floors and a fireplace and big windows and soft beds. That took away a little of the sting when I thought about how lost and deserted our old house had looked before I said good-bye and closed the door.

Mama told us the Kaufmans lived in Kisvarda, a beautiful town near Budapest with trees along all the roads and many shops. She said we would go to school, and if we behaved ourselves, Mrs. Kaufman would probably let us use her kitchen.

"I'm certain it's beautiful," Mama said. "And I'll cook all your favorite meals, bean soup, cabbage rolls, borscht."

She said we would make many new friends and go to a synagogue with huge glass windows and a cantor with a booming voice. Mina listened impatiently, sweating with the effort of carrying the tablecloth full of raspberry jars. People bumped into us when we slowed down to wait for her. Finally, she stopped and lowered the tablecloth and wiped her forehead with her collar. Then she bent down and twisted the tablecloth in her hand and tried to lift the jars off the ground, but the cloth slipped through her fingers and fell with a horrible crash. The glass inside broke into a thousand pieces, and red liquid seeped through the tablecloth.

"Oh, my God," she said. "I told you it was too heavy to carry."

Sam stood at her side and pushed at the tablecloth with his foot until it fell open. "Look," he said. "Here's one that didn't die."

Mama, Mina, and I looked down.

"See," Sam said.

He reached into the tangled mess of cloth and broken glass and pulled out a jar. His fingers were covered with fruit.

"Stop," Mama said. "You'll hurt yourself."

"The lone survivor," he said.

He set the jar on the ground, and Mama knelt down to study it.

"So it is," she said. "Thank God for such a blessing."

The jar glistened in the sunlight, as chunks of raspberry and slivers of glass slid down its sides. A sweet sharp smell filled the air, and Sam held his hand to his mouth and licked the fruit slowly off his fingers, one at a time.

THE IRON SNAKE

The train north slithered along the track in front of us like an iron snake. It stopped just short of the tiny lean-to where we stood, hissing steam from its belly. Eyes all along the side of the snake watched us from beneath half-open lids, waiting for the mouth to swallow us here in Galfalva and spit us out two hundred and forty kilometers away in Kisvarda.

A man in a blue uniform and cap jumped down from an open door at the back of one of the cars and motioned us forward. The iron snake huffed at me on the track, inviting me to come inside. I was afraid I might cry when it came time to leave, but instead I hopped up the steps to the car without so much as turning my head back toward the place where I was born.

"Go all the way to the rear," the man in the uniform said. He pointed to his right. "See those cars?" He nodded toward the front of the train. "They're full of people. This car and the next one are all that's left."

Inside the snake were rows and rows of empty seats. I followed Sam to the very end of the car, and the two of us squeezed ourselves into a seat and stood up, facing backwards, our thighs pressed against the hot leather. We were the first two people in the car, and we watched as everyone else from Galfalva came in quietly: Mrs. Davich, weighed down by a picnic basket, and Mr. Davich, carrying two big suitcases; Domino, wrestling with a couple of dresses thrown over her shoulder, and her brother Sollie, balancing pillows and sheets in his arms; our next door neighbor, Mrs. Fischer, holding on to her stomach with one hand and a loaf of bread with the other. Mama and Mina and Kati were the last ones on, and we waved at them and bounced against the squeaky seats.

After Mama pushed through the crowd and guided Kati in beside us, she said, "You two had better settle down. We have a long ride ahead of us."

She reached over and raised the window, and a large blast of steam hit me in the face. It smelled sharp and burned my nostrils. She and Mina sat down across the aisle.

As we began to roll forward, the station slid past, and the wheels rattled against the tracks below me. The train started moving faster, and trees and grass danced across my window. I held onto my seat so hard my knuckles turned white. I couldn't even stand up without falling and wondered how Lazlo could have run on top of a passenger car in the moving picture I saw with my aunt. My stomach hopped into my throat, while the train kept right on pulling the ground from underneath me. I had a sour copper taste inside my mouth and wished I hadn't eaten so much for lunch.

Sam put on his wise doctor face and pressed my wrist between his thumb and index finger. "You look a little sick," he said.

"Ouch," I said and pulled my arm away. "Stop bumping me. You'll make me throw up."

All I wanted was to lie down, but there was no room. I was pinned against the seat, with the wind beating on my shoulders and the sun burning my skin and hair. Trees blurred against the afternoon sky, and the grass turned a sickening green. I slumped forward and eased myself onto the floor. I pulled my knees to my chest and squeezed my eyes shut. My ankles bumped against warm metal, and although I wished over and over for the train to stop, it kept right on going. Finally, after many more wishes on my part, it heard me, and the wheels ground against the tracks with a terrible scream. The train slowed down for a moment and lurched forward. Then it sat perfectly still.

I remained curled up on the floor until my stomach dropped back down to its proper place and the copper taste inside my mouth faded away. I sat up and climbed back into my seat.

"What happened?" Mina asked.

Sam jumped up and poked his head and shoulders so far out the window it seemed to bite off the top half of his body. Mama yanked at his legs, and he slid back inside.

"All I can see is the train," he said. "Nobody else is on the tracks."

Everyone began to talk at once, and after a while, people stood in the aisle and formed a line to get off the snake. We filed out slowly, and when I stepped off the train, heat rose in waves from the tracks. The snake was spitting people out, three and four at a time.

"I wonder why we've stopped here, in the middle of nowhere," Mama said.

"Look!" Sam said.

He pointed toward our locomotive. Another train headed in the opposite direction sat on the track next to ours, although we could only see it once we stepped outside the shadow of the snake. The conductor of our train, a small man with dark hair like Papa's, leaned out the door of the locomotive and seemed to shout at the conductor of the second train. Pretty soon, both men climbed down and pointed at the tracks, waving their hands in the air, arguing.

"Huff, huff," the snake said.

A moment passed.

"Huff, huff," it said again, only much slower this time.

I wandered a few steps away and lay down in the tall grass beside the track.

"Don't go too far, Serene," Mama said.

"I won't," I said.

I rolled over on my back, watching two or three small clouds move across the sky. The *mezuzah* tumbled across my shoulder, and soon the sounds of people's voices talking back and forth faded into a quiet murmur. Papa sat down beside me in the grass, dressed in the muslin shirt he wore the last time I saw him.

"Aren't you hot in that shirt?" I asked.

"No," he said. "The temperature outside means nothing to me." He rubbed his chin. "So, the train ride made you sick."

"Yes."

"Maybe leaving home isn't as exciting as you thought it would be." He picked up the *mezuzah* and dangled it from the tips of his fingers. "Take it from one who knows."

"Where are you, Papa? Why don't you come back to us? We're your family, your flesh and blood."

"You are so grown up now. Maybe you don't need your papa so much anymore."

"Oh, but I do. Is that why you stayed away so long? I've missed you."

"Just look at you. Tall and sturdy, with muscles in your arms and legs. You'll be a good farm wife one day. Marry a rich man. Pay back what you owe to your parents who brought you into this world."

"But Mama says I have to go to school for many years yet so that I won't spend my life plucking chickens and milking cows."

"Your mama always did have big ideas for you girls. A good husband is all you need."

The ground beneath me began to shake, and Papa disappeared and didn't come back when I called out to him. I sat up. The other train chugged by on its way to Galfalva, and soldiers waved at me from its windows. They looked so happy, and I wished I was going home with them. I waved back at them.

"Don't forget to water Kati's rosebush!" I shouted. "And don't forget to feed the chicken we left for you in the yard."

One of them laughed at me. "We won't, little girl," he said and signaled to the friend beside him that I was crazy.

The second train seemed to stretch on for miles, and I watched it pass for a good long time before I could see Mama on the other side.

"Serene!" she said. "My God. I didn't know where you were. Don't ever go off by yourself again."

"Yes, Mama," I said and crossed back over the track to her.

Word traveled fast that we would have to stay where we were for the night. The conductor of the second train had unhooked our locomotive, over the protests of our conductor, and taken both our engine and our conductor along with him to help transport more soldiers. As the talk buzzed around us, I noticed for the first time that the snake wasn't huffing any more and that someone had chopped off its head.

"What if they forget about us?" Mina asked. "We may die here. I told you I would rather die at home."

"Can we sleep outside, Mama?" Sam asked.

"No," Mama said.

"Why not?"

"Because we'll be much safer inside the train. We can stretch out on the seats or on the floor."

"I don't want to go back inside," I said. "It smells bad in there. I like it better outside."

"Me too," Mina said.

"Come on, now." Mama said. "Let's make the best of things. We'll have ourselves a nice little picnic out here in the grass, and later on you can set up tents inside the car with the sheets we brought along."

"Why can't we just walk home?" Mina asked.

"Yes," I said. "How far away are we?"

"Fifty kilometers, give or take a few," Mama said.

"We could walk to Galfalva from here."

"We could, I suppose, but it would take days. We'd have to leave most of our food and all of our clothes behind, and each of us would have to carry Kati part of the way. Besides, the soldiers have probably already moved into our house."

"No they haven't," Mina said. "We've only been gone a few hours."

"I want to go home before the soldiers take everything," I said.

"Not me," Sam said. "I want to stay right here and go hunting in the woods."

"You'll do no such thing," Mama said. "We have to stay together. Besides, what if our conductor comes back and you are nowhere to be found? We would have to leave you here for good."

Sam smiled, as if he liked that idea.

Mina kicked at the dirt and made a circle with the tip of her shoe. Sam shuffled toward the train and sat down on the lowest step that led back into our car and poked a stick at the ground. Domino walked past and stuck her tongue out at him before climbing back inside. She almost stepped on my brother's head, but he didn't seem to notice.

Our neighbor, Mr. Fischer, sat down next to Sam, holding a slingshot in his hand.

"Let's go catch something to eat," he said.

"I can't," Sam said. "Mama won't let me. She says we have to stay put."

Mr. Fischer knelt down beside the track and pressed his ear against one of the rails. He motioned Sam to bend down and listen too.

"What do you hear?" he asked.

"Nothing," Sam said.

"There's not a train within miles of this place." He turned toward Mama. "Why can't this young fellow come along with me?"

Mama looked up at Mr. Fischer, shielding her eyes from the sun with her hand. "Are you sure you didn't hear anything?" she asked.

"Not a sound," Mr. Fischer said.

"Oh, all right. But hurry back, just in case."

She watched nervously as Sam and Mr. Fischer disappeared into the woods. An hour later, they returned. Mr. Fischer carried a dead rabbit on the end of a stick. It was fat with a thick layer of matted fur.

"Supper!" he said.

Sam licked his lips.

"Not for us," Mama said. "That's *trayf*."

"Suit yourself," Mr. Fischer said. "Out here in the middle of no-where is hardly the place to worry about keeping Kosher. God wouldn't want your children to starve to death for a dietary principle, would He Mrs. Spirer?"

"I'm certain I don't know. He doesn't talk to me about such matters."

Mrs. Fischer skinned the rabbit, and Mr. Fischer built a fire. Sam never took his eyes off the rabbit, as Mr. Fischer turned it round and round on the stick and let it cook to a toasty brown. That night, we ate a few squares of cheese and thin pieces of bread from the basket of food Mama brought along with her and let our mouths water over the meaty smell of that rabbit.

"We may be here quite a while," Mr. Fischer said. "It's a good thing I can live off the fat of the land." He slapped his belly with his hands.

"Hush, Malik," Mrs. Fischer said. "You don't want to scare those children to death."

When it came time for bed, Mama told us we had to go back inside the train to stretch out together on one of the seats. We covered ourselves with a sheet. I looked out the window at the pitch black evening sky, but I couldn't see the moon or stars. All around me, people coughed and sighed and moaned as they settled into sleep. Mina didn't move at all, and I rolled toward her a little bit to see if she was still breathing. I rolled back to my own place, and Mrs. Davich's face drifted in front of my eyes. I was too frightened to scream.

"You wanted the train to stop," she said. "Now look what's happened. Don't you realize we'll starve to death here?"

"What can I do?" I asked.

"You should never have thrown away the glass heart."

"But Domino broke it!"

"Serene," Mina said. She poked me with her elbow. "Be quiet. You're talking in your sleep."

"Shh," a voice said from the darkness around us.

I huddled in a corner by the window and didn't close my eyes for the rest of the night. In the morning, I changed my dress quickly and escaped from the snake just as Mama, Mina, Sam, and Kati were beginning to stir. As I stood beside the tracks, Mrs. Davich crept up behind me. I felt her there and spun around to face here.

"I didn't mean to do it," I said. "It's not my fault."

"What are you talking about, child?" she asked.

"Maybe I'm not the one who stopped the train. Maybe you're really the one who sent our conductor away."

"You're delirious. Don't you have enough to eat? Perhaps Mr. Davich and I can spare a morsel or two."

The ground beneath us began to shake, and I jumped into the tall grass at the side of the empty track. A train appeared, going north like us, and I crossed my fingers and begged it to stop and give us food and take us to Kisvarda.

"Don't leave me here to die," I said to the train.

But it just laughed at me. "You hated the snake," its wheels sang, as they rolled over the rails. "And the snake knew it." The train was gone in a few minutes, and when I looked toward the place where Mrs. Davich had stood, she was gone, too.

I walked toward the front of the snake, its lifeless body gathering dust under the hot morning sun. Adults stood in silent groups all along its side, and even the children were quiet. I sat down on the tracks in front of the first car.

"What are you doing out there?" a man shouted.

I stared at the ground between the rails. Something shiny there caught my eye, and I saw that it was a shapeless, rough piece of pink glass. When I picked it up, it fit perfectly inside my palm, and I was certain I had found a piece of the glass heart I'd thrown away so carelessly all those years ago. I thought I heard Mrs. Davich sigh.

Every day, I watched the empty tracks in front of me until they narrowed down to a thin line and disappeared into the trees. The dead snake lay behind me, and not a leaf stirred in the quiet air. Even my stomach had stopped rumbling, although it always craved more food than tiny bite of cheese and thin wedge of apple it was allowed at each meal.

At night, we all tried to keep our spirits high. Mama made a game of dividing our food for the next day, though I knew she worried about how quickly our supplies were shrinking. One afternoon, she sent me with a pitcher to the lake at the edge of the woods. Just as I was bending over to scoop up some water, she tiptoed behind me and put her hands over my eyes.

"Is that you, Mama?" I asked.

She took her hands away, and the two of us watched our reflections in the clear lake.

"Twins," I said.

"Yes," she said.

I smiled at the lie, because Mama and I looked nothing alike, and people often teased her and said I was adopted.

Once after dinner, Mr. Fischer told us how he saw people fly in a circus when he was a child, and another time the mayor talked about how he set a tree on fire when he wasn't much older than Sollie. Sam told everyone the story about how he cursed Uncle Mihai for spanking him, how Uncle Mihai had been shot in the very hand that struck my brother and sent Sam the bullet in the mail. He untied the bullet from his neck and passed it around for everyone to see. When I said I had seen moving pictures on a wall, no one believed me.

"What kind of pictures were they?" Sollie asked. His voice was hard and mean.

"Of a man on a train," I said. "He ran along the top and fell off."

"Did he die?" the mayor asked.

"No, he bounced off the ground and jumped right back on," I said.

"He couldn't do that," Sollie said. "He would be dead, or his leg would be broken. You're lying."

"I am not. I saw him do it in a room with a lot of other people and a man who was playing the piano."

"Well, I never heard of such a thing in my life," Mrs. Fischer said. "I can tell you that."

In spite of all the games and the stories we told one another, though, the bottom of our food basket was getting closer and closer with each passing day. After lunch, one afternoon, Mama and Mrs. Fischer sat together figuring something with a stick on the ground. That evening, Mama said we might have to start eating rabbits, after all, if our conductor didn't come back soon. She said maybe Mr. Fischer was right, and God would rather her children had enough to eat than starve to death in order to keep Kosher.

Each day, I made sure the tiny piece of my glass heart was in my dress pocket where I could reach it, and, whenever I was alone, bent my ear to the hot iron track and wished for the head to return and bring the rest of the snake back to life. Sometimes a train roared by, and I waved and yelled, along with everyone else. But it ignored us and kept right on going.

By the time we had been on the tracks for a week, my dresses were all filthy, and my socks were full of holes. I barely had enough energy to wash my face at night, and my hair was so badly knotted Mama couldn't get a comb through it. I finally began to lose hope of ever getting to Kisvarda.

On our eighth morning, a breeze rustled softly through the branches of a tree. I put my ear against the track, and it groaned a little, but otherwise remained deadly quiet. Mama and Mina sat under a tree at the far end of the tracks, and they both looked too tired to move. Kati cried, and Sam broke apart twigs and formed them into a small fort in the dirt.

"Where have you been?" Mama said, as I walked toward them. She scratched at her scarf and wiped beads of sweat from her forehead.

"Nowhere," I said.

I sat down next to Mama and, resting my head on her shoulder, closed my eyes and finished a pretend glass of fresh milk.

"Serene thinks she can bring our conductor back if she stares at the track hard enough," Sam said.

"Leave her alone," Mama said. "I'm glad someone in the family has enough spirit to keep on wishing."

I was about to start on an imaginary piece of honey cake, when the tracks beside me rumbled softly. Just beyond the last set of visible trees, a tiny black dot inched forward.

"Look!" I said.

There were shouts all up and down the train, and soon people began to gather at the front of the snake and watch breathlessly as the dot grew larger. It was on our side of the track, and at first, I thought I must be dreaming. But everyone else saw it too, so I knew my mind wasn't playing tricks on me because my stomach was empty.

"Thank God," Mama said, pressing her palms together in prayer.

The mayor crossed himself as the black dot moved toward us. Soon, it formed itself into the shape of the snake's head, and it hissed and chugged before squealing to a stop a little way up the track. Sam and Sollie and I and some of the other children walked forward slowly at first and then faster, shouting at the conductor to wait for us so that we could catch up with him. His dark head leaned out one side of the locomotive.

"Papa!" I said.

A smile spread across his face. He waved at us, and his whole body shook with joy, as if he were our lost father who had come home after a long journey and we, his children, were still alive.

REFUGEES

The iron tracks groaned. The snake coiled backwards, and the head joined itself once again to the body. Then the entire snake came to life, billowing clouds of steam from its sides and inviting us to come back inside. I climbed the steps one at a time. Sam was already in his seat with Mina opposite him, and I slid in next to my brother; my skin stuck to the leather. Pretty soon, the snake began to slither along the track, going faster and lurching and shaking. Mama offered me a tiny wedge of apple, but I waved it away, sick to my stomach again. I listened to the sound of the wheels scraping against the tracks, and my eyelids drooped. Sam poked my ribs, but they felt like they belonged to someone else's body. I heard Kati cry in the distance, and the air was stale, as it would be in a room that had been sealed away from the world for a hundred years.

An instant later, Sam poked me again. "We're here, you baby," he said.

"We are not," I said. "We just got back on the train."

He pressed his palms against my ears and twisted my head toward the window. Sure enough, outside the window was a platform with a sign over it that read "Kisvarda." I was surprised at how quickly we had arrived after being stranded on the tracks for so many days. The snake finally slowed to a stop, pitching me forward in my seat, and huffed on the track while I made my way down the steps. It hissed at me as I walked away.

The sun was about to set, and a hot evening breeze stung my face. Mr. and Mrs. Fischer were right behind us, and the moment they got off the train, a fat jolly woman introduced herself to us and gathered Mrs. Fischer in her arms and hustled her away. Mr. Fischer was too big to fit inside her arms with his wife, so he followed behind and waved good-bye, ready for his new life. Other people came to greet our neighbors and take them away so that, after a little while, we were the only ones left on the platform, except for three men with dusty pants and ragged beards.

"I wonder where Mr. Kaufman is," Mama said. "Maybe he didn't know when to expect us. Yes, I'm sure that's why he's not here."

We waited a few more minutes, and when no one else appeared, Sam told Mama he was going to ask one of the men where to find our benefactors. The first man smiled and reached into his trousers and pulled out a penny for my brother. Sam palmed it happily into his pocket. The second one pushed Sam away as if he was a beggar, but the third one rested one hand on Sam's shoulder and pointed down the road from the platform. Sam nodded and walked back toward us.

"The Kaufmans live down the main road and to the left," he said.

Mama picked up Kati, who sobbed and put her thumb in her mouth. Big tears rolled down her cheeks, and when Mina stuck out her tongue, Kati began to wail. Mama patted her until she quieted down. My eyelids were heavy again, and I would have been content to lie down on the floor and sleep on the platform for days. I had no desire to wander up and down the streets of Kisvarda, dragging my heavy pillowcase behind me.

"It's getting dark," Mama said. "We should go."

I shifted my pillowcase between my feet and leaned against Mina to keep from falling over.

"We'll stay here," Mina said. "You can come and get us in the morning, after you've settled in."

The snake hissed again and began to glide along the track headed north, and I sank to my knees and rested my head on the pillowcase.

Then I stretched out on the floor, wrapping my arms around my few sorry possessions. At that instant, I didn't care if we never found the Kaufman's house. I didn't want them and their big kitchen and their fancy synagogue. I wanted my own house, with my dusty yard and shed. I wanted my own synagogue and my own school, and as sleepy as I was, I would have walked all the way home that night to see them, if only for one second.

It was dusk by the time we reached the Kaufman's, a big white wooden house with a verandah and two huge windows in front. It smelled of fresh paint and was nearly hidden behind tall, thick shrubbery. We made our way up a dirt path and stood for a moment in front of a heavy wooden door carved with horses and birds before Mama knocked softly on it. She held herself back and lowered her head shyly. When no one answered, she knocked a little harder, and an older woman wearing a black wig that fit her head like a cap answered the door. All of the Jewish women I knew in Galfalva and Marosvasarhely covered their heads with scarves, as Orthodox custom demanded. But Mama often told me stories about wealthy Jewish women in the cities who wore fancy wigs made of real hair, not like Grandma's wig, which looked as if it had been pieced together with straw. Instead, these fancy wigs curled away from the forehead and twisted themselves into tightly-braided buns that rested neatly on the neck.

That evening in Kisvarda, both Mama and I stared at Mrs. Kaufman's wig with our mouths open. The front formed a perfect wave, and not a single strand was out of place. The hair was dark and shiny, and I thought the wig was the most wonderful thing I had ever seen. It was too bad Mrs. Kaufman wore such a sour expression on her face because it spoiled her beautiful hair. Her eyes were hard, and her mouth was so tight it looked like a tiny crack above her chin.

"Yes, what is it?" she said. "If you want a handout, go to the back of the house."

"No, I'm Mrs. Spirer, and these are my children," Mama said. "We've come such a long way, and we're tired but so thankful to you for giving us a home."

Mrs. Kaufman glanced at each of us and said, "tch, tch." We must have looked pitiful to her. I had a huge hole in the sleeve of my dress, and Mina's collar was ripped almost completely off. Kati had smudges on both of her cheeks. Sam's pants pocket was hanging by a thread, and two buttons were missing from his shirt. The edges of Mama's skirt were frayed, and her scarf was dirty. When I thought of how we looked, I started to laugh. I was too tired, had come too far, and didn't know what else to do. The more Sam pushed at me to make me stop, the harder I laughed, until he joined in, too. I sat down on the verandah, and Sam threw himself on top of me and tried to jam his fingers in my mouth. Still, I kept on.

"Please excuse my children," Mama said. "They've been through quite a lot, and they're not themselves." She nudged me with the edge of her foot.

"Wait one minute," Mrs. Kaufman said.

She slammed the door in our faces without inviting us inside and opened it a moment later, wrapping a fringed shawl over her thin shoulders. We marched after her to the edge of her backyard, and she nearly slapped Sam's wrist when he reached over to pull a leaf off one of her shrubs.

"Stay on the grass," she said. " And don't dig in your heels."

We stopped in front of a tiny shed. "In here," she said.

"There?" Mina asked, her eyes wide with disbelief.

"Mama?" I asked. "This can't be it."

"Be quiet, children," Mama said, nodding toward Mrs. Kaufman.

She opened the door, but there was no light in the shed, and it smelled moldy and stale, as if it had been sealed for many years.

"There's a candle by the stove," Mrs. Kaufman said. She turned on her heel and bade us a curt good night.

"Good night," Mama said and hurried us inside.

We stood by the door, while Mama felt around in the dark for the candle and a match. When she lit the candle, I saw our new home for the first time, not a rich man's house but one tiny room with two windows and a stove in the corner, smaller by far than our home in Galfalva.

"I can't believe you made me come," Mina said. "And you told me Aaron's room was too crowded."

"Where are our beds?" I asked. "Where will we eat?"

Mama ran her hand across her forehead. "I don't know," she said. "I just don't know."

"I'm going home," Mina said.

"No, you're not. You have no home. None of us do."

"We could run away," Sam said. "Maybe go to Budapest and live with Auntie Ilke and Uncle Isaac."

He was talking about Mama's youngest sister, who married a man Mama said did even less work than Grandpa. Once Uncle Isaac threatened to drown himself in the river because Mama's family wouldn't lend him money. Of course, the river was only a couple of feet deep in the place where he jumped in, and all he did was get his pants legs wet. In spite of that, Aunt Ilke stood on the shore and yelled for help at the top of her lungs, until Uncle Mishi dragged him out again.

"Uncle Isaac, indeed," Mama said. "He can hardly keep himself and Ilke from starving to death. How do you expect him to feed five extra mouths?"

Sam shrugged.

"I want to go to Budapest, too," I said. "And see the hand of St. Stefan."

"What are you talking about?" Mina asked.

"It's a mummified hand, hundreds of years old, hidden in a vault. I'm going to find it and wear it around my waist with a rope."

"You children are so tired you don't even know what you are talking about," Mama said. "Mina, Serene. Help me spread our blankets over the floor so we can all go to sleep. Tomorrow, we will decide what to do."

That night we huddled together, our arms and legs twisted around one another, and slept fitfully on the hard floor of our new home. I awoke early the next morning with no covers. It was hot, and my throat was dry, and there was a terrible braying noise outside.

"Shut up, Daisy," a scratchy voice said. "You could wake the dead."

I crawled to the window and saw an old woman sitting in a wagon and trying to coax her mule forward.

"Only a couple more steps," she said. "We need to be right in front of the door."

Her wagon was full of scraped and broken furniture and old barrels. The woman stood up and pulled the mule's reins, and it brayed even louder and almost yanked her out of the wagon. She sat down and straightened her dress and shook her head, mumbling something in a language I didn't understand.

"There's someone outside," I said to Mama. "An old woman with a mean mule and a wagon full of junk."

Mama sat up, barely awake, slipped her dress on over her nightgown, pushed her tangled hair into a bun, and tied her scarf on her head. She got up and opened the door.

"Who are you?" she asked. "And what are you doing here?"

"Pleased to make your acquaintance, too, Mrs. Spirer," the old woman said.

"How do you know my name?"

"I'm Mrs. Rosen. The synagogue sent me to bring you things for your new home and give you your weekly living allowance."

The old woman smiled a broad toothless smile that opened like a gaping hole in the middle of her face. Mama smiled back at her, and she and I went toward the wagon to help the woman down, while Mina, Sam, and Kati gathered in the doorway.

"Forgive me for being so rude, Mrs. Rosen," she said. "Everything is so new to me yet. I hardly know who are friends and who are enemies."

"Yes, well, sometimes friends come in strange packages." She slapped her knee and took Mama's hand and stepped down.

I climbed inside the wagon where I found three sets of dishes, one for milk meals, one for meat meals, and one for Passover. There were napkins and tablecloths, an old wooden rocker missing one of its arm rests, and a small table and five chairs. All the dishes were nicked or cracked. I wondered whether the people who owned them before had died and whether they were meant to be thrown away. I missed the pots on the old stove at home and the table by the window covered with dishes and silverware. These new dishes seemed shabby by comparison, broken down by too much use, and besides they weren't even ours.

Mrs. Rosen walked over to the wagon and looked at me. "This one is a worrier, I see," she shouted at Mama. "Wait a little while. You'll get used to us in the end."

"No, I won't," I said and jumped down from the wagon.

She winked at me. "What do you think of our Mrs. Kaufman?" she asked. "Quite a piece of work, isn't she?"

Mama nodded "Still, we're grateful to her for the roof over our heads," she said.

"Some roof!"

"Yes, but it's the only one we have right now."

Mrs. Rosen saw the *mezuzah* hanging around my neck and dangled the string between her fingers. The brass caught the light of the sun.

"What have we here?" she asked. "Ah, I see. It's a good thing you brought it with you."

She reached into her pocket, felt around, and pulled out two nails. She got a hammer from the front of her wagon, and Mama slipped the *mezuzah* over my head and untied it from the string. She handed it to Mrs. Rosen, who nailed it to the front doorpost of the shed and put the hammer in her pocket after she finished.

"Now it's official," she said. "This is really your home."

"Yes, it is," Mama said, trying to smile.

I stared at the *mezuzah* for a long moment, so shiny and strange on that splintered, dusty doorpost and thought, even it could never make such a terrible place into a real home.

GHOST BOY

On our second morning in Kisvarda, I lay on the grass behind Mrs. Kaufman's house and closed one eye. I fixed the other one on the sky, and a ghost boy drifted in front of me. He had white hair and skin and eyes so pale they were almost drained of color, and his smile twisted itself into a monkey grin. By the time I sat up, he had vanished.

Not long afterwards, Mama made me go with her inside the Kaufman's house, where we scrubbed the kitchen floor and helped the maid wash Mrs. Kaufman's clothes. I kept an eye out for that boy, and just before lunch time, he tiptoed into the kitchen and stole an apple from the counter. The maid pretended not to see him, and Mama did, too. I began to wonder if he was a real boy at all. Later, when I asked Mama who she thought he was, she told me it would be best for us not to poke our noses into Mrs. Kaufman's business; I didn't understand how asking about the boy could possibly make Mrs. Kaufman angry.

I saw him again a couple of days later. Mama sent me to Mrs. Rosen's house to pick up some eggs, since we weren't allowed to have chickens in the yard and couldn't raise our own. I knocked on her front door and she greeted me with one of her toothless smiles and invited me inside.

"You look tired, and you have dirt on your cheeks," she said

She took a cloth from a bucket of water, wiped my face with it, sat me down at the table, and gave me a glass of water and a cookie that tasted like a sweet lemon. She collapsed into the chair next to me. I ate the first cookie so quickly that she hardly had time to offer me a second one before I wiped the crumbs off my lips.

"Are there ghosts in Mrs. Kaufman's house?" I asked, my mouth full of cookie.

"There weren't the last time I checked," she said. "Why? Did you see one?"

"Maybe."

"Really? What did it look like?"

"It was a boy. He had white hair and pale skin and eyes with no color in them."

"Did he speak to you at all?"

"No."

She threw her head back and laughed. "Child, you have some imagination. That's no ghost. It's only Daniel, Mrs. Kaufman's grandson."

"Well, he looks just like a ghost. He's so pale."

"He doesn't have much color. That's true." She tapped her head. "But he's a little slow up here, if you know what I mean. Has never said a word since the day he was born. Didn't even cry as a baby. I'm surprised she lets him go anywhere where people can see him."

"What do you mean?"

She stood up and quickly gathered a dozen eggs into a basket. "That's all for today. Tell your mama there are plenty more where these came from."

On top of the eggs, she put three more of those delicious cookies wrapped inside a cloth napkin for me to eat on my way back, which I did without saving a morsel for my sisters and brother.

I shuffled toward the Kaufman's house, and just as I turned the corner onto the dusty path that wound toward our shed, the ghost boy bobbed in front of me again. He smiled the same strange monkey grin and ran into the woods beside the house, weaving in and out between the trees. I wanted to run after him, but inside my head, someone whispered, "Not today."

I watched until I couldn't see him anymore and turned slowly back toward the path to the shed. I shook the crumbs out of the napkin and brushed them off my dress. I had no plans to tell Mama about the cookies or about Daniel, either.

Early the next morning, after I finished my chores, I went into the woods to look for him again.

"Where are you?" I shouted. "Come out. I won't hurt you. I want to be your friend."

The branches above me swayed softly in the wind, and I put my hand on the trunk of a tree and circled around and around it until I was dizzy. I dug into my pocket and pulled out a boiled egg I had taken from the table when Mama wasn't looking and held it up high for Daniel to see. I could feel him watching me. I set the egg down by the roots of the tree and started to leave, although I wasn't at all sure how to find my way back to Mrs. Kaufman's yard. I walked around the trees and up and down the narrow paths between them, not sure whether I was retracing my steps. I wished I hadn't left that egg for Daniel and worried I might starve to death before I ever found my way out. I wandered around for what seemed like hours, before Daniel appeared out of nowhere, grabbed my arm, and dragged me along behind him.

"Are you sure you know where you're going?" I asked.

He didn't answer, but in the next instant, he pushed me out of the trees and into the yard. I turned to thank him, but he was gone, although I could still feel the warmth of his fingers pressing into my skin.

One afternoon a couple of days later, Mama and I went back to Mrs. Kaufman's house to do more chores. Of course, Mina and Sam didn't want to go, so Mama took me instead. She said we had to do something to earn our keep and pay back Mrs. Kaufman for putting a roof over our heads. She said we didn't want to accept charity, if we could help it, because a person always had to pay for what she ate and wore and where she slept. She reminded me of Grandma when she talked like that. I busied myself sweeping the back porch and kept out of everyone else's way. Inside, I heard water running from Mrs. Kaufman's sink, and I knew Mama was cleaning the fireplace in the front room. Suddenly, the water stopped running, and I stepped toward the back door and stood there with my broom in my hand, staring into that beautiful kitchen, with its marble counters and heavy wood table. Daniel cowered in one corner, his head bowed.

"Daniel," Mrs. Kaufman said angrily. "Have you been outside again? You know you aren't allowed. I won't have the neighbors talking about you. Pointing at you. Making fun."

Daniel kept his head down and fingered a crude knife he had taken from his pocket.

"Do you understand me?" Mrs. Kaufman asked. "Well, do you?"

She stepped forward until she was practically on top of him. She was breathing heavily. He looked up at her, bared his teeth, and pushed his tongue hard against them. Saliva trickled down his chin, and a braying sound escaped from his mouth.

"Good," Mrs. Kaufman said. "I wish we didn't have those people living in the back yard. I won't have you mixing with them. They're poor, homeless. Not like us."

Daniel brayed again, this time more softly. He wiped his mouth with the back of his hand, and I moved quickly out of the doorway before he had a chance to see me.

Later that afternoon, I went to Mrs. Rosen's for more eggs. "Why doesn't Mrs. Kaufman want Daniel to go outside?" I asked.

"He's slow," she said. "He doesn't understand things like you and I do, and Mrs. Kaufman is afraid people will gossip about him. She thinks he's a disgrace to the family."

"Why? Because he can't talk?"

"Partly. Something is missing in that family's bloodline, and Mrs. Kaufman doesn't want anyone to think too hard about it. She's something of a mystery herself. She moved to Kisvarda when she married Mr. Kaufman, and as far as I can tell, no one around here knows who her people were or where she came from. There was talk for a while that her father deserted her mother and that she was a poor orphan who married for money."

"But where are Daniel's mother and father?"

"Ah, now that's a story. The father was no good—a drifter who never worked a day in his life. They say he drove Daniel's mother to an early grave because he wouldn't stay put. Got the poor girl pregnant, then married her and went around telling everyone he wasn't really Daniel's father. Vanished right after Daniel's mother died. No one has head from him since." She gave me two sugar cookies that tasted just like the ones Mama used to make for our tavern at home. "I probably shouldn't be telling these kinds of tales to such a little girl. Your mama wouldn't like it."

"Oh. She won't mind. Besides, I know all about men and women."

"You do?"

"Yes. My aunt told me I was a born matchmaker. I saved her once from Karl, this man who helped in my grandma's store, and got her to marry Tibor instead."

"A matchmaker? That's quite something for one so young."

"Tibor is rich. He gave me a gold Star of David, but a Gypsy stole it one night on the road when I ran away from Grandma's."

"I see."

"My aunt and Tibor have twin boys now. My aunt used to write to me every month, and I'm going to visit her when I go home. I don't do matchmaking anymore, unless you count sneaking Mina's letters to the rabbi out of the house back in Galfalva. But Mama broke that up."

"She did?" Mrs. Rosen opened her eyes wide.

"Uh huh. She said the rabbi was too poor, and besides, she wants Mina and me to finish our education."

"Your mama is very wise. You should listen to her."

"I do." I dug the piece of glass out of my pocket and put it on the table.

"What is that?" Mrs. Rosen asked.

"It's part of a glass heart," I said. "Mrs. Davich gave it to me. She's our neighbor at home. Mama doesn't like her. She says she a witch. The glass heart is magic, and you can make wishes on it."

"What happened to the rest of it?"

"A mean girl in school broke it, and I threw it away. But I found part of it later. Only now it doesn't work as well as it used to."

"That's a pity."

"I know. I have a lot more wishes I would like to make."

She counted out a dozen more eggs for us and filled another plate full of cookies. I grabbed one and took a big bite.

One evening after dinner, Mama gathered us around the table and announced she had found us a school. "It's at the very end of the road that runs in front of Mrs. Kaufman's house," she said. "Close enough that if there's fighting here in Kisvarda, I can come and take you right away. There's no chance we'll be separated. None in the world."

"I'm tired of school," Mina said. "Besides, I'm too old."

"Oh no you're not, my girl. You have a lot to learn about this world. Trust me, you do."

Mina rolled her eyes.

"I have to tell you one more thing about your new school," Mama said. "It's right next to the Catholic church."

"What?" Sam asked. "You mean we're going to Catholic school. How can we? You wouldn't even let us eat rabbit when we were starving to death. How can you let us go to school with Catholics?"

"Listen to me, young man. How do you ever expect to become a doctor if you don't complete your education, Catholic or otherwise?"

"I don't like Catholics," I said.

"How do you know whether you do or you don't?" Mama asked.

"You always told us to stick with our own kind. Besides, Domino is a Catholic, and she's mean."

"All I know is the school is the best one in the neighborhood, and the nuns are very nice."

"But what if they try to stop us from being Jewish?"

"They promised me you won't have to say their prayers. I told them how devout you are, how we've always kept a Kosher home, and they said they were happy to take you in. Such smart children."

"I still don't want to go."

That night, I dreamed Daniel tapped on the window beside my mattress. He put his finger to his lips and waved me outside. I was wearing my nightgown, and I slipped from beneath my covers and crawled around Mina and Mama, trying hard not to knock over the small kerosene lamp on the floor. The front door creaked on its hinges, and I closed it carefully so it wouldn't wake anyone up. I walked around outside in the dark with my hands in front of me to keep from falling. Finally, I felt cool, dry skin brushing against me.

"Daniel, is that you?" I asked.

He stepped out of the shadows and into the moonlight, as pale as ever. We went into the yard and sat down on the grass, though I could hardly see his face. He leaned back and looked up at the sky.

"How did you know my name?" he asked without moving his lips.

"You're talking," I said.

"Yes. I use my thoughts, not my mouth, if I want to say something. Now, answer my question. How do you know my name?" His voice sounded tinny inside my ears.

"I heard your grandmother the other day in the kitchen."

"So you know. You know what my real voice sounds like."

"Is that why you can't speak, because you don't have parents?"

"Mama died." He touched my hair with the tip of his finger. "She was blonde, like you. My father disappeared one day."

"So did mine. I don't think he'll ever come back. I think he's dead, though no one in the family will say so." I watched while a cloud drifted across the full moon. "I bet you could talk with your mouth if you tried."

He opened his mouth and moved his lips, "I bet I could, too." His voice was soft and flat.

"Am I dreaming?"

"Do you think you are?"

I leaned over and kissed him on the cheek, and he took my hands and pulled me off the grass. We held onto each other and twirled around in a circle, until our fingers let go. The muscles in my legs shook, and I fell to the ground breathless. I closed my eyes and heard Daniel's feet glide back and forth across the grass. Every once in a while, he called my name. I was surprised the next morning when Mama shook me awake. The sun was already high in the morning sky, and I was alone outside on the grass. My head rested so heavily on my arms that they were numb, and Mama stood over me, her hands on her hips.

"You'll be the death of me yet," she said. "You scared the wits out of me when you weren't in your bed this morning. Since when have you started walking in your sleep?"

"I don't know, Mama," I said. "I had a dream, and I followed it out here."

"Well, that's enough foolishness about your dreams for today. Thank God you're all right. Come inside and get dressed. We have a lot of work to do. You start school tomorrow."

When she lifted me off the grass, my arms ached pleasantly, and the sound of Daniel's laughter tickled my ears.

SISTERS

Snow was falling behind the stained glass window of the school chapel. Mina, Sam, and I sat on a long bench far away from the altar. The room filled with the sound of morning prayers.

"I believe in one God, the Father Almighty," the rest of the chil dren recited in unison, "Creator of heaven and earth, and in . . ."

The son of God, the name we Jews weren't supposed to say. After they finished the prayer, they began to sing in Latin that slid easily over their tongues. I could only make out a few of the words I had heard before in class, "Lamb of God . . . mercy."

I swung my legs back and forth and Sam bumped me impatiently with his shoulder. Only Mina was perfectly still. She hardly blinked at all and stared straight ahead. Finally, the chapel grew quiet, and Sister Magdalena, who was leading the prayer, raised her arms to signal the end of the morning service. We filed quietly out of the chapel and into the hallway.

"Sister Magdalena leads the prayers so beautifully," Mina said. "I wish she was our real mother. Don't you?"

"No," I said.

I didn't like the sister very much. She had a pinched face and tiny eyes, and her robe frightened me. It was long and black and pleated, and I was afraid I could get lost inside. So I tried never to let her get too close to me.

"Mina loves the nuns," Sam said.

"I thought you wanted to marry a rabbi," I said.

"Besides, you're supposed to be Jewish, and Jewish people don't love nuns."

"Leave me alone," Mina said. She shook her fist in our faces.

Each evening after dinner, we lit a candle and sat at the table with our homework. At least, that's what Sam and I did. Some nights, Mina slid a sheet of paper from beneath her homework assignment, when she thought Mama wasn't looking, and bent over it, covered it with her arms, and wrote letters to Rabbi Aaron. I wasn't sure how she mailed them, and whenever Mama caught her, she took the letter away and hid it somewhere or tore it up. Mina never heard back from the rabbi. When I asked her why, she said he was probably too busy taking care of the congregation, now that the fighting had spread further south. She cursed Mama and said she would much rather be in Szereda with Aaron than here with us. She said most girls her age were already married, and she wanted to be married, too.

After a silence of many months, Rabbi Aaron finally wrote a letter to Mina. None of us knew how he found out where we were living. Mina swore to Mama that she had never mailed the letters she wrote, but I knew she was lying. Mina grabbed Rabbi Aaron's letter out of Mama's hand and dashed out of the house. I ran after her and caught up with her on the road to school, where she stumbled along, reading her letter with tears in her eyes.

"What does it say?" I asked.

"He's leaving Szereda," she said. "He's moving to Budapest, and he may go somewhere outside Hungary after that."

"How can he, with the war going on?"

"I don't know, but he's taking the train early in the morning, a week from Sunday. He will pass through here, and he wants me to meet him. He says he has something important to tell me." She folded the letter neatly and tucked it into her coat pocket, trying hard not to leap up and down and act too excited. "I can hardly wait."

"What do you think he wants to tell you?"

"I'm sure he's going to ask me to marry him. I may even go away with him that very day." She looked up at the sky and smiled.

"Mama will never let you."

"Who says we have to tell her?"

"We do, don't we?"

"Don't be such a child. Do you have any secrets from Mama?"

"Yes."

"I don't believe it. The two of you are like one person. Anyhow, if Papa were here, he would put Mama in her place. He would understand about Aaron and let me go with him. I'm old enough to make up my own mind, and Papa would know that. He always liked me best and took my side. Not like Mama." She grabbed my collar and twisted it a little in her hand.

"Don't. You're hurting me."

"You'd better not say one word to her, or you'll be sorry."

I pulled myself free. "All right."

"In fact, I think you should come with me to the station."

"Why? Aaron doesn't like me."

"There has to be someone from the family to say good-bye when I leave."

"Mama will kill me."

"Oh, no, she won't."

Mina stayed late at school every afternoon the next week to talk to Sister Magdalena. I waited for her in the school yard, when the weather was warm enough, or in the hall beside the chapel door, when it was cold and rainy. Most days she came out of the chapel with a dreamy look in her eyes, full of plans for her new life as a married woman.

"How can you stand to talk to Sister Magdalena?" I asked one afternoon.

"She's nice," Mina said. "Besides, I can tell her things, and she doesn't get mad, like Mama."

"What kind of things?"

"About how much I love Aaron."

"Did you tell her he's coming to see you?"

"No. But I told her how serious the two of us are."

"What did she say?

"Not to let my feelings run away with me. I told her I hated Mama, too, and she said anger is bad for my soul. Then we prayed together."

"What kind of prayer?"

"Something I made up on my own. She's not trying to turn me into a Catholic, no matter what you think."

I laughed. "Aaron won't like you to be such good friends with a nun."

"I'm not going to tell him, and neither are you."

A couple of afternoons later, I stood in the silent, empty hallway outside the chapel and waited almost an hour for Mina. It was a cold, snowy day, and the sky was gray and cloudy. I was tired and hungry and wanted to hurry Mina along, so I crept softly into the back of the chapel. Sister Magdalena stood by the altar with Mina at her side. She took Mina's hand, and the two of them knelt together and bowed their heads.

"Stop!" I shouted.

Mina clenched her fist. "Be quiet," she said. "We're praying."

"No, you're not." I ran toward her and tugged at the end of her sleeve.

"Let go of me."

Sister Magdalena put her hand on my shoulder, and I froze. She bent down next to me, and I took a step backwards, afraid of being swallowed in the folds of her robe. She smelled like incense.

"Mina and I were only sharing a moment of reflection," Sister Magdalena said. "Your sister has quite a bit on her mind these days, like most young women do."

"But she's not supposed to be here," I said.

"Why not?"

"Because we're Jewish." I looked straight into the eyes of the Son of God, whose painting hung above the altar. "And because of Him."

She smiled softly. "We're each children of God, after all, so it doesn't matter what we call ourselves. Why don't you kneel here with the two of us and pray to your God in whatever way you wish?"

The room began to spin, and I leaned against a pew to keep from falling over, although Sister Magdalena must have thought I was getting ready to pray.

"That's very good," she said.

"No!" I said. "I can't. It's not right."

The sister laughed. "Well, my dear Serene, I fear you will never make a good Catholic."

"I know." A cold sweat trickled down my back and sent a shiver through my body. "I don't want to be a Catholic. Mama says Jews are Jews, and Catholics are Catholics."

"Not always."

Sister Magdalena cupped my elbow in her hand to steady me, and the Son of God gazed down on me.

I was dreaming about our future. Mina and I were in a foreign land, in a room with red carpeting so deep our feet disappeared when we stepped on it and with photographs of men, women, and children I'd never seen before on the walls. The room was richer than anything in Mrs. Kaufman's house. Mina was perched on the arm of a black-and-white checkered couch, and I sat in a wooden rocking chair in front of a huge fire. My sister looked much different. She was an old lady, and there were wrinkles under her eyes and folds under her chin. Her hair wasn't black anymore. It was straw-colored and pasted across her forehead in thin wisps. I glanced into a mirror above the fireplace, and my face was full of wrinkles, too. My hair was the same color as Mina's and cut short above my ears. Mina began speaking in English. I recognized the language because Papa used it once in a dream.

"Remember?" Mina asked.

Someone shook me. I opened my eyes, but the beautiful room with the red carpet was gone, and Mina was kneeling over me. Her hair was black, and her skin was perfectly smooth, and I was lying in the shed behind Mrs. Kaufman's house. Oh, how I yearned to go back to that other room again.

Mina put her hand over my mouth. "Shh," she said. "You were talking in your sleep."

I looked out the window and saw that it was pitch black outside.

"Come on," she said. "Get up and don't make a sound." She took her hand away from my mouth. "It's time."

I slid from beneath my blanket and slipped silently into my dress and shoes.

"Tomorrow at this time, I'll be in Budapest," Mina said.

"Don't you want to take anything with you?" I asked.

"What for?"

It was bitter cold when we opened the front door a crack and eased our way outside. We walked quickly up the road toward the train station. Soldiers in shabby uniforms milled around on the platform, in spite of the early hour, and most of them were gaunt and had black rings around their eyes. Some looked as if they hadn't eaten in a week.

Mina stood by the tracks and blew on her hands. Her eyes sparkled, and the tips of her ears were red, because, of course, she never wore a hat or scarf, not even on the coldest days of winter. The sun began to rise, and the day grew brighter, although the train from the south was nowhere in sight. Mina asked several of the soldiers when the train was due to arrive, but none of them seemed to know.

"I want to go home," I said. "I'm hungry, and I'm sure Mama has missed us by now and she's worried."

"Who cares?" Mina asked.

She hooked her arm tightly through mine so that I couldn't slip away. The tips of my fingers and my toes were numb before we finally heard the train whistle in the distance. Mina dragged me to the far end of the platform and squeezed my arm. The train approached slowly, and when it stopped, people hopped off in twos and threes. Mina and I walked up and down the cars, searching for Aaron, and at long last, she spied him shuffling down the steps of a car at the very front of the train. She let go of my arm and dashed toward him, screaming his name and waving her hands in the air. He ducked his head down when he saw her and pushed her gently away when she tried to run into his arms. He took her hand, and the two of them walked toward me. Although Mina leaned into him, he stood straight and stiff and smiled when he saw me and held out his other hand in greeting. We pushed our way through the crowd of people who had gathered on the platform to an empty space close to the small lean-to in the center.

"I knew Mama couldn't keep us apart," Mina said. "I love you."

Rabbi Aaron pursed his lips.

"What happened in Szereda?" I asked. "How is Galfalva? Have you seen our house?"

"It's madness," he said. "The world is mad."

"Are we losing the war?" Mina asked.

"Who can say? But our own soldiers are worse than the Romanians. They destroy everything. They took over my synagogue. Used the pews for firewood. Burned all of our candles. Desecrated the Torah." His mouth formed into a tight "O" of pain. "Nothing is left."

"Where are all the people in the congregation?" I asked.

"Gone or dead. A congregation of ghosts." He let go of Mina's hand. "So I decided to go, too. First to Budapest and after that, who knows?"

Mina's mouth dropped open, and she let go of his hand. "I thought you came here for me," she said. "I thought that was what you wanted to tell me."

He squinted at her, as if he hadn't understood a word she said. "How could I have come for you, when I don't know what to do with my own life, whether I even want to be a rabbi anymore? What good is God in a world where soldiers rip apart synagogues of their own people?"

"But you still love me, don't you?"

"Your mama was right. I'm a poor man with nothing to offer a girl like yourself." He patted her arm. "Yes, I still love you. Of course, I do. How could I not love you?"

"Then I don't care. I'm going with you."

He kissed her gently on the forehead and looked over her shoulder at a vision of his own future that was very different from our own. It had nothing to do with speaking English or sitting in the wonderful room I had dreamed of that morning. Mina cried and stamped her foot and pleaded with him to take her with him, but he said he had no money for her train fare and no idea how he would live, once he arrived in Budapest.

"So this was your big news," she said. "That you're a poor man and a ghost."

He wrapped his arms around her, nuzzling her hair, and she collapsed into him. The two of them stepped away from me and talked quietly, until the conductor announced that the train was about to leave. Mina hung onto the rabbi for as long as she could, and when he pushed her gently away and stumbled up the steps to his car without looking back, she cried and ran along the length of the platform, shouting good-bye to the empty windows of the train.

"He would have married me, if Mama hadn't changed his mind," she said, after the train was finally out of sight. "I'll pay her back for this. Just you wait and see."

She wouldn't talk to me on the road home and was so silent and sullen when we arrived back at the shed that Mama didn't try to ask where we had been or press me about it later. I think she knew, in the way a mother will without having to be told, what had happened.

As the winter wore on, Mina spent more and more hours after school with Sister Magdalena, yet had barely a word for Mama and not many more for me. Once I described to her my dream of the future, the two of us happy, full, warm inside a rich man's house. She pinched my arm and said never to talk to her about the future because she didn't have one. She said she only had a past, and it was gone forever, thanks to me and thanks to Mama.

GLASS HEART

We struggled through the winter months and that spring were especially hungry for news from home. We went to synagogue every Saturday anxiously in search of Mrs. Fischer, our next door neighbor from Galfalva, who always seemed to keep such careful track of everyone in our village. One Saturday, we swooped down on her with all of our questions, and she told us that the Daviches had settled for good in Budapest and that Mr. Davich had had a heart attack, that Domino was so unhappy living in Debrecen she stopped eating for a month and nearly died. Sam asked her about the fighting at home, and she said the Germans and the Hungarians defeated the Romanians, sent them packing into the hills. She didn't know whether the soldiers were still in Galfalva, but she thought the fighting would soon be over.

"For myself," she said. "I love it here. Malik has steady work, and we eat regularly. In fact, we're so happy we may stay on after the war."

"We won't," I said. "We're going home as soon as school is over. I wonder what our house looks like now?"

Sam asked after Mr. Fischer's gout, and he complained about his swollen knee. Afterwards, we walked home, each of us lost in thought.

The next few weeks were like a dream to me. My body was in Kisvarda, but my mind was in Galfalva, on the hill that led to our house, on Papa's blacksmith shop and the tavern, on Kati's rosebush, on the road that wound around in front of Mrs. Davich's house. I was more homesick than ever, now that I was certain I was going home soon. Even Sister Magdalena noticed how dreamy I was one day and stopped me in the hallway before prayers.

"Are you here with us or somewhere else?" she asked.

"I'm here, Sister," I said.

I blinked and took a long look up the hall. It was full of children whose names I knew, though none of them were friends. They came from rich homes and wore beautiful clothes that didn't have patches and that were bought only for them and not three or four of their brothers and sisters, as well.

One morning toward the end of the school year, when Mina seemed more irritable that usual, Sam decided to embarrass her. Just as Sister Magdalena signaled the children to begin the usual recitation of the "Hail Mary," Sam started to chant the Hebrew blessing on the Sabbath candles. Each time the chorus of children paused, he said a Hebrew phrase out loud. By the time he reached the end of the blessing, he was yelling at the top of his lungs.

"*Le-had-lik Nayr Shel Shabbos!*" he shouted.

Sister Magdalena stood frozen in front of the altar. Her arms stopped flapping, and her mouth was fixed in a hard line. The Son of God stared down at us with blank eyes. The other children grew quiet for a moment before giggling softly and whispering among themselves. Sister Magdalena clapped her hands, and the chapel was silent. Mina grabbed Sam's elbow and yanked him off the bench where we sat at the back of the chapel.

"*Hav-he-nu Sho-lom Ale-chem,*" Sam sang.

Mina dragged him backwards out the door, and I slipped from the bench and followed my brother and sister outside into the bright May morning.

"If you keep this up, Sister Magdalena won't take us back next year," Mina said.

"I don't care," Sam said. "I don't plan on becoming a nun. I don't want to say Catholic prayers, and I don't want to sit in the chapel and look at the picture of the Son of God, Sister Mina. I think you love Sister Magdalena more than you do Rabbi Aaron," Sam said. "And I think you love making Mama angry more than anything else in the whole wide world."

After prayers, Sister Magdalena scolded Sam in front of all the other children and told him he would have to wait in the hallway outside the chapel every morning for the rest of the week. She said she would have sent him home for good, if he weren't such an excellent student and if she didn't know what devout Jews we were. Sam stood in the hall, not the least bit unhappy at being banished from the morning prayers. None of us breathed a word to Mama about what had happened, and Sister Magdalena didn't say anything, either.

Early on the Sunday morning before the last week of school, it was raining hard outside. Kati was asleep, and Sam huddled in a corner reading a book about chemistry he had borrowed from the school library. Mina had slipped off while it was dark, and I knew Mama was worried about her, although she didn't say so. Mama and I sat at the table and busied ourselves shelling peas.

"I'm sorry I let her go, Mama," I said.

"That's all right," she said. "You can't watch her every minute. None of us can. She'll come back soon. She can't have gone far in this rain."

But I wasn't so sure, and I hoped Mina hadn't taken it in her head to go after Rabbi Aaron. I glanced up at the door, expecting to see my sister, not the ghostly presence who stood there. I gasped, and Mama and Sam looked up, too.

"Who is that?" Mama asked.

"Daniel?" I asked.

I jumped up and led him inside. Sam stared curiously at him, and Kati stirred under her blankets and began to cry. Mama went to pick her up, and Sam studied Daniel with his doctor's eyes.

"I've seen him around here before," Sam said. "Why can't he talk?"

"He was born that way," I said. "You can't fix him. No one can."

I took Daniel's hand in mine, and Mama held Kati in her arms and smiled at Daniel.

"The two of you look like you are old friends," she said. "Why don't you invite your friend to sit down at the table?"

I nodded toward the chair, and Daniel slid silently into it. I reached for an apple, polished it on my skirt, and gave it to him. He jammed it into his pocket.

"It's all right," Mama said. "You can eat it now, if you want."

He shook his head and sat stiffly on the edge of his chair, ready to fly away at the first sign of anger.

"What a sad case," Mama said.

"Don't talk about him like that," I said. "He can hear you."

Mama patted Daniel on the arm, and he hopped out of his chair, waving his hands in the air and gesturing toward the door. He covered his lips with his fingers and formed his hands in a circle. I heard him say Mina's name inside my head.

"Where is she?" I asked.

He pointed toward the road in front of the Kaufman's house and wagged his finger.

"What is wrong with him?" Mama asked.

"Nothing," I said. "He's trying to tell us he saw Mina walking on the road."

"How do you know that?" Sam asked.

"I just do."

"Is she in danger?" Mama asked.

"I don't think so."

Daniel bolted out the door and disappeared into the woods. Mama left Sam in charge of Kati, and the two of us set out on that wet, rainy morning to find Mina. Mud stuck to our shoes so that it was hard for us to lift our feet at all. We stopped by the side of the road, and I rubbed my shoes on the grass and ran a stick along the soles.

"Does Mina love Sister Magdalena more than she loves us?" I asked. I dropped the stick and stood up straight.

"It seems that way sometimes, doesn't it?" she asked.

"But why? We're her family."

"Your sister is a young woman now, and when you are her age, you may find people you want to be with more than your sisters and brother and me."

"No, I won't."

"That's a generous thought, but why don't you wait and see? It's the way of the world. Children grow up and leave their parents behind."

"I won't ever leave you. Ever."

"Oh, my dear Serene, I won't hold you to your promise."

As we rounded the corner by the school yard, we saw Sister Magdalena and Mina standing by the front door of the church. The sister's hand rested on Mina's shoulder.

"Excuse me, Sister," Mama said from the far end of the yard. "Mina left home early this morning without a word. We have been worried sick about her."

"I'm sorry," Sister Magdalena said. "I had no idea."

"We need her at home now."

Mina looked at the Sister. "Do I have to go with them?" she asked.

"Mina!" Mama said.

Mina stared at her, and Mama took a few steps forward until she was right in front of Sister Magdalena.

"You've taken my children into your school, and you have only asked for butter and a few eggs in return," she said. "I thank you for that, but you promised you wouldn't try to change them or turn them against their religion."

"This has nothing to do with religion," Sister Magdalena said. "Your daughter is troubled, Mrs. Spirer. You should talk to her."

"I have tried. Believe me, I have. But what do you do with a child who doesn't want to talk and doesn't want to listen?"

Mina looked at Sister Magdalena for a long moment. My sister wouldn't take the hand Mama offered her and marched ahead of us without speaking. Mama thanked Sister Magdalena, and the two of us turned to follow my sister home.

On the last day of school that year, Mama sent me to Mrs. Rosen's house for extra tea and sugar.

"The Romanians are gone, and the fighting is over," I said. "So we're going home."

"Well, my dear," she said. "I'd be patient, if I were you. These things take time."

"But I'll die if I have to stay here another year."

I turned in a slow circle in front of her and fell to the floor. I rolled onto my back and crossed my arms over my chest and stopped breathing. Mrs. Rosen clapped her hands, pulled me up, and sat me down at the table.

"You are quite an actress, too," she said. She poured me a glass of lemonade. "What a talent. I hear you had a visit from your ghost not long ago. Since then, Mrs. Kaufman keeps him under lock and key. Apparently you're a bad influence."

"How? I hardly ever see him."

"But you know how to talk to him, your mama says. I would be careful, if I were you. It's best not to get in that old woman's way. You don't want to lose your happy home."

"It's not my home, and it's not happy, either."

"Well, it's better than living on the road."

On my way back to our shed, I stopped by the edge of the woods in the yard to rest for a moment. I set down the tins of sugar and tea Mrs. Rosen had given me. It was a hot, muggy afternoon, and the smell of the grass made me lonely. Daniel glided into the yard in front of me and glanced quickly toward Mrs. Kaufman's house, before he took my hand and led me into the woods. We stopped at a clearing and sat together on an old stump.

"I miss you," I said.

He nodded.

"I'm going home soon," I said.

"Why?" his voice asked in my ear.

"Because the fighting is over, and I want to see my aunt. Maybe I'll find Papa, too."

"I thought he was dead."

I slid to the ground and crossed my arms over my chest and held my breath, like I did for Mrs. Rosen.

"No," I said. "I'm the one who is dead."

Daniel laughed silently and shuffled through the leaves behind me. Pretty soon he was dropping twigs all over my arms and legs and yellow wildflowers that grew deep in the woods away from the sunlight. Branches swirled above me in a brown and green blur. After a moment or two, I stood up slowly and brushed the leaves and flowers off my dress. The two of us walked to the edge of the woods.

"Meet me right here tomorrow," I said. "I have a gift for you."

He his eyes opened wide with pleasure, and he nodded before vanishing into the trees.

The truth was I had nothing to give to Daniel, who was much poorer than we were, though his grandmother was a rich woman. I thought about taking the *mezuzah* off the door, but Mama would never let me do that, not even for Daniel. That evening, after I hung my dress on a hook and put on my nightgown, I decided the only thing I had to give him was the last piece of my glass heart. I hoped he might be able to coax more wishes from it than I could and fell asleep, certain I had made the right choice for Daniel.

The next afternoon, as I sat on the stump, he slipped behind me and put his hands over my eyes.

"Here!" I said, brushing his hands away.

I held the piece of glass out to him. My voice sounded harsh, though I knew I was just excited and afraid Daniel might not like my gift. I saw then that Daniel was much smarter than everyone else for not talking, for not letting others misunderstand him. I knew how often words got me into trouble by not really saying what I meant. Daniel took the piece of glass carefully from me, as if he were afraid he might drop it, and hugged it to his chest.

"It's magic," I said. "You can make wishes on it. I used it to make chickens fall asleep, and once I even gave my teacher at home a rash with it."

He sighed.

"It was beautiful once, before it was broken," I said.

He squeezed the glass in his palm and slipped it into his pants pocket. He took my hand gently in his and said "thank you" with his eyes. We sat together for a while, but he grew restless and afraid his grandmother might miss him. He stood up and bolted into the woods. I looked for him for several days afterwards, until I went to Mrs. Rosen's house and she told me that Mrs. Kaufman had sent him to Kallo, a city far to the north where he had relatives.

"That old lady just wanted to get him off her hands for a little while," Mrs. Rosen said. "Poor child. No one wants a boy who's not right in the head."

"But he is right in the head," I said. "I know he is."

"I'm sure you do, my dear Serene. You know quite a lot for a girl your age."

She busied herself at the stove and handed me a plate of sliced apples. I ate all but one of them without another word.

One morning, not long after Mrs. Kaufman sent Daniel away, I saw him running into the woods. I chased after him, calling his name, but he didn't seem to hear me. I went into the woods after him and wound my way around the trees until I came to the stump where Daniel and I last sat together and the small clearing where I had played at being dead. For a moment, I thought he was lying on the ground, his arms crossed over his chest, a faint smile on his lips, my glass heart stuck between his fingers. But as I drew closer, Daniel transformed himself into a pile of dried leaves and flowers.

"I know you're here," I said.

The woods were silent, except for the shrieking of crows high in the air.

That afternoon and for the next two days, the Kaufman's house was dark and empty. Not even the maid appeared at the back door to throw out the dirty dishwater. On the third day, Mrs. Rosen stopped by to tell us about the terrible rumor that had circulated around town. Daniel was traveling on the train to Kallo with his grandfather when he jumped out the window and died as he fell onto the tracks.

"The passengers on the train said there was a terrible argument between them," Mrs. Rosen said.

"How is that possible?" Mama asked. "The poor soul couldn't even talk."

I was numb and slipped out of the house, before Mrs. Rosen had a chance to finish her story. I went into the woods, found my way to the stump, and sat there for a long time, Daniel's quiet presence beside me. Finally, I started to cry, and he whispered in my ear that I shouldn't be sad because he was at peace.

I returned to that clearing in the woods many times that summer, feeling sad, but more often angry and hurt. I began to wonder whether I should ever have given Daniel such a valuable gift, if all he was going to do was die. Besides, I needed it now more than ever: Mama never talked about going back to Galfalva and made plans for another year in Kisvarda; Mina sneaked off most mornings to see Sister Magdalena, even though school was not in session; Sam kept to himself and read his chemistry books all summer long; worst of all, Papa never once showed his face.

My mind was full of all kinds of dreams and wishes that were lost now that Daniel was gone and had taken the last piece of my glass heart away with him forever.

THE BOOK OF LIFE

So I began the second year of my exile. I went to school as I was supposed to and sat silently through morning prayers. Sam did, too, though he often poked me in the arm or made a face. I helped Mama with all her chores, kept a careful eye on Mina, and went to Mrs. Rosen's house each week to collect eggs for Mama, eat cookies, and swap stories about people in the neighborhood. I even swept the back porch of Mrs. Kaufman's house every Sunday, though she was likely to sneak up behind me, rap me painfully on the head with her knuckles, and scold me for being lazy.

By the time *Rosh Hashanah* came around, I knew Mrs. Rosen was right. I would have to be patient and hope that, although the fighting in Galfalva was said to be over, there was a good reason why we had to remain where we were. It wasn't easy, but I tried not to ask Mama every day when we could go home or complain about the poor way we lived.

Mama always told us about a special book on *Rosh Hashanah* eve, and what she said always frightened me, because, according to her, it was my job to pray for the welfare of all the Jews, even though I was just a child.

"God will be watching you every minute for the next ten days, between now and *Yom Kippur*, when you atone for all your sins," she said. "He'll be deciding whether to put your name in the Book of Life for the next year. So you had better behave yourselves, or He may leave you out."

We all knew what that meant.

"Nonsense," Mina said.

But I noticed she didn't complain too loudly about missing school during the holidays or sneak out to visit Sister Magdalena. She even helped Mama wash the dishes the morning before services and smiled at her once or twice. I was on my best behavior, too. I combed Kati's hair gently and put a ribbon in it for synagogue. I gave Sam a glass of water and an extra piece of bread for breakfast, though I didn't think ten days would be enough to make up for a whole year.

On the first day of *Rosh Hashanah*, I sat peacefully at Mama's side during services while the rabbi read from the Torah. I knew just enough Hebrew to follow what he was saying. The synagogue was beautiful, and I was full of hope for the coming year, in spite of all my fears for my family and the loss of Daniel.

"There is one God, and only One," the rabbi said. "All of His creatures should do His will with a perfect heart."

He blew the *shofar*, a ram's horn that was supposed to remind us of the Jews being exiled from Egypt into the desert. Then he began to speak about the Book of Life.

"Blessing, peace, and good sustenance may we be remembered and inscribed before Thee, we and all Thy people in the house of Israel, for a happy life," he said.

As I listened to him, I wondered how I had been able to get my name written into the Book of Life for the last nine years, since I wasn't a well-behaved child and had more than my share of bad thoughts. I was certain I would have to make an extra effort if I didn't want to be left out this year, considering all the secrets I kept, the fear I had that Mrs. Kaufman sent Daniel away because of me. I often thought about our *mezuzah* and the words of Rabbi Akiva it contained. I knew I was too willful and selfish, and I knew I should accept God and the ways of my family and Mrs. Kaufman without worrying so much or trying to change things. As the service ended, I called upon Rabbi Akiva to teach me how to be a good daughter and a good sister. I begged him show me how to obey God.

"Please, can you help me, Rabbi?" I whispered.

"Yes," he replied. "But you have to be quiet and do what I tell you and not ask questions or argue. Do you promise to do that?"

"I promise."

For the next ten days, I went everywhere with Rabbi Akiva watching over me. I awoke on the second morning of *Rosh Hashanah*, and he was heavy on my shoulder.

"Remember to feed your baby sister some of your mush for breakfast," he said.

"Why?" I asked. "She never eats it. She just likes the idea of taking something from my plate."

"If you have to ask why, we have nothing more to talk about, and I will be on my way."

"Don't go, Rabbi. I'll give her some."

After Mama put mush in a bowl for me, I spooned half of it into another dish and pushed it in front of Kati. Mama looked up at the ceiling and nodded a grateful thank you to God.

A couple of days later, on the way to school, Sam turned off the road and started running across a field.

"Stop him," Rabbi Akiva said.

"How?" I said.

"Don't ask how. Just stop him."

"But he never listens to me."

"That is something that must change. Provide him with a good example, and he will follow."

I sighed, thinking Rabbi Akiva didn't really know Sam, and ran across the empty field after him.

"Stop," I said.

Sam kept right on running.

"You have to come back," I said.

"You can't make me," Sam shouted over his shoulder.

"Don't you want your name in the Book?"

Sam threw back his head and laughed. "You and your book. You go on to school like a good baby. Don't worry about me."

As I walked back across the field, I wondered why Sam had chosen this day to stay away from school. I thought perhaps Rabbi Akiva was testing me.

"You will have to do much better than that, young lady," he said.

During prayers that morning, I was sure Sister Magdalena saw the rabbi perched beside me, wearing his *yarmulke* and *tallis*, with its white fringes and the Star of David embroidered on both of its ends. She opened her arms wide so that she looked like a bat. I watched her lips rise and fall over the words of a prayer, until my body went limp and I forgot that I was a Jewish child in a Catholic church with a famous rabbi sitting next to me, judging my every word and deed.

"Hail Mary," I said.

"What did you say?" Rabbi Akiva asked.

"I'm sorry." I put my fingers over my mouth. "Sister Magdalena is evil. She has tried to turn us all into Catholics ever since we started school. She put a spell on me."

"God does not believe in spells. He believes in discipline and self-control."

"Please. I don't want to die."

"We will have to see about that."

I walked to and from school with Mina every day during the time between *Rosh Hashanah* and *Yom Kippur*, and once she got angry at me and told me how much she hated Mama. I stepped on her foot to make her be quiet, afraid Rabbi Akiva had overheard her remark.

"Ouch," she said. "Watch where you're going."

"Then don't talk about Mama that way," I said. "Do you want your name to be left out of the Book of Life?"

"You don't really believe that story, do you? I don't, and I'll say what I want to about Mama. I might even recite the 'Hail Mary,' if I feel like it."

On *Yom Kippur* eve, before the meal that began our twenty-four hour fast of atonement, I walked to the edge of the woods in the yard. For the first time since Daniel's death, I saw Mrs. Kaufman standing on the back porch, her arms crossed tightly over her chest. I waved politely to her and approached her slowly.

"I'm sorry," I said.

She nodded slightly and turned to go inside.

"Please," I said. "I miss him, too."

She closed the door in my face.

"She is a very unhappy woman who gave away her future because of you," Rabbi Akiva said. "You must learn to mind your own business from now on."

"Yes, Rabbi," I said.

"Do you remember the time you fell down in the woods and pretended to be dead for your mute friend?"

"He wasn't mute." I was crying hard.

"Answer the question."

"I remember."

"Do you want to play dead again today?"

"No." I trembled and wiped away my tears with my knuckle. "Death isn't a game."

"Precisely."

That night, Mama prepared a wonderful meal of cooked carrots and turnips floating in a rich broth and baked chicken, but I had trouble eating. I was afraid it would be my last meal, and I knew how badly I had let Daniel down, how miserably I had failed in Rabbi Akiva's eyes.

"You look pale," Mama said. "Are you sick?"

"No, I'm fine," I said. "I'm not hungry right now."

"That's not like you at all. Besides, you have to have something. You won't be able to eat all day tomorrow. *Yom Kippur* is the most holy day of the Jewish year. How can you pray for forgiveness with a full heart when your stomach is so completely empty? You must eat."

"Listen to your mother," Rabbi Akiva said.

So I finished my broth and tore off a little piece of chicken. That set Mama's mind at ease.

"There," she said, as we cleared the last of the dishes from the table. "Now you are ready to atone for all your sins."

On *Yom Kippur* morning, my stomach growled for breakfast. I went to the well to wash my face, being careful not to swallow any water as I had done in past years, and I was proud of myself for not giving in to my thirst. I hoped Rabbi Akiva was watching.

I felt faint all through the service and nearly fell asleep, letting the rabbi's voice wash over my mind. I wasn't paying much attention until I heard him say something about inscribing the names of the congregation into the Book of Life. I sat straight up and leaned over to Mama.

"Are we all right?" I whispered.

"Shh, be quiet," Mama said.

"But did God put our names in His Book? Will we live for another year?"

"I expect he did. So hush."

I was beyond being hungry and secretly glad to bid good-bye to Rabbi Akiva, now that I was safe for another year. I was light-headed and closed my eyes, offering a silent thank you to the rabbi for his guidance.

"Who is this Akiva?" Papa whispered in my ear.

Papa, I thought. Where have you been?

Suddenly, he filled my head with pictures of big cities and wagons that ran without horses, like the ones I read about in a book at school.

"I'm waiting for you," Papa said. "Join me here."

"I will," I said.

"For the last time, Serene," Mama said. "Be still. You don't want God to erase your name from the Book, do you?"

"No, Mama," I said.

The rabbi blew the *shofar* and took the ram's horn from his lips and set it carefully on the pulpit. He bowed his head to let us know the service was over.

"Next year in Jerusalem," he said.

"Next year in Jerusalem," we repeated after him.

Israel, the homeland of the Jews, where God lived closer to His Chosen People than He did here in Hungary. I wondered if that was the new world, the place where Papa lived now and where I was to meet him again.

Part Three
THE NEW WORLD, 1918-1919

HOME TRUTHS

The war in our part of the world was over, and we were weary of being refugees and made our plans to go back home. Mama said she was sick of living off other people's charity and looked forward to re opening Papa's tavern, once we returned to Galfalva. I bade a tearful farewell to Mrs. Rosen, who assured me her life wouldn't be nearly as interesting without me around to entertain her. Even Mina seemed glad to leave, though she stayed a long time after school on the last day before winter break to speak to Sister Magdalena. Lately, the Sister had begun to encourage Mina to take up teaching as her natural calling in life. I thought Mina had no intention of becoming a teacher and simply wanted to go home because she still secretly held out the hope of seeing Rabbi Aaron again. As far as I knew, she hadn't heard from him since that morning at the train station, but that wasn't enough to stop her.

On the first day of 1918, with our few meager possessions in hand—I had barely enough to fill half a pillowcase—we closed the door for the last time on Mrs. Kaufman's shed. None of us regretted turning our backs on that mournful place. We said a brief good-bye to Mrs. Kaufman, who barely nodded when Mama thanked her for putting a roof over our heads for the last year and a half and walked quickly to the train station in Kisvarda.

We boarded the iron snake heading south and began our journey home, except it wasn't really home anymore since it belonged now to the Romanians. Still, our family was there, and Mama had written to Grandma to tell her we were coming back. I was sick again on the train, as I would be for the rest of my life on any vehicle that went faster than forty kilometers an hour. I slept on the floor most of the way, curled into a tight ball to keep from throwing up my breakfast, until Mina nudged me with her foot and told me we had arrived. I sat up and let a wave of dizziness pass before I lifted myself off the floor and looked out the window. I couldn't see much. Everything was covered with snow. I felt suddenly better and jumped up, standing impatiently in the aisle as the people ahead of me filed off the train.

When it came my turn to leave, I bounced off the last step and threw down my pillowcase. I ran to the side of the track and fell to the ground and rolled around in the snow. Our snow. Galfalva snow. Sam fell down beside me and rubbed his cold hand on my cheek.

"Ouch! That's freezing," I said.

"Look at those two," Mama said, laughing. "Aren't they crazy?"

Kati bent down and ran her fingers through the snow, and Mina slapped her arms with her gloves to keep out the cold. Sam and I threw snow in each other's faces and sat up, and Mama said it was time to go. I checked to be sure the *mezuzah* was still hanging around my neck and brushed off my coat. I let Mama pull me to my feet. The train belched large white clouds of steam that melted quickly in the air, and it began gliding along the tracks. I hopped up and down, waved good-bye to it, and decided then and there never to leave Galfalva again.

I picked up my pillowcase, and we began the long walk home. We passed by our old school house. It looked the same, but smaller somehow and dark and deserted. Several of the front windows were broken and part of the roof had caved in. I can't say I was entirely unhappy about that, since I wasn't excited about returning to Miss Kovacz. We turned toward the synagogue, and it was dark too, which was strange because it was Friday afternoon and the rabbi should have been inside preparing for Sabbath services. Then I saw that the heavy swinging doors leading into the sanctuary were gone and that someone had

chopped down the beautiful old oak tree in front of the building. All
that remained was a splintered stump. The statue of Franz Josef was
still standing in the village square, but one of its eyes had been poked
out, and its nose was chipped. A hand was missing, as well as most of
its right foot. The brewery where Mama used to buy beer for the tavern
was all boarded up, except for the front door which hung on one hinge.
The whole building leaned to one side. The wooden stalls in the out-
door market next to the brewery had been chopped to bits, and only a
few sorry piles of sticks were left. The front of the general store across
the street had caved in, and sharp pieces of wood stuck out of the rubble
like broken bones.

"My God," Mama whispered. "It looks like a ghost town." She
hugged Kati tightly to her body.

"Did the Romanians do this?" I asked.

She shook her head. We huddled together and walked toward home
in stunned silence. Only Sam seemed to be enjoying himself, racing
back and forth between the empty buildings and calling excitedly to
Mama.

We formed ourselves into a single line behind Mama and climbed
the hill to our house. I followed Mina and concentrated on fitting my
feet into the prints she left behind. Finally, we rounded the last corner.

I stopped walking, glanced up at the empty wreck that used to be
our home, and screamed. The wood shutters had been torn off all our
windows, and one of the posts on the verandah had been sawed in two
so that it tilted sideways and made the house look like a sinking boat. A
few of the window panes were broken, and the front door had a huge
gash in it where someone had hit it with an ax. Papa's blacksmith's
shop had collapsed on top of the shed where Mama used to bake bread
and honey cake.

The inside was even worse. We found a few sticks of wood that
looked as though they had once belonged to our chairs. The stove was
covered with dirt, and straw from our mattresses was scattered all over
the floor. Our dishes and silverware were gone, and all that was left of

our cupboard were a few broken shelves. I found a couple of rags on the floor with two or three embroidered threads, and I was sure these were all that remained of Mama's tablecloths and napkins. Mama's candlesticks had disappeared, and so had our clothes.

Mama pushed Kati behind her and bent down to pick up a piece of wood. She turned it around in her hand, almost as if she didn't recognize what it was.

"What will we do?" I asked.

"Build a fire for now and stay warm tonight," Mama said. Her eyes darted from one end of the room to the other, and she pulled some blankets from beneath a pile of dirt in a corner and shook them out. "Help me with these."

After we spread the blankets on the floor, Sam and I went outside to search for more wood. There were a few small branches in the yard, and we pulled at a loose board off the side of Papa's blacksmith's shop that clung stubbornly in place. We pulled harder, and when it came off, it knocked us to the ground. Mama started a fire in the stove from the wood we found, and I sat in a corner with my knees drawn all the way up to my chest, trying to get comfortable and not think too hard about what had happened to my beloved home.

We piled our belongings in the middle of the room and huddled together under the blankets on the floor in order to stay warm.

I fell asleep hungry, yearning for a big breakfast the next morning, and dreamed that our kitchen table was the way it used to be, clean and covered with plates of fruit and loaves of bread and bowls of steaming chicken broth. When I woke up and looked over at the table, it was uneven and tilted to one side, and there was no food on it. The room was cold, and the fire in our stove was almost out. Sunlight crept through our mud-caked windows. It was Saturday, and since it was the Sabbath and we weren't supposed to work, I didn't know how we would be able to find anything to eat. I slipped from beneath the blankets and put my coat on over the dress I had slept in the night before. I went outside to pull another board off Papa's blacksmith shop for our fire. I wrapped my arms around a loose board and tugged at it, but it didn't budge. As I sat down in the snow to rest for a minute, I heard wagon wheels crunch in the snow behind me, and a familiar stooped figure leaned over one side and called out my name.

"Tibor!" I shouted.

I ran to him and offered him my hand to help him get down. He hugged me.

"I thought I might find you here," he said. "Your aunt made me come every day, since my mother-in-law received your mama's letter." He blew on his hands and rubbed his cheeks. "It's much too cold out here for me. You know, I'm the warm weather man. Let's go inside."

Mama and Mina and Kati were busy folding the blankets, and Sam stirred the cold ashes in the stove. Tibor and I walked hand-in-hand through the door.

"Why, who could this be?" Mama asked.

"Tibor," I replied. "Aunt Gizella's husband."

"Of course. Serene has told us so much about you."

"My ears are stinging. All of it good, I hope."

"Naturally." She bowed her head and brushed the dust off her collar. "Come in. I'm sorry everything is in such a terrible state."

Tibor stepped forward and guided Mama gently to the table. She sat down on the only chair that was left, rested her head on her arms, and seemed to cry for a moment. Then she wiped her face with the back of her hand.

"As you can see, we have no home," she said. "I don't know what I'm going to do with my children. How will I feed them?"

Tibor leaned over her and patted her gently on the arm. "You can't stay here," he said. "It's too cold, and besides, everyone in Galfalva has gone elsewhere. I don't think many people will be coming back."

"Why should they? Nothing is left."

"That settles it, then. You children roll everything up in these blankets. You're coming home with me."

"We can't do that."

"Why not? We're family."

Mama smiled weakly at him.

We stuffed our belongings into Tibor's wagon, and Sam and Mina and I sat in the back, while Mama and Kati sat in front. We bounced our way toward Marosvasarhely, where Tibor said there hadn't been any fighting and everything was much the same as when we left. He tried to cheer Mama up by telling her how Grandma's cow had gotten stuck inside the house for almost three days during a snowstorm the week before and made a complete mess of things. There was so much snow that they couldn't open the front door.

"Did the cow study the Talmud with Grandpa?" I asked.

"No doubt," Tibor said.

It started to snow, and Mina and Sam and I huddled closer together under one of our blankets. Tibor covered Mama and Kati with the other one.

"Are you all right back there?" he asked.

"Yes," I said. My teeth were chattering.

Tibor leaned toward Mama. "Can you believe it? This land doesn't belong to us anymore. I never thought I'd live to see the day I'd call myself a Romanian. Never. You know, nothing has been the same since Franz Josef died two years ago."

"Yes, I remember it just like it was yesterday," Mama said. "I felt as if I had lost one of my own. Many people all over the country said the *Kaddish* for him in synagogue. He was always so kind to the Jews."

"He actually offered to open one of his palaces to those of us who lost our homes."

"That doesn't surprise me. Such a wonderful man. No one will ever take his place."

"If he were still alive, we'd have won the war."

"We would have. I'm sure of it."

When we arrived at Aunt Gizella's, Tibor helped us out of the wagon and sent everyone inside but me. The two of us stood beneath the gateway he had built for his first wife and told me about years ago. It was painted white and full of beautifully carved birds and fish. He guided me to one corner of the gate and bent down to brush aside the snow. There in the hard ground was the largest footprint I had ever seen in my life, left there by the Romanian who had tried to steal Tibor's chickens. I stepped into it, and both my feet fit inside. I crossed my arms over my chest and turned around and around in a circle, until a shock went through my entire body and I hopped back out. Tibor began rubbing his bad leg, and I was sure the man who owned the footprint had come back at last to reclaim it.

Aunt Gizella and Tibor lived in a house with five rooms, which was much bigger than we were used to, though Mina and Kati and I had to sleep on blankets in a room with Anna, who seemed less ill-tempered than in the past. Tibor said that was due in large measure to my aunt's patience. His older daughter, Ruth, had married, and, of course, Aunt Gizella had her twin boys. Mama said she hated to make everyone change beds, and she thought it wasn't right for us to take charity, even from our family, when she had no hope of ever repaying the debt. Mama, Aunt Gizella, and Tibor discussed whether we should stay indefinitely, but Mama insisted we had to find a place of our own and a business to support ourselves. Aunt Gizella reminded Mama constantly that she was glad for the company, even though she ran out of chairs at the kitchen table and we had to take turns eating.

After we had been at Aunt Gizella's for a week, Mama rose early and went to town to look for a place of our own. She left me and my sisters and brother at home with Aunt Gizella. Mina sat at the kitchen table, staring down at her plate. I was used to her silences by now and went on eating a piece of apple without paying much attention to her. Aunt Gizella took the chair next to Mina and rested her hand on top of my sister's.

"What has happened to you, my child?" she asked. "You used to be so full of life. Are you ill?"

Mina shrugged.

"She's lovesick," I said. "But I don't think the twins can catch it."

"I see," Aunt Gizella said, taking a deep breath.

"Shut up, Serene," Mina said.

"Who exactly are you in love with?"

"No one."

"In Kisvarda, she was in love with a nun," I said. "But that was because Rabbi Aaron ran away."

Mina reached over and bumped my elbow off the table.

"A rabbi," Aunt Gizella said. "That's very interesting. I should think your mama would have been delighted."

"Mama," I said. "Not hardly. She chased him away because she said he didn't have enough money."

"What is this rabbi's name?"

Mina sighed angrily, and Aunt Gizella leaned forward and stroked my sister's cheek gently. To my surprise, Mina didn't push her hand away.

"His name is Aaron Lebov," Mina said. "We met him one day about four years ago at a funeral in Szereda where he was the rabbi. He used to visit us at home in the summers."

"Lebov?" Aunt Gizella asked. "That name is familiar." Her face turned pale. "Ah, yes. I've heard of him."

"You have?"

"Isn't he the one who moved to Budapest during the war?"

"The Hungarian army destroyed his synagogue."

"That may be something of an exaggeration. The story circulating around here was that two soldiers had too much to drink one night and broke one of the stained glass windows."

"That can't be true."

"No matter, my dear." Aunt Gizella stood up and occupied herself clearing the dishes from the table.

"He's not dead, is he?" I asked.

"I never meant to give you that impression," Aunt Gizella said. She glanced up quickly from the dishes she was washing. "Nothing so terrible as that. Serene, your imagination is much too active for your own good."

"What is it, then?" Mina asked. She rose to stand beside Aunt Gizella, and although my sister was just past her sixteenth birthday, she was already several inches taller than my aunt. "Is he hurt?"

"No." Aunt Gizella set a dish slowly down on top of the counter and wiped the edges with a towel. "Are you absolutely certain you want to know?"

"Yes. I'm not a child anymore. Tell me."

My aunt folded the towel in her hand, measuring her words carefully. "It seems your rabbi is married."

"What?"

"He found himself a wife in Budapest and came back to Szereda a couple of months ago."

"But how can he be married to someone else? He loves me."

"I'm sure he does, Mina, but in this world, in these hard times, marriages aren't always built on love. Sometimes money is more important."

"What are you saying? That his wife is rich? Who told you?"

"Mama. It seems your rabbi and his wife stopped by her store on their way back to Szereda. Mama hears lots of gossip in her store, and that's how we found out he left in the first place."

"I don't believe you."

"Suit yourself."

Mina glared at my aunt. "Mama made you tell me that story." She picked up the towel Aunt Gizella had just folded and flung it at the wall. "He doesn't love her. I know he doesn't."

She grabbed her coat from a hook on the wall, but my aunt blocked her way and guided Mina gently back to the table.

"Take your time," Aunt Gizella said. "Don't do anything rash. These things have a way of healing themselves. Trust me."

"Yes," I said. "Listen to her, Mina. She knows what she's talking about."

"Hush, Serene."

I woke early the next morning, but Mina wasn't under the covers beside me. Her coat and gloves were missing from the hook in the kitchen, as well. I went outside to look for her, but all I found were a pair of footprints that wound under Tibor's gateway and down the road toward Szereda. I ran back inside the house to wake everyone.

"Mina's gone," I shouted in the hallway.

My aunt and Tibor stumbled out of bed, and one of the twins began to cry. Mama shuffled out of the room where she had been sleeping, with Kati trailing close behind. Sam poked his head out a door at the far end of the hall.

"You have to go after her," I said to Tibor.

"Where is she?" Mama asked.

"On her way to Szereda," I said.

Aunt Gizella turned pale.

"Is that what she told you?" Mama asked.

"She didn't say a word to me," I said.

"Then how do you know?"

"It's my fault," Aunt Gizella said. "I should have been more careful when I talked to her yesterday about the rabbi. Girls like Mina never want to hear that the men they think they love so wholeheartedly don't love them back and care too much about worldly goods. It's a rare young woman who is lucky or unlucky enough to share her life with the first man to capture her heart."

Tibor grimaced.

"Don't worry," she said to Tibor. "I have no complaints about the way my life has turned out. Now, let's get dressed and go find my niece."

Tibor set out alone in his wagon, over Mama's objections. She wanted to go with him, but Aunt Gizella talked her out of it.

"Mina will be upset enough as it is," she said. "Best to let Tibor take care of matters. She doesn't know him, and it may be easier for her to admit defeat to him and let him bring her home without a fight."

The morning melted slowly into the afternoon, with no sign of Tibor or Mina. Mama paced up and down the kitchen, glancing out the window every minute or two.

Once when Aunt Gizella was able to coax her to the table with a cup of tea and honey, Mama said, "This is my fault. I should have let her go with him and starve."

"It does no good to worry about the past," Aunt Gizella said. "How could you have know she would take him so to heart?"

"It's my business to know. She's my child."

"Yes, she is, and you did the best you could for her. None of us is perfect. None of us has all the right answers. Perfection belongs only to God, so don't trouble yourself with regrets over choices you might have made."

Just as the sun started to go down and the sky grew dark, Tibor drove his wagon under the gateway in front of his house with Mina sitting beside him. We ran to the door, and when my sister came inside, I threw my arms around her and hugged her. She didn't resist.

"What happened?" I asked.

"Your sister is tired," Tibor said. "She has had a long day, and she needs to rest."

Mina allowed Tibor to lead her down the hall to the room she and I shared. He shut the door behind her and motioned us to be quiet. We went into the kitchen while Aunt Gizella warmed some soup for our dinner and Mama set out the dishes.

"Rosa," Tibor said. "Your Mina is fine. Maybe a little worse for wear, but we all have to learn the lessons life teaches us sometime."

"Did she see him?" Mama asked.

"I gather she did."

"Good. Perhaps that will get him out of her system."

"Who can say? I found her sitting on the front steps of the synagogue."

"How was she?"

"Quite composed, actually."

"Hmm. That's surprising."

We ate dinner and tried to talk of other things. After we were finished, I asked Mama if I could take some soup to Mina. Aunt Gizella agreed that that would be a good idea, so I carried a steaming bowl down the long hallway to our room and pushed open the door with my shoulder.

"Mina?" I asked. "Are you awake?"

"Yes," she said.

"Would you like something to eat?"

I set the bowl down next to her and lit a candle. She sat up slowly under the covers and brushed her hair out of her eyes. I knelt beside her.

"Are you all right?" I asked.

She smiled a tight smile. "I made him squirm," she said. "I found out where he lived and paid him a little visit."

"You didn't! Did you meet his wife?"

"I most certainly did. She's blonde and fat, and didn't she wonder what I was doing there? Aaron turned white as a sheet when he saw me and tried to keep me from coming inside, with his wife breathing down his neck and yelling, 'Who is that? Who is that?'"

"What did you do?"

"I yelled back that he was mine and that she'd better watch her step."

"You didn't really mean that."

She shrugged. "Aaron slammed the door in my face. I kept banging on it until he came back outside by himself." She reached over and touched my arm. "Can you believe it? He told me he still loved me."

"No!"

"I laughed in his face, and that was when his fat old wife crept up behind him. He has a lot of explaining to do, thanks to me."

"You shouldn't have run off like that and worried Mama." I tapped my chin. "Still, good for you."

"Good for me?"

"Yes. Now you can forget about him."

"I can?" Tears streamed down her cheeks, and she coughed and tried to swallow a spoonful of my aunt's soup.

TICKETS

Mama enrolled us in my old school in Marosvasarhely and rented two rooms for us in town. For a little over a year, we lived in the big back room, which only had one window and a high ceiling and opened onto an alley that ran to the center of town. Mama turned the front room into a tavern with three small tables and a tiny bar. After more friendly arguments, she accepted a loan from Tibor to pay for our first two weeks' rent and to buy beer and cognac for the tavern. The most wonderful thing about living where we did was the smell of cooking meat that always filled the air. Across the street was a market where people watched a man who roasted pigs over a fire in a large hole in the ground at all hours of the day and night. I was ashamed that the scent of this forbidden food made my stomach growl, although I was hungry the entire time we lived in those rooms.

One cold rainy afternoon in early February, 1919, right before supper, Aunt Gizella and Tibor came into the tavern. It was usually deserted that time of day, and the truth was we didn't have many patrons in the evenings either. Mama said that was because people were unhappy over losing the war and being turned into Romanians, and they didn't want to come to the tavern and share their misery with their friends. My aunt and Tibor were both dressed in black and looked worried.

"My God," Mama said. "Someone has died." She rushed over to Aunt Gizella and put her arm around my aunt's shoulder.

"No, my dear Rosa," Aunt Gizella said. "Why do you always expect the worst?" She dug a thick envelope out of her pocket. "It was mailed to Mama's, with the instruction to forward it to you. It comes all the way from America." She pressed it to her chest for a moment before she held it out to Mama.

"Shumi."

Mama took the envelope and collapsed into a chair, turning the envelope around and around in her fingers before finally tearing it open. She shook it hard, and tickets and paper money fluttered onto the table. Mama blew into the envelope and reached inside and pulled out a letter. Papa's ghost slid out after it. He drifted into the room and sat across from Mama, his elbow on the table and his chin resting in the palm of his hand. This was the first time I really saw him since I left Galfalva for Grandma's house.

I could almost hear the sound of Mama's breathing as she read the letter. She dropped it on the table.

"A voice from the grave," she said.

"What do you mean?" Aunt Gizella said.

"Only that it's been so long since I've heard from him. I was afraid he was dead."

"What does he say?"

"He's sent us boat tickets to America and money for train fare to get to the boat." Mama picked up the letter again and began reading. "My dearest Rosa, How are you and the children? I've never stopped thinking about you. I am writing to you from the kitchen of my home in America—soon to be our home, my wife. You will love it here. I have many wonderful things to show you. I miss you and pray for the time you and the children will join me here for a new life."

She stopped reading, dangled the letter from her fingertips, and looked up at my aunt. Papa bounced off his chair and melted into a corner of the room.

"Why, that's wonderful news," Aunt Gizella said. "All my brothers are so lucky to live in such a place, and now you, dear Rosa, are going, too. I'm green with envy."

"I don't see what's so wonderful about it," Tibor said. "Or what's so terrible about living here."

"That's because your feet are planted in Hungarian soil, whereas my brothers chose to dig themselves up and plant themselves elsewhere."

He frowned.

"Don't worry, dearest," Aunt Gizella said. "I'm happy staying here with you, but that doesn't mean I can't be excited for Rosa."

We stared at one another in silence for a long moment before Aunt Gizella laughed and joined Mama at the table. Sam grabbed my arms, and we danced around the room. Then he picked up Kati and spun her around. Everyone said the idea of going to America made my brother crazy, but we continued to dance around the room until we ran out of breath and fell to the floor giggling. Only Mina, who stood in the shadows by the bar, had no smile on her face at our antics. Mama locked the front door of the tavern and announced she was closing it for the rest of the day in honor of Papa's letter and the new life it promised to bring. We all gathered around a large table in the middle of the tavern.

"Where has Shumi been all this time?" Aunt Gizella asked.

"He was living in America in a place called 'O-hi-a'," Mama said. "Is it a city?" I asked.

"What's he doing there?" Sam asked.

"Working in a factory," Mama said. "Making metal cases for guns."

"For the other side?"

Mama shrugged.

"Who's Papa?" Kati asked.

"Why did he wait so long to write?" Mina asked angrily.

"You are right to ask about that," Mama said, her voice turning bitter. "We have suffered, and it wasn't fair of him to leave us alone like that without a word."

"Why can't he come back here? Why do we have to go there?"

"I understand what you are saying. We have lived here all our lives, and now Papa, who has left us on our own all these years, snaps his fingers and we are supposed to drop everything and go to him."

"Yes. It's not fair."

"But on the other hand, what's here for us now?"

Aunt Gizella bit her lip, and Mama reached forward and grasped her hand.

"My sister," Mama said, "You have been so kind. I meant no offense. It's just that I can barely make enough money to keep a roof over these children's heads. Besides, they need their papa, now that we know where he is."

"I want to go," Sam said.

"Of course you do, but out of fairness to your sisters, let's think about it for a while, about the welfare of everyone in this family. I know it will be difficult, no matter what we decide. I want what is best for my children. I don't want to see them dressed in rags, hungry all the time. What parent would? Ah, Shumi."

"He's not the easiest of men to be married to," Aunt Gizella said.

"No, indeed."

Over the next two or three days, we argued over whether to stay or go. Mina swore she would never leave Hungary, but Sam said he was counting the hours until we could get on the ship. He had read about America, where the streets were said to be full of magicians who performed tricks for men who hurried to jobs in tall buildings and women who wore elegant costumes. Sometimes I sided with Mina and thought Papa should come back to us, since there was only one of him and five of us. Other times, I was filled with excitement and a thrilling fear at going so far away from home. Mama listened patiently to each of us, but I knew from the moment she received the letter that she had made up her mind. She saw a better life for us, a warm house, new clothes, enough food on the table, and, most importantly, a father for her children, no matter how bad his temper was or how uncertain his prospects remained.

One of the most important things we had to do to get ready for America was to have our photograph taken so that Papa would be able to prove to the people in his new country that we were his family. Mama fussed over us and told us repeatedly we had to look nice for America. She scratched her head and inspected each one of us from top to bottom. We were too tall for our clothes, even Kati. The sleeves of most of her dresses only reached her elbows, and her skirts were high above her knees. Our patched clothes were missing buttons and pockets.

Several mornings after the letter arrived, Mama went across the street to the market and bought a few pieces of gray and light blue cotton cloth. She spread them out on one of the tables in the tavern to show us when we came home from school that day.

"They were just left over from the end of the bolt," she said. "I got them for a song."

Over the next two weeks, Tibor picked Mina and me up after school in his wagon and drove us to his house so that we could sew our new dresses from the material Mama had bought. Aunt Gizella did the measuring and cutting, and Mama joined us most afternoons, since business at the tavern was slow. We were supposed to make new dresses for Mama and Mina and me. After we were finished, we were going to cut one of Mina's summer dresses down for Kati. It was a rich blue color, and there was enough of it to make a long-sleeved dress for my little sister.

"It's so much like Shumi to book our passage in April, before the school term is over," Mama said one afternoon. "I worry about whether the children will be too far behind their classmates next year."

"That's a problem," Aunt Gizella said. She folded and refolded the cloth in her lap.

"Will I have to speak English?" I asked.

"I'm afraid you will," Mama said.

"But how? I don't know a single word."

"You will have to learn. You are young, and it shouldn't be so difficult." She turned toward my aunt. "Isn't it strange how easy it is to talk about Shumi as if he hasn't been gone all these years?"

"Yes, it is," Aunt Gizella said.

"Still, I can't help wondering if he cares about these children's education at all. I used to think he could hardly wait for them to grow up and go to work so that he could sit at home on the verandah and collect their pay each week."

My aunt laughed softly. "That's Mama's influence, no doubt."

Mama nodded. "No doubt."

My aunt stuck her needle into a piece of gray cloth, stopped for a few seconds, and then pulled the needle out the other side. She turned toward me. "Do you know why I'm going so slow?"

"No," I replied.

"Because maybe if I don't finish, you won't have to leave." She rested her hand on top of mine for a moment, and I bent down and brushed my cheek against her knuckles.

"I'm going back to my school in Kisvarda to become a teacher," Mina said. "Or else I'll stay right here."

Mama shook her head, annoyed by now with all my sister's threats and complaints.

"There's nothing I'd love more than to have both of you girls with me," Aunt Gizella said. "But your mother is right. You children have a chance for a brand new life. A chance to be with your papa again, to become a whole family."

Mama dropped her sewing in her lap and stared hard into my sister's eyes. "Has it ever occurred to you that I might want something better for you than what I had for myself?" she asked. "That I don't want any of you children to have to count every penny the way I did?"

"I'm still not going." Mina said. She jabbed her needle in and out of the dress she was sewing.

"We'll see about that. Now be quiet and finish your work. Honestly, you children don't know how lucky you are."

Grandma warmed her hands by the stove in Aunt Gizella's kitchen. Whenever she was there, she always took up so much space in front of the stove that she soaked up most of the heat and left the rest of us to freeze. Mama and Aunt Gizella and I were sitting close together, hemming a dress, and Mina stood staring out the window.

"I've been wondering what Sam is going to wear in the photograph," Aunt Gizella said.

Mama stopped sewing. "I don't know," she said. "I've been so worried about these girls and myself I haven't given nearly enough thought to Sam."

"I wish I could help, but he's much too small for Tibor's things, and my boys are still babies."

"Tch, tch," Grandma said and shook her head. "Do you have a pair of his pants and a jacket I can use for a pattern?"

"Yes," Mama said.

"Well, then, give them to me, and I'll take care of it, and let's have an end to all this talk."

Mama and Aunt Gizella glanced at each other and smiled.

The day before we were to have our photograph taken, Aunt Gizella gave Mama a package from Grandma. We gathered around Aunt Gizella's kitchen table, while Mama tore the wrapper off Grandma's package. Inside was a brand new camel-colored suit for Sam. Something about that suit looked familiar, and I tried hard to remember where I'd seen it before. I ran my finger along the jacket pocket, and the material scratched my skin and made me feel sorry for my poor brother for having to wear such a suit. Mina looked at the suit, too. She fingered the lapel of the jacket and rubbed it against her chin. Suddenly, I knew where I had seen that material before.

"Neigh," I whispered loudly.

"What?" Mama asked.

"Neigh!" Neigh! Neigh!" I galloped around the table.

"Oh, no," Aunt Gizella said. "That's Papa's horse blanket."

"Dear God," Mama said, twisting her lips, trying not to smile.

Aunt Gizella rolled her eyes. "Poor Sam."

Mama wrapped the suit back up and took it home, never saying a word about it to my brother until the next day, right before she made him put it on to go to the photographer's studio. He jumped around the room, scratching his arms and pulling at his sleeves and pants pockets. I busied myself tying the sash on my dress and wouldn't let myself look at Sam for fear I would start laughing and reveal the true identity of the suit Grandma had made for him.

"I can't go," Sam said.

"It's too late now," Mama said. "We have an appointment with Mr. Groscz to take our photograph in a few minutes."

It was a cool sunny day, and we walked carefully down the alley toward the center of town. None of us wanted to get mud on our clothes, except Sam, who rubbed his back and legs against the walls of the buildings we passed and told Mama he was going to take the suit off and be photographed without any clothes on.

Mr. Groscz was waiting for us when we arrived at his studio. He showed us into a large empty room with a chair by the window and a box resting on top of three skinny legs. The box stood in front of the chair. He sat Mama on the chair with Kati on her lap. He took my sister off again and stood her next to Mama. He moved me behind Kati and told me to rest my hand on Mama's shoulder. He put Mina on the other side and placed her hand on Mama's other shoulder. Every time Mina let her hand drop, Mr. Groscz put it right back again. He puzzled over what to do about Sam. First, he had my brother kneel down in front of Mama and then stand behind her. He moved Mina over and elbowed Sam between her and Mama. My brother was hopping around and scratching his neck and knees.

"Stand still, young man," Mr. Groscz said. "Otherwise, I'll never be able to take your photograph."

"I don't care," Sam said. "I'll die if I can't take off this suit."

Mama touched him gently on the arm. "Try," she said. "Just for one minute."

Sam struggled to stay in one spot. "Hurry up!"

Mr. Groscz pushed us each a little closer to one another. I stared at him wide-eyed with my mouth open, and at that moment, a flash of light blinded me. I closed my eyes tight and still saw stars as bright as the sun.

"All finished," Mr. Groscz said.

Sam ran out of the studio and down the alley toward home. The rest of us followed slowly behind. We found his suit jacket in front of the tavern door and his pants on the floor beside his mattress, though my brother himself had vanished completely.

A week later, Mr. Groscz delivered the photograph to the tavern. I could hardly wait to see how beautiful I looked in my new dress with the white collar and thought about Papa holding the picture in his hand and showing it proudly to the people by the boat, while he waited for us to arrive.

"I think you'll be pleased," Mr. Groscz said, as he set the photograph on the table.

We gathered around him and stared at the first picture that had ever been taken of us. The camera caught me moving so that my dress and collar faded into one color of gray. My eyes were half closed, not wide open, and my mouth and nose were so blurred I hardly seemed to have a face at all. Kati's head was tilted toward Mama, and her eyes and mouth were turned sideways. Mina's hair fell over her forehead and hid her eyes and cheeks in the shadow. Mama sat perfectly still, her hands in her lap and a half-smile on her lips. I thought she looked beautiful in her new flowered scarf and jumper, but Sam stood in front of her, almost blocking her from the camera. His back was rigid, and his hands were jammed into his pockets. His eyes were open, and his mouth was stretched so wide it pushed his nose out of place.

"I hate it," Mina said.

"So do I," I said.

I turned away from that terrible photograph, afraid of what Papa would think of it and us after so many years. We looked like poor, ugly creatures, and once he saw it, he would probably throw it away, forget we were ever his family, and tell everyone in O-hi-a he didn't know us. Then we would have to sail back across the ocean, come home again without a father and stay poor and hungry for the rest of our lives.

THE AMERICAN FLAG

Mama mailed the photograph to Papa, even though we begged her not to. She made each of us write a sentence or two to him in the letter she included with the photograph. Mina just said hello and signed her name, while Sam asked whether Papa had ever driven a horseless wagon. My hand trembled as I wrote to him about how often he had been in my dreams. I told him I couldn't believe I would be seeing him in only a few short weeks. Kati printed her name at the bottom. Mama sent me to the post office with the letter and, afterwards, occupied herself with trying to sell the beer and liquor that remained in the tavern to help pay our expenses on our trip to the boat.

One of the last things we had to do before we left was to see Dr. Kuncz, the town physician, so that he could give us a piece of paper that swore none of us had any diseases. Mama said they wouldn't let us into America if we were sick, and she made an appointment for us during the last week in March. We arrived nervously at his office.

This was the very first time we'd ever been to a doctor's office. In Galfalva, our doctor lived at the end of our street and went to synagogue with us and came to our house whenever we needed him. Sam threw snowballs at his window in the winter, and I pulled on his beard when he made me swallow medicine I didn't like. In Kisvarda, we never saw a doctor because we had no money. But Dr. Kuncz lived on the other side of town from us and wouldn't come to our house just to give us a piece of paper. Besides, he wasn't Jewish, so when we got sick or hurt ourselves, Mama said it was better to let our bodies heal on their own or give Sam a chance try some of the remedies he was always reading about in books.

Mama, Mina, and Kati went in first to see the doctor, while Sam and I sat in the waiting room. Pretty soon, Kati began to wail.

"Don't tell the doctor that you burp after you eat or that chickens make you sneeze," Sam said. "Or about how sick you get on the train."

"Why?"

"You want him to sign the paper, don't you?"

The door to the doctor's office opened, and Mina came out with a frown on her face.

"What's wrong?" I asked.

"Nothing," she said. "I'm perfectly healthy, so I can go."

"What's the doctor like?"

She shrugged. "He's an old man. He has thick glasses."

"Yes," Sam said. "And they'll burn holes in your skin, if you're not careful. Did you have to take your dress off?"

"None of your business." Mina sat down next to me and folded her hands in her lap.

A minute later, Kati came into the waiting room. She jammed her thumb into her mouth between sobs.

"What's the matter, Kati?" Sam asked. His voice was soft and teasing. "Did that old man hurt you?"

"Yes, I hate him," Kati said and started to cry.

"Did he stick you with a big needle?"

"Uh huh."

At that moment, Dr. Kuncz opened the door to his office and called my name. I stood up slowly and walked inside, staying by the door with my arms wrapped tightly around my waist. Dr. Kuncz sat on a chair in the middle of the room, and Mama sat in a corner behind him. She motioned me toward a table near the doctor, and he peered at me over the top of his glasses and patted the table with his hand.

"Sit up here, Serene," he said. "Let's have a look at you. I won't hurt you. I promise."

I backed onto the table and kept my arms up. Dr. Kuncz's glasses caught the sunlight and blinded me so that I couldn't see him or Mama. I felt faint and leaned forward to put my head between my knees."

"I'm sick," I said. "I can't go to America now."

Dr. Kuncz took off his glasses and lifted my head up slowly. "Why don't you let me have a look?" he said. "Then we can decide."

He put his glasses back on and made me open my mouth so wide I thought he was going to stick his head inside. He touched my neck and eyes and ears and asked me to lie down and poked my stomach and ribs. He asked me to sit up again and poked my knees and elbows. Finally, he turned to Mama.

"No signs of disease," he said. "This is one little girl who won't give you any problems." He pinched my cheeks. "Nice and rosy. You're finished. You can go."

"But where's the needle?" I asked.

"What needle?"

I stepped down from the table, and he smiled at me. That's when I screamed at the top of my lungs, hoping to make Sam think the doctor had sliced open my stomach or pulled out my teeth. I wanted my brother to be afraid of what the doctor might do to him next.

"Serene," Mama said sternly. "What on earth is the matter with you? Go on now, and get out of here. Send in your brother."

"Yes, Mama," I replied.

A few days later, Mama received the piece of paper from Dr. Kuncz that said we were fit to go to America. I found my name with a few check marks behind it.

"What do these marks mean?" I asked.

"That you're ready for the New World," Mama said. "You're in such perfect health you can leave Hungary and become an American. Now you can be with your papa. Don't you remember what it was like when he lived here? Oh, you were probably too young."

Then she sat us down and told us the story of how Papa had run away from the Hungarian Army the month before he and Mama were to be married because he missed her so much and because his lieutenant wouldn't allow him leave to visit her.

"That was when your papa loved me so much he could hardly stand to be out of my sight," Mama said.

The day after we received the paper from Dr. Kuncz, I followed Sam home from school. He had something stuffed underneath his shirt and ducked into the alley behind our rooms. I went in after him, because I wanted to know what he was hiding. Our teacher told us about a series of thefts from the storeroom at school, and I wondered if my brother was responsible.

"What's back there behind that pile of rags?" I asked. "You'd better let me see, or I'll tell Mama."

He grabbed my arm. "Nothing," he said.

That night, I heard someone moving inside our room. I sat up and rubbed my eyes and looked into the darkness, but I couldn't see anything. I slid under my blanket and crawled back toward sleep and a dream of Papa and me playing tag in the front yard of our new house.

The next afternoon, when we arrived home from school, Mama sat at a table with her head in her hands. On the table in front of her lay a red and white striped flag with a blue patch covered with white stars.

"What is it?" I asked.

"An American flag," she said. "Over our front door. Who would do such a thing? Perhaps some envious neighbors. Could they have stolen it from somewhere?"

"That's right," I said. "My teacher—" Sam pinched my arm, and I cried out.

"I had no patrons at all today, a market day. Not one. I knew something must be wrong, so I opened the door, and there was the flag, hanging from a rusty nail. Who do you suppose put it there? Not that nice Mr. Hirsch who bakes our bread. Or what about Mr. Herzl?"

"He couldn't have done it. He likes us. He gives me a free apple every day on my way home from school."

Sam lowered his head and, for the first time I could remember, didn't have a word to say for himself.

Mama stared hard at him, and I thought she knew the truth, in the way she always did without our having to tell her. "Think about all the people in this town who aren't as fortunate as we are and have to stay here the rest of their lives," she said. "Think about how they will feel buying a drink from the friend of an enemy."

On our last Sunday in Marosvasarhely, we went to visit Aunt Gizella and Tibor. We drank tea and ate up all of my aunt's honey cake. Tibor gave us two suitcases for our trip, and Aunt Gizella ruffled Sam's hair and told him to take good care of his new suit. Sam squirmed in his chair.

"What will we do without you?" Mama said.

Aunt Gizella sighed. "What will *we* do without you?" she asked.

Mama kissed my aunt on the cheek and began washing the dishes, and Sam disappeared into the shrubbery in front of the house. Aunt Gizella took my hand and asked Mina to watch the twins, since Anna was off for the day visiting her cousins.

"Serenc and I are going for a walk," my aunt said.

We turned down the road that led toward school. I remembered the many times we had walked on the road together, talking about school, magic, love, life.

"I had hoped to meet your husband and be an old aunt to your children and grandchildren," Aunt Gizella said.

"But I'm not ever going to get married or have any children," I said.

"Why not?"

"Because." I didn't want to talk about Karl.

"That's not a very good reason. I don't believe you anyhow. You have to swear you'll send me photographs of your husband and every single one of your children."

"I swear." Though I crossed my fingers behind my back, certain that was one promise I would never keep. "Will you and Tibor ever come to America?"

"Probably not. Our families are here."

"We're your family, too."

She patted my hand. "Yes, you are. But Tibor is my husband, and he says he's too old for big changes, or even little ones. He wants the twins to grow up to be Hungarians."

"Sometimes I wish I could stay here all my life, too."

"Why? Just think of the adventures you are going to have, the new people you will meet. You'll learn to read and write all over again. You'll speak two languages, instead of one. I can hardly imagine what that will be like. I've always lived here, where one day is just like the next. Even the war didn't really change anything."

"You're lucky. I wish things would go back to the way they were before we left Galfalva."

"But then you wouldn't get to see your papa so soon. You do want to see him, don't you?"

"Yes . . . I don't know."

"Ah. You're afraid."

"When he was here with us, sometimes he acted like he hated me, but since he's been gone, whenever I dream about him, he's always nice and looks after me."

"Well, then, the Papa in your dreams is the real one." She hooked her arm through mine. "He's the one who's waiting for you in America."

We arrived at school and sat down on one of the benches in front where Aunt Gizella used to wait for me until classes were over.

"I was the one who sent Miss Zora away that time with the Russian soldier," I said.

"What made you think of that?" my aunt asked.

"Sitting here with you. Do you remember Sophia Gorgei? She had this eye. She said her mama dug it out of a dead cat."

Aunt Gizella cringed. "I wouldn't put it past that woman."

"Sophia said that the eye was magic and that I could make one wish on it, so I wished for Miss Zora to be in love with her Russian soldier. But I forgot the part about her having money and a home."

"So the cat's eye did exactly what you asked and no more?"

"Yes."

"It wasn't a very smart eye, was it?"

"I guess not."

Aunt Gizella took my hand in hers.

"Sophia's mother told me Tibor might be a Gypsy," I said.

"What foolishness," Aunt Gizella said. "You know, of course, that Tibor got my beautiful scarf with the Star of David back from Mrs. Gorgei."

"I should never have given it to her," I said.

"True enough. That woman wreaked havoc on us the first two months we were married. First, our wagon tipped over on our honeymoon trip to Debrecen and scattered our belongings everywhere. It took us almost a day to find everything, and Tibor wrenched his back searching through the grass for a bracelet he gave me on our wedding day. I wanted to leave it behind, but he wouldn't hear of it. He was afraid it would fall into the hands of someone who might use it against us."

"Like Mrs. Gorgei?"

"Exactly."

"Did he find it?"

"Yes, and he could hardly walk for a week afterwards. While we were in Debrecen, Ruth fell in love with the son of her mother's fourth cousin, a poor country rabbi with no congregation and no money, and slipped off and married him. That made Tibor's back hurt even more, and he was laid up for two weeks afterwards, so we didn't return home until the middle of July. By that time, your grandma had worked herself into quite a state over your running away."

"She still doesn't speak to me, if she can help it."

"That's Mama for you. She's like an elephant. She never forgets. Of course, once Anna found out you ran away, she had to try it, too. Tibor was out one entire night looking for her and came home with an awful head cold. He was feverish and kept saying he could feel something evil in the air. I said the only thing evil in the air was the smell of Mama's onion soup. She'd made it for him when she found out he was sick—she didn't know that onions make him break out in hives."

"Mrs. Gorgei again."

"Who else? A few weeks later, he ran into her and Sophia on the road to Szereda. Mrs. Gorgei had the scarf around her neck."

"But she told me she gave it away."

"And you believed her?"

I nodded.

"Tibor recognized the scarf right away and demanded that she return it," Aunt Gizella said. "He told her she had caused us enough trouble already."

"What did she do then?" I asked.

"She ripped it off her neck and threw it on the road, as if it had burned her skin. She told Tibor to take it, because it brought her nothing but bad luck. Then she and her daughter vanished into the last light of day, and no one has laid eyes on them since."

"Is that true? Did Tibor really see them disappear?"

"That's what he claims. They grew thinner and thinner until he could see right through them."

"I hope they don't show up again."

"So do I. Still, I'm glad to have my scarf back. I have big plans for it. I mean to give it to your sister. I want her to have some peace, and I want her to give your mama a rest, too."

"So do I."

"Don't you think a scarf that has survived such a terrible ordeal with no damage has some kind of special power? Besides, maybe that power can help Mina mend her angry feelings."

"Do you think she'll use it to cover her head, like other girls her own age?"

"That would be a blessing."

I leaned on her shoulder and stayed there until a cool afternoon breeze raised goosebumps on my arm and my aunt said it was time to go.

"I don't want to leave yet," I said.

"But we have to," she said. "Everyone is waiting for us." She took my hand in hers. "Miss me a little."

"I will." I kissed her on the cheek, half knowing I would never see her again.

OLD CLOTHES

Mama raised the white flag so that the train to Budapest would stop for us at the tiny station in Marosvasarhely. We stood by the tracks with our two suitcases and the baskets of food Mama had prepared for the four days we would need to get to France, where the ship to America was waiting to take us across the ocean. Mama studied the letter Papa had sent with directions to the ship. Mina rested her foot on a suitcase and stared back at the town. Kati played in the grass beside the station platform. Mama made Sam wear his new suit, and he pulled at his pockets and scratched his legs. I kept glancing up the tracks, and after a while, I spotted a puff of smoke in the distance.

The train rumbled onto the track in front of us and ground slowly to a halt, hissing steam out its sides. I climbed the steps to our car, took my seat by the window, and pressed my lips and nose against the cool glass. I watched every tree and shrub glide by until I couldn't see our town anymore. Then I pulled myself away from the window and leaned back and let my body sway with the movement of the wheels along the track. My stomach turned a somersault.

During the next four days, we switched trains five times, and on each new train, I'd lie down on the floor, not looking out the window at the countries drifting by. The inside of my mouth tasted sour, and I barely managed to eat a few crusts of bread and drink warm water to keep myself alive. That was all my stomach would allow.

Sam was in agony, tortured by Grandma's suit, the only decent clothing he owned. Early on the third morning of our journey, after he ate a quick breakfast, he threw his jacket over his shoulder and announced he was going for a walk. Ever since we'd been on the train, my brother liked to go up and down the cars, talking to people, even when they couldn't speak Hungarian, and giving them free medical advice. Usually, he wasn't gone long, but on this morning, he didn't come back for almost two hours. Mama was beside herself with worry. The train stopped at a small station in the middle of a field and let off several families. Mama glanced out the window to reassure herself that Sam hadn't gotten off, too. Just as the train was about to start, Sam waltzed into our car wearing a new pair of brown pants with a vest to match.

"Where did you get those clothes?" Mama asked. "And what happened to your new suit?"

"I traded it," he said.

"For what?"

"Nothing. I helped a lady two cars back who had a stomachache, and her son gave me these clothes."

"What did you give him in return? A black eye?" She put her hands on Sam's shoulders.

"I did not. These clothes are mine. I earned them."

"I'm sure that's a matter of opinion. You have to give them back."

"I can't. The boy who owned them got off the train"

We leaned our heads out the window, and at the very end of the train, on the grass beside the tracks, stood a family with a boy about Sam's size who didn't have any pants on. In the grass a little way beyond them, was Sam's suit. The whistle blew, and the train started and pulled away from the station, leaving the boy without pants and my brother's new suit far behind.

"Take your pants and vest off now," Mama said.

"I can't," Sam said. "I don't have anything else to wear."

Mama grabbed my brother by the ear and dragged him to the seat in front of her. "Sit here and don't move until we get off this train."

Sam didn't seem to mind.

On our last afternoon on the train, I crawled into the seat beside Mina. I was still sick to my stomach and tried hard not to look out the window. Mama, Sam, and Kati were at the other end of the car. My sister and I rode together in silence for a few minutes, and then I slid off the seat and stretched out on the floor.

"Do you really think we're going to see Papa?" Mina asked. "What if Mama made this whole thing up? The letter? The tickets?"

I sat up, dizzy, and held on to the edge of the seat. "Why would she do that?" I asked. "And where would she get the money?"

"I don't know. Tibor, maybe."

"He wouldn't make up a lie. You're crazy."

"Am I?" She stretched the ends of her mouth with her fingers and crossed her eyes.

"Don't." I laughed. "You'll make me sick."

I curled back up on the floor, and she poked me with the tip of her shoe.

"Stop it," I said.

She poked me again, and I slapped at her shoe.

"You told her to give it to me, didn't you?" she asked.

"What are you talking about?" I asked.

"Aunt Gizella. You were the one who put her up to giving me her scarf. Or Mama did. She's always trying to get me to cover my head."

"It was Aunt Gizella's idea, really. I didn't have anything to do with it, and neither did Mama. Aunt Gizella is so kind, and all she wanted was to give you a gift that might bring you peace."

"Well, I don't want any peace, and I don't want that scarf, either."

I rolled over on my side and stared up at her. She slid a suitcase out from under her seat, hoisted it onto her lap, and rummaged through it until she found the scarf. She set it carefully on top of the suitcase, patting out the wrinkles and folding it neatly into a square. Then she flung it at me.

"It's yours," she said. "Aunt Gizella should have given it to you in the first place."

I grabbed the scarf, to keep it from falling on the floor, and leaned forward on my elbow. "She wanted you to have it," I said. "I can't take it away from you."

"Oh, don't be such a ninny. Besides, I'll never wear it. I doubt Jewish mothers in America make their daughters cover their heads."

"But it's yours."

She put the suitcase back under the seat without bothering to close it, hopped up, and sat down on top of me. "You're impossible. I'm trying to be nice."

"Oh."

She poked me gently on the shoulder, took the scarf from my hand, and tied it around my neck. "There."

She got up and collapsed back into her seat. My stomach ached, but I fell into a restful sleep, fingering the fringes of my aunt's scarf, feeling in its soft cotton her love and good wishes for my new life. When I awoke, Mina had tucked her legs under her skirt and pressed her nose against the window. I reached up and tapped her knee.

"It's so beautiful out there," she said, nodding toward the window. "It's too bad you can't enjoy it."

"Mama says some day, when I'm an old woman, I'll tell my grandchildren how I traveled across Europe in a train," I said. "They'll ask me what it was like, and I'll feel silly and have to say, 'Well, the floor looked nice.'"

Mina frowned and pressed her nose against the window again. I pulled myself up into the seat beside her, and she moved closer to the window.

"Thank you for the scarf," I said. I lifted one of the edges to my nose. "It still smells like her."

Mina turned toward me. I tried to reach over and hug her, but she pulled away.

"Go on, now," she said. "Go back to Mama, and leave me alone."

I stumbled out of the seat. "Thank you for this," I said. "I'll never forget it."

She shooed me away.

Late on our fourth afternoon on the train, the conductor walked up the aisle, punching tickets. When Mama handed our tickets to him, he said something in a language I didn't understand. Mama told us she thought he meant we had arrived in LeHavre, the city where we were to meet our ship. She fussed over Kati's dress, and as she leaned over to pick up one of our suitcases, the train screeched to a sudden stop. I sat up slowly.

"Mama, why didn't you tell us Papa was in America all this time?" I asked.

"What?" she asked, tightening the strap on the suitcase.

"Why didn't you tell us before about Papa?"

She let go of the strap. "I didn't know where he was. We had no word for over a year, and I thought he was dead. Then he wrote a note to your grandmother."

"Why didn't he write to us?"

"He wasn't sure where we were. He thought we had left because of the fighting. Later on, your Uncle Mihai got a letter from your Uncle Yankev in America saying Papa was there, working in a factory. A good job, Yankev said, that paid five times what Papa could make here. Then two months ago, the letter with the tickets came."

"He should have written to us more. We're his family."

"I know he should have, but that's your papa."

"But Mama, it's not fair."

She sighed. "Who told you life was fair?"

"What if Papa doesn't like us anymore?"

"Where did you get such an idea? Of course he likes us. Otherwise, why would he send for us?"

"Maybe we should stay here."

"You are starting to sound just like Mina. Listen, it may be hard at first. Everything will be so different, even Papa. But you'll see. In the end, you will be very happy. Now go and help your sister with the other suitcase, and stop worrying."

After we got off the train, Mama gathered us together on the platform and told us to hold tightly to one another so we wouldn't get lost. We were going to follow the directions Papa gave us to a boarding house where they spoke Hungarian and where we would spend the night. Our ship wasn't going to leave until the next afternoon. Mina carried one suitcase, and I held on to her free hand. We trailed along behind Mama, who carried the other suitcase and held Sam's fingers firmly in her fist. Sam held onto Kati.

We wound around the narrow streets of LeHavre. They were shaded by taller buildings than I'd ever seen in my life. From time to time, a woman with a baby at her breast would lean out a window and smile and wave at me, and I waved back. The thing that amazed me the most, though, was the laundry dangling high above the ground, pinned to wires stretched between two buildings. At each of the ends of the wire was a wheel, and whenever someone turned one of those wheels, red and yellow dresses and blue pants and fresh white nightgowns glided across the sky in a straight line before folding themselves neatly into the nearest window.

Mina said it was my turn to carry the suitcase, and she dragged me along behind her. My arm was numb with the weight of the suitcase, and the streets grew darker. People sang out to one another in the same language the man who took our tickets on the train had used, and birds swooped down from the tops of the buildings to peck at chunks of dirty bread that had fallen to the ground. We finally turned into a courtyard with a big fountain in the middle and a house with five or six stories at one end. Several women were rinsing clothes in the fountain and hanging them to dry on wooden stands, like the ones we had in Galfalva.

Mama walked up to one of the women who was wringing out a dress and pointed to Papa's letter. The woman said yes, and after a moment or two, Mama and the woman began talking together like the best of friends. Mama turned toward us and told us we had arrived at our home for the night.

Inside the house, another woman greeted us in Hungarian, though she spoke with such a strange accent it was difficult to understand her. She showed us to a big room with rows and rows of hammocks, three deep in some places, and we each claimed one in the same corner of the room. Sam jumped into his and started swinging back and forth. I eased into the one next to him and tumbled out as quickly as I could because it made me dizzy.

Mama put her hands on her hips. "I hope you're not planning to do that all night," she said.

Sam began to swing harder, and Mama came up behind him and stopped him with her arm. Kati pulled herself up into her hammock and sat there sucking her thumb. Mina fumbled with one of the suitcases, and fell into one of the hammocks, staring at the ceiling, while Mama began to unpack the few things we would need for the night.

"Come and give me a hand," she said to Mina.

My sister gave Mama a sharp look and went back to studying the ceiling. Mama marched over to her and bumped her out of her hammock.

"Get up, you lazy girl," Mama said, wiping the sweat from her forehead.

She took Papa's letter from her pocket, folded it carefully, and placed it on her hammock. Mina stood behind Mama, her arms crossed tightly over her chest. I went to the window and opened it and stared at the dark courtyard below. The air was close and stale, more like someone's damp cellar than an open yard.

I looked all the way up and down the street, back and forth across the tall buildings that blocked out the sun, hoping for another glimpse of that wonderful clothing floating through the sky on a wire so thin you could barely see it at all.

THE STRIKE

Early the next morning, I followed Sam down one dark street after another, until I finally heard water lapping and smelled the sharp odor of fish.

"This way," Sam said

He ran so fast I could hardly keep up with him. Once or twice, I almost lost him around the corner of a building, but pretty soon I came racing into the sunlight and saw gray water stretching out before me forever.

A ship was docked on the water, and there were several small boats around it. The ship reminded me of pictures I'd seen of Noah's Ark, but it was much bigger. When I looked up at the railing, I felt as small as an ant. No men walked around the deck of this ark, and no animals peered out of its tiny windows. A man in a black uniform and cap stood by the gangplank, pacing back and forth, eyeing the dock and rubbing the wooden stick that hung from his belt. Sam walked up to him and pointed to the ship. The man took a step backwards. Sam reached for the man's hand and examined it carefully, before pulling a handkerchief from the man's pocket and wrapping it around his wrist. The man had obviously hurt himself, and Sam was playing doctor again.

The two of them gestured at one another for a little while longer. Then the man shook his head and rested a finger on one of Sam's vest buttons. After a minute or two, Sam turned away from him and walked around the dock, kicking at the papers scattered there, bending down to pick up a piece and stick it in his pocket. He stopped at the waste baskets that were placed every few feet and searched through them, as well.

I cupped my hands over my mouth. "What are you doing?" I yelled.

Sam glanced up at me. "Come here," he said. "I've already found two coins. Now I'm looking for stamps or anything else I can trade or sell."

I joined him in his search of the dock. "What did the man by the boat say? Why aren't there any people on the ship yet?"

"There's a strike. The men who load food, suitcases, sugar and other things on the ship say they won't work until they're paid more money."

"What will we do? Papa is expecting us in Newyork in ten days. If we don't leave today, we'll be late, and he may go back to O-hi-a without us."

Sam shrugged and waved good-bye to the man in the black uniform, whom he called Jacques.

We raced back to the boardinghouse. Coins jingled in Sam's pocket as we wound through the dark streets, and when we arrived at the courtyard, Sam circled the big fountain, helping the women gathered there wring out their clothing, taking a penny for his trouble when one was offered.

Mama buried her head in her hands when we told her about the strike. Then she reached into her pocket for the small purse where she kept her money and counted what she had left. Sam held out the coins he had collected that morning and begged her to take them. He lied and said he had been saving them from odd jobs he had done for some of our neighbors before we left home. Mama closed Sam's fingers around the coins and told him she didn't need the money.

Early every morning for the next six days, Sam dragged me out of my hammock, and the two of us walked to the market a few streets over to buy a loaf of long, crispy bread. Sometimes, if we were especially hungry, we nibbled at the ends. We also bought sharp-tasting cheese that had blue spots in it. We purchased this strange food with coins we found at the docks and took it back to the boardinghouse for our family breakfast. Mama accepted the bread and cheese gladly and didn't question us too closely, after Sam convinced her he didn't have other plans for his hard-earned savings.

Each morning after breakfast, we went to the docks to talk to Jacques in the hope that he would give us money or a fresh apple. That way, we didn't have to work so hard going through the trash cans, searching for coins or stamps we could sell. One morning, Mina accompanied us, and she proved to be better than Sam and me at finding pennies and other things of value scattered around the dock. But she tired quickly and told us she didn't want to go again, when we asked her to come with us the next day.

The boat was always deserted, and Sam and I developed a kind of sign language to make ourselves understood to Jacques. Sam would pretend to steer the wheel of a boat and shrug his shoulders. That meant, will the boat leave today? Jacques would shake his head no and move his index finger in a circle. That meant, it will be many, many months before the boat leaves. It wasn't long before Sam learned the French words for hello and good-bye, morning and night, and tomorrow. When Jacques puffed out his stomach, seemed to count out his money, stooped forward and frowned, and counted out even more money, Sam took that to mean the men who owned the boat were still arguing about how much money to pay the men who loaded it. Of course, we kept this information to ourselves and didn't even tell Mina.

All of us had night clothes and underwear, and Mama and Mina and Kati and I each had one change of clothes. Every second or third afternoon, we had to go to the fountain to rinse our clothes. Mama enjoyed these visits to the fountain because she had a chance to talk to the other women who were washing their clothes there. Most of them were like us, stranded in LeHavre, waiting to go somewhere else. One of the women had been in the city for months because her husband had not yet sent her money for her passage on the ship. In the meantime, she washed linens for our landlady and mopped the floors.

"You see how fortunate we are," Mama said. "Papa has taken care of everything for us. Suppose he hadn't sent us enough money for the boat. Suppose we had to stay here forever."

Of course, whenever Mama asked Mina to help with the laundry, my sister said she didn't want to, but Mama wouldn't take no for an answer. She pushed Mina out of her hammock and loaded her down with dirty clothes, scolding my sister, who was now a half a head taller than Mama, for giving in too easily to her own bad temper. Most afternoons, Sam disappeared on his own down one of the side streets near our boarding house, but if Mama happened to catch him in his hammock, she made him take his pants and vest and shirt off so she could wash them. Then he had to stay inside the rest of the day while they dried, since he didn't have any extra clothes to wear. Sometimes I helped Mama with the wash, and I struggled down several flights of stairs, nearly invisible under a pile of my sisters' dresses and nightgowns.

On the sixth afternoon of the strike, Mama and I were up to our elbows in water at the fountain.

"Do you think Papa will wait for us in Newyork?" I asked. "He doesn't like for people to be late. What if he thinks we decided not to come, after all?"

"I'm certain they've already telegraphed to Newyork about the strike," Mama said. "The man at the boat there will tell Papa he has no choice but to wait for us." She laughed. "Besides, the train fare from O-hi-a to Newyork is very expensive. Papa will stay put for at least a month before he turns around and goes back home again, because he'll want to get his money's worth."

"Are you sure?"

"Trust me. I am."

I slept fitfully that night, while visions of Papa's angry, impatient face flashed inside my head. His hair was ruffled; his beard was overgrown, and his mouth had tightened down to a thin black line. The next morning I woke with a terrible headache and would have stayed in my hammock, if Sam hadn't grabbed my wrist and shook me until I yelled at him to let go of me.

"Get up," he said. "It's late."

"Oh, all right," I said.

We skipped breakfast and went directly to the dock. There were people around all the boats, and the deck of our ship was covered with men.

"How did you know about this?" I asked.

"I came back yesterday afternoon, and some of those men were already here," he said.

We saw Jacques, and he counted out more fake money for us and patted us on the shoulder, smiling broadly. I guessed that meant the men who loaded the boats were happy with the money the men who owned the boats agreed to pay them. Jacques pointed excitedly to a group of men who were repairing the railing of our boat. Then he tapped his watch.

"*À demain, à dix heures dans le matin*," he said.

"What is he saying?" I asked.

"That must be when the ship leaves," Sam said. He pulled on Jacques' arm. "*Départ?*"

Jacques leaned forward to show Sam the exact time on his watch the ship was to depart.

"*Merci*," Sam said.

"*À demain*," Jacques said and rushed away to answer the questions of the large group of people who had assembled on the dock.

On our last day scouring the docks of LeHavre, we found four copper coins and went to the market to buy two long loaves of bread and yellow cheese with holes in it. Afterwards, we went back to the boardinghouse to share the good news with Mama. She smiled, thanked us, and stared out the window for a moment.

"What's the matter, Mama?" I asked.

"Sometimes it's frightening when your most treasured wish is about to come true," she said and sighed heavily. "In the meanwhile, we have a lot of work to do, children."

She gave each of us a long list of chores to complete before we went to bed that night, and we groaned and complained and tried our best to do what she asked of us.

I never saw so many people in my life. They stood crushed together in front of our ship, held back by a rope. The crowd swallowed up Sam, and Mama was frantic, although she couldn't move because of all the people around her. She called out Sam's name, but her voice was lost in the sound of people talking around her. Kati hung on to Mama's skirt so hard her knuckles turned white. Mina and I clung together, and I wrapped the fingers of my free hand around the waistband of Mama's shift.

"Where is he?" Mama asked. "I warned him not to wander off like that."

"Don't worry, Mama," I said. "I'm sure he's here somewhere."

I jumped up and down, trying to see the top of my brother's head, but people on all sides of me stepped on my toes and poked me with their elbows.

"Stop it," I said and poked right back.

Pretty soon, someone next to me pinched me. I never took my eyes off Mama, since I was terrified of losing her. The person next to me pinched me again.

"Ouch," I said.

"Ouch," the mocking voice of my brother said.

I had to let go of Mama's shift because the crowd pushed her forward, and now there were three people in between me and her.

"Mama!" I shouted. "Here's Sam."

She didn't seem to hear me, and she didn't turn around. Sam hooked his arm around mine and pulled me through the crowd. I had to let go of Mina, too.

"What are you doing?" I said.

He kept right on pulling me forward. We ducked under some people and shoved others aside, until we reached the rope that kept the crowd in place. Sam bent down. I followed him, and we crawled underneath all those people into the open, with the gangplank only a couple of feet in front of us. Our friend Jacques was at the other end of the crowd, pointing toward the ship and yelling something.

"What's he saying?" I asked.

"He must be telling them to wait," Sam replied.

The two of us tiptoed to the gangplank, ran quickly up to the deck of the ship, and turned to watch what was happening on the dock below. Jacques untied the rope and held it in his hand to form a small passageway for the people in the crowd. At the top of the gangplank, a man in a uniform and big blue hat approached us and shouted angry words at us.

"*Maman!*" Sam cried. "I want my *maman.*"

I understood immediately what Sam was doing. "Mama!" I cried. "Mama! Mama!"

"Shh," the man in the uniform said.

"*Maman!*" Sam yelled.

"Mama!" I said. "Mama! Mama!" I pointed toward the crowd.

The uniformed man leaned down, ignoring the row of people who had begun to march up the gangplank. Most of them wore dresses made of silk and fur coats, even though the day was very warm. He spoke to us in French, and Sam gestured back, repeating over and over that we had lost our mother in the crowd.

The man frowned and said something else to Sam.

"Do you want her name?" Sam asked. "Rosa Spirer."

The man stumbled over Mama's name several times until he finally said, "*R-r-ose Spi-rey. Maman. Oui.*"

He turned and walked down the gangplank, swerving to avoid the people coming up the other way. Soon the man in the uniform was talking to Jacques, and together they began to yell into the crowd. We stood on the deck and hung over the railing and waited, sweat streaming down our foreheads, stinging our eyes. Soon the crowd parted, and the man in the uniform went up and down the rows of people.

"He's looking for her," Sam said, leaning so far over the railing I was afraid he might tumble to the dock below.

After several minutes, Mama emerged from the crowd with Kati glued to her side. Mama turned to Jacques and pumped her arms up and down, and Jacques cupped his hands over his mouth and called to someone in the crowd. Soon, Mina pushed her way past a row of people. She was carrying one of our suitcases.

The man in the uniform offered one arm to Mama and the other to Mina, and Sam and I called out to Mama until our voices were hoarse. Mama, Mina, and Kati inched their way up the gangplank and, at long last, reached Sam and me on the deck. Mama's face went white, and she wiped her hand across her cheek.

"My God, I've lost our suitcase," she said. "It's got to be on the dock."

"I'll go and get it," Sam said.

"So will I," I said.

"Oh, no you won't," Mama said. "I won't have you children running off again. Besides, you would never get back on the boat. They were boarding people with first-class tickets before everyone else. Ours are second-class, so we are out of turn."

"But we need our clothes," I said.

"No, we don't. We can replace them easily enough in America, and until then, we will just have to do without."

The ship's horn blasted behind us and sounded just like the *shofar* the rabbi blew in synagogue at the end of the *Yom Kippur* service. I heard the low rumble of the engine below us. The last of the people climbed up the gangplank, steerage passengers who had to make the trip below deck. Jacques and two other men lifted the gangplank, and Sam leaned over the railing and called to him and waved good-bye. Jacques glanced up at us, smiled, and waved back. Mama stared out at the city of LeHavre.

"You had better look hard now," she said. "I think it will be a long time before we see this place again."

I knew she was right.

The sun went behind a cloud, and the air was suddenly chilly. I never took my eyes off LeHavre, as the ship backed slowly out of the dock. More and more of that gray, lapping water separated us from the land. My stomach began to roll with the waves around the ship, and I leaned hard against the railing.

We found our way to the cabin Papa had reserved for us, and it was much better than we could have imagined. There was one small room for the family and tiny individual sleeping rooms for each one of us. We had our very own bathroom, but it was so narrow we could hardly stand up in it. We didn't mind, though, and counted ourselves among the luckiest people in the world for the abundance Papa's money from the new world brought into our lives.

I already felt sick to my stomach and opened the door to my room and fell into bed. My bed. In my room. If I hadn't had such a big rock in my stomach, I would have jumped and down on the bed and yelled to my sisters and brother through the walls.

I was sick that night and the next day, too. Sam said fresh air would help, so I staggered around the deck, trying hard not to throw up. The third day on board the ship, after my stomach had settled a little, I searched through our remaining suitcase for a clean dress. Luckily, the one Aunt Gizella and I had sewn for the photograph wasn't in the suitcase we had lost, and I steadied myself and slipped it over my shoulders. The fringes of her scarf stuck out from beneath one of my nightgowns and a couple of pairs of Kati's socks. I decided to leave it where it was, to save it for special occasions when I needed to feel that my aunt was near.

I couldn't imagine what it would be like never to see the mountains that rose in the clouds beyond Marosvasarhely, never to hear everyone around me speaking Hungarian, never to take my blanket to the shed behind our house in Galfalva and sleep on top of the warm oven inside. I wanted to see Aunt Gizella's face and smell the forbidden meat cooking in the market in front of our tavern in Marosvasarhely. I wanted to go home.

I didn't tie the *mezuzah* around my neck, as I had done in the past when we left home, because this time we had suitcases. So I thought it would be safe to pack it away. That morning, I tore through our suitcase, looking for our *mezuzah* so that I could hold it in my hand and let it take me back to all the houses where we had lived. I dumped piles of clothes and shoes on the floor and searched through the pockets on the inside of the suitcase. I was sure that I had stuffed the *mezuzah* in the side pocket of the same suitcase with my dress and scarf, but when I looked for it, all I found were a few old buttons and a tarnished penny. I knew Mama had taken it off the door in Marosvasarhely and given it to me for safekeeping.

"This little container carries with it many treasured memories of our old life," she had said. "It is important for us to take those memories with us to our new home."

I had wrapped the *mezuzah* in an old handkerchief and stuffed it into the suitcase, checking on it several times before Mama finally strapped the suitcase closed. Between then and now, though, it had somehow slipped away from me and stayed on the other side of the water, lost forever.

I went outside on the deck to breathe in the fresh ocean air and settle my poor stomach. It was a warm morning, but the breeze from the ocean gave me goosebumps. I glanced over the railing and into the water.

"Please forgive me, Rabbi Akiva," I said.

He had been strangely silent since the *Yom Kippur* service after Daniel's death, and this time he didn't answer me either. All I heard was the empty sound of waves as they beat against the side of the ship and raised a thin white foam in its wake.

BAR MITZVAH

By the fifth morning of our voyage, my stomach settled down enough that I was able to walk around in the fresh air without feeling too sick. I ate a small breakfast and went by myself to the deck. All I could see for miles was gray water, but I was glad to escape from our tiny stateroom, where tempers were short and elbows flew into ribs and arms. I stood on the deck and let the sea breeze whip my hair off my face.

I wondered what it would be like to live with Papa in America, go to school with strangers who spoke a language I didn't understand. They would probably make fun of me and think I was stupid. I might even be in a class with children much younger than I. Or maybe Papa would make me get a job, and I wouldn't have to go to school anymore. I hoped he and Mama wouldn't have too many arguments about that.

The ship pitched underneath me. I leaned against the railing and held onto my stomach, when someone pinched me from behind. I jumped and turned around, and there stood Mina, laughing at me.

"Are you on the boat or somewhere else?" she asked.

"I'm here," I said.

"You had that look on your face, like you were a poor lost child who couldn't find her mother." Her voice was mocking.

I shrugged. "Do you think we'll have to go to school right away when we get to O-hi-a?"

"I'm through with school. I'm much too old."

"You're sixteen. My teacher in Marosvasarhely was almost eighteen, and she told me she went to school right up to the time she took over our class."

"I don't care what she did. I'm going to get a job and save up all my money so I can live somewhere by myself."

"You can't do that."

"Why not? Who's going to stop me?"

"Papa."

"How can he? I'll have my own money."

"Oh, Mama says Papa won't let you keep it. She says he plans to collect our money from us every week. Anyway, who ever heard of a girl like you living alone?"

"I'm sure girls in America do that all the time, and I've had enough of this family to last me a lifetime."

"Maybe you can find yourself a rich husband."

She threw her head back and laughed again. Her thick black curls swirled around her face, and when she brushed them away, her eyes were fiery, and I saw how beautiful she had grown over the last year.

"Aaron was stupid," I said.

"Was he?" she asked. "He has a rich wife, plenty to eat, warm clothes, his old congregation back."

"I'm sure he's not very happy."

"So what?"

I leaned over the railing a little and peered into the water. Sam told me I shouldn't do that because it would make me even more seasick than I was already. He was right. A wave of dizziness almost knocked me off my feet and into the ocean, and I had to sit down and put my head between my knees. Mina sat down beside me. Passengers from steerage milled around the deck and bumped us with their heavy boots. There was no sunlight in steerage, so the people traveling below came onto the deck whenever they could to get fresh air. They were much poorer and unluckier than we were and had no beds to sleep on, no place to wash their faces and hands.

I began to shiver, and Mina slipped off her jacket and wrapped it around my shoulders. I glanced up at her.

"What do you think Papa looks like by now?" I asked.

"How should I know?" she asked. "You're the one who always used to see his ghost."

"What if he has white hair and walks with a cane and looks like Grandpa? What if we don't recognize him?"

"Honestly, Serene. You can worry a thing to death, can't you?"

"I just want him to remember me, to like me. That's all."

"Don't be foolish."

She stood and pulled me up beside her, and we pushed our way through the crowd on deck and walked back to our stateroom.

That afternoon, I went with Sam down to steerage, where my brother had befriended one of the passengers, Mr. Lazar. He was a farmer from Debrecen who had lost his land and who suffered greatly from a sore throat, until Sam prepared him a salt water gargle. He gargled religiously twice a day. Mr. Lazar was a talkative man and, being grateful to Sam for restoring his voice, invited us to sit with him while he entertained us with a story.

"Have you ever heard of the Ba'al Shem Tov?" he asked.

"Mama told us about him," I said. "He was a holy rabbi who was born in Russia two hundred years ago."

"That is correct. How smart you are. Now, the Ba'al Shem Tov wasn't an educated man. The truth was he could hardly read Hebrew at all."

"How did he ever become a rabbi?" Sam asked.

"He believed that prayer wasn't so much a matter of reading the words on the page as it was an act of reaching through the individual letters of each word to God. You had to forget who you were in the real world. A banker, a beggar, a doctor, a thief. It made no difference. Rich or poor, you had to stare at the letters until the words blurred and narrowed down to a single point. Then you weren't a thinking man anymore. You weren't sending words up to God. God was sending His thoughts down to you."

Sam squirmed a little and frowned. "I don't understand."

Mr. Lazar reached over and patted my brother on the back. "You will. I know Friday is your thirteenth birthday. It is time for you to learn how to pray like a grown man, like the Ba'al Shem Tov."

"I'll try." Sam sat up on his knees and scratched the side of his head.

"Come to see me this Friday evening at sundown. I'm certain we have more than enough men for a *minyan*, so we can celebrate the Sabbath, the day you become a man. The day you begin to follow the path of the Ba'al Shem Tov."

On the last Friday of April, 1919, Sam celebrated his thirteenth birthday. We woke early, and Mama gave my brother a small magnifying glass. None of us knew where she got it.

"Happy birthday, my fine young man," she said. "My gift is to help you see germs better when you're doctoring people." She reached into her pocket and held out a watch on a thin gold chain. "And this is from Uncle Tibor and Aunt Gizella so you'll always be on time and never keep any of your patients waiting."

Sam hung the watch from his vest pocket and caressed its stem and smooth case. He walked from one end of our cabin to the other with the magnifying glass in his hand, inspecting the walls and the wood around the doorways. When he turned toward me, his eye was enormous, and Mina called him bug eye. He chased after Kati with his magnifying glass and nearly convinced her that his eye was about to fall off his face, before Mama intervened and reminded him that, according to Jewish law, he was a man now and should stop acting like a child.

That evening, Mama, Mina, Kati, Sam, and I climbed down the narrow stairway to steerage. It was darker there than during the day and filled with people, talking together in small groups. Mr. Lazar came quickly forward and led us to a corner where about thirty people were gathered. Mr. Lazar stood at the front of the group, many of whom seated themselves on the floor, the men on one side, the women on the other. Ten men remained standing around Mr. Lazar, and they made up the *minyan* for the Friday night service. The Sabbath candles sat on top of a trunk behind Mr. Lazar.

"*Bo-ruch Atto' Ado-noy,*" he said.

His voice was deep and rich, and he hung onto the end of each word before beginning the next one with a sigh.

"*Le-had-lik Nayr Shel Shabbos,*" he said.

He struck a match and lit the Sabbath candles. Next he recited the prayer to inaugurate the Sabbath. Afterwards, he went on and on, quoting from the Torah, closing his eyes and going deeper and deeper inside himself, burying his chin in his chest. Finally, he stopped speaking, took a deep breath, and opened his eyes. His glance came to rest on Sam's face, and he called for the mourners to rise and say the *Kaddish*. Out of habit, I chanted what I remembered of the prayer silently inside my head, since only the men were supposed to say it out loud during services. Although Papa wasn't dead anymore, the Hebrew words of the prayer were still beautiful to me, sad and full of longing for those people who were left behind.

The mourners sat down, and Mr. Lazar smiled at Sam.

"We have in our midst this Sabbath a young man who is celebrating his thirteenth birthday," he said. "My young friend, who is kind and quite skilled in the healing arts and who has eased my journey to the new world, becomes a man today. As you know, the *Bar Mitzvah* ceremony dates back to our ancestors in Asia during the thirteenth century."

Sam hung his head.

"It is my great honor to call my friend, Mr. Samuel Spirer, to the Torah for the first time on this day," Mr. Lazar said. "Sam is an excellent Hebrew student, I can assure you. He and I have discussed the Torah on several occasions, and he possesses a knowledge well beyond his years. Therefore, as a birthday blessing and for his *Bar Mitzvah*, I am going to ask him to read one of our additional Sabbath prayers."

He motioned Sam forward, but my brother sat rooted on the floor, until the man next to him poked him in the ribs. He rose unsteadily to his feet and balanced himself on his heels before walking slowly forward. Mr. Lazar placed a *tallis* around Sam's neck. A star of David was embroidered on each of its ends, and its fringes quivered. Mr. Lazar pointed to a place in his prayer book and handed it to Sam. For a long moment, Sam didn't speak. His face was deathly pale, and he raised his eyebrows, as if he were confused and didn't know how to read. The people on each side of us stirred uneasily, rustling their skirts and clearing their throats, and Mama, whose hand had been resting lightly on my shoulder, pressed her fingers through the thin cotton of my dress. They felt hot on my skin.

At long last, Sam bent forward and began to read, so softly at first that we could barely hear him, and then louder and faster, as though he was galloping to the end of the prayer.

"And thou shalt love the Lord thy God with all thine heart," he said. "And these words which I command thee this day; thou shalt bind them for a sign upon thy hand and write them upon the doorposts of thy house, and upon thy gates."

Mama stared at him, her hand on her heart. She seemed to have forgotten all the tricks my brother had played on her over the years, all the coins he had stolen, all the black eyes he had given to other boys, and only to want to thank God for giving her such a son. Mina smiled, and I knew she was proud of Sam, in spite of herself. Kati leaned into

Mama and twisted inside her arm. As I watched my brother, standing in front of all those people, I felt as if I hardly knew him. The boy who used to tease me with spiders and frogs and kick me under the table was gone. In his place was a tall, thin young man with narrow shoulders that stooped a little, a few hairs above his upper lip, and a voice that cracked every third or fourth word so that it was beginning to sound like it belonged to a grown man. Tiny worry lines were just starting to crease his forehead, as he squinted at the prayer book in the dim candlelight and went on and on with his birthday recitation.

HOUDINI

Early on the tenth morning of our journey, I heard Sam burst through the door of our cabin.

"Mama! Mama!" he shouted. "Come quick."

"What's wrong?" Mama asked.

"Come on!"

Mama knocked on my door. "Serene, are you up?"

"Yes, Mama," I said.

"Well, then, get dressed and let's go to see this wonder that has your brother so excited."

I stumbled out of bed, slipped into the dress I wore the day before, and rubbed the sleep out of my eyes. I followed the rest of my family onto the deck where crowds of people had gathered, talking excitedly among themselves and looking across the ocean. I looked, too, and saw a most unbelievable sight, a giant woman on a pedestal in the middle of the water. The Statue of Liberty. Sam had read about her in a book and showed me a picture, but the real statue was far more fantastic. She wore a huge crown and carried a torch in her outstretched hand. English words of welcome were carved on the pedestal, and Sam told me they meant America had enough food for all the hungry people in Europe.

We glided closer to the statue, and I saw that she was ten times as tall as the statue of Franz Josef in the village square of Galfalva. She smiled such a friendly smile that I wanted to touch her torch, climb into her arms, wrap my hands around her neck, and fall asleep beside her.

Mr. Lazar squeezed in between Sam and me.

"Isn't she magnificent?" he asked.

"Yes," I said. "I love her."

"She's like a goddess," Mama said.

"Indeed," Mr. Lazar said.

As we sailed closer, I reached up and stretched my arms out to her.

There was a small island of red brick buildings beside the Statue of Liberty, and all around her were rows of docks that jutted out onto the water like long bony fingers. Behind the docks were buildings of different sizes and shapes as far as I could see.

"That's New York," Mr. Lazar said. "Have you ever seen anything like it?"

Mama squinted into the sunlight.

"My papa is waiting there for us," I said.

"You are very lucky," Mr. Lazar said. "For myself, I have no family here, so I have to go to that island beside our beautiful Miss Liberty and stay there until they decide whether to let me into the country."

"Do you mean you might have to go back to Hungary?" I asked.

"I certainly hope not," he said.

As I watched the beautiful statue sail by, she smiled at me again and wiped my mind clean of longing for my old home. I only wanted to get off the ship and start exploring the wall of buildings behind our wonderful Miss Liberty.

Mama took Kati's hand and went back to our cabin to pack our few dresses and shoes and coats into our one remaining suitcase. I said good-bye to Mr. Lazar and ducked under the people gathered on the deck and pushed through the crowd until I pressed against the railing. I shaded my eyes with my hand and stared at the island in the distance. My papa was on that island. I had dreamed about him, wished for him for almost six years, and worried that he was lost forever. But somehow, he managed to find us and bring us to this new world where we could begin our lives all over again. From now on, I would have my real papa, not the one who had floated in front of my eyes in the dark or melted into stained glass windows. Not the one who had tickled my ear with his laughter and sometimes spoke in a language I couldn't understand. The papa who waited for me just beyond the water had arms and legs, and I could hold his hand and rub my cheek against the sleeve of his shirt.

After the ship finally docked at the very tip of Newyork, we had to stay on board a good long while. Finally we began to line up to get off, but the people in front of us only inched forward a step or two at a time. I wanted to scream at them to go faster. I poked a woman who stood in front of me, but she didn't move.

After what seemed like hours, we arrived at the gangplank. I looked for Papa but couldn't see him among all those people. A man waited for us at the bottom of the gangplank. I wondered what kinds of questions he might ask and decided I wouldn't tell him how seasick I was on the voyage.

Mama was the first one on the gangplank, and she held her hand out to Kati. Mina and I were next, and Sam followed closely behind. All I could see was the back of Mama's shift. At the bottom of the gangplank, the man glanced at our tickets and motioned us toward an iron fence. He didn't really look at us, and when I tried to tell him how well I was feeling, he pushed me gently toward the fence and turned to the people behind us.

A second man in a blue uniform and a cap stood at an opening in the fence, and I thought he was a policeman. Mama handed him our tickets. "Spirer!" he shouted.

The people on the other side of the fence stood perfectly still, as if they hadn't heard the policeman. I pushed my way next to Mama.

"Mama, what if he's not here?" I whispered. "What if he didn't wait for us after all?"

The policeman pursed his lips and returned the tickets to Mama, but she pushed them back at him and shoved me behind her.

"Spirer! Spirer!" the policeman shouted. "Spirer!"

This time, the crowd behind the fence rustled, and some people moved to the side. A small man with thin shoulders and streaks of gray in his hair and coal black eyes emerged from the crowd. He was wearing a new black suit and carrying a hat in one bony hand and a photograph and some papers in the other. He bowed his head, moved forward, and whispered something to the policeman.

"Spirer," the old man said and patted his chest. "Spirer."

Mama stared at him with her mouth open, her face drained of color. "Shumi?" she whispered.

"Papa?" I asked.

My papa was an old man. He held up the photograph to the policeman and showed the policeman a long piece of paper. The policeman looked at it and shook his head, and Papa stood beside the policeman with the photograph in his outstretched hand. The policeman motioned us forward, one at a time. Mama went first, and the policeman touched her shoulder.

"Rosa," Papa said.

"Rose," the policeman said and wrote her name in a tablet he had pulled from beneath his arm.

Mama walked forward, and after Papa took her hand in his, she collapsed against him and sobbed. He let go of her hand and put his arm around her and hugged her.

Kati came next. The policeman touched the top of her head, and there were tears in Papa's eyes for the daughter he had never seen before.

"Kati," he said.

"Kathy," the policeman said and wrote her name in his tablet.

Mina followed Kati. The policeman touched her shoulder, and Mina tried to brush him away.

"Tch, tch, Mina," Papa said.

"Myra?" the policeman said.

"Mina," she said. "M-i-n-a."

"Mina," the policeman said and wrote her name in his tablet.

Sam pushed his way through, and the policeman put his hand on my brother's head. "Samuel," Papa said.

"Shmuel?" the policeman said.

"Sam," Papa said.

The policeman nodded and wrote Sam's name in his tablet.

Finally, I stepped forward, and when the policeman touched my head, I felt weak and afraid I might fall down and be sent back to the ship.

"Serene," Papa said.

The policeman frowned at Papa and held his pencil above his tablet, because my name seemed more difficult than the rest to say in our new language.

"Serene," Papa said and licked his lips. "Es-ss-er-r-r—" He looked nervously at the policeman and stopped speaking before he finished the last part of my name.

"Esther?" the policeman said.

Papa nodded in agreement.

"No, no," I said.

Papa put his hand on his hip. "Es-sth-er," he said, his voice stern.

"But I don't want that name."

Suddenly, I remembered the name Mina gave me when we ran away from Grandma's the year Kati was born. Sarah. Back then, I dreamed about a new life for this girl called Sarah. I liked the name because it was soft and sweet and easy to say.

"Sarah!" I patted my chest. "Sarah. Sarah."

Papa shook his head, but the policeman just repeated my new name and wrote it in his tablet.

We walked up and down the streets of Newyork. There were carriages everywhere, some drawn by horses and some not. I had only seen pictures of horseless carriages in Hungary, but no one ever told me how noisy they were and how their horns blasted in your ears. People crowded the streets, and the sounds of horses hooves and carriage wheels never stopped, not like at home where the whistle of a train or the banging of a branch against a window were all that broke the silence. Endless rows of brick houses with ten or twelve huge stone steps up to their front doors lined the streets. Iron stairways hung flat against the walls to the upper stories of these houses, and when I asked Papa what they were, he said they were fire escapes for the people who lived on the top floors. Wagons like Tibor's and Shifty's stood along the streets, and once a man approached Mama with a piece of red cloth and held it an inch from her nose and barked at her in a strange language. He followed us down the block, until Papa laughed at him and shooed him away.

I kept watching Papa out of the corner of my eye, trying to get used to him. The longer I watched him, the more I could see the Papa I remembered, hidden underneath this new person. I had to let my eyes get used to him, and finally, I took his hand. Once he stopped to point at a long, skinny building that ran along one street and turned the corner to run along a second.

"That's a funeral parlor," he said. "Can you believe? The Italians carry their coffins out the front door, and the Jews carry theirs out the side door, with a rabbi and a priest in the middle. Can you imagine such a thing in the old country?"

A little while later, we stopped in front of the most beautiful synagogue I had ever seen. It was made of yellow brick and was at least three stories high. It had arches everywhere, a heavy wooden door, and a huge circular stained glass window that gave off an orange glow.

"A rich man's synagogue," Papa said. "It costs many hundreds of American dollars just to sit inside. More than we'll ever see."

I wanted to go inside that synagogue and sit in one of those seats and see what it was like to pray to God in such a place. We stood in front of that synagogue for a long time.

"Can we go inside?" I asked.

318

"Not today, little one," he said. "But maybe some day."

"When?" I asked.

A small frown crossed his face. "Still asking questions that can't be answered."

"I'm sorry, Papa."

He took a deep breath and patted my arm.

"You know," Mama said. "Of all the children, Serene—"

"Sarah!" I said.

"Excuse me, Sarah, was the one who worried about you most. From one day to the next, she'd never give me a moment's rest. 'Where's Papa? Did he fall into the ocean? Is he in America with his brothers?' For a while, she even said the *Kaddish* for you."

"What bad luck," he said. He spoke Hungarian more slowly than I remembered, with an odd, clipped accent. "Let's hope the deed doesn't follow the prayer too closely."

"No, Papa," I said. "I wasn't wishing for you to be dead. I was afraid you were, and I was praying for your soul to rest in peace."

"We all thought you were dead," Mina said. "We were worried because you didn't have a proper burial."

Papa's face flushed, and Mama rested her head on his shoulder.

"They meant no harm," she said. "They only wanted to see you again."

"Indeed," he said. "Is God punishing me with such children?"

"Dearest, Let's talk of more pleasant things. Sam had his *Bar Mitzvah* on the boat. You would have been so proud of him."

Papa remained silent.

"Please, Shumi," she said. "The children never wanted you to be dead. They missed their papa." She hooked her arm through his. "Why don't you tell us a story about our new home?"

"Please, Papa, tell us a story," I said. "Please."

"Oh, yes," Sam said.

Papa slowed down a step or two so that we had an easier time keeping up with him. "All right, if you want me to," he said.

We all leaned toward him so we wouldn't miss a word.

"This is a story about clothes," he said. For the first time since we got off the ship, he seemed to relax and fall into his old way of talking.

"An interesting subject," Mama said.

"Your Uncle Yankev lived in this country for about ten years before I arrived. That's why none of you children know him. He considers himself a real American. He has an American wife who doesn't speak a word of Hungarian, and they have an American son."

"Who doesn't speak a word of Hungarian either?" Mama asked.

"Correct. Anyhow, I lived with Yankev for a year after I arrived, and at dinner Bess, his wife, would stare at me, and she and Yankev would talk to each other in English, which I didn't understand very well."

"Can you speak English now?" I asked.

"A little, but very slowly. It's difficult and hurts my tongue."

"Say something for us."

Papa sucked in his breath and made a sharp barking sound followed by a few coughs. We all laughed, and Papa puffed out his chest.

"Was that it?" Sam said.

"What did you say?" I asked.

"I said, 'Welcome to the new world'," Papa replied.

"That's enough, children," Mama said. "Let Papa finish his story."

"Good," Papa said. "So, let's see, I would be eating my dinner in my old muslin shirt which I brought with me from home, and Bess would give me such a mean look that I'd yank my elbows off the table."

"What was wrong with her?" Mama said. "Didn't she like you?"

"That's what I thought. She's very fat, and while we were at the table, I would make Yankev laugh by saying in Hungarian that it seemed like people in America always had plenty of food on their plates, not like at home. I was afraid Bess knew I was making fun of her, but it turned out it was my shirt she didn't like, not me. One evening after dinner, Yankev took me aside. 'You dress like a greenhorn,' he said."

"What's that?" Sam asked.

"Someone like you who just got off the boat," Papa said. "You don't want to be a greenhorn because you don't want anyone else to know you came from another country. Everyone here wants to be an American."

"Oh," Mama said. She frowned.

"Anyway, Yankev grabbed my sleeve that night said, 'Bess tells me everyone in synagogue knows you're not from here. We'll have to buy you a proper suit to stop people from talking about you so much.' The very next evening we visited Yankev's tailor. Uncle Yankev had four suits back then, and he fussed over them more than he did his baby son David and loved to brush them off and take strict turns wearing them to Sabbath services."

"What color was your new suit?" I asked.

"Black, like the one I'm wearing," Papa said. "I picked up my new suit from the tailor, and not a week later, Uncle Yankev's house caught on fire in the middle of the night and burned to the ground. Bess's screams woke me up, and I ran to rescue David. When I went outside, Bess was standing in the street, pulling her hair. A couple of neighbors were pouring buckets of water on the house, but I knew that was hopeless. The fire was everywhere by now"

"Where was Uncle Yankev?" Sam asked.

"That's what Bess wanted to know," Papa said. "I had quite a time keeping her from running into the house to find him. We waited and waited and called his name, and still there was no sign of him. At last, he staggered out the door. He was wearing his own four suits and mine on top. 'Yankev,' I said. 'Are you insane? Forget about the clothes.' 'I can't do that,' he said. 'Tomorrow is the Sabbath, and I have to have something decent to wear.'"

We all laughed.

"So that's your new home," he said. "You may not have a roof over your head, but if you have a freshly-pressed suit to wear to synagogue, everyone will think you're an emperor."

I looked down at my torn pocket and frayed hem and my shoes with the holes in them. "Does that mean I can have a new dress?" I said.

Papa smiled. "I think you can have one, as long as you behave yourself."

We stopped at an open air market. The smells made my mouth water, and I was suddenly hungry for the first time since we had left France. On one block, stand after stand sold fresh fish, although no one in our family ate it because of our great Uncle Ziggy, who choked to death on a fish bone before he had the chance to fulfill his destiny and become a doctor. Behind the fish were rows and rows of roasted chickens. There were bushels full of apples and pears and oranges and berries of all kinds. Papa bought two apples and two oranges and a pear and pointed at one of the chickens, holding up two fingers. The woman who was selling the chicken held up three fingers. They argued for a little while in loud, angry bursts, before Papa finally bought a chicken wrapped in brown paper. He stopped at a shop and argued some more with the owner there and bought several slices of bread. They didn't smell nearly as yeasty as the kind Mama baked at home.

"Be careful when you eat this bread," Papa said. "It sticks to the roof of your mouth."

We passed through a park that was surrounded on all sides by tall buildings. There weren't many trees and only a few benches, but since it was the first of May and the afternoon was warm, we sat down to eat our delicious lunch. Papa pulled some meat off the chicken and put it on top of his bread and ate the whole thing at once. The rest of us watched in amazement.

"That's how they do it in the New World," he said and licked his fingers clean. "I have to eat like this to show everyone I'm a real American and not some stupid foreigner who doesn't know his way around."

I bit on the pear, and the sweet juice trickled down my chin. I couldn't ever remember eating anything that tasted as good to me. After Sam finished his apple, he tried to steal the rest of my pear, but Papa patted him lightly on the hand and gave him another piece of fruit.

"Leave your sister alone," he said. "There's plenty here for every-one. Not like in the old country."

Mama smiled at each of us, and tears rolled down her cheeks. Papa reached over to wipe them away.

"I thought I'd never see you again," she said.

"Don't be silly," he said and waved his hand in the air, as if all our troubles until that very moment had no meaning at all.

"You can't begin to understand what we've been through."

"Shh." He put his finger over her lips. "The past is the past. Today is ours to enjoy in New York. Tomorrow we go home."

Mama nodded her head slowly. "Home . . ."

Mina sat at one corner of the bench by herself and ate her chicken first and then her bread and wouldn't mix the two as Papa had done.

"Still the stubborn one," Papa said. He smiled, and she gave him a hard look. In that instant, I saw how much alike they were.

Every once in a while, when Papa was busy peeling an orange or cutting up an apple, Kati would scoot off the bench beside Mama and wander toward him and watch him. When he looked up at her and held out his hand, she ran back to Mama and hid behind her skirt.

"Such a beautiful child," he said to Mama. "What's wrong with her? I don't think she'll ever love her papa."

"Of course she will," Mama said. "Give her a little while. She's just a baby."

Papa wiggled his finger at Kati, and she hid her face in her hands.

"Not like Serene," Mama said.

"Sarah," I said.

"Sarah. She loves her papa. There's no doubt about that."

Papa ran his hand lightly over my head before turning his eyes back toward Kati. I put the rest of my pear down on the bench for Sam to eat.

After we finished our lunch, Papa stretched out his legs to warm himself in the sun, and I watched the reflection of my face in his shiny new black shoes for a moment. There were deep furrows in his forehead and more lines around his eyes and mouth than I remembered. He wasn't much taller than Mama, really, though I'd never noticed that before, and his shoulders were stooped now. His fingernails didn't have half-moons of dirt under them as they used to, but his hands were rough and callused. He saw that I was staring at him, and he smiled, closed his eyes, and raised his face to the sun. Mama leaned against him and warmed herself.

I was dozing in the sunlight, with a full stomach, when I was awakened by a commotion at one end of the park. Sam jumped up and ran toward the noise, and the rest of us followed. We walked out of the park and onto a street that was jammed with people. Some of the buildings that surrounded us had stone columns and fifteen or twenty steps up to their doorways. In front of one building was a huge bronze statue of a man who stood on a pedestal, holding a tablet and wearing leaves on his head. There were so many people crowded around the three horseless carriages that had stopped in the middle of the street that only their glass windshields and roofs were visible. The crowd grew silent and looked up at the sky. I glanced up too and saw a most amazing thing. High in the air, hanging upside-down from the top of a building much taller than any of the ones in LeHavre, was a man. His feet were bound, and he was wrapped in something that looked like a jacket and held his entire body prisoner—a magician, like the ones in Sam's book about America.

A breeze started to blow, though the rope from which the magician hung stayed still. Someone in the crowd screamed, and I screamed too and covered my eyes, because I was afraid the man would come crashing to the ground.

"Houdini!" several people shouted.

"Is that his name?" I asked.

"I read about him," Sam said. "He can escape from any jail in the world. Sometimes he locks himself in a box full of water and escapes from there, too. They say he can even talk to the dead."

Everyone grew silent, and Houdini dangled above the crowd without moving.

"Watch out, Houdini!" I shouted.

The people around me laughed, and Papa took my hand and glanced down at me.

"I love you, Papa," I said.

He patted my shoulder.

"Please don't hate me anymore," I said.

"What are you talking about?" he asked.

"You were always angry at me at home, and I think you still are."

"Ah, well. I wasn't angry with you then, and I'm not angry with you now. You see, you were such a happy child. Everything to you was fun, and I wanted to show you that life was no joke, that a person had to be careful of what she did."

"But I am careful."

"Do you know that of all my children, I worried most about you while we were apart?"

"Why?"

"Because Mina and Sam are stubborn like me, and when the world bites, they bite back. Kati is your Mama's youngest, and I knew Rosa would protect her. You are so gentle and open, with a heart so easily broken. I was afraid you might not survive without your papa, so I tried to make you harder."

"But I *did* survive, and I'm here with you."

"Yes, you are." He hugged me close.

All at once, the entire crowd began to cheer and call out Houdini's name. Still, he made no move to get out of the jacket, and I wondered whether he was frightened of letting go at the wrong time and plunging to the ground.

"I'm scared," I said to Papa. "I don't want him to die."

"Don't worry, little one," Papa said. "I'm sure it's all just a trick." He squeezed my hand.

Suddenly, Houdini started to wiggle and bob his head up and down. Little by little, he began to twist and turn his way out of the jacket that bound him, moving first his shoulders and next his arms and hands and finally his waist and legs. No one in the crowd said a word. At last, the jacket floated slowly to the ground like ducks landing on a pond, and the magician hung in the sky far above us, with his arms straight out, a free man.

"What did I tell you?" Papa asked, laughing and pointing the air. "You see."

I leaned closer him, slowing my breath to match his, and kept my eyes glued on Houdini. "Yes, Papa," I said. I was laughing, too. "I see."